THE
SHALLOWS

THE
SHALLOWS

HOLLY CRAIG

THOMAS & MERCER

Text copyright © 2023 by Holly Craig
All rights reserved.

Published by Thomas & Mercer, Seattle

www.apub.com

Amazon, the Amazon logo, and Thomas & Mercer are trademarks of Amazon.com, Inc., or its affiliates.

ISBN-13: 9781662508165
eISBN: 9781662508172

Cover design by Lisa Horton
Cover image: © Alessandro Colle © Bilanol © Happy Stock Photo © ASDF_MEDIA / Shutterstock; © Alexandre Rotenberg © Lois Adomite / ArcAngel

Printed in the United States of America

To Kurt, for transforming my whole life. And to Milly and Emme, for brightening it daily.

PROLOGUE

I have no idea why he's brought us here or how he knows about this place, but I've learnt to stop asking questions.

The boat pitches, coming down with a hard slap. My son, Cooper, clutches my leg, with a sour stink of acid bile wafting from his mouth. It's a seasickness that won't disperse. I clutch the rail, steadying him. Every now and then I wipe his mouth with a tissue, making him spit into it. And then I throw the tissue into the foaming wake and wait for his little body to convulse once more. I can picture his ribcage when he does it, the clenching effort of relentless vomiting. But I don't want to leave this small, swaying craft. Yes, he's sick and Kiki keeps pulling a face whenever her brother brings up more of his breakfast, but to leave the boat would mean admitting defeat. They don't know this, they don't understand what this means for us, but I do. It means we've reached the end point.

This boat isn't meant for the open ocean, not like the last one. Kiki joins me and her brother and I kiss her head while a seagull flies overhead, scoping us out. It seems to delight in the gusts carrying it. It swerves and swoops, horribly cackling over the rumble of the engine.

Charles gazes out over the ocean, his fringe swept back off his forehead. I used to think he was handsome. A memory of him feeding me wedding cake flashes in my mind and I want to spit at it. The number of times I've investigated my husband's childhood psychology would have most wellness coaches scrutinising *me*. The fact is, even after ten years, I don't know my husband. But do we ever really know anyone?

We're slowly approaching a forested point, and from what I can see, the beach is pristine white, enough to dazzle and blind. The tropical palms stretch up onto a hill, dense and rising from the beach. I want a guide, someone to explain what every nook leads into. I want Charles to stop making this seem like an adventure. The kids are guessing now, so he can cut the bullshit. Instead, he stares in front as the boat moves over the shifting waves. I cannot face him any longer.

Beyond the point is a rocky headland, boulders stacked in a jumble. Dark cavities indicate openings.

If this had been a holiday, a trip I'd planned with the kids after flicking through a brochure, I'd delight in this tropical location. Sultry heat. Turquoise sea, fanatically glittering like one of my diamonds. But it's not a brochure. It's difficult to breathe with a hard stomach. My neighbour is dead, I'm complicit, and I don't know where my husband is taking us. So I hold my children a little too tightly, as the waves harass the hull, as the sea smacks the boat.

PART ONE

Three Months Ago

You have to watch out when someone tells you they're happy in their marriage. Anyone who calls their husband lovely is lying. You have to watch out for the 'nevers' and the 'always' people spill from their mouths. They're wanting to prove something to you, to themselves. That's why I didn't believe my neighbour, Ariella, when she told me her and her husband, Mateo, *never* fought, had *always* been in love. No one's that perfect.

When they first moved in, from my bedroom window, I stood watching my new neighbour for minutes. Her garden and life looked so idyllic. The sun had a way of dappling itself over her skin, filtering light over the lush grass and terrace, which screamed to invite me onto it. I imagined sitting there, bouncing my legs and drinking rosé in ice-cold glasses with French cheese and pickles. I imagined this woman telling me how wonderful her life was without kids. She had a husband who kissed her like they were newly dating. The house had been empty all year, the garden neglected and bare. To have a neighbour would hopefully lead to having a friend. I've never had many female friends – you can't always trust them. But I wanted her to smile at me like *we* were friends.

My new neighbour wore a floppy straw hat when she worked in the garden. Bent over coriander, patting the soil, watering the earth like Mother Nature, she prided herself on her herbs, I could tell.

As soon as they moved in, she knelt there on the grass, squeezing seedlings out of pots and making room for them. I found myself ordering a trailer of new plants to surround the pool. I don't know why.

The neighbour and I waved at one another from our cars in the driveway and I briefly said hello, catching her name. *Ariella*. The kind of name I'd have wanted as a child.

Ariella. She appeared so perfect it was painful. Her princess name. Her curved frame. The way she sipped her iced water.

But just like any perfect person who you admire from afar, you can't invite them into your own house, otherwise they'll notice the imperfections and the fragilities of your *own* life. We can't have people comparing. It's best to shut them out until you find a crack, a tiny fault in them that levels out the playing field. Then the invitation gets sent out. The olives are poured into ceramic bowls and champagne into flutes. We're equal, we're no better than each other. Now we can be friends.

I saw her crack; I saw her weeping into a tissue one morning when Mateo left for work. Two hours later, I pulled out a gold sheet of paper.

The invitation was placed in their letterbox in a gold envelope with their names scrawled in fine writing. Three times I attempted to write it and couldn't get the handwriting perfect enough, so I eventually made my housekeeper, Georgia, do it while I dictated. 'No, six o'clock, not seven. Don't bring a thing. We are so looking forward to having you. *We're*, not we are. It's too formal, I don't want her to think I'm like that.'

I made Georgia run next door and post it and watched through my upstairs living room window as she padded out the front garden gate, gold envelope glinting. I'm not sure why I chose gold. I wished I'd chosen pearl. The invitation itself was too formal. I wish I'd never sent it.

In between online clients that day, I'd asked Georgia to check the letterbox for a reply, but there wasn't one, yet I got something better. I got a knock on my door. And that's the first time I really met Ariella.

Now

The sun is almost too lazy to show up this morning and I'm guessing most of Sydney relishes it. The lie-in, the snug cosiness under the covers, the darkness. Outside will be chilly, even with it being spring. The hedges around the yard are stiffened by the cold, not yet ready to shake off winter.

Charles is still deeply sleeping, unaware that in fourteen short minutes, the alarm will startle his resting heart.

Once he wakes, the noise of him readying himself for work will rouse Kiki and Coop. And then the day will begin. That's why I need to allow myself these short fourteen minutes of silence before the day starts. It's what every mother needs.

The heaviness of my belly and the tickling beneath my ribs woke me. It's reached that time in the pregnancy, five months, where I'm feeling the baby a lot more.

If I roll over to get up, Charles might feel the weight of me and he won't need the alarm to wake him. However, there's something I do every morning and if I don't get the chance to do it, my whole day will be set off-kilter.

Charles' breath is deep, cycling one after another. I've read about the body becoming paralysed during deep sleep. If he's in a coma-like sleep, then he shouldn't feel me move. Regardless, I roll off the mattress until my feet touch the old oak floor. I sneak a glance back at Charles, who doesn't stir, and then make my way over to the side table beneath the bay windows.

Our side table holds our history like a display cabinet. My phone, his keys, a crystal vase his mother gifted us on our ten-year anniversary – holding white David Austin Roses – a silver box with gold trimming, the photo of our kids, Charles and I underneath the Eiffel Tower, a book on country manors and a carefully polished candelabra all sit together like a museum of our lives. Sometimes I stare at this old memorabilia, feeling tempted to knock it all down with my forearm, slide the objects off the end until they satisfyingly smash. If there's something I hate being, it's false.

I'm standing there for only one object. My phone. I lift it and type in the password, as my face heats. I click on WhatsApp and gaze down at the name with one new message. Reading the message, a sickly arousing tingle shoots through my stomach. I'm not sure whether passion affects babies' movements, but the baby slides inside me and I have to grab the side table for stability. I erase the message and place the phone down. Now I can concentrate for the rest of the day.

A yellow light pierces the crack between the heavy velvet curtains. The neighbours' outdoor lights are on, illuminating their large, stretched garden, which isn't too dissimilar to ours. Our homes are the same too. Five levels, overlooking the river.

Next door, Ariella and her husband Mateo sleep in a house much too big for the two of them. But it's crowded with security. Testosterone crams the space so she can't breathe. Once upon a time, I thought I could help her. But that's the thing about neighbours, you have to be careful with how much you know, how involved you become in their lives.

Three Months Ago

When someone embraces you upon meeting them, and the aroma of cookies or vanilla or some sort of baking wafts off their hot skin and their hair seems to wrap itself around your nose, while the smile on their face brightens the morning, it catches you off guard. The last time I felt the skin of a woman, it was my mother's. The last time I felt skin from a human was two nights ago, caught between curled bed linen with the weight of him crushing my stomach. Ariella holds the type of loving energy I envy. How can someone just be so nice?

'You cannot imagine how happy I was to get this invite.' She smiles, holding the golden envelope to her heart. 'It's felt so weird coming here from Bondi. And I know we're not far, but we are.'

'I get you,' I say, not knowing where to place my hands. It's because I only have two friends. It always seems strange to meet friendly females. My mother is cold. She never taught me that some women are warm. I fold my arms. 'It's so good to have a neighbour now.' I try to smile naturally. 'Your house has been vacant for over a year. And the family on the other side are always travelling internationally.'

She looks over her shoulder. 'It looks like a friendly street.'

I shrug. 'People tend to keep to themselves.'

'Well, I'm just as thrilled as you.' Her eyes squint and she means it.

I nod to the invitation and a hot spread of red hits my cheeks. I feel stupid about the invite now. All the gold. All the instructions to Georgia. 'So, you're free for dinner?'

'Absolutely. Matty will be thrilled to meet our new neighbours.'

I've already seen her house. The first day I knocked, her house-keeper answered and Ariella wasn't home, but I got a glimpse into the foyer and from that alone, I built a picture of these people. He's the poser, while she's the naturalist. He drives a flashy black Range Rover with tinted windows while she drives a hybrid, eco-friendly car. They have gold-trimmed mirrors hanging in the foyer with frames so thick and curly they make me cringe. Their floors are polished marble that freeze the foyer and brighten it so that the walls and ceiling and floor all collaborate in a shiny mesh of white. I'm guessing he chooses their furniture. I'm guessing by the denim overalls she's wearing and the brown scrappy sandals and the floppy straw garden hat that Ariella is a coffee-drinking, juice-cleansing hipster who'd rather be sunbaking on the beach than attending stuffy dinner parties. That's why ours won't be stuffy. I already have it planned. I, too, want to be a juice-cleansing hipster. Although I just don't fit into that bunch.

'What can we bring?' she asks.

'Absolutely nothing. Just your husband.'

She gives a chime laugh, throwing her head back slightly. 'Just my lovely husband,' she says.

And in that, I hear the lie.

Now

When Charles gets out of bed, the whole household follows suit. The home runs like a machine of routine and predictability. Charles complains about his tie mismatching with his shirt and Georgia quickly irons him another. Kiki sits at the kitchen bench with scrambled eggs, flicking through her latest videos of sunsets, her bedroom, her new jumper, the golden leaves in our garden. She mirrors her dad and he doesn't even realise it.

I want the kids to hurry up and get to school. I want ten am to come faster.

Ariella has something major to tell me today. I still have the note upstairs, tucked inside an empty candle, lid shut, with the rest of them. These notes are our only way of communicating honestly and I have to hide everything from my husband. I'm chewing my lip, because things are getting serious now and she needs me more than ever.

Coop sits up piling cornflakes in his mouth while Georgia microwaves hot milk for him. And I sit back observing my household, yet not really feeling connected to the running of it. My ginger tea is weak and lukewarm, like sweat. I tap my manicured fingernails against the porcelain china, its intricate blue and white patterns glinting beneath the chandelier.

Charles barely sees me. Kiki only sees herself. Coop sees Georgia, the housekeeper who could easily pass as his mother. I see myself in the reflection of the polished kettle, warped and defaced, looking for a way out of this mess.

◆ ◆ ◆

I think mothers all over the world would judge me for Kiki's YouTube channel. At first, I hadn't exactly condoned it. Kiki got an obsession over some crafty influencer and every time I'd buy her slime, she'd open up the packet and pretend she was being filmed while prying open the bubblegum-coloured plastic. She'd comment on the squishiness of it and speak with an American accent. And then one day, she secretly filmed herself and posted it on YouTube. She gained quite a few likes and comments and I urged her not to share it with Charles. He's the owner of a security company for Sydney's elite, so I didn't think he'd be thrilled to have his daughter displaying our backyard and home to the world. I think that's why once Kiki hit the one thousand mark I started feeling less blasé about it and more freaked out. You never know who's watching. And that's when I told my daughter to stop.

◆ ◆ ◆

Kiki and Coop are at school and I'm home with Georgia. She's like a piece of old furniture who blends into the family. I hear her occasionally humming through the hallways, upstairs and from the room beside my study. She sounds so happy while she goes about her days in my house, cleaning, sorting, vacuuming, cooking. I love her; I just hate that we need her.

She makes me the lesser mother, as though my children should be hers, my husband should be hers. Somehow, I just don't fit into this narrative.

◆ ◆ ◆

After school drop off, I'm in my study, sipping a green smoothie when I hear the sirens outside our house. I'm meeting Ariella soon and I'm desperate to speak with her. Apparently, Georgia heard her crying behind the front wall this morning and the note she passed Georgia means it's something serious, something we've been waiting for and searching to find. My friend from work, Tracy, is somehow involved and I cannot focus on the computer screen.

I know everything. Tracy told me. Meet me at 10 near the fence. A x

As soon as I read the note, my stomach twisted. What has Tracy told Ariella? I haven't seen Tracy at work for a week, and I've been trying to phone her, but she won't answer or call me back. It's clear she's avoiding me. I've been wondering what she saw that night. What happened to her? It was my fault for taking her, dragging her along when she wasn't comfortable with the idea. And now she hasn't spoken to me. Instead, she's bypassed me and passed on information to Ariella. The computer screen blurs. I can't focus until I find out. A piece of spinach gets trapped behind my tonsils, hanging there, and I gag into a tissue. I hate spinach and the way it does this. It never mixes well enough in the blender, and I only drink this for the baby and to balance out my iron levels.

I'm blinking at the computer screen, trying to stay focused, distracted, occupied, reading an email from one of my clients, who claims to be busy tomorrow afternoon and can't make his

14

appointment. He's missed five in a row, so I think I need to terminate the sessions with him. Clients can only be clients when they're ready to commit to salvaging their health. I'm not their mother and will never nag them to continue seeing me, therefore I write that he needs to think clear and hard about why he wants to heal himself. However, I'm waiting for Tracy to phone me back; I'm waiting for ten am. What does Ariella know? What did Tracy tell her?

The sirens. They're louder now, and when they hang around, I push my chair back from the desk. Car accident? Robbery? I'm someone who always assumes the worst. But being where we are, on one of Sydney's most exclusive streets, I've often wondered how long until one of the homes along here would be broken into.

Georgia's out on the landing, carrying a bucket with disinfectant wipes that fill my nose with strong lemon.

'Car crash, no?'

'I'm not sure,' I say and open the guest bedroom door. Through the windows, I gaze down and see blue and red flashing lights bouncing off the newly cleaned BMWs parked along the side of the street. The sun shows off, using the water's reflection to glitter and wink. Three cop cars. And two officers who almost run to knock on Ariella's front door. The sirens stop, yet the lights continue flashing. And I realise I'm tasting blood, because I'm biting down hard on my tongue.

'What is it, Mrs Drey?' Georgia says from the hall.

'Something's happened next door.'

Three Months Ago

Mateo swaggers into our house, disregarding the standards of polite social etiquette. He briefly mutters hello to me before concentrating solely on Charles. It's the energy he lets off matching his heavy cologne that'll take days to clear, overtaking everything – the winter air, the cooking garlic in the kitchen. His personality is so large it's as though our house is his.

The two men slap shoulders, recognising one another instantly, realising they're linked by acquaintances. Ariella looks at me like we're suddenly family. Can you believe it? Of all streets in Sydney, of all neighbours, Charles knows this one. They laugh about the coincidence and rattle on about who they both know, bonding in a superior energy, a testosterone display of shaking hands, slapping shoulders, laughing loudly – everything I despise in Charles. Mateo says, 'Come work for me. I hear your team are one of the best.' It's an order, not a suggestion and it's amusing the way Charles nods and repeats, *yes, yes, yes,* like a maître d' trying to accommodate a high-paying guest. My husband is ex-military, owns a company that provides security for high-risk targets such as dignitaries, international travelling CEOs, and celebrities. It's all I tell people when they ask because it's all I know. I don't dabble in Charles' work and he never asks about mine. When you're married to a man who used to kill for a living, you're hardly going to bring up emotional clients and how to deal with depression at the dinner table.

Mateo and Charles are equals, both in money and egos. They match like a mirror, seeing only one another. The obvious back and forth competitiveness keeps the conversation between them rolling like two schoolboys comparing penis size. And while this happens, one upping each other in cars, jobs, success and goals to take over the world, Charles ignores my presence, ignores his wife. I can sense Mateo is a man's man who isn't too fond of females.

So, Ariella and I form our own intimate conversation, leaving the men in the foyer. We stroll outside as the setting sun coats the river in a pink milkiness. The heavy fog of gardenia musks the winter evening air with a promise of spring.

On our terrace, the table's set, with fairy lights hanging above us. Caterers dart in and out carrying champagne and oysters. Kiki and Cooper are playing hide and seek somewhere in the garden, their squeals echoing past the traffic of boats and picnickers setting up barbeques on the foreshore opposite us. We're at a higher vantage point and we can see the public below, yet they can't see us. This is what Charles reminds Ariella and Mateo while circling the table with champagne, filling glasses until they bubble and froth over the edge.

'The best position in Sydney,' he says.

Mateo chinks his glass against Charles', agreeing that Bondi was filled with tourists, backpacking hippies who wanted nothing more than one-night-fucks on the beach. He doesn't mind cursing. I'm guessing he's the type to say cunt in front of kids.

'This is the neighbourhood to be in, Charlie.' A pet name has quickly been assigned to Charles and I already despise this human.

Ariella and I leave the table and walk to the end of the garden and the air feels lighter, less choking. I ask about her and Mateo, how long they've been married. Polar opposites, the two of them.

17

He's gold chains, designer labels and close-shaven. He's everything I find unattractive in a partner. She says, 'Practically since we were sixteen. We're high school sweethearts.' That makes a lot of sense.

I've always been jealous of those types of people, the ones with a bond that's been formed since childhood. They'll never break. But there's also a flip side to that. You become accustomed to your partner's bad behaviour.

I don't know how to talk to Ariella, so I start with a common subject. 'It doesn't feel like winter,' I say.

Ariella sips her champagne. 'We're never usually here in winter.'

'Where do you go?'

Kiki runs between us, beetroot face glistening with sweat and Ariella tickles her hair as she passes. 'Here, there and everywhere. Mateo's family are back in Lebanon, so we sometimes go there.'

Cooper is down on the bottom lawn, forgetting to search for his sister. Now, he swings on the tyre hanging from a thick branch, jabbering to himself.

'So, you're a wellness coach,' she says, and it's not a question. Ariella says it in the way that someone may say, 'So, you're a criminal.' Like she's scared of my occupation, yet also hesitantly intrigued by it. She takes a sip and stares out to the river and I follow her gaze. White yachts, like floating kites, sail by on a river so flat it mirrors the pink sunset. It's a perfect winter evening. No wind. Sunny all day. Now people are celebrating by sizzling lamb chops on the foreshore barbeques and kicking footballs under peppermint trees. Charles is right about our postcode. It really is one of the best in Australia.

'I've never been to a wellness coach,' Ariella says.

'You should try it sometime.'

'With you?'

I shrug. It seems to me that she's asking me to ask her. 'People normally come to me with their problems. I'm halfway between an intimidating psychologist and a life coach. I'm guessing you don't have any problems.' I sip the champagne and it tingles my tongue and Ariella watches me, her brown eyes no longer smiling. A child over the road screams as though they've hurt themselves, interrupting the tranquillity. There's a shift in the mood when Ariella says, 'Even if I don't have problems, could I still speak with you?'

'Of course.' I smile, trying to restore the calmness in her, the ease in me. It works and she continues down the stone steps to the lower garden. I've never done this before, had an acquaintance, especially not a neighbour, ask to talk to me. I've never agreed to it. It's a barrier that I wouldn't normally cross. Ethically and professionally, I just don't want to take the blame for dishing out advice to someone close. Things like that backfire. But it's her – the woman in the garden, the neighbour with the perfect life. I want to know her faults, her issues, her insecurities.

Something about knowing hers makes my own seem less frightening.

Three Months Ago

The mothers at playgroup blame the woman who leaves her husband for another man. The women in my wellness class criticise the single mother. The group of friends fault-find the mothers who selfishly leave the father of their children. A single mother, a single *female* disrupts everything for the happily married crowd. Dinners consist of fewer husbands, upsetting the ratio at the table. And no one wants an ex-wife around miserable husbands. This is the golden rule of mother friendships. A recently single wife sets off a chain of subconscious, unquestioned thoughts.

Am I happy? Are we happy? We're happy, aren't we? We fuck once a month and that's considered 'normal' right? I mean, who defines 'normal' anyway? The newspapers? Sex and the City? *Normal means what's right for us. I gave him a blowjob for his birthday, and surely that's all that's expected, right? After all, we have kids. And we're married. Everyone knows that sex lessens after saying our vows and popping one out. He knows that too, doesn't he? Although he hasn't looked at me like I'm sexual lately. The look he gives me is the same look he gives his mother on Sunday roast night. Does he see me as someone who just cooks his dinner? No, we're happy. Aren't we?*

Those thoughts set off a conscious chain of female bullying and fables.

She's a slut. No, I heard he was really prudish. I heard she always fantasised about his best friend. Whatever, she's a slut. She left her husband for another man when her son was only two. And he's rich, comes from old money and his mother fucking hates her. So, she's a gold digger. She's a slut and a gold digger and we need to keep her away from our husbands. Why would our men want her anyway? We're happy. But she's a maneater. She'll come for my hubby next.

When those women who flee the marital nest come across hardships, it's karma, apparently. They should have stayed with their ex-husband, and simply put up with the marriage. If they meet another partner, they're neglectful and too interested in sex. Their partner will never be invited to dinner parties, even if the ratio at the table is upset.

I see it, I shy away from it. That's why I've put up with my marriage. That's why most people do.

Not all marriages stem from love or wanting to be with one another. Ours was practically arranged and simply needed to happen. I needed a baby, in fact, I needed more than one. All I wanted in my life was to fill a home with children who I'd make sure I'd raise differently from my own upbringing. I could live vicariously through their childhoods, apply their memories and experiences as my own. I'd laugh when they laugh and share delight in things like a dove coo, a loud motorbike, the wheels on a tractor, the sparkles on a ballerina tutu. We'd gaze at the clouds and make shapes and read books until we all fell asleep together. I just needed to meet my lost inner child once more. Scrub over the neglect with bubble soap baths and coloured paint. Charles was simply the tool to make that happen. I needed him to create my children and once they arrived, I wouldn't need him any longer.

I was lucky. Because my husband didn't need me either. He wanted the look of perfection, the look of happiness, the wife to boast about, the house to drool over. I filled the need for his social approval. And that was it.

I never knew Charles exactly. What books had changed his life growing up, why he wanted to be in the special forces, how he'd first learnt to change a tyre, where he'd always dreamt of travelling, when he planned to retire. No, I only knew he liked his steak medium, always with mushroom sauce, his coffee with two sugars, a cigarette in the morning and how he folded his socks.

The sex required to make the kids was quick, awkward and uncomfortable, lasting no longer than three minutes. It was disappointing, mainly because I thought Charles looked quite good with his shirt off. But on the night we married, I knew I'd never enjoy sex with my husband, and this would never change. He was prudish, wanting the light off and made no noise. That was the time we conceived Kiki.

Still, even if we loved each other dearly, can you really ever know a person fully? I know Charles suffers from PTSD and he'll never disclose why. It's a disability he'll never admit to. I know he's a serious person who sometimes doesn't come home until four am, reeking of beer and perfume and it's the only time he lets loose. I think he fucks hookers. I know I don't care. I hear him laughing to himself and the next day, after the hangover's worn off, he's back to his serious, solemn self, avoiding us.

And that's when the unknowing began, the eluding of one another. Lack of eye contact, sidestepping around the kitchen counter, the hiring of Georgia to break the silence, the ducking between showers and bed, all in the dark. Sleep became a game, a pretence of deep breaths rolling into one another, a feigning of night-time murmurs to avoid conversation and intimacy. I was lucky if he made it there before me. I was lucky if I made it there before him.

But the kids were there, and that's all that mattered. The kids were the salve for me, the nourishing balm over a neglected soul.

Now

It's not the same as rolling slowly past a horrific car accident to observe human remains, a bleeding temple, a distraught driver crumpled over the steering wheel. It's not the same as listening in to a couple arguing in a pub, a pint of beer sploshing over a face. The urge to barge through the neighbours' door and push past police to find Ariella is as strong as picking at a crusted scab. I have to do it, because I believe something bad has happened to my neighbour, client, friend. These three relationships link us together like an umbilical cord of trust. I know all.

I thought I did.

Georgia steps up to the window with her spray and a faint hint of basil loosens itself from her hair. She's been chopping vegetables, dicing them into perfect squares for a stew. She's like a cosy, well-worn blanket, a body of mushy comfort. When I smell cooking on her skin, I'm eight again and cooking with my grandmother, acting as sous chef. I want to cling to her now as more police in unmarked cars pull up with a skid, and gentlemen in suits step out with precision and focus. God, this does not look good.

'Quick, Georgia, hand me the phone,' I say, clicking my fingers towards the office.

She waddles out, mumbling words about robbery or theft and my breath fogs the glass, coming out in short, sharp clouds that evaporate and reappear. Bystanders are collecting on the sidewalk, some with prams and coffee. This is not a daytime soapie. I want to knock on the glass and tell them to move on. The juxtaposition between them, casually drinking coffee with hands in pockets, and my neighbour, house suffocated with cops, is disjointed, making me angry.

Georgia returns with the phone. 'Here, Mrs Drey.'

My fingers swipe the screen, pulling up the message icon instead of the contacts. I'm a rambling mess, unable to focus. When I get to the numbers, I'm blank. It's like forgetting Coop's school lunch. It's like forgetting to wear knickers. Ridiculous how the brain cannot form logical steps during fight or flight. And anxiety is coursing through my body, limbs becoming jelly, ready for running. Because I know all. I thought I did.

Georgia blinks up at me, and points to the screen with the spray bottle. 'You check her name, Mrs Drey.'

Georgia's brain still works. Because she's not frightened. We were supposed to meet for our talk in the garden in fifteen minutes. She finally knows everything, and Tracy told her. Told her what? About Mateo? About his business? About what happened to her the night she disappeared from the club? The fact I have absolutely no idea – whether it's good or bad – tightens my throat.

Scrolling through names, I press her and Mateo's residential number. Ariella. Her name reminded me of my favourite princess when she first told me. Ariel the mermaid. Such a delicate, feminine, divine name, perfectly suited to the perfect woman next door.

Georgia is back by the window, spray bottle leant against the glass. She's commenting like a football commentator in her accent. *Here comes another police. Here comes an ambulance. Too many people watching.*

24

The phone rings for a hundred years until her voice – light, cheerful, bubbly, princess-sounding – tells me that they're not home right now, that she or Mateo will call back as soon as they can. I call again and when the phone is picked up, I hold in a lungful of air.

'Hello.' It comes out as a statement. A man's voice. Already accusing. Already direct. It's one of them, a cop. I hang up.

Three Months Ago

Before Ariella comes to visit me for our 'talk', I make the kitchen area as inviting as I can. Vanilla candles and white roses in a short vase. Cold jug of water with ice and lemon. Teapot on a tray with chocolate cookies and sugar cubes. Cream for coffee, or soy, or almond, or low fat, depending on which she prefers. I have the radio playing, and then switch it off when the ads blaring about half-price fridges come on, attacking the serenity I'm trying to create. I switch to café music. Not bistro – the lounge type that can be heard in a swanky wine bar. I have a plate of banana bread slices spread with butter. And the doors to the terrace are open, allowing the river breeze, carrying the distant hum of boats, to enter.

Everything has to be perfect to welcome the imperfections in people. It's the same in my wellness studio. Conditions must be met with temperature control, plush cushions that clients can cuddle, squeeze and embrace. We provide blankets and slippers and tissues – not the eucalyptus type – the fabric softener scent reminding clients of washing and mothers and home and childhood. When Ariella rings the doorbell and Georgia goes to answer, I hold in a deep breath for ten seconds before releasing. I don't know what to expect. I don't know why I'm nervous. I guess I want her to think I've got my shit together. It's what everyone wants everyone to think.

◆ ◆ ◆

Ariella arrives at my door with a tall, burly man stuffed into a dark suit wearing sunglasses, which he doesn't remove as they enter. I introduce myself and he nods, and she laughs nervously and says, 'Mateo thinks I need a minder.' Minder, security guard, bodyguard – I've never seen anything like it. It's hard to form a normal conversation after this.

Tea gets poured and the reflection of the chandelier spins around in bubbles. Her ring is bigger than mine. Her skin is more youthful, hydrated. Her nails real and dipped in pearl shellac. We face each other.

'Thank you,' she says.

I don't know how she expects me to respond but I nod and sip my peppermint tea. Cups of tea are good for hiding your face. Behind us at my dining table, the minder sits flicking through his phone. Should I offer him a tea? I've never felt more awkward. Ariella seems to pick up on this and steers my attention to the banana bread. Mentions how light and fluffy it seems. Says she'd like the recipe. My gaze drifts back to the stranger in my home.

'Help yourself.' I push the banana bread towards her, and she lifts her shoulders and accepts a piece. She makes a *mmmm* sound and nibbles a bit. Her minder is listening and watching. His wrap-around glasses are black and serious, hiding his eyes. He plays the part well. No smile. No voice. A walking weapon. I fidget a little on the bar seat. The only people who I imagine requiring minders are celebrities, royalty and the mega-wealthy.

'What does Mateo do? I'm embarrassed to think that Charles stole the conversation the other night and I never heard Mateo mention what he did.'

She clears her throat, but it doesn't sound like there's anything to clear. 'He does everything. Business owner, mainly.'

'Which business?'

A quick glance over her shoulder at the minder, who seems to have stopped scrolling. 'He owns nightclubs and bars in town.'

'That's cool. Which ones?'

Almost choking on her banana bread, a tiny crumb pops out of her mouth, landing on the counter. She flicks it away and waits to swallow before talking. 'You wouldn't know them.'

I laugh. 'I don't know about that. I used to get around a bit in my day. Where are they?'

She brushes an imaginary strand of hair off her face. 'Kings Cross.'

'Oh.'

'Some gentlemen's clubs.'

The word *some* means all or most of them. And the elimination of the word 'strip' is obvious. It's information and humiliation that she didn't want to disclose. I take another deep sip, scalding my tongue. I'm shocked by this revelation, only because I didn't expect it. She's nothing like the owner of a strip club. I want to know why they need so much security around them. I've seen a driver, two men who seem to lurk around in the garden on their phones a lot and another man in their foyer when I knocked that first day. Now this? Her own personal minder. Is Mateo more than a club owner? Perhaps they have too much money to handle, but I can't imagine a club owner earning enough to warrant protection. The minder coughs into his fist and Ariella rapidly blinks. Is this a signal? A cue? He coughs and she stops talking?

'What about you?' I say, taking a piece of banana bread. My heart pulses a little quicker. 'What do you do?'

She lifts one shoulder, and her gaze falls to her plate. 'Nothing really. I want to be a mother.'

'Oh, that's great.' I haven't told her about my pregnancy. I'm only eight weeks pregnant and this baby comes with giant consequences I'm not willing to face yet.

Ariella presses her lips together in a tight, thin line. She lifts her chin and looks down her nose at me, then sighs. 'I'm trying to convince Mateo to have one.'

This is why she's here. She wants a baby, and her husband doesn't. This is the problem she wanted to discuss with me, but it's going to be hard to help her with this. Parenting is a personal choice, and I don't know how I'm supposed to support Ariella with her husband's differing opinion. I go to say this when Ariella stands, brushing crumbs from her jeans. 'Could I use your bathroom?'

'It's through that door and down the hall. Third door to the left.'

Her minder stands too, following Ariella, and I'm left shaking my head. The way he stalks her, anyone would think an assassin lurks in the bathroom, waiting to take out Ariella. How does she maintain composure with a security detail trailing her every move? Is he always around her? Shopping, lunch with friends, family dinners? I suppose if royalty can get used to it, so can she, but still – this is bizarre and totally over the top. The fact I'm supposed to accept this behaviour – her minder, his rudeness, him occupying my kitchen area – as normal is also unsettling. The air is hot and suffocating and the banana bread leaves a burning glugginess on my tongue. I push the plate away and then see it.

A tiny, folded piece of paper no bigger than my thumbnail hidden under the banana bread plate. I look to the door where they had both disappeared through and swallow. Did she leave this here? It wasn't there before, I know that for a fact. I'd sprayed kitchen cleaner all over the bench just before they had rung the buzzer. My pulse jumps slightly again, my eyes flicking up to check the door. It could be a folded receipt, a tag of some sort, even rubbish. I have no idea why my heart is beating so rapidly. I lick my upper lip, unfolding the paper and realise it's not a receipt, nor a tag. It's a note, handwritten in tiny blue writing. And on it is a message that makes me hold my breath.

They are always listening. Don't ask about my husband. The topic of pregnancy must be our only discussion together. I need your help, Emma. A.

I pore over the words again, carefully, trying to invent and comprehend another reason for the note. Is it a joke? No. The threatening references of the minders, *they are always listening*, the instruction not to ask about Mateo. She needs my help. Oh God, Ariella needs my help and I have no idea why. How will I help her if they're always listening? Scrunching the note into a small ball, I slip it into my shorts pocket and busy myself with another pot of tea, hands quivering. Calm. Calm. I can't let him detect the shift in my mood. These men are like sniffer dogs, alert and ready to scout out trouble. Drop another scoop into the pot and boil the kettle, but when that door opens, I have to act normal. I'll change the subject and ask about Bondi Beach and their old house. And then she'll leave, and I'll figure out what to do. That's if I even want to get involved. There's only one person who'll know what to do. Jack. I'll ask Jack.

The door opens and Ariella comments on the abstract painting hanging on the wall. An ugly piece of art that Charles had chosen. She mentions the quick brushstrokes of red, the muted blue. How it reminds her of a fire in the ocean, 'If that can be possible.'

Her minder takes his same seat, starts scrolling and Ariella spins around and she stares at me pointedly. I give a slight nod and she knows and blinks slowly as though relieved, or in pain, or about to cry. Gulping down a burst of emotion with the tea, I'm unable to imagine what she's feeling. But I'm betting she's good at hiding. Play-acting the good wife. And now, if I'm to help my new neighbour, I'm going to have to do the same.

Now

I'm stepping out onto a stage with audience members, neighbours gathering, mothers pushing prams, sheepishly speaking behind cupped palms into phones, watching me. This sort of thing doesn't happen on our street. Private drivers unloading intoxicated dignitaries, yes. A CEO who brings home a new woman every night, yes. But not this. I'm half expecting boats along the river to chug up and anchor with binoculars blazing. How long before the media gets a hint?

I'm dressed in crumpled home boots with a rumpled jumper and frumpy pants. Because this is how I dress before ten am. I can wear homebody clothes because I'm five months pregnant. Pregnancy means living comfortably for nine months. It's amazing the way insecurities about appearance flash up, regardless of the circumstances next door.

Georgia is staying put, but I sense her snooping stare from one of our windows while I march down my front steps and along the path to Ariella's gate. I have to know that she's safe. My neighbour, my client, my friend. My throat's thick when I'm met with a woman at their door wearing a tight face, with crossed arms, hair pulled severely back. Plain-clothes detective? And a man dressed in forensic gear is handing her a police tape to block everyone out. Medics rush out of the ambulance, carting boxes of equipment and that's when I know – whatever Ariella had to tell me has now been kept hidden.

Three Months Ago

The invitation to Ariella and Mateo's comes the day after our talk, after she presented her crisis in the form of a note. The idea of visiting her prison, enjoying dinner and pretending I'm unaware of her vulnerability has left me with a day-long migraine that won't recede. Because, ultimately, I don't know if she's in danger. I don't know anything. I haven't had the opportunity to phone Jack, and Charles is the last person I'd ask for help.

Firstly, how am I going to communicate with Ariella? Notes, like being back in high school? There's a temptation to alert the police, but, whatever's going on behind our neighbours' closed door, I'm guessing Mateo is well equipped at hiding it. What could the police do anyway? And what would I even say? My neighbour left me a note asking for help?

Organising a walk with her along the river might tease out clues as to what Ariella needs from me. Hopefully if we become walking buddies and Mateo gets to know us better, her minder will leave us alone and I can get to the bottom of her dilemma.

Charles is elated about the dinner invitation. In fact, he and Mateo have exchanged a few phone calls leading to meetings in the city. I'm more invested in knowing about that. What did they talk about, where did they meet, were there strippers involved? As usual,

Charles is secretive and tells me to mind my own business. This is why I'd never seek his support.

We're the same in that way. Secret-keepers.

Coop bounces on our bed in his plane pyjamas while Kiki films a video with her phone and my jewellery box by her side. 'So today, guys, we're going to be trying on our mum's special jewellery. Who else loves doing this?' She puts on a slight American accent as she speaks to her phone, tilting her head like an influencer.

Charles has dressed in a dinner suit and is comparing various ties while he talks down the phone to a client. He really wants to impress Mateo. I've never seen him care so much about his appearance. He used to be handsome once upon a time, back when he'd returned from his first overseas deployment. A friend had set the two of us up. Apparently, I'd love the masculine soldier-type who didn't care about money. I think they only said that because they knew I had it and didn't want a money-hungry leech. I'd tried the rich pompous types before Charles came along. And his pompous name never did quite match his personality. He would be much more suited as a Gus, or a Brett. Charles seems too regal, too snobbish.

Even now, as he sprays cologne over his thick neck, I don't see him as handsome. I see him as a stranger who visits the house every now and then to eat dinner and fall asleep earlier than me. He's not my husband anymore. He's the 'should man'. The man society says I 'should' have; 'should make happy' and 'shouldn't' divorce, no matter how unhappy I am. I pierce the earring through my earlobe and wince when it misses the hole.

'Coop, off the bed,' I say. He goes to jump, and I shake my head, 'Absolutely not.'

Giggles bounce his shoulders, and he leaps off, wrapping his arms around me. I kiss his blond curls. 'Go and ask Georgia to read you a book.'

'When will you be home?'

I kiss him again. 'When you're asleep, bub.'

'Kiss me while I'm sleeping,' he says.

'I always do.'

'This tiara is fetching,' Kiki says from the floor. A tilted crown falls over her eyes and I tell her to stop filming. I bend to kiss her head.

'Remember, don't you upload that,' I whisper.

She gives a wink and smiles. 'I never would.'

Now

Georgia's stopped her cleaning. The kitchen is infused with coffee as she makes me one to help ease my nerves. I take the mug, sipping it slowly while closing my eyes. She talks through scenarios, ridiculous ones like, 'It's only a break-in, it's only a robbery and Missus Ariella is fine.' Her little chubby hand finds my arm. But it's not a break-in. What I saw is something much more serious. I think Ariella is hurt, possibly dead. No. I shake my head. This is not my fault.

'They'll be here soon,' I say into my mug. 'The police. They'll come to ask questions. Whether we saw anything.'

Footsteps come echoing down the hall towards us and Charles storms into the kitchen with a briefcase. Sweat glistens over the bumps on his brows. I laugh slightly and then don't know why I do. Because that look he's giving me is unfamiliar and more than a little disturbing. His eyes are round black holes like he's high on drugs, only worse – he's trembling. Fear. Could he be scared of something?

'We need to leave, right now.'

'Charles, I think something happened to Ariella—'

'Emma, listen to me.' He drops his briefcase with a smack, clutches my shoulders with the hottest palms. His fingers dig into my upper arm and his breath is sour. This is when I take him seriously. He would never do this in front of Georgia, grip me so hard.

Charles always wants to be seen as lovely, doting. To me, he's a cold, hard slab of concrete. 'We need to get the kids from school, grab your purse, keys and nothing else because we need to get the fuck out of this house.'

My gut pulls up in an uncomfortable motion. I don't understand this urgency, but I'm frightened it's linked to Ariella. 'Why? You're acting so irrational.'

Charles doesn't answer me. Everything about my husband is a secret. So, Georgia tries asking, 'Why, Mr Drey, why?'

And he turns to her, finger pointed in her startled face. 'You tell no one that we've left, you hear? No one, Georgia.'

'But—'

'No, no fucking *buts*. Tell no one.' He swirls to me. 'Hurry up, Emma, get your purse.' He roars like I've never heard him. And I, all of a sudden, cannot for the life of me remember where my keys or handbag are. I'm just standing there. Crying. Like a baby who needs guidance from their mother. And Georgia is hysterical, grabbing on to Charles' arm as he marches off with the briefcase. Why can't Georgia tell anyone? Are we leaving because of Ariella? He scrambles to collect his briefcase and I want to vomit because what if I'm right? It's too coincidental. A commotion next door and now this. Something major has happened and what if Charles is associated with it?

'I don't know, I don't know where my purse is,' I say staring blankly at the coffee cup. 'Is this because of Ariella? What's happened to her?'

Charles frantically moves around the house to find my purse. And I hear his footsteps sprinting from room to room, collecting whatever he needs while I'm standing beside Georgia, who's speaking Spanish, tears collecting above her fat cheeks. Why can't she tell anyone? My bag's hanging on the kitchen stool and I just stare at it. Because I know that we're in danger somehow, and so time just stops. And I know my bag's there and I need it, yet I can't move. There's sniffing beside me. And steam slowly curls from the coffee, a sensual movement my eyes are attracted to. Charles comes back and flings my bag over his shoulder. He's got Kiki's teddy and Cooper's blanket and a backpack that I've never even seen before. He grips my wrist, shocking me out of this state and tells me we're going. 'Get in the car.'

Three Months Ago

There's a certain scent that's sprayed throughout the lobby and floors of five-star hotels, and it's the same in our neighbours' home. A rich, earthy cologne taking me back to holidays in Europe. I assume the table would be set decadently with either gold-rimmed plates and faux diamonds or fragrant white flowers with petals opening like thighs. It'll either be over-the-top glam or down-to-earth Ariella.

It's neither. Severe, white, sterile and lacking. The food is the same – prepared by their chef and delivered by mute waiters – a scallop atop white foam, decorated with a silver sliver of endive. White, everything so white and barren. It makes me uncomfortable. I'm watching Mateo scoop up the scallop in one hit and suck it off his spoon, then wipe his slithery lips on the napkin. And mine sits like a perfect round coin, and yet I can't eat it. Not yet, at least. I take a sip of sparkling water and think about the note.

'What do you do, Emma?' Mateo asks, chewing. 'Other than frequent the society pages in newspapers.' It's a joke, but it's underhanded.

'She's a wellness coach,' Charles says.

'I'm a wellness coach.' Who can talk for herself, wanker.

'A good one.' Charles smiles at me and it's a performance. We're not happy, we're not happy and he's not proud. Don't pretend. All the things I'd love to say to anger him.

'I've looked you up,' Ariella says. This *makes* Mateo look up. As though he doesn't want his wife to consider a wellness coach. I find that men who are threatened by their partners seeing a wellness coach, healer or intuitive mentor, are always hiding something shameful. 'One of the best in Sydney. You work with big companies, right?'

I don't like to brag, so I give a small shrug. I do work with big financial companies, training their staff to create safer workplace environments. I see people in government, celebrities and CEOs. But I'm also involved in charities affiliated with women's health, domestic violence awareness and poverty. Still, none of this makes my life any better. People only see success by who they know and associate with. Where they work and live. What car they drive. They never see the woman crying in the shower, the drinking to get drunk, the bingeing after starving, the relentless running to burn off the pent-up anger.

'It's an interesting job,' I say.

'I better behave around you, then.' Mateo flicks his napkin and grins. No need. I already know what I need to know about you. Ariella and I look at one another. What is he doing to you?

'She's off-duty,' Charles says and when he places a hand on my shoulder, I have to resist the urge to shift away. It's weighted, hot and riddled with meaning, words he wishes he could say.

I scoop the scallop and pop it into my mouth. Lemon, salt and a sweet chilli tang coats my tongue. Utterly delicious and a great distraction.

'Wellness coaches are all about confidentiality, right?' Mateo chews. 'Client loyalty?'

I nod. 'Of course.' I don't know what he's alluding to, but I'm getting a strange vibe off him as he watches me, nodding. And then Charles changes the subject to security.

When Mateo decides he has to show Charles a new painting he's purchased in between courses and they leave the table, it's like the room softens into a warm dim glow. We can rest, loosen up and talk. Ariella tops up my water and sighs. I feel for her. I really do. And then her minder steps closer to the table and I'm pretending not to notice. Will there be another note tonight? Perhaps I should have written her one back.

'Did Charles tell you Mateo is employing him to do our security?' she says.

'No, actually. We don't really talk business. When did that happen?'

She sits back down and flicks the brown curls off her shoulder. Ariella is in a simple black dress with a trendy coat over the top, whereas Mateo and Charles are dressed to impress. She and I are opposite to look at. She's all clear skin and hazel eyes and brown, bouncy hair. Earthy, curvy and tanned. I'm paler, Vitamin D-neglected with eyes that sting in the sun and limbs that bend to the point of appearing boyish. 'Mateo contacted Charles last week. Your husband and his company have made such a good impression and our security has been a bit sloppy recently.'

I really want to ask why they need it. Despite our obvious wealth, we don't exactly have security guards roaming our gardens and greeting us at the front gate. I'm guessing they are next level wealthy. We have cameras and PIN codes and all the usual gadgets, but so far, I've spotted at least three men outside. Perhaps that's why I'm constantly checking the time on my watch with an urge to leave and go home. It's like sitting in a targeted home. Part of me fears helping Ariella. What is she involved with here? I don't know what I can possibly do for her.

'Sloppy how?' I adjust my napkin over my lap.

She tops up her own wine and I'm realising how good we are at this. Normal chit-chat. Under the table, my toes are curled tightly. 'Someone tried to break in when we first moved here. Security caught them up by these doors. They shouldn't have even got as far as the boundary fence.'

I'm surprised. In all the time we've lived here, that's never happened to us. 'That must've been terrifying.'

The two waiters are standing by the wall like Grenadier Guards at Buckingham Palace, eyes up to the ceiling. They must be listening. What do they see here? A security guard lingers out by the terrace doors and a downpour of rain sprays his feet. He kicks it away and leans up against the glass. But Ariella doesn't seem to notice or care. She's used to being watched, overheard.

'It was scary,' she says and I'm wondering if this has something to do with the note. *I need your help, Emma.*

'Let's go walking this week,' I say. 'I usually go during the morning before the kids are awake, around five thirty. I need a walking buddy.'

She sips her wine. 'I'd love to.'

I'm trying to read her eyes.

'We could go tomorrow—' Ariella cuts herself off when the men return to the table, clapping each other on the shoulder like two long-lost friends who've just made a deal. And the mood shifts like the weather outside. Colder, tight air, as if you can't breathe. And Ariella resumes her straight pose. And I look at the watch around my wrist, willing it to beat quicker to get home to my babies. I'm looking for a note. Under my plate, behind the salt-shaker, under the bowl of risotto the waiters have passed me. But there's nothing.

'Ariella mentioned someone tried to break in here a few weeks ago?' I ask Mateo. Obviously, it was okay to talk about this with the minder present. Mateo sloshes some wine in his glass and gives her a quick look. Now I wish I hadn't said anything. Fuck. What if I've overstepped the line?

'Yeah.'

'That must have been horrible.' I turn to Charles. 'But apparently you're doing the security here now?'

'That's right.' He clinks his glass against Mateo's. 'We'll be taking good care of you. Who was your last chief of security though, Matty? You never mentioned what company?'

Matty? He's calling him Matty now? I almost want to laugh.

'Nah, you don't want to know about that.' Mateo chews on a dinner roll and rips another chunk with his teeth, smiles up at the minder standing by the wall. 'Fucker went missing. Vanished. Boom.'

If he's insinuating his chief of security is dead, then I'm disturbed by the smiling. I want to leave here. I want Jack. Jack is the only person to make things right. Charles laughs like a nerd to the class clown and it's a childish, skittish laugh. The minder smugly smiles at his boss and Ariella stares at her plate. I'm so tempted to ask what he means by *boom*. Blown up? I'm betting Charles is regretting signing with this man.

The third course comes, followed by the dessert and, still, there's no note. There's talk of Sydney, money, businesses, luxury yachts and collectable watches. But no note. Ariella passes around wine, asks for another bottle. Mateo kisses her bare neck. I sit and listen and Ariella and I talk between ourselves about yoga, recipes, my kids and fashion. She laughs, getting merry, and the men crack jokes, lighting cigars. Dessert is a wobbly sickly custard which Ariella feeds to Mateo. And as Mateo shows us out with his arm around Ariella, and the door clicks shut behind us and the gates open and lock her in, I'm staring over my shoulder and frowning. Ariella is just so damn good at pretending, it's almost as though I've imagined the note.

Three Months Ago

How many people are miserable in their marriages? I'm betting a lot. How many couples say *I do* and already question the paralysing thought of being trapped with that person for the next sixty years? How many get married because their friends are? How many want to leave but don't? Even before Charles started working for Mateo, we were miserable. He's never home before ten pm. Now, with his buddy Mateo, it's sometimes four am. The excuse of eating separately works for both of us. We've become good at pretending not to despise one another.

If he's ever home early, Charles mostly eats at his office desk, spilling spaghetti sauce over his notepad while I'm putting the kids to bed, reading them stories, asking about their days. I do the parenting while he lives a life of solitude in a house we begrudgingly share.

After showering, I watch television in the other loungeroom while he claims he's tired and needs to sleep. He's had a busy day. He says running a business is hard work and I wouldn't know. I wouldn't understand what it's like to run a business.

The bed is king-sized and still too small. I place pillows in between us to stop our skin from touching and only go to bed when I know for a fact that he's asleep. The snoring is the most obvious indication, except it has to be the *way* in which he snores.

If he's pretending to sleep, a person simply can't keep up the dryness of breathing. Eventually you succumb to swallowing and I know because I've tried it. But that little tell-tale swallow indicates he's awake, so I grab a hairbrush, my slippers, a bedside table book and leave the room.

We can't have that. We can't go to bed with the other awake.

It's only happened a few times. We've been in bed, pillows between us, awkwardly coughing, sniffing, staring at the ceiling and trying to sleep knowing the other is listening. And sleeping is such a personal business. It's been this way since Cooper was born. No touching, no goodnights, no eye contact. It's been this way since I had a son Charles has to compete with. Something happened with his father and brother and although I've always wondered what that is, I'm also secretly terrified of it.

I actually prefer his ten pm late-night arrivals. By that stage I've eaten dinner with the kids, bathed them, bathed myself, watched my programmes and gone to bed without even having to speak to him. The pillows are there, an undercover barrier, my very own Iron Curtain.

Most would wonder why I don't sleep somewhere else, but I can't. Imagine if the kids saw. Imagine if they told their friends. No, as soon as the parents sleep in separate rooms, you can kiss the marriage goodbye. And I'm not ready for that. *Yet.* Things must be put in place first.

When you marry a person, they are always the best kind. But Charles is no longer the husband who leaves tea-stained cups on his work desk for Georgia to clear and wash, the man who presents his charming persona to the world and the grumpy bore to me. The man who gets more excited by whiskey than he does by my nudity, more enthusiastic towards politics than the upbringing of his children. This man is the warfighting, hooker-loving, four-am-arriving man I feared he was. He's the man my mum appraised with that twitch at the corner of her lips which alluded to her utter dissatisfaction. He's that kind of man.

That's why, when Charles swings the bedroom door open at ten past ten, smacking it into the wall and chipping the paint, I jolt up in bed and see him fully as that man.

◆ ◆ ◆

There's no time to open my eyes properly or stretch away sleep. He's by the door, swaying and pointing in my direction, his voice angry and strained. 'You were disrespectful to Mateo at dinner.'

I lean on my elbows and stare. 'Pardon?'

'You need to stay out of his business, you fucking hear me?'

'I have no idea what you're talking about.'

Charles lurches towards the bed, clambers on the mattress until his face is inches from mine. His breath reeks of whiskey, cigars and a spicy perfume I don't recognise. His finger juts into my collarbone. 'He is my new client, and you will respect him in his house, do you hear me? No talk of break-ins. No talk of dealings with him. You are to play respectful wife and that's it. Get it?'

I nod. I want to stab him. If I had a knife under me, I think I probably would. That's how much I hate my husband.

I'm going to leave him. I'm just waiting for the right moment. And isn't that the worst part? That I *have to* wait. For my future to be set up, to be prepared financially, for the children's stability. I have to wait, even now when he's scaring me. In the dark, his eyes are wild saucers. He's taken drugs in the past, been on benders lasting whole weekends, returned on a Monday, and slept all day with Georgia bringing him cups of coffee and Vegemite toast. He's high now. It's in his sporadic, bursting energy and the chemical reactions popping his neurons, making his mouth squirm. His jittering finger. His head cocking from side to side. I'm done with this repulsive marriage, done with him.

'Mateo doesn't like your attitude,' he continues.

I pull up against my pillow and smirk. 'And what Mateo wants, Mateo gets, right?'

I didn't see the slap coming, but the sting on my cheek is sharp, shocking, quick and over in a blink. Still comes as a jolt. I don't hold my cheek though. Don't say, ouch. Don't cower or whimper. I don't give him the satisfaction of admitting pain. I already plan to sting him back in the best way possible, later.

'Mateo is my client.' He grates his lip with his teeth, eyes searching my shoulders, ear, forehead, neck. He looks like he'd do anything for his new client. Either that or he's terrified of fucking up. 'Very important man. Stay out of their business. I mean it.'

Swinging himself off the bed like a gymnast about to do a twirl, Charles' body wants to run, pump weights, exercise and burn off the chemical cocktail he's swimming in. I hate him with all my heart. And now, that hate galvanises me to help Ariella with whatever she needs.

Now

We exit the driveway slowly, and Charles instructs me not to look at the police or whoever stands outside Ariella and Mateo's property. It's a hard thing to do. I sense their eyes on us, suspicious stares, and Charles clears his throat, an idiosyncrasy that appears whenever he's uncomfortable. I've swallowed three times in a row and wiped my face and I'm thankful for the tinted windows. However, Georgia is inside our house, and he's asked her to lie, and I don't know what that means, or why she even has to. As we drive away from the house, the sensation of someone chasing us bears down on my spine.

I go to ask questions and Charles passes the phone. We've turned off our street and I give a short exhale. While speeding through the leafy streets to Kiki and Cooper's school, I swipe the screen and Kiki's YouTube video flashes up.

'What? But she's stopped doing this, she promised—'

'Well, she fucking breaks promises, doesn't she? She's a liar like her mum.'

I ignore his abuse and say, 'I don't know what this has to do with Ariella—'

'Take a look and see, why don't you?'

Why is he showing me this and how does Kiki have anything to do with what's happening right now? His rage is keeping me quiet. It's something I've seen more and more over the past few months, since he's met Mateo. I've learnt to keep silent and let him cool down. The close proximity, the speeding through the streets, the tight paleness of his knuckles on the steering wheel reminds me of how he slapped me that night.

The footage has already been uploaded. Seven hundred viewers have already watched Kiki's latest episode. In her treehouse, with the sheer curtains drifting on the early breeze and the sun casting that morning light, that yellowish, golden filter across the newly sprouting foliage around her, Kiki had her phone positioned half on her and half on the neighbours' property. It was filmed just this morning. She said she was taking pictures of the river. She lied.

Kiki fumbles around in her dress-up chest, while the phone wonkily displays a picture of the neighbours' garden: Ariella outside in her floppy straw hat, rugged up in gumboots and a stripy scarf, pulling vegetables from her patch, which have grown tremendously since she planted them three months ago. Then there's some movement on the left of the screen and my brain struggles to make sense of what I'm seeing. It's a man in a balaclava striding purposefully towards Ariella with his arm raised, holding a gun pointed directly at her. I hold my mouth, unable to look away from what I'm watching, yet equally disturbed by it. Creeping up behind her, the man silently shoots my friend in the back of her skull.

I blink away, letting out a sob, realising how many times I've fretted over something like this happening to Ariella. Charles says nothing. He's focused on the road and his hands grip the steering wheel, unfazed, serious and solemn.

'She's dead,' I say to him. He stares in front. 'Do you not care about this?'

He glares. 'Why else do you think we have to leave? Mateo's coming,' he says, turning at the traffic lights so fast the car leans to the side. 'That's all you have to know.'

49

'Pull over,' I say.

'No.'

'I'm going to spew.'

The car brakes alongside a bus stop, of all places, but I couldn't give a shit. Flinging open the door, I lean out while sour, coffee-mixed vomit chunders out of my mouth. It's revolting, quick, and I don't feel better. I see her skull explode again and another gush pumps up my stomach and from my open, quivering mouth. Tears drip from my eyes. I thought I was equipped for anything. I thought I was strong. I'm not equipped for *this*, not murder. Wiping my mouth with my fingertips, I flick vomit from them and use my sleeve as a tissue. The footage was quick. But the person who shot her . . . I hang my head, blinking tears. I swear his frame, his stature, his movement reminds me of Charles. I swear it looks like Charles. I cough and splutter, trembling.

'Get in,' he snaps behind me.

I wipe my mouth again, slamming the door shut, and slump back into my seat.

'We need to go to the police.'

My shrill voice hangs in the car and he breaks it with a, 'No. Leave this for me to deal with.'

'But why are we running? What has this got to do with us?'

'Stop asking questions,' he screams, belting the steering wheel. I stop asking and become quiet. That anger flares in him. Even if it makes me sick and distraught, I need to study the footage again to make sure. What if it was him and that's why we're leaving home? My husband could have killed my friend. Oh my gosh, she was going to tell me something. It could have been something about Charles. Is this why she's dead? Ariella and I were going to meet for our talk at ten am. *I know everything*, she said in the note.

The car speeds under a leafy canopy of trees and my chin shudders as my body shakes with the dread of knowing too much.

Two Months Ago

Bondi Beach is surprisingly quiet and I can only thank the weather. Overcast days tend to keep the backpackers and hipsters inside for selfcare Sundays. Netflix bingeing, reading under woollen blankets, takeaway coffees in bed with nail polish remover nearby is preferable over beach walks under threatening skies.

Some of the cafés are occupied with the smashed avocado bunch, flicking through newspapers over long macchiatos, blearing hangovers making them quiet and groggy. I've chosen one of the popular ones. It feels good to be here among normal people, even if her minder is trailing behind us. Ariella suits this environment, with her scratched denim overalls, sandals and wide-brimmed hat. I want to fit in, order a green juice with extra ginger and lemon, but I can't seem to match the place. I'm ordering an almond flat white and a piece of sourdough toast with extra jam, and I never do this, I never pick the carbs, but I'm foolishly nervous and carbs are the only thing to comfort me. Once the bread is in my belly, snug and hefty, I'll relax into the vibe here. I'll be able to sit back on the couch with one leg folded on the pillows, and not worry about her hulky minder listening in, or the threat of Charles telling me Mateo disapproves of my behaviour. I haven't seen her since the dinner, where she acted like nothing was wrong.

But this time I've come prepared with a tiny note of my own clasped in my sweaty palm, ready to covertly deliver.

Tell me what you need help with. E

Already, I feel like chickening out, hollering for the cheque and bolting. But then I remember Charles, the slap and how much I actually want to help my new neighbour.

It takes a while to adjust to the flow of conversation. Ariella starts the dialogue with a look in her eye that reveals everything: *He's listening in.* Her minder takes the seat right beside her, wide shoulder to small shoulder. To anyone else, he would be her dismissive partner who has some sort of beef with the world. Crossed arms, tight jaw, eyes scanning the customers and waiters like he's about to jump them and steal their wallet. Perhaps that's why I ordered the sourdough toast. I need something comforting and warm like a pillow. When it comes, I cut it into squares and chew on one square while cutting another, spreading dollops of jam like on a scone. And we resume conversation like normal, regular clientele.

Ariella asks about my wellness centre, my job, how I help people. I tell her it's nothing like this place. This café is filled with trendy hipsters. In my Paddington wellness centre, I don't tend to get the hippies walking in. I'm more for the rich housewives who want to be seen as earthy, without having to adopt hanging plants for their home, without having to send their children to schools outside of the curriculum, without having to purchase organic face creams that never work. My clients only want to perform yoga poses in expensive active wear, sip cucumber juice with mountain-fresh water and complain about their husbands afterwards. They want to say they've been to see me. They want to say they are a part of my tribe.

We have bubbles and bitch nights, where women come to drink expensive champagne, eat good food and vent about whatever they need to get off their chests. We have presentations from world-renowned wellness coaches, wellness leaders who you see on American morning shows. We don't have sweat-infused yoga mats, incense or wicker furniture. If they want that, they can go next door to Tracy, the yoga instructor.

'I would love to visit sometime.' Ariella smiles.

'You definitely should. Listen, thanks for dinner the other night. It was fantastic.'

She clasps and unclasps her hands. 'Thank you for coming.'

'You two sure know how to host a dinner party.'

'Do you think?' She sips her green juice so the froth coats her upper lip. Her pink tongue licks it off as I face my toast, stuff the crust in. I hate this. Polite, meaningless conversation about dinners and jobs. I'm waiting for another note. And yet part of me wonders why I'm even bothering. What would happen if I just let her get on with her strangely insular life and don't ask her to meet with me anymore? We have a walk planned tomorrow. If I cancelled on her, how would it make me feel? She stirs her green juice with her straw in a childlike manner, then clutches the glass with both hands. I barely know her. I chew my crust, eyeing her arrogant minder. Can't she ask someone else? Why choose me? Her minder's cheek bounces in and out. My lower stomach clenches. Whether I feel conflicted about this or not, I'd feel horrible letting her down. Still, I need to know what she needs help with. Mateo? Or is it the minder himself that's intimidating her? She possibly can't tell her husband, or her minder may threaten her. I'm trying to sift through imaginary scenarios, seeking the most likely issue. And the only way I'm going to know is if I hand her the note. But I'm not sure how or when I should do it. He's close, too close.

'How long have you and Charles been married?' she asks, and in that instant, we've reversed roles. She's a wellness coach and I'm a client. Perfect. This wasn't supposed to happen.

I suck the jam off my index finger. 'Ten years.'

'Amazing. How do you keep the love alive?'

I almost laugh and can't find the words to respond. She sees it and takes another sip. My neck's sweaty under the scarf and I yank it off, unravelling it from my neck, careful not to drop the folded paper. The coffee's making it worse. Like Ariella, I should've ordered a green juice.

'Marriages aren't perfect, are they? There's no secret. You're either compatible or you're not.'

My eyes do not meet hers once, yet I sense her, sense her targeting me. Does she know about my own little secret and how I plan to leave Charles? Women's intuition is stronger than words. I slather jam over another piece of toast and bite into it, scanning the café past Ariella's head. And then her warm hand reaches to clasp mine and I finally look at her. She can feel it, hot and damp tucked under my fingers. Her eyelids squint. I either let her take it or pull her hand away. We stare at one another. Her minder scrolls through his phone.

'It's fine,' she softly says and I don't know what that means. 'I'm going to be pregnant soon.' She releases my hand, without taking the note. But it was there, she must've felt it, she could've taken it. But Ariella is all smiles again, sucking at her straw. 'Hopefully Matty will be convinced. He'll make such a wonderful father, so I'll need all your parenting tips.'

We're back at this – the pregnancy conversation. *The topic of pregnancy must be our only discussion together.* It's all we can talk about, apparently, but Ariella's acting so authentic, I don't know whether she means it or not. Is she genuinely wanting a baby? Should I tell her about this one in me? I haven't told anyone yet.

Or is this just a performance for the minder? I'm searching for a hint, a clue, a lie. But it's not there. Where's the danger I witnessed when we had tea together? Was the note some sort of sick joke or has she changed her mind?

It's such a momentous struggle to appear happy for her. Stretching my lips, forming a smile, gleaming my eyes with the satisfaction of happiness, all comes off in a grotesque parody. It's false and I'm a phoney and a fake. But still, I perform this ritual of smiling, happy neighbour and congratulate her. Because it's hard being a woman sometimes. And even harder when you don't know how to act. 'So, he's starting to come around to the idea of parenthood?' I ask, watching her eyes for emotion. 'That's great.'

She mixes the green slush with a knife until the dark bits collide with the light, spinning the liquid into grass green. 'I think so. He'll be happy.'

No, he won't. She's forgotten what she told me when we first met: Mateo doesn't want a baby. Funny the way we forget the lies we've told others. Why even begin the lie? To coat our shitty world in romance. And it occurs to me then. We both have a lie, a secret that only I know. But unlike mine, she gave hers up so quickly, so easily, so trustingly.

Once Ariella has slurped up her green juice and the waiter has cleared our table, I'm wondering what Ariella's motivation was for coming here. There's been no note, no indication of threat and her minder spent most of the time on his phone, once we'd settled into the conversation of parenting and schools around the area. She didn't take my note, but she felt it there. So, I'm left baffled, staring up at her as she loops her bag over her shoulder and blows me a kiss, her minder like a bullterrier barrelling behind her.

Now

I don't judge people who have affairs. A relationship is two sides of a gold coin. You can't have the royal face on it without having the value on the other side, just like you can't have respect, unless you have trust. Trust is the treasure breeding safety, communication, intimacy, friendship. Lose the trust, and the partner strays. That's what happened with us. I strayed. Perhaps that's why I don't judge people who have affairs.

Jack, my affair, blew life into my wilted being like a summer breeze, lifting up the petals of a daisy. I started spinning, twirling through life with the genuine smile that makes one wonder why. Holiday planned? Got a new diamond ring? Hubby agreed to those kitchen renovations? No. None of that. What I got was human connection, skin rubbing skin and noticing it. I got the stare to end all stares with the kiss to die for. I got sex. Hard, powerful, all consuming, human, loving sex. From my affair.

I'm five months pregnant and it's Jack's. I know this because Charles and I don't have sex anymore. When I discovered I was late, I quickly did a test, saw the positive line sprout up and made sure I fucked Charles that night. The baby will come four weeks 'early'. I've already planned for that and he's stupid, so he won't know.

The morning after I took the test, Coop seemed to sense the baby in me, leaning his fluffy blond curls against my stomach. His hand stroked my belly in round motions and I sat there, coffee mug hovering over his head, unable to move. He *knows*. He knows it's there.

Kiki, just that little bit older, had lost the link between herself and any foetal energy. Perched on the iPad and biting chunks of chocolate toast, she sat scrolling through YouTube with sticky fingers smudging the screen.

They never came from loving Charles. They came from a primal need to have babies. That's why I tell my clients: don't get married, don't have kids until you really know him. Don't get married because society says so. In fact, just don't do it.

◆ ◆ ◆

Jack is a silent business partner in Charles' security firm. Charles is ex-military. Jack isn't. He's into finance and accounting. Charles is everything you'd expect in someone who's spent his twenties abroad, obeying orders from hyper-masculine men with weapons.

Jack's different. Jack's kinder. Jack's the type of man who cares when you tell him you've had a migraine that's lasted longer than two days. He's the person who stops over for a coffee and asks if he can have the recipe for the carrot cake. He asks after the kids and comments about the dangers surrounding technology and social media. Charles doesn't listen and Jack shrugs and says things like, 'When I have kids, they're not having technology. Not with all the freaks out there.'

He's helped me in the garden to move a heavy plant pot. He knows my mother's name. He's that sort of person. He's the sort of man to not have affairs, so when he did, I excused him for it and blamed myself for taking advantage of him. He's not married. I'm the miserable one in the loveless marriage. I'm the preying leech.

I don't like to call it an affair. Affairs are short, slutty and all about sex. We have a relationship. Jack strokes my hair while I lie naked on his hairy chest and he kisses my skin and we hold hands, joining and connecting fingers and talk about one day moving to the country and forgetting city life and owning horses and sitting beside a fireplace. We don't discuss Charles. And when I see him at dinner parties, Jack is no longer my lover, Jack is Charles' silent business partner who speaks fondly, yet distantly.

It happened in the most uncliché way. Usually, affairs or secret relationships happen because you're drunk and you're both horny and one makes the move and the other agrees and you fuck. No, I don't do cliché anything. I was in the pantry, pulling out the coffee-pot and he was at the counter while Charles was dressing upstairs, and Jack said he loved my hair, and I said I loved his stare and then we smiled and knew. I poured the coffee and slid it towards him and touched his curled fist, running my index finger over every knuckle bump. The touch was electric and my insides swelled. I bent my head to the counter and kissed the hairs on his knuckles and breathed in the oiled scent of man.

A week later, I was out on a girls' night while Charles was away. Though I wasn't on a girls' night, not really. I was walking through the botanical gardens with my hand nestled in Jack's, discussing the price of farms, the price of our future.

Now

The script was written on my tongue. I was bursting to deliver the monologue with Charles and Jack as my audience. Jack and I are ready to tell Charles about our relationship soon. *I'm leaving you. Jack and I are having a baby, it's not yours and there's nothing you can do to stop me. No control, no financial abuse, no threat will ever stop me leaving you.*

To watch his face fall. To have Jack protectively by my side. To have informed the children with a lawyer and therapist present. To have every safeguard in place. To have Jack's new accounting firm set up. Our house is ready for us to move into. A vacant space with polished wooden floors and much-needed light. Kiki has a mauve room and Cooper, green. Our furniture's being delivered next Saturday. We have uninterrupted views over the ocean with the warming sun filtering into each room. Georgia would come with us, because she dotes on me and the kids like the devoted mother and grandmother we never had. None of this can be done now.

Kiki often asks why we're married. Aren't parents supposed to kiss, cuddle, love one another? Aren't fathers supposed to build Lego, roll around on the grass, throw and catch you in the pool? Why don't I ever see my dad?

That's how I know she'll be okay with this decision and thank me for it later. They deserve a happy mother, a light, bright house.

Anyway, Jack and I will make it right and give them all the love and support they need. She'll see me laughing, her mother smiling and that's all kids ever want to see. It'll be fine. It's a new life.

And now, now what?

Kiki and Cooper sit in the back seat of the car, and my mouth tastes of sour vomit, and Charles' eyes are stuck to the road, beeping when a car pulls out in front of us, and his phone vibrates in the centre console like an alarm. The video footage rolls in my mind of the man, possibly Charles, shooting Ariella in the back of the head. Rain washes the windscreen in a blurry pattern, and I've just told the kids we're going on a quick holiday to visit a friend who's sick. The questions rotated around like I knew they would, and it will only be a matter of time before Charles yells at them to stop talking, so I answered them quickly. A dear friend they didn't know, we couldn't pack everything, but we'll buy stuff when we get there, it's happened so suddenly. Mummy really needs to see her friend.

But are we really going anywhere or are we just going to drive around awhile, stay in a rental or hotel until we figure out the next steps? Charles won't tell me and I'm too frightened to ask.

And when Coop asks where we're going, I look at Charles, picking my nails, hoping he'll take over and finish the lie. I want to know where we're going. What's the plan? How many people are after us? He's distracted and shoots me a sideways glance.

'Hmm?'

'Where is it? The place where Mary lives?'

We've chosen that name and this story while standing outside Cooper's classroom. It'll be one night, two nights max, surely. Just until we form a plan.

'Queensland.'

I swallow. What? Why there and why so far? We know no one in Queensland. And Jack. When will I see Jack again? I place a hand to my belly and fight the urge to spew over my lap. He doesn't know where I am or what's happened and there's no way of texting him without Charles seeing.

'We're driving all that way?' I ask.

'Boat.'

The kids cheer in the back while I sink further into the seat, chewing the inside of my cheek until a copper taste forms. Boat. Ours? Is he serious? We're sailing to Queensland? I don't believe this. Water rises behind my eyes, so I blink it away. The kids can't see this. I have to pretend we're okay and this is the plan and keep on pretending. I know nothing yet. I only know what Kiki uploaded to the world. Still, why are we in trouble? Is Charles the killer of my friend? If not, then why can't we call the police? And Ariella is dead. That's all I know. Ariella is dead.

Our boat is kept at the bottom of Rose Bay. A seventy-foot luxury cruiser that we haven't sailed on together for months. Charles takes Kiki and Cooper out to the harbour every now and then, yet seasickness prevents me from enjoying regular outings. It's used for Charles' business meetings, a place to coax deals and sales out of potential clients. Has Mateo been on the boat with Charles? How many strippers and sex workers have partied on here with my husband?

I start to ask Charles how long we'll be gone for, but he holds up a hand and mutters, 'Shush.' It's ever so light and quiet and the kids don't hear. But it's a sign. He either has no idea of timeframes or he's deliberately keeping me in the dark.

Two Months Ago

Jack is warm skin and warm smiles. He's powerful thrusts and gripping fingers. He's the breath in my open mouth, the nest to sit in, the arms to land in, the home I fit in. Jack is everything I'm not. He's selfless and kind. Unruffled and solid like a rock. He's patient and unassuming, making cups of coffee with the brand of almond milk I like. I sometimes stare at his back, sharp, an upside-down triangle and just want to own him. But Jack won't be owned because he's his own man and that makes me want him more.

Like with every new relationship, I want to know about his past loves. That way I can compare myself with them. I want pictures, anecdotes and to study his eyes to guess whether the emotion still lingers there. Though with Jack, I see nothing but my own reflection staring back. There is no one before now. I am now and I am all that exists in him.

And a love like that just ruins a person as insecure as me. It's not knowing what to do with it that troubles me.

That's why, when we meet in the Four Seasons Hotel, over-looking Sydney Harbour with the lights of the bridge and city leaking out over the water's surface like coloured streaks of paint, I don't ever want to leave. Not for Kiki, not for Coop, not forever. Happiness when you're unhappy is easy to find in thick bedsheets, chocolate cake, privacy and time. Now, this is the only place where I smile. Our hotel nights are getting trickier and can only be achieved when Charles is away, out of the state, and Georgia's caring for the kids. If anything ever breaks us apart, I don't know where I'll go to find happiness.

◆ ◆ ◆

Jack's filling a glass with water and his arse cheeks are tighter than the skin on an orange. I follow him on all fours and, laughing my head off, I sink my teeth into them, hearing him crack up.

'How dare it be tighter than mine,' I say, kissing over the saliva. Jack turns, lifts me to my feet and sets the glass down. A shimmer of water over his lips makes me lick it off.

'And all I do is work out.'

I laugh. And then we kiss like hungry teens.

'Please,' I say.

He shakes his head, pulling away again to get the chocolate cake from the coffee table. It's so freeing, standing naked in front of an open window. Balls and breasts, naked with happiness.

'Please,' I say between bites of cake, accidentally puffing some out of my mouth. We both laugh again. And then I stop pleading, because I already know the answer and no amount of pleases will change his mind. I haven't told him about our baby yet. I'm afraid if I do, he'll change his mind. He can't be with me properly, not yet. Not with Charles and their partnership. He's scared of what my husband is capable of. And now, with Charles' mood shifting like a pubescent, angry teen, I'm also questioning that. He'll never forgive Jack for being with me. He'll disregard and shift any responsibility over our failing marriage and will plant the blame, hatred and hostility on Jack and me.

First, Jack must quickly establish his new business before he can leave theirs. Once that's organised, we'll be together. I'll finally be free of Charles.

I don't tell Jack about the slap. If I do, he'll sacrifice setting us up properly. A hotel will be booked, the kids ripped out of their home and our carefully crafted plans may as well be tossed to the wind. I want to leave Charles now, I really do. Everything about our house feels dirty, tainted and spoilt, a waiting room between where I once was and where I want to go. But Jack's meticulous preparations and my children mean more. Jack always says, 'If we're going to do it, we going to do it right,' and that's what I love so much about him.

'What do you know about our new neighbour, Mateo?' I ask him, feeding him another spoonful of cake.

He speaks with a full mouth. 'That's Charles' new client, right?'

I nod and slump down at the end of the bed. 'His wife and I are getting close. I'm wondering if you've heard any rumours about them.'

He shrugs and sets the plate down. 'You know I don't deal with that side of the business.' Although he's a silent partner in the firm, Jack isn't actively involved in the management of the company.

'But have you heard of him? Apparently, he owns strip clubs.'

He shakes his head, brushes the crumbs off his chest. 'Why do you ask?'

'He smothers his wife with twenty-four-hour security. Even when she comes to our house for coffee. Can you believe it?'

Jack wipes his mouth with the napkin. 'Talk about overkill.'

'Why would she need that level of security?'

He shrugs again. 'Who knows? Kidnapping threats?'

'Maybe. They even follow her to the bloody bathroom.'

He blows up his fringe. 'Like I said, overkill.'

'Jack, she secretly gave me a note.' Standing, I move to my bag and fish the note from my purse. It's hidden behind my health

64

insurance cards. It's still folded the same way. I hold it up to his face and Jack takes it off me, reading with a deep line between his eyebrows.

'Okay,' he says.

'I know. And the weirdest thing is, I've seen her twice since and she's pretended like nothing's happened, like she never gave me the note. She acted happy, fed Mateo his dessert, laughed, mentioned having a baby with him. I gave her a note asking what she needed help with and she didn't even take it off me.'

'No, don't do that.' Jack hands it back to me. 'Don't get involved, Emma.'

'But how can I not? What if she's in some kind of trouble?'

'Then she can go to the police with her minder.'

'Very funny. But what if she can't? What if she's physically trapped?'

He shakes his head, still frowning. 'I don't want you getting caught up in all this.'

'Okay, I won't.' I stuff the note back behind my cards. 'But why would she have given me this and then nothing since?'

He holds his hands up. 'I have no idea. Maybe she's a little loopy. I mean, you don't know these people. It's best you stay away and let Charles do his job.'

'But could you look into Mateo for me?'

He inhales and nods and then pulls on a shirt. 'If you promise to keep your nose out of her business.'

I don't know whether I can keep his promise, but I nod anyway and kiss his chest before he can pull the shirt down. Ariella may not ask for my help again, but if she does, I can't simply ignore her. His hairs curl against my nose and he laughs as I slide his shirt off his shoulders. 'Again?' he says, standing naked before me. I throw the shirt on the ground and nod.

'Again.'

Two Months Ago

It's the second time I've invited Ariella to the bar near my wellness centre. The women who work beside me usually go there on a Friday evening and I join them. We play stupid games like would-you-rather and watch Tracy, the yoga instructor, chat up married businessmen. I can't wait to get to the bar, sink into the warmth of a booth and order mini pulled-pork burgers and slim-cut chips.

I'm the only one here and already the after-work crowd forms around the shadowy bar, ordering chilli margaritas and deep shiraz. I order a bottle of red for them all, a sparkling water for me and a bowl of frites. I pick our usual booth by the fire and use the cushion behind my back.

Our drinks come before the women do, so I slouch back and relax. I'm not expecting *her* to come. We haven't seen each other since our Bondi coffee and, like Jack said, I should probably be avoiding her predicament. Still, when she was backing out of the gates yesterday, I quickly told her our plans and part of me wants to see her again. I'm intrigued now more than worried. If she did just do it as a one-off, then what was the purpose? Isn't she embarrassed about it? And yet, in the driveway yesterday Ariella was ordinary, smiley, behaving like any woman driving to the shops for groceries. And I'm not sure whether her minder was with her, either.

Tracy arrives first, flicking her golden curls from her shoulder. She's a walking incense bottle of hippy oil. The type that lingers long after she's gone and seeps through every fabric she touches.

'Sorry I'm late,' she says with a kiss.

'That's fine. Ariella, my neighbour, might be coming.'

'Great. The more the merrier.'

Barbs is next, stepping through the bar and creating a cold draught that sneaks through the warmth. She gives me a wave, notices Tracy at the bar and goes to her. By the time they reach the table, I can see how hard Barbs' day has been. Her lipstick has faded around the edges and a few flecks of mascara have fallen from her lashes. She pours a great big glass of red wine and sips it slowly.

'Would you rather work or be at home all day?' she starts.

'Work,' Tracy and I say.

I glance at my watch. Ariella is fifteen minutes late. Odd. She seems the punctual type. I pull my sleeve back over my watch and take another sip of sparkling water. 'Would you rather chocolate or wine?'

'Wine today,' Barbs says, slugging it back.

'I'm in a bit of a chocolate mood. I'm not loving this wine.' Tracy pulls a face and gazes around the room at the men at the bar. She's often on the lookout. I want to tell the women about Ariella, especially if she's not coming. What would *they* do about the note?

'Listen, I have to tell you—' Someone taps me on the shoulder, making me turn.

It's her. Ariella's here. And there's her minder, stepping in, clad in a dark trench, glasses surprisingly off and perched on his skull. Ariella looks at me with a twisted face. She's been crying. I can tell. I know puffy eyes and pink cheeks anywhere.

'Hey, how are you?' I say, rubbing her arm. I stand to embrace her, and she holds me a few seconds longer than usual. I feel her hand scrape my pocket. My body stiffens. She's inserted something in there. A note? What if he sees?

And that's what this friendship has come to now. Her insecurities, her sadness, boosting my fascination in a sick and twisted way that would have my colleagues worried if they knew. My heart thuds. It's not that I'm enjoying the sight of her sad eyes, or the covert passing of information. It's more that I'm disturbingly intrigued by it. Ariella really does have issues she needs help with, and I want to console her like I would a client, though I can't do that here. Not with Tracy and Barbs watching. Not with her minder lurking like a shark. So, I sit back and observe the way she plays with her lip, pulling at it and twisting it and taking sips of wine in between introducing herself to the women. The women don't notice Ariella's minder. He blends in with the regular patrons. Ariella sucks back her wine like water, barely joining in on the conversation and then, when there's a break in stories and laughter, Ariella leans in with a berry breath and says, 'I can't stay. I'm going for dinner with Mateo.' She bangs the empty glass down a little too loudly, jittery.

'But you've only just got here.'

She blinks rapidly, wiping her red-stained lips. 'Thanks for the wine.'

Ariella rises, says goodbye to the other women and pushes through the crowd with her minder following. And my friends look at me, puzzled, questioning why she came, why she barely spoke. But only *I* know the real reason why Ariella visited, downed her wine and withdrew like a quick breath. And it's sitting in my pocket torching a hole through the fabric.

Now

The car pulls up at the bottom of the hill beside Vaucluse Yacht Club. We never come here, so it doesn't make sense that he'd bring us to this location. The small weatherboard clubhouse mainly hosts sailing championships and doesn't hold boats the size of ours. It's quaint, wooden, and old-fashioned; the type of venue for weddings and family gatherings.

Kiki's little nose presses against the window, warm breath misting the glass. The thought of anything happening to her or Coop churns my stomach. I don't mind what Charles has planned, as long as it's to protect them. I still don't understand what's happening and my fingertips are stroking my phone, so tempted to text Jack. Maybe he knows what's happening and we're meeting him.

'Where's our boat, Dad?' I'm relieved Kiki's asking the questions.

'It's moored out there.' He climbs out of the car and slams the door shut. It's such a final sound.

In the rear-view mirror both my children are staring at me, hoping that I'll have the answers. This responsibility of 'mother' sometimes feels too overwhelming.

'Come on,' I say with a forced grin. We step out of the car and the wind collects my hair. It's a freezing day and the river is moody, sloshing up the banks and gurgling between the boards of the jetty.

Beyond the yacht club, there's a large luxury cruiser, moored on the river. It's our boat and there's a man on board peering back at us. For a second I think it's Jack and I go to wave. But upon squinting, I don't recognise him. Charles has either hired this skipper or he's a friend. I'm guessing our boat is moored at this yacht club so Mateo won't know where we are. I stare down at my phone and swipe the screen. I need to speak to Jack. If he doesn't know about this, then what the fuck am I going to do? I could be trapped indefinitely with Charles. I didn't think we'd really be getting on the boat. My head is pounding so badly, I want to throw up again. And then I feel little Cooper's hand on my hip.

'I'm excited to go on the boat, Mum,' he says.

I kiss his hair. 'Are you, baby?'

Charles is leaning into the boot, tugging our bags out. I drop the phone in my pocket. He passes a bag to me, while Kiki and Cooper pull their backpacks on. Charles' face is white and tight. I want to watch the footage again. He hasn't made Kiki take it down yet and I think he has something to do with Ariella's death. That's why we're running. What did my neighbour learn from Tracy that could affect Charles? Our notes, our regular, secretive correspondence never mentioned Charles, but that doesn't mean what Ariella had to tell me today wasn't linked to him. I think that's why she's dead. I want so badly to cry but can't with Kiki and Cooper at my side, excited about going on a cruise.

Without a word, Charles marches down the slope towards the yacht club. He didn't even bother locking the car, he didn't even look back. The kids follow him down. Peeking inside the window, a silver cluster of keys rests on the driver's seat glinting back at me. He's left the keys. That can only mean one terrifying outcome.

We're not coming back.

Two Months Ago

It's considered and folded the same as the last one. Her writing is small, blended in a neat scrawl. I read it in the toilet cubicle with my head leaning on the subway tiles, and it doesn't make sense.

I don't think we should meet again.

No explanation as to why. No kiss; nothing. I'm gritting my teeth, embarrassed by how annoyed this tiny note, these seven words, make me feel. Only seven words, but they carry intense meaning. Did someone coerce her into writing this? There can only be two explanations for her switch in behaviour. Either her husband doesn't approve of me, forcing her to send this, or she's regretting the first note she hid under the plate in my kitchen.

Regardless of her intentions, this note isn't preventing me from delving further. If anything, I'm even more invested in Ariella and what she's deciding to keep hidden. I can't stop now. She's already hinted at her unconventional life, at whatever mess she's involved in and the curiosity in me is firing hot. She's come here tonight red-eyed and puffy, like she's had an altercation. With her minder or Mateo? Which one? Or is it something else? Why even bother coming here, just to leave me a note?

Staring at the words, their hidden meaning, I imagine what she really wanted to write. *Help? They know? We have to be more careful? Things are getting worse?* I believe Ariella doesn't mean what she writes. This is a cry for help and attention.

I stick the note behind her first one and step out of the bathroom and back into the dimly lit bar. Jack's not going to like this, but I've never been one to let sleeping dogs lie. My neighbour came to me for help, arranging our first meeting. My ethos and business model are based around supporting women and Ariella requires this most. I'm not stopping.

The bar's crowded and hot and Tracy and Barbs are out the front with a taxi ready to take me home. I push through the bodies, elbows and shoulders and head to the door. When I open it, a gush of cold air clears away the bar's foggy, boozy stuffiness. Tracy and Barbs are climbing into the cab, and my bag catches on the door handle. Unhooking it, eyes lifting to the crowd by the bar, my breath catches as I spot him. Ariella's minder, or someone a lot like him, leaning against the bar. Watching me.

'Hurry, he's about to go,' Tracy calls from inside the cab.

I face the cab and then turn back to the bar. The man hasn't shifted his attention from me. Solemn face, no drink in his hand, no one around to talk to. He's clearly alone and unfazed by my noticing him. Even with me glaring at him, he continues to stare and it's a threatening sign, a warning. It's hard to know if he is Ariella's minder. I've only ever seen him with his glasses off tonight, while it was dark, and I barely looked at him. This man may just be a sleazy weirdo who hasn't learnt social rules or manners. But if he is, if he *is* one of Mateo's men hired to also watch me, I'm suddenly aware of how careful I need to be.

Two Months Ago

It's always hard to broach the topic of pregnancy. If you're trying for the baby, then it's a celebration of achievement. Yes, the routine sex without passion worked and we've won the baby race. When it's with your husband and you've slightly discussed the option, you can be met with a silent gulp and a 'What are we going to do?' And in that moment, you're not a mother anymore, you're an inconvenient carrier of a human that's going to fuck up your plans.

The hardest time to broach the subject of pregnancy is to a lover, a man who's out of the family, yet in the picture. A man who you see in your husband's office, signing business transactions. A man who isn't supposed to touch your hip while you're making him and your husband a coffee.

I meet Jack at a spot on the river where only families go to have barbeques and kayak. We park a little away from one another and he carries two coffees to a tree trunk where we're hidden from others. We kiss softly, his mouth tasting of mint gum, and I sit between his thighs and lean my head back against his solid chest. And we just sit there like that for a while, just loving the connection of oneness. I sip a coffee and he comments on the yacht sailing past, the birds above us, how he hopes they won't shit on our heads; the nice jumper I'm wearing, the smell of my hair. He kisses my hair. And then I tell him.

'I'm pregnant, Jack.' And it always sounds so silly when you say it. Like a character in a movie, waiting for the 'right time'. But it's true, and perhaps that's why they do it like that in movies, make it such a big deal. Make the silence between words long and unbearable for the viewer. Will he respond with a grunting, *fuck*? Or will he embrace his woman and tell her how happy this makes him? How could such a personal, intimate, natural moment become so formulaic?

I'm holding the coffee cup between my teeth while I wait for him to respond the way that only Jack can respond. And it's exciting in a way. Because the way a man responds to this sets the tone of his fatherly responsibility. If he utters, *fuck*, I'll get rid of it. If he says, *yes*, I'll love him even more.

'I knew this would happen,' Jack says. And I'm not quite sure what to do with that. I'm not yet ready to look at him. It's much easier gazing at the water, nature, greenery and picnicking people.

'You knew?'

'The sex we have is pretty passionate.'

'I agree.' Extremely. Addictive. Consuming. Unique. But that doesn't make one pregnant. 'It's my fault. I forgot to take a pill.'

He gathers a breath of air and I'm waiting for the drawn-out sigh that tells me how unhappy this makes him. But instead, he holds it in there and my body leans towards him.

The words funnel out in his mouth. 'I'm so happy about this.'

So, I tilt my head to stare at him. His eyes travel out to the river and I want to kiss his lips. He told me he was in love with me four weeks after we'd kissed. In our hotel room with Netflix playing and a bowl of hot, salty chips between us on the bed. I'd fed him one and he'd accidentally bitten my finger and I pulled it back, sucking on it and he'd kissed it better and said, 'I love you, you know?' And no, I didn't know. But the way my body responded to that was like a drug addict chasing the next hit. His words flew through my loveless, deprived body like lightning. And I kissed him long and hard, whispering into his mouth that I loved him too.

'You're happy?' I say.

He nods slowly and his eyes flick to me.

'But what about Charles?' I ask.

He looks at me for a long time and I wonder whether he's thinking what I am.

'I'll have to pretend it's his, but we don't ever—'

He nods. 'I know.'

'So, I've had to—'

Jack intakes a sharp gasp as though in pain and chews the edge of his mouth.

'You really want this baby?' I ask.

His fingers find the back of my head and stroke my scalp. 'I want you.'

So, I rest back against Jack and the warmth of coffee fills my belly while the warmth of his love radiates through my back and the sun has decided to filter through the trees, dappling warmth over my legs. Everything's right and real. Everything will work out the way I want it to.

Now

Our yacht is called *Lady Luck*. Yellow and white roses poke from a vase on the outside table while a huge Australian flag flaps against the wind. The boat is polished to perfection and varnish, rubber and leather fills the warm interior. Kiki and Cooper bolt to the comfy velvet lounges, flinging themselves around and knocking off a few cushions and throw rugs, but Charles doesn't seem to mind. The engines are running and the skipper, a guy named Scott, dishes out a small, nervous smile.

I nod. 'Nice to meet you.'

Does he know what's happened? That we're on the run from a man who I believe to be dangerous? That my husband could also be the dangerous one? He's got a kind, youthful face that doesn't appear tainted enough to deal with this situation. How does Charles know him? I'm starting to realise there's a lot about my husband that's been kept from me.

'If you need anything, just let me know.' He places his hands in his pockets and then takes them out again quickly.

'Thanks.'

Everything on this boat is prepared for us to just hop aboard. Food in the fridge, another double fridge stocked with top-shelf alcohol. Our cruiser is luxury with a capital L. And I can't enjoy any of it today. Not the royal-blue velvet cushions with embroidered double Ls, nor the library of books beyond the galley. Our boat is four levels with guest bedrooms below, and yet all I can do while Kiki and Cooper lounge around the living area is stare back at Vaucluse Yacht Club and wonder where Jack is and when we'll return.

'Mum, this is awesome,' Kiki squeals. 'I haven't been on our boat in ages.'

'Neither have I.' I gaze around at the finer details of the main deck. Woodwork finish, huge plasma television, separate living spaces with glass coffee tables, gold accents and nautical furnishings. Books on islands are splayed beside large shells and coral pieces. I don't think the shock of all this is sinking in yet. Ariella's head hidden behind a pink mist. Ariella slumping over into her vegetable garden. I drop my luggage and exhale heavily as my head throbs with tension. I can't remember the last time I drank water or went to the toilet or ate. I'm light-headed and queasy and utterly exhausted.

Charles has probably packed the bag with useless items. Mismatched underwear and summer wear even though it's freezing. And the boat starts moving. Kiki and Cooper run back onto the deck, holding the railing and staring out. We're headed for the open ocean, headed away from Sydney. And somewhere back over the hill, police are swarming in Ariella's home.

Pulling my phone from my jacket pocket, I quickly tap on WhatsApp and find the name Janine, my secret name for Jack. He hasn't written back since my last message this morning. I'd told him something was happening next door at Ariella's. Then I'd told him the police had arrived. Nothing. No comment, even though his icon rests beside my message with the word *seen* next to it. So why isn't he texting back?

I don't know what he'll think when I write this next line, however I hope he does something about it.

My neighbour, Ariella, has been shot and I think Charles is involved somehow. He's taking me and the kids on a boat to Queensland and he won't tell me where. The skipper is a man I've never seen. You have to help. I think we may be in trouble.

Waiting to see if two blue ticks appear, I chew my inner cheek. But the message remains unread. And when I look up, Charles is standing before me. In two quick seconds, I flick my screen off WhatsApp and he glares at me.

'Who are you contacting?' he says.

'No one. I was checking if Georgia has said anything.'

'Give me the phone.'

I hesitate for a second and his eyes flash as he lunges forwards, breath touching my nose. Stale coffee and a hint of nicotine. I haven't been this close to him in a long while. Grey hairs flare from his nostrils. He really is unattractive. I hand him the phone, praying he doesn't look on WhatsApp. What if Jack texts back right now?

He asks for my password and types it in, scrolling through messages, not WhatsApp. He hasn't thought to look there. I lick my lips, waiting for him to catch me out.

'If anyone knows where we are, Emma, you're putting those kids in danger,' he says. 'It'll be your fault.'

'Tell me what's happening.' I step backwards, voice wobbly. 'What have you done to Ariella?'

'What have *I* done?' he whispers hotly. His eyes glance out to the kids. '*Done* to Ariella? What the fuck are you saying, Emma?'

'Our neighbour is dead and we're on the run. It looks a tad suspicious, doesn't it?'

He's too angry to pay attention to both me *and* the phone. He's checking the screen on my messages, finds nothing and then throws the phone overboard. Just like that. I imagine the plop. And I feel myself drop. It was the only way I could communicate with Jack.

Shaking my head, I glare at him. 'Why did you do that?'

'To stop you blabbing. Mateo hired me to guarantee his and his wife's safety, so now we're all fucked. You have no idea who we've been living next door to, Emma. Mateo will never let this go.'

'So, we go to the police and tell them.'

He holds a hand up to my face and spins around. 'You need to let me deal with this.'

It doesn't make sense. People who avoid police are criminals. There's a point Charles isn't admitting. He's connected to her murder somehow and now he's scared. I've never seen him scared, not since he started working for Mateo. Not when I was giving birth, not when Cooper choked on a grape as a one-year-old, not when our old car crashed into the back of another. But he's scared now, and this makes it more unsettling.

'We can't just keep running,' I say, holding my stomach. His eyes flick down to it and then back up. I see it there, behind the lazy lids, behind the clenched jaw. I don't think he cares. He's never been connected to this baby and he made it clear the minute I told him. Two was enough. Two was what we planned for. Why do you marry a man, ignoring all the signals? They were there and they were obvious, yet the prior, failing long-term relationship and the looming inner-baby-timer ticking had me rushing, had me rushing into marriage with him. The rebound became the one, the father of my children. And then you're stuck in the collective cycle of marriage, house, kids and you can't leave it. Because if you do, then you've failed. But I want out. I am close to getting out. One week, that's all. One week until we're supposed to move into the beach house.

But that failure of a choice, of a husband, stares at me now, unwanted, unattractive, nothing like Jack. And he says through gritted teeth, 'We disappear until I can figure this out.'

Two Months Ago

Trippy dance music beats through the house like an electric pulse. The bedside clock reads 2:24am and if it doesn't wake the kids, I'll be surprised. It's Charles. Off his head and forgetting his responsibilities, his commitment to family and respect. My heart races with shock and fury. Sure enough, in the hallway, Kiki rubs her eyes with matted hair while Coop shuffles to my bedroom, squinting.

'Back to bed, come on.' I usher them to their bedrooms, down the hall from mine.

Kiki yawns. 'But what's the music?'

I kiss both their sweet soft cheeks and lie, protecting their reckless father. 'I think your dad's accidentally broken the stereo and it's come on too loud. I'll go and ask him to turn it down.'

Cooper snuggles under his covers with his beloved rabbit teddy and Kiki rolls over, pulling the bedsheets over her shoulders. And I'm fuming with an anger that matches the pulse of the beat. What the hell is he doing now?

Downstairs, the music is so loud, the glass around the lampshades vibrates. I have to hold my ears. Charles sprawls in the loungeroom, smoking a cigarette, shoes off, business attire rumpled, a whole bottle of brown liquor at his feet. I march to the stereo and flick it down, making him lift his head. Absolutely fried. Worse than a month ago when he slapped me. A total mess.

White pasty face, clammy with sweat. Dark eyebrows and eyes that stand out like they've been drawn onto his face with black ink. Scary doesn't begin to describe him. I should've taken the kids and run.

'Don't turn that down, I'm thinking,' he yells. *Please be quiet*, I want to hush him. I don't want the kids overhearing us. I hold my hands up as though he's about to shoot me and give the warmest smile I can offer to someone I loathe.

'The kids woke up. It's a little loud.'

He rubs his temple, ash sprinkling to the white carpet in a neat grey clump. 'I'm . . . I'm needing this time. Don't you need time?' I don't know what he means but he sucks his cigarette like a total addict, three puffs in, and then says, 'He's riding me so hard, you know. He wants my soul.'

'Who?'

'Who do you fucking think?' he snarls and swigs the bottle of liquor. It sloshes down the neck like liquid gold. Mateo? Is this who Charles is talking about? He's got Charles wrapped around his little finger and it's playing on my drug-clouded husband. A trickle of booze dribbles down his chin and I'm staring at the staircase, willing Kiki and Cooper to stay upstairs, away from their disaster of a father. If they see this, it'll stay etched in their minds forever. Their father high on drugs and stressed like I've never seen him. Rave music matching his mood. Their mother scared out of her wits and trying to appease a useless drunk. He's changing before my eyes, and it's all because of Mateo.

'Why don't you have a nice warm shower and a tea—'

'Turn the music on.' He flicks his hand to the stereo. 'I need to think.'

I'm wondering who I should phone. The police? Jack? 'I'll call Jack.'

Charles shoots off the couch like a bullet, points to me from across the coffee table – a barrier I've deliberately placed between us. 'You leave this alone, you hear?'

'Okay. I'll go upstairs.'

He grunts at me like I've just said the most ridiculous thing in the world. 'No, I'll go.'

Charles collects his keys from beside the bottle, stubs out his cigarette and leaves his shoes. And it looks like he's going to vacate the house, and I know I should stop him from driving, *I know I should*, but I can't. Because I just want him out of the house and away from my babies and away from the new baby in my stomach.

Staggering to the foyer, jabbering about pressure, being over-worked, how he needs to think, Charles steps outside the door while I run to my spare key above the coffee machine. I bolt to the front door, deadlocking it from inside. And the relief that comes with the click of the lock, the revving of the car, the opening of the garage, the fading engine, is exhausting, making my legs wobble. Kissing the key in my clammy hands, I lean my head against the door for a moment, wondering how much longer I can hold on.

I hate my life. The neighbours look in on it with vintage-filtered lenses, the ones on Instagram that subtly alter the pictures of acai bowls, a lazy Sunday moment of black coffee and the newspaper, a daisy in a blown-glass vase. Take the filter away and you're left with a brightness so blinding that something as delicate as a daisy now seems disfigured, ugly, too colourful. Our life looks like the vintage-filtered version. The neighbour can imagine tinkling jazz always playing in the background while I'm tossing garden salads, flipping pancakes and fucking my husband. We all live vintage-filtered lives on the outside, we're conditioned to live that way. But

I hate my perfect life. I chose kids and marriage with another baby on the way. I chose 'wellness coach' as my identity. I chose the five-level home overlooking Sydney Harbour, the one that people enter to attend dinner parties every weekend.

But lying in bed with my eyes wide open, wondering how much more I can bear, I didn't choose this.

Now

Charles has left us alone and while the motor yacht sails out of Sydney and into the open sea, Kiki and Cooper follow me around the huge space, exploring the levels and staircases to the upper and lower decks. It's easy to get lost on our boat.

The main cabin is behind the dining room, complete with an ensuite bathroom fitted with marble benches and brass taps. Staircases, lined with lighting, curl down to a level of five bedrooms and four bathrooms. From there, another staircase branches up to a kitchen scullery and large pantry, the size of another room. We use a door that leads us outside and Kiki takes the lead. We follow her along the wooden corridor until she finds the other staircase and we trail up to the windy deck, complete with a jacuzzi, bar and sunloungers. I already know it's going to be enough space for me to avoid Charles and him to avoid us.

One more staircase up leads us to the bridge, where Charles is talking. Coop runs up to find his dad while Kiki and I wait in the loungeroom. It's a Sunseeker, worth at least thirty million and Charles shares it with five other families who we meet for Christmas and summer holidays. I never got to choose it, hardly ever use it and Charles had to borrow five million off my father to buy his portion of it. What will they all think about this now?

Charles has practically stolen their boat. What will my friends and family think of what's just happened?

The views back to the mainland are hidden by a swell that I hope will die down. It's a large boat, but not immune to rolling. When Cooper skips back down to us, we continue following Kiki through the huge boat, past crew quarters, laundry and engine rooms. Cooper delights in the machinery, yet I'm growing tired and hungry. I need to eat before I pass out. The boat rocks and Kiki stumbles against me.

'Let's go find something to eat,' I say. 'And put our bags down.'

Swinging back to the kitchen and pantry, I open one of four fridges and spot a bowl of fresh fruit. Bananas, apples, oranges and kiwis. I lift the whole bowl off the shelf and scour the pantry cupboards for chips, crackers and sweet cookies. I hand Kiki a few packets and look around. I'm not sure why I'm needing to hoard food. I suspect it has to do with anxiety. I'm unsure what's going to happen out here.

We venture back to the main deck where the master cabin sits. I don't know where Charles is planning to camp, but I want the kids near me. We carry the food to the bed and I ask Kiki to grab the luggage.

'Can we have a cookie now?' Cooper asks, jumping onto the quilt.

I nod. 'I'd like one too.' Sugar will give me some much-needed energy. He rips the plastic open with his teeth and pulls a chocolate cookie from the bunch, handing it to me. I crunch into it and Kiki comes back and I offer her one.

'Unzip your bag, bub,' I say to Kiki.

We spill crumbs over the silky doona cover. Kiki unzips her small backpack and I study the contents. One jumper, one pair of pants, some odd socks, dirty knickers from last night. Great. He's literally picked everything up from her bedroom floor, everything she wore yesterday and stuffed it in here. Kiki's t-shirt is wrinkled and stained from yesterday's hot chocolate. He didn't have time to think. Surely we can pull in somewhere up the coast and get more supplies? I'll chuck the clothes in the wash later. I'm just too tired to deal with it now.

I eat another cookie and Kiki and Cooper pull out the drawers, commenting on the little bars of soap and shampoo. Leaning back on the mattress, I unzip Cooper's bag and pull out his belongings. Same deal, only his dirty clothes from yesterday have been packed. I dread to think what Charles packed for me.

Kiki's phone buzzes and I quickly tug it from her pocket, swiping furiously. I didn't know she had her phone on her. In the rush to collect them from school, I thought she'd left it behind with her teacher and forgot to ask. This phone is our lifeline.

She whines as I finger the surface. 'Hey, Mum.'

It's Georgia, and her text is chilling.

I have tried contacting you, Miss Drey. But Mr Drey said not to call. I thought I would try Kiki. They come asking questions. Mr Mateo says it's Mr Drey who did it. They are taking me to the station. Mrs Drey, please come back? I will delete this now. G.

I stare at the screen for a while, blinking until the words blur behind tears. Mateo said Charles did it? Charles killed Ariella. Hopping off the bed, I leave the kids in the cabin so they can't see my reaction. My body moves itself in shaking waves. He killed her. But why? To hide something from me? To prevent our friendship from continuing? For Mateo? As a sign of loyalty? I understand how preoccupied he's been with impressing his new client, but would Charles really do this for Mateo? I don't know about Charles and his other clients, but his obsession over assisting our neighbours seemed to take precedence over anything else. The drug-taking, the late nights, the two am music thumping downstairs, all points to the stress Charles was feeling towards his relationship with Mateo.

I swipe the snot from my nostril and head into the bathroom for a tissue. Tracy saw, experienced or heard something that night. And I know I'm to blame for her ignoring me. Ariella said she knew *everything*. And then a few hours later, she's shot in the head. It can't be a coincidence. Whatever Tracy told Ariella got her killed. A tight knot sticks somewhere in my chest and I respire into it. These aren't just stories I'm inventing, the same way that my clients invent stories of phantom fears. I feared this would happen to my friend. And I'm seriously worried about Tracy.

Yet I also can't believe what Georgia said, not without evidence. Mateo's a criminal who could easily implicate Charles.

Still, the nagging thought teases me in the corner of my mind like a bratty child. The man in the footage, his swagger, the way he lifted his arm, he *looked* like Charles. And his behaviour has changed so dramatically ever since meeting Mateo. Also, why else is he running? Why aren't we going to the police?

After wiping my nose, I place the phone back in my pocket and head to the bedroom. I pull the kids into my lap. It's hard to hold them like I used to, cradled under my chin, sniffing their baby scent. It's hard now with this baby kicking inside me. I try to do it anyway. 'It's going to be okay.'

It sounds like I'm speaking to them, and Kiki's frowning up at me. But I'm reassuring my own frightened inner child.

Two Months Ago

I've started drinking my coffee in the morning with the curtain slightly drawn. I've started peeking through the gap into Ariella's garden, hoping to catch a glimpse of her. There was a moment, a few days ago, when I was just about to set my coffee mug down on the side table when a movement outside caught my eye.

I almost knocked my coffee mug over with my hand as I pried open the curtains to her life. My breath obscured the glass as I peered through the sheers while Ariella strolled through the garden in her leggings, sneakers, earbuds. She seemed so well-adjusted and content that the sight of her annoyed me. It's almost as though our fast-lived friendship bears no impact on her. She's still running, exercising, enjoying life while I'm upstairs, in my dressing gown, wondering why she needed my help and then didn't.

Today, as I'm standing at my usual spot, I thank the universe when she comes out into her garden and brings a tissue to her nose, blowing it. Her fluffy dog, who I've never cared to ask the name of, trots behind her, and they both end up against the trunk of her plane tree. The dog hops into her lap and Ariella is crying, or has a cold. Either way, she doesn't look good.

It's nine am. Mateo left for work an hour ago. In that time, she could have gone jogging, done some gardening, perhaps meditated on her lawn like she sometimes says she does, however, she's still in tracksuit pants and her hair is in a messy bun and, are those slippers? Yes, she's wearing slippers. It could be a cold. Yet I don't think so.

I want to run over and hug her and assure her that everything will be okay. She's patting her dog and starts crying into her tissue and that's when I decide to quickly change into jeans and a jumper and tug a brush through my hair. I clean my teeth and leave the coffee sitting on the side table. And then I scribble something on a note and fold it.

Ariella needs me. And when she sees me, she'll thank me.

I'm invited in and that's only because Ariella's housekeeper doesn't know Ariella doesn't want anything to do with me. She knows I'm a neighbour and she's seen me before and that's why the door swings open for me to enter. The foyer is just as white and polished as I remember, with the same expensive scent running through it. In the golden-framed mirror, I'm like an out-of-place imposter here. I should be dripping in diamonds, with gold bangles up my arms; instead, I'm dressed like a mother working from home.

'Miss Ariella is outside, Miss Drey,' the housekeeper tells me. We move through to the kitchen area, where the housekeeper has been wiping orange spray over the tiles. There's someone vacuuming down the halls and outside, by the terrace, the usual beefy bodyguards notice my approach. I still don't understand the need for all this security. Anyone would think Ariella is royalty the way they hover over this property.

The housekeeper opens the door to the terrace and I stand there a moment, unsure how Ariella will react when she sees me. I just want to wish her well, make sure she's okay. I fiddle with the paper in my hand.

When Ariella spots me, she stands from the tree trunk, brushing something off her lap. Swiping her nose, Ariella knows how to transform her expression from snotty, red, sobbing to happy, lovely, bubbly. She raises her eyebrows, opens her mouth and says, 'Hey,' as though well-rehearsed in feigning happiness. 'Don't get too close to me, I have a cold.'

I just saw her crying through my window. It's not a cold. Her watery red eyes and pink cheeks are the result of sobbing. It embarrasses me that she's lying. But sometimes you've got to allow people to hide the truth from you.

'I was wondering if you want to go walking with me later? It's such a beautiful day.' I stare up into the glare. 'The sun's out. And I have something exciting to tell you.'

I'm planning to admit the pregnancy. Perhaps if I divulge my dirty secret, she'll reciprocate and share hers. I wait for her response like a person asking for a first date.

'I can't today,' she says, and I press my lips together. 'But tomorrow?'

I beam. At least she's agreeing to meeting me. Will the wine bar, the note, what she wrote be forgotten? I cannot read her face. Somewhere between regret and remorse. So I quickly say, 'Perfect,' before she can pull out.

Ariella gestures towards the house, as though eager to have me gone. 'I'd invite you in for a coffee, but I have a hair appointment in an hour.'

'No, that's fine, I just came to give you this.' I hand over a recipe with an image of banana bread on it. Inside the recipe is my note. She stares at me for three seconds and says, 'Thanks.' Then she accepts it, tucking it in her pocket, blinking away from me and whoever watches our exchange.

'You said you wanted the recipe, so I printed it out.'

I've checked her social media. There is none. We haven't swapped numbers. I cannot text or call her because she doesn't have Messenger or WhatsApp. She doesn't have an email address or website. She's a disconnected citizen in a modern and connected world. And this is the only way we can do it. Exchange notes, knock on doors, act like housewives, talk about pregnancy.

Therefore, I leave Ariella's house with my message clear and explicit. She may rub it out, burn it, flush it down the toilet, but it's there. My words, words that I mean.

I want to help you. You can trust me. Tell me what you need.

Now

We've been on *Lady Luck* for five hours. Night cloaks the sea in muted grey. The ocean is swelling and mad. Even on a boat of this size, the hull crests and falls over the swell in a sickening movement I can't get used to. If I stare at the lights on land, I'll stay level.

Shrek plays on the big screen and Kiki and Coop are snuggled up in pyjamas on one of the lounges with bowls of crisps and eyes glued to the movie. They don't notice the rocking and rolling. I'm outside on a cold leather lounger with a thick woollen throw over my body and a large glass of red wine. I haven't drunk alcohol since being pregnant, but if I don't relax somehow, I'll find myself diving off this cruiser and leaving them all behind. So, it's quietening me. Even if I just take little sips, and don't finish the glass, the knowledge that it's there, sedating me, benefits me greatly.

Charles hasn't come down from the bridge since our tense conversation and I'm pleased. It's allowed me some time to settle alone. I even managed to doze off for an hour while Coop and Kiki played Nintendo. How that was possible in my state only came down to the pregnancy forcing me to rest. We'd eaten a banana each and half the biscuits and the sugar-induced coma washed over me like a wave I couldn't ignore. When I woke, they were still playing and dusk had pushed the daylight away. So, I crept down to the kitchen, made them a cream-cheese-and-tomato sandwich each, filled two glasses with juice and balanced them back to the galley. And then I went down there again, this time to search through the cupboards until I found the knives. Long, sharp, good-quality knives that I may need. I slammed the drawer shut, shaking my head for even considering it, and padded back up to the kids.

I've used Kiki's phone to call Tracy and messaged twice. Nothing. She's been ignoring me for a week now. Ever since that night. And guilt gnaws at me, so I block it out. Still, I'd like to know that she's safe. I'm sure what she told Ariella is the reason for my neighbour's brutal murder. So many unanswered questions. Is Ariella's death on the news? Are the police after us? After receiving Georgia's text, I've been too nervous to check. And the reception out here is patchy, dropping in and out. I can ask Charles for the Wi-Fi password, but then he'll suspect I'm communicating with someone. Cut off from Jack, the internet, only leaves me with one option. I'll have to call his phone. Yet I know what consequences that could entail. I've heard Charles drop the idea of bugging a wife's phone to catch them cheating. What if he's bugged Kiki's too? If Charles got even a hint of our relationship and plans for the future, there would be a reason to start searching. My husband is unfortunately the hardest person to hide anything from. If he discovers details about our new house or how I plan to leave him, or about Jack and my baby, I truly believe now he might kill me.

I can't risk it, especially being isolated at sea with just the kids. So, I check the internet one more time. I have a couple of bars out here. They could drop out at any time, so I quickly type in *today's breaking news*. And it springs up like a toxic friend you've been trying to avoid. Our names, faces and address plastered all over the story for the whole of Australia to scrutinise.

Suspicious Disappearance of Reputable Drey Family After Daughter Films Neighbour's Murder.

And the article is riddled with accusations that makes the wine slip out of my hand and slop over the white leather lounge like blood. 'Daughter accidentally filmed and uploaded neighbour's murder.' 'Housekeeper told to keep silent.' 'Children taken from school.' 'Neighbour a client of wellness coach.' 'If anyone has seen, or has any information about the whereabouts of this family, please contact Crime Stoppers.'

Two Months Ago

We're meeting after school drop off. We're going to do a river walk and kick off at the bottom of my steps. I told her I'll bring a thermos and she said she'll bring ginger tea. We'll probably take a break later on and grab a coffee at the café and then I'll invite her back to my place for lunch. I'll prepare a salad and fish.

I'm ecstatic that Ariella wants to meet me, and emotionally relieved, especially after leaving her the note. I've never been one for conflict, particularly with new friends. It feels good, it feels right, to have her trusting me. I want to be part of her life and I may be wrong, but I think I understand why she needs help. She's trapped, like me, in a loveless marriage. I can help her with that. Once she decides what she wants to do with Mateo, I'll be there supporting her. I can picture him losing it and he'll blame her in some way. And when he does, I'll have the guest room in mine and Jack's new house ready with towels at the end of her bed, a fresh linen closet emptied for her clothes to be hung in and Netflix installed onto the guest-room TV.

Ariella's on the path at the bottom of our garden. She's wearing the latest jogging shoes and a coat with fur around the hood. We carry flasks of hot tea and our breath swirls along with our voices. The sun hasn't really lifted the morning dimness yet.

It's hard to be vulnerable and conversational with an employed stalker behind you. His footsteps match ours. He clears his throat. It's like having a husband crash a girls' dinner party. Always having to watch what you say, how you act. His relentless presence is so irritating, worse than someone eavesdropping at a café, a stranger pushing against you in a shopping line. I don't know how she stands it. I'd like to stop abruptly and have him knock into me. I'd like to accidentally spill my scorching tea over his chest.

Ariella doesn't mind. She chats away about the river, the morning, the stillness. What changed her mind to meet me? Was it my note? My authentic warmth in wanting to help her?

Still, even after meeting hundreds of clients a year, I've never encountered this – someone so wary, secretive, able to adapt and adjust their personality to fit the room. She can switch from alone and sobbing to joyous and bubbly in a blink of an eye. Ariella should be sitting on the couch in my office.

'Come to my centre and we'll do some breathwork. You know, reiki, meditation—'

'I don't need to.'

I slurp my tea and poke my hand into my pocket. 'You looked really upset that Friday night,' I whisper, staring ahead at the path. Moreton Bay fig trees arch over us like a safety bridge and our shoes squelch the berries, bringing up a pungent perfume. I don't want him hearing.

'No, not really, why?' she quietly says.

It's that tone. That forced, *there's nothing wrong with me* tone, that's starting to bother me. It's the type of tone I hear in women who are abused or controlled and pretending to be content.

I laugh. 'You can open up to me.'

She mimics the laugh. 'There's really nothing wrong.'

'Have you been trying for a baby?'

She brushes off my question by saying, 'You said you had exciting news to tell me.'

'Yes, I do. I'm pregnant.'

She stops, mouth open in a genuine smile. There's no hugging though. No kisses on the cheek. 'Really? That's fantastic.'

'Are you still trying?'

She shrugs and keeps strolling, yet my footsteps are getting louder, faster. I take another sip, burning my tongue.

'I don't really know yet. I run hot and cold with the idea.'

Ariella changes the topic to regular conversations. The price of broccoli, the growing seasons, an avocado dressing she made the other day. We're back to this. Talking about meaningless subjects and not getting to the bottom of her problems. And I've given her every opportunity to open up and accept my support.

'God, it's cold,' I say. I wrap my hands around the flask and stare over at the yachts stuck on the river like they're trapped in ice. It's that tranquil. So still you want to ditch a rock into it just to create some ripples.

Ariella's gone quiet and so have I and it's not until we reach an exercise group laying yoga mats out on the lawn that she talks again about maybe trying it out. It's that kind of conversation now. So, I agree we should try it out. She goes up to the trainer and requests a business card, and she asks so nicely.

But I'm on the path and I'm stuck on wanting more information. Why was she upset that Friday night? Why won't she tell me?

When Ariella returns down the hill, she hands me a business card with white paper poking out beneath it. Another note. Pressing my lips together, I side-glance to her minder, who's kicking a berry with his foot.

'This looks interesting,' she says brightly.

'It does.' I nod. I smile. I know. I've got it. 'We'll do it together.'

Giving a loud sigh, Ariella keeps on walking. I stick the business card and paper note inside my pocket, and suck on my thermos. This is how we'll do this. The minder resumes tracking us. We'll do this behind the bastard's back. We pretend to talk about life. But the obvious message is there. Finally, Ariella's letting me in.

Now

Scott, the skipper, is seated at the helm steering *Lady Luck* when I climb the stairs to the bridge. Soft music drowns the engines, and he almost looks asleep up here, staring out at the black moving picture. I want to ask why we're not stopping to moor somewhere for the night, but after reading the news, I now understand why.

At first, I hesitate by the stairs, my fingers hovering over the door. Charles isn't here. So where is he? Scott yawns into his elbow and I knock, accidentally startling him.

'Sorry. I was just looking for Charles.'

'He's in the captain's quarters.' He nods behind him to a shiny wooden door. He considers me for a moment and I wonder what he's thinking. What does he know? Is this guy employed by my husband to carry out dirty work?

Leaving Scott, I twist the doorknob and close it behind me. The captain's quarters are a whole suite in itself, complete with a loungeroom, dining area, and a bedroom off to the side. A stupid sitcom plays from the television and the forced laughter makes me cringe. Since when has he watched shows like this? Steam and lime-infused soap wafts out from the bathroom. And then I spot Charles with a towel around his hips, shaving in the mirror. Hair combed back like a mobster. White back, like a sheet of A4 paper. He sees me in the reflection and drops the razor into the bowl with a rattle.

'What are you doing in here?'

I stamp forwards with Kiki's phone up and out. 'This. We're on the run. And they all know it. The police have Georgia, they're questioning her. You're a prime suspect and—'

Charles knocks the phone out of my hand and slaps me across the face like a bastard. It stings and the first instinct is to slap him right back. But he grabs my wrist like a vice and bares teeth that are ugly and yellowing with age, nicotine and too much whiskey.

'I told you to stay the *fuck* out of this,' he roars into my face, spit landing on my tingling cheek.

He lunges to grab the phone from the tiles, his towel falling off his hips, exposing a swinging penis and floppy balls. He doesn't care. He gets Kiki's phone and smashes it onto the marble counter until the screen cracks and splinters.

Every beating of the phone generates a grunt from him, so angry, so vicious, so alarming, that I step out of the bathroom, clutching my cheek.

He's lost the plot and he's wild with rage. I don't want him to hurt me, and I know what this man is capable of. He points to me, curved over so thinning skin folds at his belly button. 'You have no idea who we're running from.'

'You've lost it.' I shake my head. 'And the police are after us. That's who we're running from.'

'And Mateo,' he bellows with his arms flinging. 'Mateo.'

'What happened to Ariella? Why was she shot?'

'Why do you think I know anything about this?'

Because it was you in the footage, I want to say. You killed her for your boss or for your own personal, sick reasons. But I can't say that. I'll get smashed up like the phone.

I never expected this. This whole day, this scenario we're in. I never expected when the removalists reversed past the gates of Ariella and Mateo's property that in three months' time I'd be here on this yacht with a dodgy skipper called Scott, a naked enraged husband, along with two kids pulled out of school, on the run from police. I hate Charles. I hate him so much I'm picturing the knife in the kitchen stabbing his gut. However, I know better than to rev a client who's gone ballistic and Charles is no different. Except there are differences in his appearance that perhaps I didn't notice at first. Red circles under the eyes, red nostrils and dilated pupils. Is he high? If he is, then this is even worse than I imagined. I need to cool him down, because he's stamping towards me bristling with fury.

'Okay.' I hold my hands up. 'I get it. I won't say a word.'

'Good.' He nods. 'You're treading a very thin line, Emma, very thin.'

'I understand.' I force a quick smile and step back. 'This is serious.'

He keeps on coming, penis swaying, nipples pert and pink. 'This man is the boss, the boss.' He accentuates the 's' like a snake.

'You must feel very frightened by that, and I get it.' I swallow, almost against the lounger. 'I won't interfere. I trust you.'

He swipes his nose and nods over and over like the drugs have him dancing. And it's worked. Charles is not moving towards me any longer. He believes my bullshit, my soothing voice, which covers the fear like a phoney Band-Aid. And it's only now, noticing him naked without his suits, without his armour, without that charming persona that comes with clothing and cars and credit cards, that I see who this man really is. And is he capable of killing? Capable of killing Ariella?

I swallow, hand pressed on my cheek.

One Month Ago

Ariella wants me to spy on her husband. She hasn't said why yet, but I'm guessing she thinks he's having an affair. The note was simple and quick.

> *Listen to Mateo's conversations when he's out smoking in the morning. Please. I need to know what he talks about.*

I've started peeking out my windows when Mateo smokes in their garden. At first, while I'm working in the office, his dull murmur irritates like a mosquito, a trapped fly on the windowsill. I'm deep in work and I hear his laugh outside, a repetitive *ha ha ha, ha ha ha*. It's false, forced and actually sounds the way its spelt. Pushing the blinds up, I peer out as cigarette smoke fogs over his head. He's with one of his men.

Sunlight sputters in patches over Ariella's immaculate herb garden and Mateo stomps his cigarette butt into the grass. I already envision the conversation between them when she spots it there later. Her garden is her pride and joy. That's why he spoils it.

I've even left the study on three occasions and crept downstairs – avoided Georgia – pushed the terrace doors open, taken the next level down to the pool area and stood by the fence, listening. A tickle in my throat had teased me into a cough, which I had to contain by swallowing multiple times, because I didn't want him catching me.

Sometimes he's alone, just puffing and scrolling through his phone. At least he has the decency to smoke outside. Filthy habit.

But today, as I leave the study and make for fresh air, I'm like a peeping, prying mother; like a peeping, prying wife.

I'm staring at the crisping orange leaves from a dying bush, which needs pulling out. Avoiding the leaves, stepping carefully and quietly around them, I hear Mateo speaking to the beefy bodyguard about the catch last night. It's like uncovering a scandal meant for me.

'Legs up to armpits, cock-sucking lips.' I can hear he's smiling. *Ha, ha, ha.*

'How long you have it?'

'Who gives a fuck about timing,' Mateo mutters. One of them spits, a phlegmy chunk that lands on a leaf. He could be talking about one of his strippers, but I doubt it. I hate the way the bodyguard calls the woman *it*. I hate the way they spit without caring. Pigs.

'Anyway, I gotta go back down there tonight,' Mateo says. Shoes shuffle on the pavement. Cigarette smoke wafts over my fence, the stink of nicotine strong. Who and what is he talking about? *Timing, how long have you had it, legs up to armpits, gotta go back there tonight.* He could be talking about a fling, but I can't be certain. I'm uncertain what to tell Ariella. That her husband speaks badly about women? I'm sure she's aware of that. I'm grinding my teeth, eyes staring at a yellow star leaf, golden, not ready to die and crisp. And then Georgia steps out and sees me. And I know he'll hear when she calls me. I put a finger to my mouth, but she doesn't see.

She calls out, 'Mrs Drey, you want a coffee brought up to the study or out here?'

I flap my hand, holding my finger up to my lips. And the footsteps behind the wall scuffle, there's murmuring, and I start hopping over the wilting leaves, avoiding the sound of my feet crunching down on them.

I've been caught out as the snooping neighbour, the prying gossip. And with someone like Mateo, I've likely crossed a boundary.

One Month Ago

We won't have moments like this for much longer. Our sex is a connection that ties us together like the leash of a straying dog. Life will soon get in the way and that connection will unclip, distancing us further into an unknown future. These moments are precious and need to be handled carefully. One slip and this bond can break into silent shards of grief that can't be addressed or spoken of. If Charles discovers us, this could all be over.

This is what I tell Jack as I step out of the shower, the dull ache of my vagina proving how well he took me from behind. The lights of Sydney Harbour flash through the sheers as Jack listens flat on his back from the hotel bed, also naked and spent.

In the bathroom mirror, I examine myself. Cheeks creased. Mouth pulled. Lips burnt from kissing and stubble scratches.

'I'll only have myself.' I speak to the reflection. Behind me, Jack's face turns, and he laughs. It's not funny though. I'm hormonal and annoyed. He has no idea what it's been like living with Charles. Things are getting worse. Charles is getting more stressed, coming home later, drinking and smoking. I don't want to tell Jack, because he would leave everything right there and then. Even though I'm sulky, the truth is, I want our relationship to start the right way. Our kids settled, our life organised, his new business set up. I just have to hold on a little longer. But keeping it hidden from

Jack is proving difficult. It'd be easier to tell him, pack the kids' bags and book a hotel for a month.

'I don't know why you're saying this. It's not like you to be so melodramatic.' He adjusts the pillow under his head.

I gaze over my nakedness. What does he see in someone like me?

'It's all going to be sorted in the next month,' he says. 'We'll have our house, our life, we'll have each other.'

'You don't know what it's like to have a baby.' I lick my chafed lips. 'If our house and plan don't get sorted, I'll be raising it alone.'

'That's never going to happen.'

'What if Charles finds out about us sooner?'

'He's never going to find out.'

I lift a swollen breast, considering the purple engorged veins. My breasts will soon carry milk. 'I'll be alone with this baby.'

In the mirror, I see him lean up on his elbow to stare at me. 'Emma, stop it.'

'If he finds out and we don't go through with our plan, that's what will happen.' I brush my hands over my stomach, inspecting the belly button that'll soon pop. 'I'll be alone.'

That gets him out of bed. That gets him stepping over to me. He's behind me and I feel his heat. We stare at one another in the mirror. He made this baby with me. I don't know why I feel like arguing with him, provoking a fight. My mind feels muddled and agitated, jumping and jerking, wanting to cling to security.

Two hot hands on my shoulder. 'We're not prepared yet. But we almost are, and I've been sorting this out ever since you told me about the baby. Four more weeks, that's all we need. I have to get everything sorted first. You want a house to move into? Somewhere for our baby and the kids to live?'

Ignoring his face in the mirror, I open my lip balm, apply some to my lips. 'I can live anywhere. Hotel. Apartment. My parents—'

'But you know what Charles is like. A dog with a bone. You want to be a few steps in front of him, don't you?'

I huff to myself. 'What if it never happens? What if you change your mind?'

'That's bullshit.' Dropping his hands from my shoulders, he moves beside me to the sink, where he turns on the tap, splashes water over his face. He's annoyed with me and I'm being hard on him.

'I'm sorry,' I say, passing him the hand towel. Jack rubs his face with it. His eyebrows bristle and I smooth them down. We face the mirror, then he takes my hand and guides me back to the bed, onto his lap where his lips trace down my shoulder.

'Four more weeks, okay?' His breath is warm and tickly. 'Everything will work out. Promise.'

'I know. I'm just tired. Did you look into Mateo?' I ask.

'I did, actually. Apparently, his last chief of security went missing a little over five months ago and hasn't been seen since. That's why he's employed us.'

'We knew that. Mateo openly told us at dinner. Did police look into it?'

'Apparently.' He squeezes my waist. 'He's now a missing person who's literally disappeared without a trace. And you.' Jack bounces his knee. 'Keeping away from his wife?'

Leaning back onto his chest, I nod, hiding my face, hiding the lie. 'What could that mean? Why would he just disappear?'

'Look, I don't know much about Mateo, but if he's linked to anything or anyone down at the clubs in Sydney, it's usually dirty business, if you ask me. Those men demand loyalty and respect. Maybe the chief of security let him down, somehow.'

'And Mateo got rid of him?'

'I can only surmise.' He kisses the base of my neck. 'Stay clear, okay. Don't get involved.'

Ariella wants me to spy on her husband, but I can't tell Jack about the notes. I hate lying to him. But what I'm doing is practically harmless – standing outside in my own garden, listening in. I could be watering, weeding, it's not so devious. If I'm not worried, then neither should Jack be. So, I agree and kiss his hand.

Now

Once Charles picks up his towel, I quickly let myself out of the captain's quarters. Scott gives me a glance and I'm sure he heard us. It bothers me though because he never came to check on my safety. Well, he wouldn't, would he? He's only here for Charles. Still, the glance and quick smile doesn't go unnoticed.

I don't bother saying anything. My legs are jelly, finding it difficult to hold up my weight down the steps to the level below. I use the railing for support, holding a brick of emotion in my belly. I need to let it out before I burst.

There's a door leading to the outside deck, so I travel between soft lounge chairs and golden lamps, past a bouquet of fresh yellow roses and towards the windows.

Once outside, I slam the door and I can breathe again. The air is briny and cold, sharp in my lungs. There's salt on my lips and I lick it.

We're travelling at quite a pace. The waves roll past and the cruiser slices through the water, creating a foamy wake. How easy would it be to jump off and float on my back, to let the black current take me away? The stars are covered by thick clouds, and the lights of New South Wales blink back. We're here, we're not going anywhere, you're safe. I hold myself, touching goosebumps under my hot hands and inhale deeply.

Poor Ariella. It comes before I can stop, and why would I want to? Stress is an emotion that needs to be released and this is what I teach my clients. I step towards the railing, gazing overboard and my tears leak over the edge, meeting the salt sea like companions. And I stand there, holding the railing, head on my arms, crying. The ocean is loud, blocking my sobs and I'm free to do it, let it out.

It's good to release tension: face scrunched, fisted hands, bawling. It's the responsibility that has me choking. What if this was my fault? Getting involved with Ariella, passing notes back and forth, trying to support and boost her courage to leave Mateo, bringing Tracy into the mix. All Ariella wanted was freedom from marriage, freedom from a controlling, domineering man who'd been watching her every move since they said, *I do*. She only had me. Just me. Friends and family were forbidden, because like any dictator, you can't have people forming alliances, connections. I was her saviour and I failed her.

Now the gravest threat surrounding me and my children is their own father. Charles asserts he had nothing to do with Ariella's death, we're simply running from Mateo. But I do not believe my husband. If he did kill Ariella, then there are a number of possible reasons why. Firstly, Ariella was going to tell me everything she knew, and I truly believe that information got her shot. Did Charles shoot her to protect himself? Or did Mateo order him to shoot Ariella before incriminating Charles? He's had my husband's head under his shoe since we all met. I believe Charles would do this for Mateo. But maybe whatever Tracy divulged to Ariella had her killed? It's up to me to unearth the reason and who did it. But black engulfs me and this cruiser, this never-ending voyage, is worse than any cell. Jack's not coming. No one is coming for me. How will I escape with my children from a floating prison? How will I save them from my murdering husband who's kidnapped us?

Three Weeks Ago

Stop listening. Two chilling words that I read over and over as though unable to comprehend their meaning. And I do, only it's just that I'm scared by them. So, I dissect the handwriting, the quality of paper, the way he wrote my name on the envelope, the type of envelope he chose, the black pen over blue. In it, perhaps I'll find a hint of humour, a joke, a nice way of saying, *Stop snooping, Emma.* His handwriting is blocky, considered and definitely not rushed. He's ripped the tiny piece of lined paper from a notepad I guess sits on his desk. It's ripped perfectly, as though he's folded it and torn it on the edge of a table. He didn't fold the paper. It sat neatly inside the blank white envelope with my name, blocky, scrawled in the middle with a full stop at the end, like a tiny bullet hole. Like he'd dotted it in anger. There's no licking of the envelope. He didn't want to waste his spit. Instead, he's slipped it inside and directly pushed it into the letterbox, unfazed by the possibility of Charles reading it.

He hates me. And I hate him. For what he stands for, the way he treats Ariella, the colour of his car, his snicker, his grin. He doesn't even know what he has in someone like Ariella.

I drop the paper so its floats like a feather to the kitchen bench, as though those words hold no weight. But they do. I've noticed how tight I'm suddenly breathing. So, I scrunch it up in my fist.

My coffee's developing a skin and I push it away and head to the kettle, where I flick it on again. His threat hurts, but it won't stop me. It's like I *need* to know what he's up to. She's relying on me and my strength is powering my own courage.

The kettle clicks and I scoop a spoonful of instant decaf into a new mug and pour the water in, mixing it. It's an early spring day where the sun's warm and the shade's cool and you have to pick the point in between. Outside, I choose the sunny upper step, overlooking the clipped lawn and rectangle pool area. A group of mothers are over by the river on picnic rugs, prams parked in a line, babies lolling around them like jellybeans. I sip my coffee and imagine Ariella leaving Mateo. In fact, I don't want to picture it. There'll be tears and upset, slamming of doors, violence and aggression. She doesn't have to tell me; I know that's what she fears. I bet that's why she's having me snoop on him.

Over their fence, from here, the tops of their trees sway gently. I always believe it's a good idea to sit back like this and reflect upon your own behaviour. It's what I teach my clients to do and many meditation instructors who've given presentations in my field have said to practise. Self-reflection, self-analysis, self-enquiry, self-investigation. If you can do this often, then you have a higher emotional intelligence, you're not afraid to pick at your scabs and gaze at the blood beneath them. I don't think Ariella knows how to do this. That's why she struggles to tell the truth. I think that's why I care, I think that's why I was listening, why I wait for her notes. Because if she can't look beneath her scabs, then she needs someone stronger who can.

Three Weeks Ago

We attend a dinner at my parents' house and it feels different from any previous dinners. Partially because I think this is the last time we'll be doing this. Charles and me and our two children blended in a typical foursome.

Mum and Dad live on Macquarie Street in a flashy penthouse apartment with a huge balcony overlooking Sydney Opera House and the bridge. They're not the sort of parents who come with warm hugs and grateful kisses or doting voices over the kids. Mum's never offered to look after Kiki and Cooper, and it's somewhat due to the white carpets in their penthouse and somewhat because her and Dad are more sociable than me, heading out most nights for dinners, charities and shows with friends. They're just not grand-parent parents. In fact, they're not even parent parents. Half of the reason why I studied psychology, wellness and spirituality was because of the neglect I'd suffered at the hands of two extremely self-absorbed adults. I'd been raised by nannies, housekeepers and given everything I'd ever wanted. I blame them for everything I am.

'Pass the kale, Charles,' Mum says holding out a skinny, wrinkled arm. I get my disordered eating from her. A pendulum of guilty bingeing and difficult starving.

Charles passes the kale. Cooper and Kiki are sitting at the kitchen bar with their own special dinners and an iPad each. Truth be told, I'd rather they didn't develop a relationship with these two strangers. Better to block the experience out with iPads, headphones and their own plates of nachos. They don't need to end up like me: warped and worried about female companionship. I've never trusted friendships and I blame my mother. She taught me they're not to be trusted, in fact, nothing and no one is.

'How's business?' Dad asks Charles.

'Good. Busy. Just acquired a new client, a big one, actually.'

'Our neighbour,' I intervene, sawing into the Wagyu steak. I glance at Charles. 'Right?'

He nods, chewing his steak, probably wondering why I'm so invested in the conversation.

'Who's your neighbour?' Dad pours himself a large glass of yellow wine, wooded and strong, and he sloshes it around the glass before slurping.

'Mateo El-Din. Owns most of the bars and nightclubs in Sydney, for starters.'

'Why does he need protection?' Mum sniffs.

'Wealth,' Dad tells her.

Charles shrugs. 'Yeah, and other things.'

Dad stops sloshing and sets his glass down, sucking his teeth. 'Nothing dodgy, I hope?'

Charles laughs in a way that Charles never laughs and says, 'Nah. Nah. Nothing like that.' And then changes the subject to the other side of business. Partnerships, employees, monetary losses. And they haven't noticed as they pass the salt, and spoon extra jus on their meat. But I noticed. My husband is hiding a dark secret and that dark secret is Mateo.

Now

We've stopped. I wasn't meant to fall asleep. The sea created the rocking movement of a womb. And that, along with the white noise of droning engines, had me passed out deep. Only, we've stopped moving and the cruiser's engines are silent. Waking fills me with dread. It's the same when your kid is in hospital, when you've injured yourself badly, when you wake after a horrendous argument with your family. You can't go back to sleep but life just seems too hard to stay awake.

Rolling onto my side, I lean on my elbow to check the adjacent bedroom where Cooper and Kiki share a bed. Their little bodies are mounds under the bed covers, fast asleep. Thank God they're okay and they don't know what's happening. Slumping back onto the bed, I face the clock on the bedside table. Six am. Is Charles coming down from his high? I touch my cheek. Dreams had me restless and waking all night, fretting about the immediate future. Now my head is heavy with stress and exhaustion, my eyes puffy and blurred. We're fugitives on the run from a crime I'm not sure he's committed.

I swing my legs off the bed and reach for the water bottle, sculling almost half. The baby kicks three times in a row and I stroke above my belly button. Right now, this is my only connection to

Jack, yet I can't ignore the hurtful tugging every time I think of him, our house, our future. Where is he? And where are we?

A white strip of light between the curtains blinds me as I move to part them. The water is dark blue, choppy and uninviting. Beside us, a long jetty reaches out and there's a rocky mole barricading a yacht club filled with masts, a dismal collection of boats. Where the hell are we? Somewhere north of Sydney and it's not Byron Bay or anywhere in the tropics. If it was, the water would be ice blue, palm trees would crowd white beaches. But the yellow strip of beach backs onto Norfolk pines. We've been sailing for about ten hours, so I'm guessing it's Port Macquarie. We must be refuelling or stopping for supplies, yet the size of this cruiser means we can only go ashore using the tender. Perhaps Charles and Scott have already left?

The sight of land provides a conflicting mix of emotions. So close I could swim with the kids to escape Charles and wherever he's taking us. We could go to the police and tell them we were forced to join him.

My husband is kidnapping us, this much I know. Still, are the police waiting for us to disembark so they can arrest us?

Someone's descending the spiral staircase to the main deck and when I move to the doorway, I spot Charles with a backpack on his shoulder, hair dishevelled and shirt wrinkled. I don't want to step out and greet him, but I want to know what we're doing here. Are we getting off this boat?

He's still wearing his work shoes from yesterday, the same blue business shirt he had Georgia iron before his polished shoes tapped out of the house. When we first met, he didn't wear clothes like that. It was plain cotton t-shirts and army shorts. That's what attracted me to him. Simple, unassuming, unconcerned by appearance and material possessions. Boy, have things changed. He plonks his backpack down onto a table and rifles through it.

116

'Where are we?' I ask.

He looks up, startled, saying nothing. Then he goes back to his backpack.

'Coffs Harbour.'

'Are you going ashore?'

'Only to get a few things.'

'Can I come?'

He stares at me, face pale and restless. Definitely coming down. Such a vacant husband, I never saw the drug-taking before, never saw this side to him. I was blind because I wanted to be. How many women are?

'I don't think so,' he says.

'The kids need things. Extra clothing. I don't know how long you plan on running, but they need—'

'Write me a list.' He grabs the backpack and flings it over his shoulder. 'You've got five minutes and Scott's staying here to keep an eye on things.'

It's a threat. *Don't do anything foolish.* I don't want another slap to the face and I'm already calculating what I'll do once he reaches the shore.

My husband has kidnapped me. I'm being kidnapped and taken to a mystery place, and I have to pretend to be okay with it for my kids' sake. Meanwhile, the police are after us, and family and friends will be worried. My husband is the lead suspect in my neighbour's murder, a murder I've now seen being committed. A sharp stab in my gut has me holding my breath. Jack. I want Jack. Where the fuck are you? And poor Ariella. Why are you dead? What did you need to tell me?

While Charles goes ashore, Scott will be here, yet it doesn't mean I can't at least try to alert someone. I shut my mouth and get ready, writing up a list with the stationery from the desk in the master cabin.

The bag he packed for me has practically nothing in it. Two pairs of knickers, one bra, a pair of leggings, two t-shirts and a jumper. He's packed sneakers and I'm wearing boots and that's about it. There's no make-up, no toiletries and I've used a spare toothbrush from the cruiser and stuffed that, some soap and hair products in my bag in case we have to leave. Last night, I used the disposable comb from the bathroom, pulling it through my knotty hair and staring at my reflection. A washed-out ghost stared back. I'd never seen myself so miserable, so dead inside. It's frightening and I promised to not face a mirror again. Quickly, I write a list of essentials that we need. Clothes for the kids, bathers, socks and shoes. Flip-flops for us three, a proper brush and hair elastics.

I need to try and do something while he's gone. At least attempt to be useful. When I hand the list to Charles, he doesn't look me in the eye.

Shame or guilt can do that to a person. Or hate. Judging by the redness on my cheek, I'd say it was the last of those emotions.

Two Weeks Ago

It's a perfect setting for perfect people. It could be a movie set from a romantic comedy where the girlfriends come together after a one-night stand and discuss the sex, the size of his penis. I want it to be like that but it's not that kind of friendship. This is all a charade Ariella and I act out. The table is set with a basket of croissants, plump raspberries in a blue and white bowl, a carafe of fresh juice and a coffee plunger. The linen tablecloth moves and a small vase of yellow roses from her garden proudly sit in the centre, as though they've only been grown for this occasion. Without Mateo, Ariella can set the table how she likes. Out on the terrace, after school drop off, once the men have left for work. Wish it were that perfect. Two bodyguards linger nearby.

'This is so lovely,' I say, taking a seat and unfolding the white napkin over my lap. She pours me a mug of coffee and passes me the milk. All very girly and pretty. Even a lime-green leaf has fallen on cue atop my plate. I twist it around by the stem, admiring the veins.

'I've gone off coffee,' I say, finding it easier now to play-act with the men listening.

Ariella pours herself a juice.

'I've started craving carbs, though. White bread, white pasta, all the bad things.'

She laughs and the glass accidentally chinks against her teeth like a child. 'When I get pregnant, I'm going to end up like a beached whale.'

'I doubt that.'

'Here.' She hands over the basket of pastries, and normally I wouldn't, however, she's been lovely setting this breakfast up for me, so I reach for one. I wish we could have one of those friendships where we get together and discuss the woes of heartburn and aching pelvises, of babies and nurseries. Yet we're here for one reason and one reason only – to pass notes and information. Mine relates to what I heard in the garden, about Mateo's threatening letter to me. I wonder what she'll say about that? Obviously, he hasn't said anything to her. I'm here, in their garden, spreading thick jam on a croissant and biting into flaky pastry. I haven't been stopped at the door, there are no minders searching me or dragging me out. Maybe this is Mateo's plan? To listen in on our conversation as a risk assessment.

'Tell me about your friends,' I start. 'Have they had children?'

She shakes her head. 'Not yet.'

'I've never heard you speak much about them. And what about family? Sisters or brothers?'

She scrapes jam across a croissant, unable to look at me. 'I don't have family.'

I lift an eyebrow. 'None at all?'

Ariella raises her gaze and speaks with a robotic voice. 'I only need Mateo. I don't need friends or family.' It's a pointed, frightening confession and I struggle to act normal after she states it. Ariella's talking in code to me, divulging details and secrets in sarcastic vocabulary that her minders won't bat an eyelid at. She's clever and I feel smart being able to pick up on it, decipher the language, scrutinise the meaning.

I bite into the pastry and talk with a full mouth, not really wanting to swallow or eat. 'We're so lucky to have such wonderful husbands. I agree, you don't need anything or anyone else.'

I'm building a picture of Ariella and what she's going through, what she's been through. I suddenly don't feel like eating. I'm trying to go along with how wonderful Mateo is and it's difficult. Memories of him stalking through my foyer, mocking my job, *Stop listening*, the mention of cock-sucking lips. I shudder and take a sip of bitter coffee.

The minders sometimes wander around the garden to smoke a cigarette over a chat, and in those precious private moments, I try to tell Ariella as much as I can. Leaning in, I admit to the most uncomfortable part of my life, to quell and squash the discomfort of knowing hers.

'We live in a loveless marriage,' I say. 'One I immediately regretted. But my parents are still together, and they hate one another. My mum always said, *You've made your bed*. It's the way I was raised.'

I tell her how my mother always cheated on my father and vice versa. How they disappeared on weekends to screw the days away with their lovers. That it's the only way of overcoming a difficult, loveless life.

She whispers she's been married since she was eighteen: too young, too naïve. I tell her I'll help her any way that I can. And now the conversation must stop. Because the minders are returning. I shake the napkin from my lap, until crumbs of pastry fly away into the morning air.

But before I leave the brunch, there's a note under my bowl I must pocket, and I've left my own for her. A wink for a wink, a word for a word, a life for a life.

She tells me:

121

There is only one way I'll ever be able to escape him. I realise this is dangerous for you, Emma. But if you do want to help me, go to the strip club and see if you can uncover anything criminal.

◆ ◆ ◆

To be unhappy is to be selfish. How dare I hate my life. I have everything I could ever want, materially. You only have to come to my house for brunch and see how privileged my life is. There will be coffee, all types, arranged on a cart which guests can choose from. There will be every kind of fruit on expensive fine bone china. We'll have espresso margaritas and strawberries with whipped cream. If you want a wellness catch up, I'll roll out the yoga mats and offer face masks dripping with retinol and we'll stretch until we're as flexible as a newborn.

And while we eat, the views of the river will be there. To me, they're becoming a picture I see every day, an old one you recognise each time you step foot inside your grandparents' house. The only aspect that changes out there is the reflection of the sky's colour in the water. People will comment on how lovely it is and I'll agree and realise I haven't bothered to notice the trees growing across the street, or the new barbeque that's been established over in the park.

My life is so sickeningly advantaged I have bubble bath sent over from Paris. I employ a chef for most of our dinner parties. I get my hair blow-dried once a week, curled at the ends like Goldilocks. So, how dare I hate my life. I'm not allowed to be miserable when I step inside the business I've created simply because I didn't want to be a mother at home.

I'm so lucky, when I got sick of being one of those types of mothers – the ones who lived all day in active wear without being active, who bought takeaway coffee and took it back home to scroll on Instagram and watch the boats drift by on the river – I got to start up a business, pay for the marketing, invite celebrities to the opening and instantly book out my days with equally privileged women.

I'm so lucky that I could choose to be a business owner, and also the mother who made healthy lunchboxes, taking pride in the various combinations of rolled ham and cheese pita one day, and savoury muffins the next. When Georgia isn't around, I get to be the baking mum, the washing mum, the mum my mum had made fun of my whole life.

Yet misery follows me upstairs into my bedroom closet and downstairs into my bath, bubbly and scented with Paris. Karma's a cruel bitch and I know I'm being stalked by her. For this baby, for Jack. My payback is long overdue. But at least if I'm helping Ariella, karma may just compensate me.

Now

We're getting off, no matter what. But I can't operate a cruiser, let alone one this size. Besides, Scott will be guarding the bridge like Charles has told him to. My mobile phone is sitting on the seabed, and I don't know how to use a CB radio, but I'm still going to escape Charles and get the kids off this cruiser.

From the master cabin, I stare out the large windows. Charles steers the tender over small choppy waves towards the jetty. Once he's there, moored and walking off the pier, that's when I'll do it. The kids can't know, and I have to be quick before Scott notices I'm gone. Anytime from now, Kiki and Cooper will wake, wondering where they are and what we're doing stationary offshore.

There's a big cabin cruiser anchored about two hundred metres away. Every now and then, a woman steps out to the deck and goes back inside. That woman is all I have, my only hope. How strange to think she doesn't even know what's occurring beside her.

Scott's up on the bridge with hip-hop music blasting. He's on his phone, scrolling with his feet up on the opposite seat. The heater blows hot air into the space and he doesn't see me at the bottom of the stairs, watching. He's distracted and that's a good thing.

Outside, the wind is frosty, freezing my arms. I can't get warm and I can't add layers. I don't know how I'll manage it with the extra weight of this belly sinking me under the waves; still, I have to try. That cabin cruiser, that woman will be my lighthouse. But the water is dark, intimidating and I've always hated ocean swimming.

Descending the stairs, I reach the stern transom and lick the water with my toes. It's cold, very cold. I'm already shivering with the knowledge of it. The woman comes outside and I wave my arms in the air, hoping she'll look across. She's carrying items out to what appears to be a table. I picture it to be cereal, coffee, toast, a breakfast she's preparing while her husband gets ready to fish. They're anchored there and two fishing rods arch over the sides like candy canes. I wave my arms again as a gust of wind lifts my hair. Please look over. But she doesn't. She doesn't see me.

Charles is nowhere on the jetty.

I dive in. A rush of bitter water seeps into my jumper and tracksuit pants, weighing my body down. But I furiously kick through the waves, trying desperately not to think of what lurks below. It's cold – hurting my scalp cold – biting my nipples and under my arms cold. But the boat. That's all I can think of. The woman on the boat. Perhaps she heard the splash, perhaps she'll see me flailing in here.

Why didn't I grab a floatation device? Why didn't I think this through?

My arms pull through the water, but this is very hard to do. Especially wearing clothes. It's like I'm wearing weights and the ocean's sucking me under. And it's deep. So deep below me.

A surge of water lifts me high and then lowers me. I'm so far from land and I'm suddenly aware of being pulled out deeper, away from the cabin cruiser. It's me against the force of water. Flipping on my back, I decide to kick that way to conserve energy. The clouds are brimming with rain. Saltwater laps over my face, into my mouth and eyes and I gasp, swallowing a mouthful. I cough, almost vomiting from the salty taste and flip back over, blinking.

I'm praying the woman sees me out here. But when I look up, I can't see her outside anymore. What if she doesn't come back out? I don't think I can do this.

Turning my head back to *Lady Luck*, I hold my breath. There's Scott, on the bridge, looking down at me. He's on the phone and I have no hope of getting to that boat before he comes to drag me back. I want to sink under the water and hide from him.

Instead, I surrender, hoping the kids will forgive me. I tried, I really tried. Spinning back around, I float on my back, arms out and shivering. The current should take me. And then I hear an outboard motor approaching. Scott's in an inflatable dinghy. His hands grip me from behind. I'm being yanked over the rubber side and dumped onto the floor like a fish.

'You silly bitch,' he says, shaking his head. 'Charles is going to kill you.'

One Week Ago

The only way I'm going to gather evidence of Mateo's criminal activity is to go and obtain it first-hand. Ariella won't want words, hearsay, a guiding friend with concern; no, she wants cold, hard facts – a picture of him pumping a stripper with legs up to her armpits, snorting cocaine, beating someone up until they're bleeding from the temple.

It's Friday night, when we usually meet at our wine bar. The last of my clients are in the main lobby, yoga mats rolled under their arms, a faint waft of sweat lingering from after-work exertion. Why these people want to exercise straight after work on a Friday night is beyond me. Do they go home now and cook vegetable stir-fry with tofu and drink kombucha? These are the Friday-night bunch. My regular clients come on weeknights after their hard day at home, hosting charity events and luncheons. They wouldn't dare waste a Friday night doing barre. This is their night to hit Sydney and dine at the latest modern restaurants and bars. I can empathise because usually I'd be doing the same. But first and always, there's the Friday-night bunch.

After I've locked up and left the lights on for the cleaners, I wait patiently outside Tracy's yoga studio. She has a different kind of clientele. Hers pay fifteen dollars a session to work with Tracy under golden candlelight and singing bowls. Mine pay for exclusive membership and don't pay for the singing bowls and alternative therapy. They want expert trainers, blasting aircon, ice-cold cucumber water and a selection of teas. We always laugh about how different our practices are.

Barbs is on the phone, leaning against a tree trunk on the sidewalk. She waves when she sees me. We're going to have our usual Friday evening drinks, order our cheese board and eat spicy chorizo and sun-dried tomatoes and yet none of them are aware that afterwards I'm not going home to my children. Afterwards, I'm going to Kings Cross.

I have a bag packed with heels, a fur coat that hangs to my shins. I have make-up that I'll put on in the cab, that'll heighten my cheek bones and redden my lips. I need to blend in, in an environment like Kings Cross. But none of them know that.

When Tracy steps out of the studio, red-faced yet ready, all three of us walk down the cold street of Paddington, laughing, sharing our day's stories, looking forward to escaping life and entering the dimly lit world of our bar. And Tracy doesn't know this, but I plan to invite her with me, in fact, I'll insist that she join me. And after a few champagnes, she'll agree, because that's what Tracy does.

Inside is just the way we like it. Dark, moody, an atmosphere of hanging pendants, exposed-brick and velvet booths. Sophisticated men and women in business attire and good moods. It's Friday, after all.

Tracy orders champagne for the table and sparkling water for me, and I'm so nervous I'm on the hunt for Mateo that it's dizzying.

Now

Salty wet hair drips over the bathroom tiles and with it a swirl of blood. I'm woozy with pain in a hallucinogenic dream. Skin flecked with goosebumps and lips purpling like a bruise, I stare at my nakedness and hold myself. As long as he only hurts me and not the kids, that's all I can hope for. Soggy clothes are bundled by the door and the shower heat steams the mirror. I can't wait to step into it and wash away the shock. As soon as I'm under the hot water, the blood rushes like a river at sunset down my bulging belly and between my breasts.

He's pushed me hard against a doorframe, hitting my head and I'm not sure if he meant to inflict a wound or just scare me with the push, but my scalp stings as hot water enters the cut.

I wince, making sure I don't shower the wound, but I'm sure the salt will do it good. My hands quiver as I rinse the salt from my strands and, eventually, the blood peters out and all that's left is clear water. There can be no more mistakes and no more foolish quick decisions. Everything has to be strategically planned.

There's a naïve part of me convincing myself that perhaps Charles is simply tense, and he doesn't mean to be violent. He's only trying to protect us from Mateo. While the other part strongly believes that Charles is a killer, the killer of Ariella.

But that first slap months ago, when he started working with Mateo, demonstrated all I need to know: Charles is a stranger, a druggie, I cannot trust him and I need to find a way to protect me and the kids and escape this dangerous man.

Leaning my face into the water, I close my eyes, allowing it to wash over my skin. We're stuck on this cruiser. How are we going to escape? I twist the knobs and wait to drip dry for a bit.

I gently pat my cut and assess my fingertips for blood. There's none. The rage I have for him is going to be hard to manage. I'm tempted to run naked down to the kitchen, grab a butcher's knife and hold it against his throat. But the kids, and Scott. Two soldiers against me? It's never going to happen. The best thing I can do is go along with it, stay composed and rational. By doing that, he may come around, fill me in with plans. I can play sympathetic, offer support through gritted teeth. If it works, the kids and I may just have a chance of getting out of here.

I wrap a plush towel around me and roughly dry my hair with another, careful around the cut. Wrapping my hair in the towel, I pad out to the master bedroom where Charles sits on the end of my bed. I jerk back and he looks up.

'I'm sorry,' he says. His face is pallid and moist under the lights. In the opposite bedroom, Kiki and Cooper are watching cartoons in their bed.

I blink, unknowing what to say. But the voice appears like a mother's: appease him, offer support, get answers.

'I ran because I'm scared,' I admit, clenching the towel around me. It's yuck, standing here before him semi-naked. I remember his saggy balls the night before, his limp penis, and want to spew. Apart from when I got pregnant with Jack's baby, Cooper's conception was the last time we fucked, and before that, five or so years. 'You're not telling me anything and I read the news last night and

130

I need to know. Police are coming after us. Can you imagine what my mum and dad are thinking? Our friends?'

'You and I don't talk business, we never have.'

'But this isn't business, Charles. This is our lives. Kiki, Coop and the baby's lives. We're all in danger. You need to open up to me.' I hate the way I'm sounding so pathetic and warm, so wife-like and loving. It's fake and hard to use that tone, but I'll do anything to get us back on land. When I see him softening, smiling, I say, 'Where are you taking us?'

He laughs, rubs his face and his mouth pulls side to side, jaw grinding. And then I see his pupils, dilated and black. Shit, he's high again. That's why he's come in here, all apologetic and nice. He's riding a loving mood. 'I'm protecting the kids.'

'You can tell me if you hurt Ariella,' I gently say. 'I'm your wife, I won't tell.'

He scoffs into his palms and stretches his face with them before standing. He takes a few steps towards me and I grip the towel tight.

'I never touched our neighbour.' He smiles with half his mouth and he's giving me a look I recognise, lustful. I step back and he steps forwards. 'You know, I haven't even seen you naked with our baby.'

'Kiki and Cooper are just there.' I laugh. It comes out nervously.

His hand presses against my stomach and I want to cry. What would Jack do if he saw this?

'Mum,' Kiki calls out and Charles drops his hand, stepping back. I release a tightness from my belly and quickly push past Charles to the other room.

'Yes, baby?'

She looks up from her pillow. 'Can we have breakfast?'

131

'Sure.' I move to kiss them both on their heads, to avoid the man behind me.

I feel him there like a stalker, ready to strike. I don't know him and in fact, I can't remember when we stopped knowing and started avoiding each other. But the dodging comes at a price, a dangerous one.

One Week Ago

The taxi reeks of stale sweat and onions. Bad pop music thumps, vibrating the doors and Tracy asks if he can turn the music down. As well as the heat. It's cold outside, starting to drizzle, but in here, the heat only intensifies the stench of leather and body odour. We both look at each other and she pulls a face.

He begrudgingly obliges and we don't talk to him for the rest of the journey to Kings Cross. I'm too busy anyway, applying make-up, wrapping my fur over my work clothes, redoing my hair so that it falls over one eye, covering my face slightly. And Tracy's on the phone to her flatmate. At one point, the driver takes a sharp corner and tells me to put my seatbelt on. Tracy and I bump into each other.

When we reach our destination, I hand over the cash and step out onto the grimy footpath. Jack would kill me if he saw me here alone, and that's mainly why I've dragged Tracy out with me. I need an accomplice, someone who likes to have fun, without asking questions.

The streets are packed and bits of scrunched-up rubbish roll down the street in a gust of wind. There's a line outside McDonald's and some teenage girls screaming at each other while their friends huddle with thick shakes and black hoodies, watching. Our heels clip-clop over the concrete. Loud music blasts from every shop and fast-food chain along the way and I thought the rain and the cold would have pushed the crowd away, yet this street on a Friday night is where the scum lives and breeds.

An Irish pub has men smoking over the rails and surly bouncers by the door, glaring at whoever passes them. And then I pass one of the first strip clubs, with its neon pink sign flashing up a woman in a martini glass. Posters, hanging by their corners, flap in the wind, tearing others underneath them. Bits of bubblegum are holding them up against the wall. We'll go to the Irish pub first. From there, I can scope out the doorways of the strip clubs. I know which ones he owns.

'Come on, let's go in here.' I take Tracy's hand. 'They'll probably have a fire going.'

'Sounds like a plan.' She smiles, leading the way into the sweaty bar.

We find a cosy table by the window, overlooking one of the clubs Mateo owns. I've done the research; this one is his pride and joy. People pay the most money to step inside, and it's often seen on his Instagram page. Images of the bar, art deco and Parisian-inspired. Red velvet booths, red lamps and brass trimming. He doesn't show the naked women swinging from poles. The male clientele leering. From the outside looking in, you'd think his club was a classy top bar and nothing else.

'I'll go and get us a drink,' Tracy says, placing her bag beside me.

'Thanks, I'll have a sparkling water.'

She nods and walks off, the men at the bar watching her approach. However, I'm too distracted by the club over the road. Neon-yellow and pink streaks over the wet asphalt. Girls in mini dresses and leather jackets step over puddles, shielding their hair from the rain with their handbags. A group of hens in a bridal party enter the doorway, flashing ID to the two security men guarding the entrance. The men let them in, and I catch a glimpse of red velvet curtains. Has Ariella ever been inside? Her sweetheart husband surrounds himself with women all night and she's never been allowed to have an opinion about that.

When Tracy returns to the table, I sip my water and gesture over the road with my head. 'Ariella's husband, Mateo, owns that place.'

She's as shocked as I was, frowning as she stares at me. 'No way, really?' Tracy drinks her wine and gazes out the window. 'I never would have expected Ariella to be involved in that kind of scene.'

The icy water causes my brain to freeze. 'I could never be with a man who ran strip clubs. There's got to be something up with that.'

'I don't know. Could be sexy?'

'He started buying pubs and then nightclubs and now these places.' Tracy's observing the outside world when I say, 'We should go in and check it out.'

She laughs loudly. 'Yeah, right. I don't think so.'

That wasn't the reaction I was hoping for. 'I just saw a group of women go in there. A group on their hen night.'

'But why would they?' she says. 'I don't get turned on by naked women.'

'It'll be hilarious.' I sip my water and wait for Tracy to agree. She's usually so bubbly and spontaneous and up for adventures.

She looks at me hard, green eyes widening. 'Oh my God, you're serious. What if her husband's there?'

I shrug. 'We can hide and sit somewhere tucked away. I imagine it'll be dark.'

'What if she finds out we went in there?'

'We won't tell her.'

'I don't know . . .'

'It'll be the funniest thing I've done since my own hen night. And you don't get how boring being pregnant is.' She has to agree with me; it was my plan all along. 'Please?'

Tracy considers me, her mouth stretching. She laughs again and lifts one shoulder. 'Okay. That *is* pretty funny. A pregnant woman in a strip club.'

I slump back in my chair, relieved she's agreeing. What I don't mention is that I *want* Mateo to be there. That's why I've picked this club. I want to catch him in action, I just don't want him spotting me. I understand the danger, but it *is* a club, and anyone's allowed to enter, so if he does catch me in there, I'll just pretend I didn't know this was *his* club. He may not buy it, yet ultimately I'm doing this for Ariella and her freedom. I know what it's like to feel trapped. And I have the choice to leave. She doesn't. I'm doing this to witness the pig Mateo truly is, so Ariella can find her escape route.

Now

I didn't mean to be in the galley when I heard him talking. They didn't know I was there, slicing apple and arranging grapes and watermelon on a plate in the shape of a rainbow. As soon as the murmur floated through the porthole windows, I glanced up from the kids' dinner at two pairs of shoes blocking the view of the swell. The outside lights are dim and yellow, highlighting the daggy deck shoes Charles now wears. It's quite hard to hear everything with the motor going, with the waves lapping against the hull, but I get snippets, drunken snippets. Their shoes move from view, sometimes reappearing, as though they're trying to remain balanced over the swelling water. It's getting rougher, I've noticed. Even in the galley, I'm swaying a little, finding myself leaning away from the chopping board.

I know they're drunk, because Charles doesn't sound like himself anymore. He's not high, because if he was he'd have that rapid fire tone from last night and this morning, clear and precise, as though his tongue darts against his teeth. Now, it's like his tongue doesn't know where to roll. He's sluggishly speaking about Mateo as that cunt and this fuck. And Scott joins him, quieter, but there. He coughs and a cloud of smoke billows down. They're smoking and the cruiser's on autopilot.

The conversation annoyingly slips in and out like bad radio reception, and I'm closing my eyes to hear better.

'If he does, though, then at least we've got somewhere to . . .' Charles speaks.

'What about me after that?' Scott asks.

'Back home and no one will even . . .' Charles murmurs, '. . . have to make a deal with him.'

It's quiet for a while and then I clearly hear Charles talking about an island off Queensland, that Mateo knows we're at sea, but doesn't know where, that the other men will know exactly what to do, that Mateo is searching. He doesn't mention Jack. I never hear his name once.

And then there's coughing and another billow of smoke and Scott references a storm and a smaller boat. And then the shoes tap away and I'm biting my lip. A large surge of water pushes the cruiser and I stumble back against the pantry cupboard, wobbling the doors. Watermelon and grapes slide off the board, onto the floor. If they're intoxicated and smoking weed, then how can they responsibly steer the cruiser, anyway? Stepping back to the chopping board, I pick up the fruit and pull myself up, holding the bench top. Coop and Kiki could be worried about the swell; I have to get back to them. But my eyes focus on the porthole window, the distance to land, the specks of light that are growing smaller and further away than they were last night. We're bypassing civilisation. Every now and then a wave blocks the lights of the Australian coast like a black curtain. It vanishes like it was never there. And I wait a moment to see if it'll come back as the cruiser dives down into a deep trough. When it does, I swear it seems smaller, more distant. And I know Kiki and Cooper may be worried, but I can't leave this little microcosm. I can't leave the lights.

138

While the cruiser pitches and rolls, we eat fruit in front of the big screen with Kiki in her new pink pyjamas and Coop in too-big slippers. Charles came back with five giant shopping bags and instead of rejoicing in the coconut deodorant and new lacy knickers, my stomach filled with a dread so heavy I could barely talk.

Those bags the kids rummaged through, squealing at the bathers and useless flippers and goggles, needed to be thrown overboard. Those five bags signified more than shopping essentials. The bags meant we were staying away from home for a long time. They basically represented our next life. Apparently, the coconut deodorant, the lacy knickers, the goggles and flippers were essentials for island life. I'd stared at the lacy knickers, twisted on the carpet like they'd been thrown there after a one-night stand. These knickers, Charles had chosen to either picture me wearing or view me in. Even Kiki got the connotation, holding them up with an ooh-la-la. My face grew hot and I felt like stomping to the master bedroom and slamming the door like an embarrassed teen.

Charles already had it all planned out. If he'd bought jumpers and beanies, I'd know we were headed for somewhere south, so where was this place he was planning to take us?

Take me home, I wanted to scream. Take me to Jack and our new life. Take me back to my office yesterday morning in my Ugg boots and hooded jumper. If I'd known, I would've spoken to the police then and there without avoiding them. Why did I step away from that detective by the door? Why did I collect the kids from school?

A piece of salted popcorn lodges in my throat as I gasp out a sob. I cough loudly and Kiki looks at me, the light of the television coating her face in blue.

'You okay, Mum?'

I nod, coughing to clear it. The worst part of this is the lying to her face.

Charles and Scott haven't come down and now when I look outside the portside windows, I can't see the coastal lights. So, I stand and step out to the main deck, holding the bars for support. Wind funnels like a violent channel towards me, teasing my hair in irritating gusts that dry my mouth. They're there. The lights on land. Behind us, getting smaller and smaller. Pin pricks of sanity, a loss of life.

One Week Ago

The red velvet curtains hold remnants of sex, skin and cologne. This is what I think about when we push through them to the open space inside. How much DNA is embedded in the wallpaper, the fabric booths, the woodwork. I already feel icky as my heels stick to the floor. Tracy's in front, leading me to the bar, when I pull her back. I just need a moment. This place, with its sleazy music, darkened nooks and private, curtain-sheered alcoves smells, looks and tastes like sex. On stage, two naked women are performing to their audience by gyrating on and over one another. Long hair extensions flick, twirl and glide over the other's body parts.

Men of all shapes, sizes, ages, and even some women, are all viewing this performance from mini tables, lit by dull red lamps. The mood is alien, yet interesting to me. Tracy doesn't bat an eyelid.

'You grab us that booth over there and I'll get myself a drink,' she says. She's pointing to an empty booth, nestled between two crowded ones. One is taken up by the hen party, so at least I'm a tad more comfortable beside them, but the other is filled with a couple, kissing so passionately I instantly think of Jack. They don't care or mind who's looking. Their tongues are swirling inside each other's mouths, hands travelling all over her breasts, her face, his shoulders, his crotch. I look away and head to the empty booth.

A topless waitress sashays past me with a tray of drinks: expensive champagne and caramel-coloured liquor on ice. She smells sickly sweet of strawberries and vanilla, matching her fiery red hair. In fact, the whole place smells like berries. I'm wondering if Mateo forces them to wear perfume.

I pull my jacket closer around me and slide into the booth. It's dark and shadowy, which I'm grateful for. If Mateo is here, I don't want him spotting me. I finger the lamp and realise it's stuck in place on the wooden table. Tracy's by the bar and a man has already started chatting her up. She smiles and talks to him and orders her drink. I scan the area for Mateo. There are groups of men in the booths opposite and people coming and going from the private alcoves. Every now and then, an elbow, a foot or leg causes the sheers to move and jut out. I'm presuming there's a lap-dance happening in there, maybe something more. I swallow and feel the baby kick.

Maybe this wasn't such a great idea. The women on stage are getting more loose now and beside me, the hen party aren't even paying attention. They're having shots and doing a drinking game that has them squealing and laughing. The bride does a promiscuous dance and embarrasses herself, knocking over three glasses of wine. I don't know what I'm looking to find or what I'm doing here, but I'm just hoping something comes from this.

Tracy makes her way back to the booth, smiling as though she's enjoying herself. She's got that hazy, drunken look in her eyes and I feel bad for bringing her here. But I needed to see him, see what he's up to. So far, it's been the only thing Ariella has asked of me and I'm not going to let her down.

'Cheers,' Tracy says, handing me a sparkling water. She chinks her wine against my glass and takes a seat. 'What a place.'

'Not like our tapas bar.'

142

She slurps a big sip of wine. 'Poor Ariella. Is she open to her husband seeing this all the time?'

I shrug. I can't see Mateo anywhere. Not behind the bar, not at one of the tables. I sip my water, and it fizzes and pops on my tongue.

Tracy almost chokes on her drink as her eyes stare towards the stage. The women are now on top of each other, kissing and rubbing their breasts together. I glance away, as a dirtiness itches my scalp. I scratch it hard. Imagine if Jack knew I was here? I'm growing hot and I take my jacket off and then stop as a waitress with big breasts and long golden hair heads towards us carrying a tray of top-shelf champagne. She places two glasses down and her long lashes fall over her cheeks.

'We didn't order this,' I tell her. 'Or did you?' I face Tracy.

She shakes her head. 'No, I think it's a mistake, sorry.'

'It's a gift,' she says, ignoring us and placing the bottle down. 'From the owner.'

I look past her. Mateo is with a group of men in the booth opposite. He holds up his whiskey and tilts it towards me, a half-smile on his face. My cheeks and neck heat and I don't know what to do. Tracy looks at me.

'Mateo?' she says.

I nod. 'Yep. This is from him.'

Now

The water's changing colour from royal blue to sheer green, pure and almost drinkable. In some parts, you can see the white desert underneath, the sand-curves breaking and moving from surface ripples. I could stare at it all day. And the heat, it's assertive, clogging the throat. If you're outside, you're in water, otherwise you're inside, freezing in the air conditioning. The pregnant clouds don't make it any better. They work like a pot lid, blocking the humidity and steaminess in.

I need to swim, float, dunk myself into the water like a dumpling. And since the cruiser has stopped for a break, just above Byron Bay, I'm going in.

Weightless floating. There's something so delicious about floating when pregnant. The stiffness of heels and hips and joints and breasts becomes void in water. I'm one with it and I let it hold me. The water, a halo around my face, cools the heat from my head. The kids are in the outside spa, swimming in their goggles and flippers. And I'm away from them, floating like a starfish, dipping over tiny waves that bobble my tummy like a tortoiseshell. In here, I can relax, exhale, hear the rumbling of breath and the slippery sloshing.

Distant squeals of Kiki and Cooper tell me they're safe and I'm able to do this. I close my eyes, enjoying bliss. But it splinters with an image of Ariella, a week before she died, hair tied in a messy bun, chapped, dehydrated lips and trembling fingers. *'Let's meet tomorrow, okay?'* she'd said.

Pulling myself up, I paddle, gazing over to the land. What if I could have saved her? What if I knew all along what it was she was going to tell me?

I slip under the water, billowing bubbles until I start sinking, sinking, feet pointed to the depths. How easy to let it take me down, down to the point where I can't swim back. I'll run out of oxygen, my legs will thrash for the surface, but I won't make it. I'll swallow a lungful of water. I'll go back the way I came. Part of water, part of nature, mimicking the baby within.

My heart thuds and I open my eyes, viewing a lifetime of blue. I need air. I pull through the water, kicking against gravity, holding my mouth tight like a puffer fish, ready to pop. It's five seconds up and I want to make it. Air needs to quench me. When I come back into contact with the wind, I suck air in hungry mouthfuls and lean back, floating. Salt spills into my gasping mouth, along with rain, pattering my eyelids and lips, fresh, sweet.

And then I notice, I can't hear the squeals anymore. Only sloshing water, underwater sounds and an engine motor starting up. I paddle, glancing around and realise the cruiser is moving away. Charles is at the railing, watching me. He turns and steps inside.

'What?' I gasp.

And the sea doesn't seem so blissful now.

'Help,' I scream, throat hoarse. Rain pelts the surface into submission. Droplets bounce up around me, into my eyes. I scan the waves, some higher than me. And then I can't see it. And then I can. It's going. They're leaving me. I bet he's been wanting to do this, to teach me a lesson or get rid of me, take the kids and pretend that I've drowned. This is a terrifying fact. I truly believe Charles is planning to leave me here, either as a form of punishment or an easy way out of our marriage. I drown, he becomes the grieving father. Or what if it is something worse. Maybe he knows about Jack and me? Or maybe he realises I recognised him in the footage, shooting Ariella? If he could have executed her so cold-bloodedly, disposing of me like this would be too easy for him.

The coast is barely visible, and I won't be able to make it. My breathing is fast and shallow and I'm taking in water as I start to sob, realising my fate. I've seen films like this. A shark will take me, or I'll encounter some other danger, like a current that'll pull me out to sea.

'Help,' I scream again, louder.

I need a bigger wave to come and lift me higher so I can see them, and they can see me. But what if he doesn't want me to be found? How easy it'll be. The kids will know poor Mummy drowned. Oh no, I cannot believe this. My legs are getting tired and my arms are jelly, so I turn onto my back, resting a little, while I think. But childlike panic takes over, images provoking me in unhelpful, damaging ways. *What's underneath me? When does the current come through here? I'm not a strong swimmer.*

I'm lying back, rain drumming over me when underwater I hear another engine. It's dull, but grows into a growl and I quickly lean up, waving an arm through the air.

'Help,' I scream. 'I'm over here.'

And a thump, thump, thump over waves comes nearer and a large aluminium dinghy slashes through the waves with two fishermen, practically boys, on board. I wave my arms until the boat slows and one of the boys points towards me. They've spotted me. I dip my face into the water, clearing the tears and sob into it. It was too close, much too close.

'What are you doing out here?' one of them says, reaching for me. He looks about fifteen. Too young to be operating a boat out here. The other is about the same age, just staring at me as he grips the steering tiller.

'They've left me,' I say, gripping the boy's skinny arms like a vice. 'They left.'

He yanks me up while I use my wobbly legs to climb over. 'Are you from that big cruiser over there?'

From here, I see the cruiser. Kiki and Cooper are out on the deck gazing over and it's moving away. Charles leads them away, back inside the main deck. He left me here. He left me to drown.

'My children,' I tell the boys as the first one sits me down and throws a towel over my shoulders. 'We're in danger. Do you have a phone?'

They shake their heads. 'Well, I do, but I've run out of credit,' the boy at the tiller says.

The other snorts. 'His phone's a dinosaur.'

'Listen, you need to do something for me. Take me back to the cruiser and write down its name and you must, you absolutely must, tell the police to come and get me. We're going to Queensland somewhere. Maybe an island.' They aren't taking me seriously, and why would they? They're kids. And I'm an older pregnant woman who's crazy enough to swim in the deep. 'My husband is kidnapping me and my children. You have to tell them that.' When they don't say anything, I scream, '*Please*.'

'All right,' the first one says, nodding. He looks at his friend. 'We'll do it.'

'You must.' I nod, tears dripping off my chin. 'You must. We're in danger.'

The dinghy accelerates towards the cruiser, bumping over the waves and I tell them to just let me off on the transom.

The first boy keeps staring at me, chewing his cheek. He's pimply, rough-looking with a flannelette shirt and mullet hair. Uneducated, with a parent who doesn't care about them fishing out here alone. Their dinghy is small and rusted. A bucket of water

147

holding herring sloshes onto my feet. The fish swim in crazed circles, opening and closing their mouths. And the rain keeps falling.

When I step off their dinghy, the first one holds my hand to steady me. We make eye contact and he nods ever so slightly. And it's then I think maybe this was meant to happen. Maybe these boys are my young heroes.

One Week Ago

The topless waitress leaves our booth and I tell Tracy I don't think we should drink this. He could have drugged it for all I know.

'Are you kidding me?' she says. 'You dragged me in here and this is the best champagne you can get. I'm drinking it.'

Leaving her fifteen-dollar wine, she pours herself a full glass and it almost spills over the rim. Tracy sucks at the bubbles and giggles and I'm staring over at Mateo, who's talking to his friends. He seems unfazed by my presence, barely even glancing up. He's deep in conversation, although I know I've crossed a line being here. How am I going to tell Charles? Or Jack? Suddenly this all seems like a really stupid idea.

'If Charles knows we've come here—'

'Just relax, Em.' Tracy flaps her hand and chinks her glass against my water. 'It's fun. You can blame it on me. I don't think he'd care anyway.'

Tracy's getting drunk, starting to sway to the music and making funny jokes about the women on stage. She's clicking her fingers to the beat and saying she's feeling horny just watching them.

'I wonder how they got into this gig?' She downs another mouthful of bubbles.

I'm ready to leave; I wish I'd never come. This determination to help Ariella needs to stop. I'm not in danger and I can only imagine Jack's response to this.

I sip my water, then pull my jacket over my shoulders. 'I think we should go.'

Tracy wiggles her eyebrows. 'Whoops, here he comes. He's hot.'

'If you like that greasy look.'

Tracy's staring as though he's a Greek god when all I want is for the booth to collapse around me.

'Love that olive skin against white teeth,' she says. 'Also, look at his arms.'

I could never see him as attractive. Mateo struts across the floorboards, kissing a bleached-blond woman and shaking hands with a man who's sitting at one of the tables with his drinks. He smiles with deep dimples, charismatically drawing women towards him. I don't want him to come over here. I really don't. I won't know what to say. And how will I explain it to Charles? Oh, we just decided to go in and check out a live act? It's too late. He's sliding into the booth beside Tracy, flashing his white teeth. Charles is going to kill me.

'Fancy seeing you here, neighbour.' He winks at me. The note and the words appear through his smile. Shit.

'Listen, I got your note the other day,' I start. 'It probably looked bad, but I was tidying the leaves—'

'I thought you were out at the wine bar tonight?'

'We were.' I fidget in my seat. How the fuck does he know that? The minder at the bar. He's been having me watched. I can't let him see my reaction, but I'm shaking below the table. 'But Tracy and I wanted to go out. We've just been to the pub across the road and I recognised your—'

'Where's my girl?' He has a way of interrupting and making me fall silent. My voice just crumbles weakly and I'm twisting my jacket in a knot. His eyes focus on it, so I stop.

'Your *girl*.' Tracy holds his shoulder. 'You're so sweet. Your *girl* didn't come tonight.'

He looks at Tracy as though only just noticing her, although doesn't smile or introduce himself. It's a worrying look. And even Tracy gives a weak laugh and sips her champagne, hiding her face.

'This was for you.' He points to the champagne and his eyes flick to me, black and squinting. There's an aggressive tone to his voice.

'I'm pregnant, I can't drink.'

'Fucking waste,' he says, peering around the club. He's running his hands up and down his jeans and there's an awkward silence that I want to fill, but don't have the guts to. And I'm realising he's one of those people whose mood shifts as quickly as the conversation.

'I'll have it all,' Tracy says, pouring more into her glass and I want to shut her up. She's acting like a fool and I don't think he's the type of man who enjoys foolish women. In fact, he turns to her again, with gritted teeth and I'm tempted to pull her from the booth and run.

'I know you'll have it,' he says, grinning at Tracy. 'We should get you up there on stage with them.' His smile abruptly comes and then leaves again like a flickering movie that doesn't quite show the expressions changing.

'As if.' She slaps his shoulder and I tense up. Shut up, Tracy. He's not amused. He watches her and she looks away again. His stare penetrates and even though it's not aimed at me, it's there. Intense, unreadable. A serial killer about to take a life.

'Horny bitch,' he mutters. And I'm rigid in my seat. He's pulling on his lip with his teeth, dragging them across the bottom. I want to go. I want to leave right now.

'We should go,' I say.

He scoffs at me. 'Why? You wanted to come. I have no fucking idea why, but you came. So now you stay.'

'It's getting late,' I tell him and go to stand up when he grabs Tracy by the throat and kisses her forcefully, sticking his tongue deep into her mouth.

And I can't move. I'm frozen watching as Tracy first struggles and then reciprocates, kissing him back. And I'm beside them, witnessing it unfold like I'm viewing a porno and I shouldn't be. And all I can think about is Ariella imprisoned at home, holding a hot cup of herbal tea, in bed and watching *Escape to the Country*.

Now

Kiki and Cooper follow me into the bathroom while I peel the bathers off my shivering body. I'm a shaking mess, failing to hold it together for them. Kiki sits on the toilet lid and Cooper stands, eyeing me. And I want to drown under the heat of the shower.

'Why were you leaving us?' He speaks in a small voice.

I kiss his head quickly, before settling under the hot water. The warmth sweeps itself over my stinging nipples, nose and fingers. 'I wasn't leaving you, Coop. Why would you think that?'

'Dad said you were planning on swimming away.'

I close my eyes, inviting the shower to scorch my lids, because the burn is minor compared to what just occurred, to what Cooper believes. Their father wanted to kill me and then blame my disappearance on myself, and Ariella's limp body emerges under my eyelids. I'm involved in her murder somehow and so is Charles, but I just don't know how yet. How am I a threat to *him*?

After arriving back on board, I stepped along the carpet, a dripping wreck, while my husband avoided discussing his obvious plan to leave me drowning in his wake. He'd already left the main deck.

I rub the foggy shower glass so their faces appear. 'Look at me,' I say. 'Come closer.' Cooper's the only one who steps forwards, eyebrows knotted. I smile at him. 'I would never, ever, ever, ever leave you both. Ever.'

He giggles, face altering in an instant and blows a bubble on the glass.

Kiki's not so easily convinced, and I don't blame her. She's starting to interrogate me about everything, and I'm not ready to scare her with the truth. 'Dad said you wanted to leave us.'

I squirt lime and coconut soap into my palm, acting nonchalant as I smooth it over my body. 'He's being silly. The tide took me too far and Scott was trying to turn the cruiser around to come and get me. Luckily, those boys saw me first. It was very scary.'

I'm hoping those boys believed me, that they sailed straight back to shore and contacted the police like I told them to. I'm picturing them right now in the station, relaying the events. *We saw her floating there and screaming for help. She's pregnant. Her yacht took off and left her there. She says her husband has kidnapped her and the children. The cruiser's called* Lady Luck.

I imagine the police will search up my name, make the connection and they'll be on their way soon to rescue us. There's a glimmer of hope that has me smiling. Charles has no idea. Maybe this *had* to happen.

Kiki shakes her head. 'But Dad said you were leaving us. He actually said that.'

I smile. 'He was just joking, silly.'

Kiki hangs her head and plays with her fingers. 'I want to go home.'

Cooper draws a love heart on the glass, and I close my eyes again as the water showers over my body.

I start by saying, 'It's a great adventure—'

'And you took my phone and Dad said it accidentally smashed upstairs. You packed nothing of mine. I didn't even get to tell Milla I was going away. It's like you literally ripped me away from my life all because of some stupid sick friend.'

'Kiki—'

154

'No, I'm going to tell Dad I want to go home.' She stands from the toilet, and I step out of the shower, dripping wet.

'No, Kiki, wait.' She frowns at my odd behaviour, my clutching her hand. But I can't have her going to him, not now. He could be high, angry, dangerous. 'I understand what you're saying, and it really feels like that. But you don't always need your phone with you. We wanted you to have a break. We wanted to do something unexpected like this and treat it like an adventure.'

'But why are we going to Queensland by boat?'

I squeeze her hands. 'To make it a family holiday.'

'We've barely seen Dad.'

'He's really distracted with work. This is the best he can do right now.'

'It really scared me when you floated off.' She begins to cry, and I identify the baby in her: the scrunched eyes and pudgy cheeks, the sobbing sound she makes. I slide the towel off the rail and wrap it around myself before tugging her close. The shower runs behind me, clouding the bathroom. Cooper comes in for a cuddle too and I kiss them both.

'I'm sorry.' My voice is croaky. 'It won't happen again.'

I don't admit how it terrified me too. Don't point out how I gasped in a mouthful salty water watching as Charles carted them away from the deck. The cruiser motoring off from me has hit a new level of terror I never expected to encounter in my life with Charles.

This is more than the drugs, more than the aggression, more than Mateo's revenge over Charles' inability to protect Ariella. I'm a link in the chain to Ariella's murder. And he needs to get rid of me. This is obvious now.

One Week Ago

Drumming the table, an aroused Mateo orders us to stay and finish the champagne. 'Enjoy it, enjoy it,' he says with heavy-lidded eyes. When he stands, Mateo draws a line down Tracy's cheek with his finger. She smiles, sucking in her lip and this display is uncomfortable. I want to pull Tracy aside and scold her. But she's drunk, always available and I unwillingly dragged her here. This was my plan, Ariella's plan – not Tracy's, I can't blame her.

Mateo instructs Tracy to come to him later, out the back. He does all of this, understanding fully what an open betrayal of Ariella this is. My new friend, my new neighbour. What a low-life scum. His actions are loud, brash, spelling out his contempt: *Your husband works for me, there's nothing you can do to stop me. Even if my wife finds out, she can never leave me.* I excuse myself to go to the bathroom, sensing his eyes on my back. How long has he been having me watched? And does Charles know about this? Was this his little plan, too? Fuck, what if he finds out about me and Jack?

This drives me to want to incriminate Mateo even more. He needs to be locked up. People like Mateo are cunning rats, experts in deception, secrets and shonky underworld dealings. Their crimes are well hidden under satin costumes and cheap make-up, behind private booths and backstage curtains.

The bathroom's seedy, flooded in fluorescent blue, preventing junkies from locating veins and shooting up. Soap on the sink is crusted and wrinkled like an elbow, with the toilets devoid of toilet paper. I hover over the seat, avoiding the bowl, while high heels clip over the tiles, in the cubicle beside me. A strong cologne follows and the female next to me makes noises with her mouth, sighs, gasps, exhales. Zips zip, jewellery chinks, a whoosh of fabric falls to the floor. She's undressing. Another pair of clicking heels enters the bathroom.

They speak in a language I can't decipher – fast, urgent and terse. Then I hear the word *bagus* and know what that means. *Good*. Indonesian is the only second language Kiki's learnt at school, and she loves the word.

When I step out of the cubicle, one of the women eyes me up and down. She's petite, height up to my shoulder. I almost mistake her for a child. Jet-black bob cut to precision, thick black kohl batwing eyeliner and fake lashes. These eyes are glaring at me. Excusing myself to get to the basin, I try to lather my hands in the bar of soap, feeling grimier than I did before. Her friend comes out, also tiny, also so young looking. I have to stop staring. They can't be teenagers, surely? The other girl has long black hair to her bottom. She pulls red lipstick out of her bra, runs it over full lips. I know they talk about me. They laugh. About me, I'm sure.

Ignoring them, I wipe my hands on a paper towel and leave the bathroom. There's a long hall to my left, dark with doors branching off either side. I'm so tempted to head down there for Ariella. But Mateo's probably having me watched, even now, with cameras tracing and scanning every shady corner of this place. I bend to do up the catch on my shoe, hoping to hear or see something, *anything* I can pass on to Ariella.

The two girls in the bathroom are possibly strippers or sex workers, employed by Mateo. They're coming out behind me and calling down the hall. Another two females step out from the first door, breasts exposed like tiny lumps. So young. So tiny. They are blond and barely look old enough to drive. They spot me and arch back, closing the door on the hall.

Clipping my shoe, I then stand and head back out into the main bar. It's darker than before and my eyes adjust to the reddish hue of lamps, curtains, burgundy wallpaper.

The booth's empty. Tracy's not there. In fact, she's nowhere to be seen. Not in the booth, not near the bar, not back at Mateo's table. I scan the busy tables, the waiters strolling with trays, the men in groups, the hen party dancing by the stage. Where is Mateo? I can't see him anywhere, either. I check my phone and there's no text from Tracy. Where the hell is she? I don't want to leave her here, drunk and alone, but I want to escape this environment and go home. Maybe she left the club with Mateo. It'd be like him to do that, take her away and isolate me. But that's what scares me. He's capable of anything. I could wait at our booth, but the champagne bottle and glasses aren't there. In fact, another couple are filling the seats. Chewing on my lip, I stand for a moment and then phone her. The call rings out with her voicemail answering.

Shit. I feel sick. Where the hell is she? And most importantly, what have I done bringing her here?

Now

Apparently, there's a storm brewing down the coast. It's going to hit us tonight and we have to be prepared, because we're not docking anywhere, not after last time, Charles tells me. I've certainly noticed the change in movement. The increased rocking from side to side. Apparently, I have to stay calm for the kids.

When he tells me, reaching for life jackets and equipment above the dining table cupboards, I'm so tempted to kick him in the back. *Stay calm for the kids.* What else have I been doing?

Charles goes around the coffee table to place loose objects into drawers, securing them tightly, and I follow him. I'm close behind him when I whisper, 'You tried to kill me.'

He turns his face to the side, so I note the greying stubble creeping up his jaw. And he laughs through his teeth. 'You're crazy.'

'You wanted me to drown,' I say tightly.

He bends to open a drawer and places an ornamental vase inside. 'You should've thought about the risks. The tide, the current.'

'You were moving off.' I'm carefully speaking in a low tone. I don't want the kids to hear. But I want to be clear on one thing, I know what he's trying to do.

His voice is growing louder, impatient. 'Go and look after *my* children.'

I ignore his reference to *my*. 'You want to kill me.' Whispers are light, and this does not feel light. What I'm vocalising is painful and raw. And perhaps he senses it, and he's great at lying, but when he stands and looks at me, I see a stranger.

'You're trying to ruin every chance of us sorting this out.' He snatches a picture frame from behind my head and I flinch, expecting a slap. And instead of reassuring me with a gentle touch, a kind smile, Charles sniggers and leaves me standing there.

The kids are watching a movie and thankfully can't hear him, and I guess this is the reason I never act upon what I'm envisioning. Like stabbing him with a knife, like pushing him down the stairs, like shoving him overboard, like smashing a heavy lamp over his head when he's not prepared for it. Because of the kids. I want to keep them stable and I don't want them growing up with the incised memory of their mother killing their father.

But, I'd like to. I really think I could. And that thought worries me.

So, I turn away from him and head over to the plush lounge suites, hug a cushion and breathe. I relax my jaw and rest my head back, wondering how long until the police find us. It's been eight hours since they rescued me from the water. When will Jack call the police? When will my parents pay for a search? But they'll never suspect Charles of kidnapping me, that'll never fucking happen.

The kids are absorbed in a Disney movie and there's cheesy crisps and lollies in front of them, stuff I'd never give them. But they're content. And I hate that he tells me to keep them calm. Like I don't know how to do that, like I haven't been doing it all this time. I'm gritting my teeth at the sight of Charles pulling life jackets and torches down from a cupboard. Don't be the protective father now. I see straight through you.

'Tomorrow, we're changing boats,' Charles says. He's talking to Kiki and Cooper.

A Disney princess sings about being trapped in a tower, long-ing to escape. Charles leaves the life jackets on the dining table, and I stare out at the wake. Another boat? Oh my God, no. That means the police will never find us.

'Why?' Cooper says. 'I like ours.'

Charles laughs a little. 'I know you do, mate, but this one is really cool. Smaller, but it'll get us to the island.'

'What island?' Kiki says.

He blinks a few times, staring at Kiki. 'A friend's island.'

'Where?' I ask.

He spins his back on me. 'North.'

'How awesome.' Kiki beams, turning around to face me. I pull my mouth into a fake smile.

'You'll love it,' Charles tells her. 'You'll have your own little house and there's a pool.'

'Is it in Queensland?' Cooper asks.

'That's right. Tropical Queensland.'

'I can't wait, Mum.' Kiki squeals and grabs a lolly and sucks on it. Cooper claps and takes one too.

An island. A paradise prison. The wake bubbles and tears the sea in a whitewash trail. About fifty metres behind, the wake fades, returning to swelling sea. *Lady Luck*. This was the only chance of them finding us. And now they won't.

We were never here. We disappeared fifty metres ago.

One Week Ago

Ariella is the kind of woman who plants herbs for hours at a time, humming to herself and taking sips of lemon water. The kind of woman who should be hanging out with intellectual university students who study philosophy and art. She's the type of woman who would speak about her mother as though her mother were a saint, as though her mother never annoyed her as a teenager. She'd be happier riding a bike than driving a car. She'd be happier in overalls than designer jeans. She'd be all the things she never can be.

She's planting herbs, like coriander and mint, and they're all lined up in perfect rows, and from that alone I know she'll be a great mother one day. When she gets away from him. The way she carefully coaxes them out of their plastic pots, squeezing around the soil so they release effortlessly. The herbs can't wait to be in her garden and taken care of. She pours just the right amount of water over the baby leaves and brushes any bits of soil left over off their greenery. Then, with careful pats, she nestles the herbs into place like snug babies in their cots, ready to watch them sleep and grow.

I'm beside her on a chair, rugged up in a coat, boots, and clutching my mug of ginger tea, hoping to get warmer. And she's never cold. She just accepts the temperature and embraces it the way Mother Earth embraces us.

She doesn't fit this life. She's in the wrong picture book. The illustrator drew Ariella and planted her on the pages of someone else's story. That's why she deserves more than this and him and this patch of garden.

Her minder lights a smoke and heads down the grassy slope, just out of earshot. I'm only here because Charles had to come over, so I invited myself. And Mateo *had* to allow it. They're inside drinking Turkish coffee and I've come out to join Ariella.

Mateo's hungover, with black, creased eyes. When he sees me, I swear he imagines strangling me. He stares like a predator about to maul his prey, but Charles distracts him with a document that needs signing. I'm guessing he hasn't yet told Charles about my visit last night. And all I'm wondering is what happened to my friend?

'Quick, I have to tell you something,' I say, placing my mug beside my boots. It almost topples over on the grass and I steady it.

Ariella brushes her dirty hands over her jeans and I wince. I'd hate to be that dirty and wet and cold with bare sleeves and goosebumps pricking my arms. She doesn't mind. As usual. She doesn't mind at all. She swipes her hair off her forehead and then takes a sip of her peppermint tea.

'It's about Tracy, the yoga teacher who works next door to me.'

A frown. A laugh. A tilted head. 'What?'

'My friend who works next to me.'

'I know the one.'

'He . . . he.' It's very difficult to speak. I pick up my tea again but she doesn't let me pause the conversation.

'He?' Another false laugh. 'He what?'

I lick my lips and rub them together and swallow. 'He kissed Tracy last night.'

Ariella doesn't speak. She just stares at me, unmoving. Her eyes move over to the door, to the grass, to me.

'And I haven't heard from her since. I can't get hold of her—'
I stop.

She blinks and tears spill out and I want to hug her. She's gritting her teeth, showcasing saliva that gets stringy between her lips. Tears drip from her nostril to her mouth. She's utterly distraught and I don't understand. This wasn't supposed to happen. This was supposed to validate why she hates Mateo. If I'd learnt this about Charles, I'd be happy. He'd be the cheater, as well as me. Why isn't she happy about this? At least relieved to know? Surely, she could have guessed her husband was a cheat.

'I didn't mean to upset you,' I say.

Ariella shakes her hand and quickly wipes her eyes, patting the soil once more. 'It's fine. I know. But I just want to *leave him*,' she whispers. 'He's despicable.'

'I'm worried about her,' I say. 'Tracy. She won't pick up her phone. She won't text. Has he ever . . . Would you suspect that he'd ever . . .'

We have to stop talking. Ariella is staring at me with glassy eyes. She notices me looking at him and resumes gardening. The minder is turning back and walking to us.

Tracy is a party animal, often going out until four am and rocking up to work with a migraine. But this time I feel as though something sinister has happened to her. I can't get hold of her. Not by text or phone call. Because Ariella didn't know I was visiting with Charles, she hasn't got a note ready for me to collect. But I have one for her. The details of last night, the young women who looked almost underage, Mateo kissing Tracy, him having me either followed or watched. I bend to the herbs and pretend to study the tag on the coriander.

'I never knew you could grow this in our sandy soil,' I say, aware the minder is listening, smoking, monitoring her conversation. I place the note beside the tag and she quickly pinches it and stuffs it into the gardening glove.

Then she turns to me with the saddest eyes and says, 'Let me know if you find out where that herb garden is.'

She means Tracy. And she's just as worried as I am.

Now

It's hard to keep the kids distracted, but I try. I'm hoping they'll fall asleep in a sugar coma and the rocking will encourage them along. It's eight thirty and Cooper's eyes are drowsy, blinking longer. But the swell is obvious and the rain is coming down in heavy sheets, flooding the deck area, bouncing off the spa water in big droplets, flowing over the sides. If they just don't look out there, they'll be fine. If they just keep focused on the television, they shouldn't get seasick.

But I am. I'm also starting to worry. Because the rain is so intense, the swell is so huge, that I've lost my guiding lights of land. The volume of water pushes the cruiser so you tumble even when sitting. And a big one's just hit the cruiser, frothing over the main deck. And Kiki starts to cry.

'Are we going to drown?' she says, which starts Cooper off.

I pull him onto my lap. We're on the rug, because apparently if you sit somewhere flat in the centre, the roughness isn't as obvious. Whoever said that was bullshitting. 'Of course we're not. Boats like this are built to get through storms.'

'Are you sure?' Kiki asks, backing herself onto me. I have them both on one knee each and we're swaying so much, I have to place a hand down to balance us.

I nod. 'I'm sure. Let's watch this. We've got ten minutes until it finishes and then we can go to bed and it'll be like a rocking chair.'

Cooper bites his thumbnail, Kiki looks to the windows. The outside lights illuminate the dumping rain, lashing at an angle. I guide their attention back to the film. The waves thump against the hull and my stomach is really starting to churn. God, I'm nauseous, and I can't let them know how bad this is. A picture or ornament falls off the walls and smashes and Kiki screams.

'Shh, it's okay.' I clutch her shoulders. 'You stay with your brother while I clean it up.'

I'm not going to clean it up. I want to know what the hell Scott and Charles plan to do about this shit we're in. Because no craft, no matter how big, would risk sailing in this weather.

'Crawl to the lounge and I want you to sit on it and hold on,' I tell them both. 'I'll go and find Dad.'

Kiki and Cooper crawl to the lounge and with each bang, the hull shudders, the television stops and freezes, before resuming. I smile at them both and struggle to stand. When I do, I hold on to the furniture I know is secured to the deck. And I grip the rails, the dining table, the walls to get to the stairs leading up to the bridge. Each step is hard to climb as I'm brought banging against the wall. Eventually, I make it up to the men, who appear as tense as I do.

'This is really dangerous,' I say. They both turn around to me, and from this station, I can really comprehend the full fury of the storm. The waves are much bigger than us. The tip of the bow sometimes dips under and I'm shaking. 'We need to turn back and head inland.'

'We know what we're doing, okay?' Charles says.

'The kids are terrified.'

'You need to chill them out.'

'I'm trying—'

'Put their life jackets on,' Scott says to me.

167

'What?' I frown. 'Is it that bad?'

Charles clamps his lips together and their silence proves that yes, it is that bad. I can see it in the floodlights shining over the black, chaotic swell. I can see it in the green light from the control panel, bathing over Scott's wrinkled brow. I can hear it in the groans and creaks. We're in a lot of trouble. And he doesn't care. And if we don't head for shelter then we're stuffed.

'Charles, you need to think about your children. We could call the coastguard.'

He turns to me, finger pointed at my face. 'Scott here is the best skipper I know. You need to listen to him and do as he says. Go and put the life jackets on them.'

'Are we going to roll over?' I ask. It's a question they probably don't want to hear, yet needs to be asked.

Scott shakes his head. 'We just have to get through it.'

I'm not confident. And neither are they. And if they won't turn back and they won't call for help via radio, then life jackets are our only option.

And it hits me like the wave against the hull. We're in life-threatening danger, and Charles knows it too. However, whatever this is, he'd rather endure it. Because what Mateo stands for, or what we're running from, must be something far worse.

One Week Ago

Tracy lives in a two-bedroom apartment with a flatmate who wears sixties-style clothes and smokes menthol cigarettes. Their flat holds the potent power of patchouli oil, ginger and tobacco, with an awkward aesthetic of crochet blankets, brown lounge chairs and cork flooring. Her name's Mindy and she hasn't seen Tracy today. She assures me Tracy sometimes does this, goes out and doesn't come home, couch-surfs from one house to another. But Mindy doesn't know about Mateo.

'I've tried calling her,' I say, glancing at my phone. I've tried calling at least ten times. It's now 1:15pm and there's been no texts, no calls. I'm actually starting to wonder whether I should phone the police. But Mindy shrugs and offers me a coffee.

I shake my head. I've had about five coffees already today, and I'm buzzing. I couldn't sleep all night. 'If she was sleeping off a hangover, wouldn't she hear me calling her?'

Mindy pours a black coffee into a chipped mug. 'This is just Tracy.'

Yeah, I get that Tracy is a little loose. Her day job description is yoga instructor and tarot reader and Tracy switches partners like the wind, but I still can't imagine why she wouldn't be answering her phone. What did he do to her? Or did Tracy go with him voluntarily?

'Can you get her to call me as soon as she gets in?' I ask. It's like speaking to a teenager who doesn't understand the repercussions.

'Sure.' She tilts the plunger. 'Coffee?'

I decline and leave Tracy's apartment, pulling my coat tight around my chest, sneaking a glance over my shoulder. The neighbourhood's quiet, cars parked on the side of the verge, a man jogging across the road, the trees holding their breath. A car with tinted windows followed me here though, all the way from the bottom of our street. It isn't coincidental. Either Charles or Mateo is having me shadowed, for different reasons. To catch me and Jack together, or for Mateo to keep track of me and his wife. I'm scared to admit this to Jack, but I'll have to tell him I went to the strip club last night. If Charles or Mateo continue to have me stalked, Jack and I can't meet without him finding out. The cars around me are empty. Maybe it was just a one-off, but I highly doubt it. This must be how Ariella feels, day in and out, always paranoid about slipping up.

Climbing into my car, I close the door and lock it, easing back into my seat. When I pull out onto the road, I check the rearview mirror. There's no one following me, no dark cars with tinted windows. I let out a deep sigh. Mateo's all about intimidation and possibly last night's statement was a threat. *Keep away or else.* If it is Charles having me tracked, I can't imagine why he'd start now. This reeks of Mateo, and possibly Charles isn't even aware.

Driving away from Tracy's apartment, I make a promise to myself. If I don't hear from her by tonight, I'm calling Jack and then I'm alerting the police. This could be the perfect opportunity to catch Mateo out.

Now

Five hours after the storm passes, leaving the waves exhausted and the wind out of puff, the cruiser engine starts up again from the shelter of Fraser Island. We're heading back north. If the island we're saying goodbye to *was* Fraser Island, then we're not far from tropical northern Queensland. So, if we're not far from tropical islands, the next boat will be here soon, and we'll have to leave our luxury cruiser behind.

That's why I've started packing. Hair conditioners, soaps, foldable toothbrushes, dental floss, spare hand towels, crackers, biscuits, chips, lollies, chocolate, fruit, water bottles – anything I may need to survive in our new destination. I don't think we're going to Hamilton Island, a five-star resort. These will be our luxuries.

'Let's hop in the spa,' I say. In fact, let's use everything while we can. I plan to blow dry my hair and wash it. I plan to drink a glass of wine with lunch. I plan to watch a movie in the main bedroom with a bowl of popcorn, while wearing a fluffy robe and slippers. I'm going to put on the air conditioning, I'm going to blast it through the room. I'm going to layer cream, expensive cream, all over this swollen body of mine and sink myself into a bubble bath. Fuck Charles. That's my mantra. Fuck him.

Kiki and Cooper are leaping around the place, talking in high-pitched voices while they await the next adventure, so I pretend to be just as excited for them. I'm so relieved they've seen and heard nothing that'll damage their souls later on in life. I plan to keep it that way until I find a way out of this infernal mess.

'I'm going to have a bubble bath, so you two can choose one thing you'd like to do before we switch boats, okay?'

'I want to hop in the spa,' Kiki says to Cooper.

Cooper considers that option for a moment and then says, 'I want to play the games on the TV.'

I get them both organised, filling the spa with lukewarm water and firing up the jets. Kiki pulls her bathers on and dumps the towel beside the spa. She's going to snorkel under the water and play mermaids. Cooper sets up cushions on the carpet, and sits straight-backed in front of the television, ready for the games to be switched on. And I fill the bath with rich, milky soap.

I'm stepping out of my clothes, clipping my hair in a bun, when the door to the bathroom opens. At first, I expect Cooper to enter, complaining about the Wi-Fi not working or the games being too hard to play, but it's not Cooper. It's Charles. Charles with his cold hands sliding around my ribcage and cupping my bare breasts. Charles with his breath freezing the hairs on my neck. I pull away, yelling out his name.

'What the hell do you think you're doing?' I cover my breasts as my pulse throbs in my throat. Jack's face flashes in my mind and I want to cry. Only *he* gets to touch me. *Where is he? Where is he? Where is he?*

Charles' eyes are glassy and red again, however, not dilated. There's a thick tangy yeastiness coming out of his mouth. He's been drinking beer and can barely register. And all I can do is stare and think about what a useless, pathetic person he is.

'I heard you say you were having a bath,' he slightly slurs. 'Why can't a husband touch his wife?'

172

I'm exposed in front of a drunken drug addict. I should've locked the door. I'm not even going to answer his ridiculously perplexing question. I need to get him out of here and away from me.

'I need a bath. The kids are relaxed, and I want a bath alone,' I tell him. 'So, give me my space.'

Pulling a robe from the hook, I quickly wrap it around me and wait for him to leave. He's staring at me in a dream-like state. He's looking through me. Perhaps imagining I'm a woman he could have treated better. Perhaps imagining I'm someone else, someone he loves. There's a sadness to his eyes and he shakes his head and holds his face.

'I never should've got involved with him,' he mumbles behind his hands.

'Who, Mateo?'

He nods. 'I knew about his reputation.'

The fact that he's opening up to me has me standing straighter. I fold my arms, hoping to use him in this state to gather some answers.

'Did he kill Ariella?' I ask.

He stares at me, scratching his stubble, his eyes signposting confession time.

'Well?' I prod.

He shrugs, ever so slightly. 'He's accusing me to cover his tracks.'

Really though? I don't want to discuss that she had something big to tell me. *I know everything. Tracy told me.* She never mentioned Charles, but I believe he was involved in it, and I'll never trust what he tells me.

'But why would he kill her? And why would Mateo blame you?' I lick my lips and speak gently. 'Was she cheating on him?'

He looks up, face blotchy red. *Was it you, Charles?* I read his eyes, searching for the hint. A rapid blink, a twitch, a movement that'll confess his involvement in her death.

And when he smiles, it's unsettling. 'Fucking impossible,' he says.

'Why?'

'Are you kidding? She always had security around her.'

'Then who would want to kill her? And how with all that security?'

Charles shakes his head and says, 'I don't know, I don't know.' He's done. I can see he's regretting ever coming in here, talking to me, trying to have sex with me or get close, or whatever sick fantasy he was playing out on me. He peruses the bathroom as though wondering where he is and backs up against the door. And it's then I think, *I could really knock you out now. This is my chance. Grab something heavy, like the lamp on the marble counter and smash it over your head.* I bite my bottom lip, flicking my attention from it to him. From it. To him.

'Boat's coming,' he says. 'Soon.'

My heart bursts into an uneven, nervous beat and my feet tickle. One step, one grab, one smash over the head. It's methodical, quick and easy. My fingers stretch for the lamp. But a phenomenon pulls them back as Charles turns to open the door and steps out. And I'm holding my breath so tight it's making me dizzy. I exhale and clutch the counter. A vision of a newspaper murder headline appears with my startled face underneath it.

I'm a prime suspect, just as much as Charles is. And the note Ariella sent me the morning before she was shot is enough proof for the police to link me. And then I'm on the run with my kids. And then I kill my husband with a heavy lamp. And then Scott, our skipper, accuses me of planning all of this, arranging a boat, kidnapping him and taking off to Queensland. I'm sent to jail for the murder of my neighbour, the one whose husband I was seen stalking.

And then I never get to see my kids again.

I sink into the bubble bath, until the heated water cradles me. Just keep doing what you're doing. I can't hurt Charles. To get away from him, I have to play the victim.

One Week Ago

One word: *Home*

In bed, I'm blinking down at my phone. Tracy's left me a text and it's odd and unlike her. No full stop, nothing else. I need to call her, find out if she's okay. With Tracy, I'm used to love heart emojis, flowers and exclamation marks. Not this. Anyone could be writing this. Anyone could have her phone. It's not like me to think the worst, but with Mateo, anything horrible is feasible. What if she's been abducted, raped? I go to press her number when the door to my bedroom swings open and Charles stands wide in the doorframe. I lower my phone, stiffening.

'What the fuck are you doing getting involved in Mateo's business?'

Two stamps forwards and I can't see his face, only his silhouette. That suffocating load of dread has me sliding under the covers. He slapped me last time, so what will be next? A punch to the face? Charles knows. Mateo's told him about the strip club, about Ariella and my notes. What worries me most is whether Mateo knows about Jack.

I try to act nonchalant by lifting a shoulder and talking calmly. 'I have no idea what you're talking about.'

'Last night. You and that yoga tramp going to his club.'

There's no mention of Jack or the notes and surely an affair would be the first thing he'd accuse me of. I lick my lips. 'We didn't know it was his bar. So what?'

Charles' voice darkens when he says, 'You're not seeing her again, do you hear?'

'Who, Tracy?'

'No, Ariella. Never again. Stay out of their fucking business, I'm warning you.'

'Is that why you're having me watched and followed? This is all about you intimidating me.'

'What are you talking about?'

'The man at the wine bar watching me, the car shadowing me this morning—'

Charles stares at me, clearly puzzled. 'Why the fuck would I have you followed? I couldn't give a shit where you go. Just stay the hell away from our neighbour.'

Slamming the door behind him, I'm left with a cramping, tightly wound body which releases in a sob. He's right about one thing. The danger of dabbling in our neighbour's life is tangible and getting dangerous now. Ariella's regulated existence, me being watched, and now this, Tracy's unusual behaviour, just proves Mateo's capable of anything. Squeezing the bedsheets between my fingers, I stare at my phone, then at the window, wondering what I can do for Ariella. I'm scared for her life. How will she gain freedom without me?

Hopping out of bed, I head for the candle where the notes are hidden. Laying them out flat, I read over them, especially the last one she slipped through the gate. *They're watching, find something illegal, I need your help.* And now I can't help any longer. The only option left is to go to the police in case something *does* happen. They may scoff at the notes and jot down my name, shoving my statement into a forgotten box on a dusty shelf, but I don't care, I need to do something.

Now though, I stuff them back inside the candle, close the lid and move to the curtains, shifting them aside. Next door, their house is dark. No lights spilling over their garden, her herbs. Are they in there? Will Ariella be punished for last night? Tracy. I need to phone her. I press her contact number and it rings four times before she picks up. Her voice is groggy and hoarse but I'm smiling just hearing it. 'Hello?'

'I've been trying you nonstop, I've honestly been worried sick.'

She doesn't answer straight away. Finally, she says, 'I'm . . . all right.'

'Are you, though?' I gaze out at the garden, the river beyond it, the moon accentuating the treetops. 'What happened to you? I went to the bathroom and then you were gone.'

'Emma.' She swallows and there's just her breathing. 'Just. I'm all right, okay?'

No, she's not. Her voice is small and timid. My shoulders drop and my body slumps. Fuck. What did he do to her? What has he threatened her with? I play with the cord on the curtains and wait for her to talk, but she says no more. Just breathes into the phone.

'What happened—'

'I've got to go, okay? I have a headache.'

'Tracy, wait—'

She hangs up. The phone's hot against my ear and I don't want to lower it. I want her to tell me what happened. I want her voice, and yet I don't. Because the disturbing, vivid picture in my mind provokes me. Tracy with him. Being forced. Maybe there was more than one. Maybe Tracy wanted it initially. Maybe she said stop. Maybe it was too late. Maybe he kept her there. Maybe she saw something so traumatising she can't find the words, the courage, the effort to tell. But it's my fault. I took her there, dragged her there, tricked her into coming. And hot tears fall down my face.

Three Days Ago

The littlest details are heightened by love, things you wouldn't normally notice or even care about. The stitching on the towel around your wet hair, who made it? Who made this towel? And the goosebumps on your thighs. What makes them pop up? You notice the crack in the ceiling, the chipped fingernail, the fluffiest scrambled eggs and the way they dissolve on the tongue. You notice the way coffee steams exotically, swirling erotically like a Spanish dancer.

You notice the stubble over the lips, the creased lobe, the dandruff on the scalp. You notice how it felt to sleep all night in awkward, uncomfortable positions with arms locked around your shoulders, deadening the muscle, but not wanting to move, because to move means to be apart. The fluffiest scrambled eggs. The best you've ever had. He's the best I've ever had. That's what I know.

He feeds me another mouthful and I barely swallow before another forkful hovers near my lips, sheened with butter grease. I laugh, coughing some out, which he collects and sucks off his finger. He feeds me. I take it. I swallow.

This will end soon, but I don't want to imagine that yet. We've made a deal to not see one another until we're finally ready to move into our home next week. Jack doesn't understand why, and I won't tell him that I'm doing this to protect us both. I won't tell him about the strip club. Not about Mateo having me followed, not about Ariella's notes. With Mateo watching me, with Ariella forced to sever all contact with me, with Tracy taking an abrupt holiday from yoga teaching and not answering my phone calls, our relationship is too risky and I can't have Charles finding out yet.

So, I try and enjoy now. Our last time. I'm here on white bedsheets stiff with washing powder and I wonder who washed them? How many people have fucked on here too? How many couples have cuddled all night under this particular sheet and slept uncomfortably, like we did?

It's our last night together until our first night forever. And last and first nights can never be relived. That's why I notice everything, every detail. His penis and the girth. The movement of him. The way he moans. And he does everything so perfectly, which makes this even harder.

He feeds me the egg and I take it and swallow. I love him. I love him more than when we first made love. And yet I'm afraid something's going to prevent me from starting my life with him.

Now

The fifty-foot boat rocks up against the cruiser like a baby sister, barely capable of sailing on its own through the swell. This is the first time since we started my invented adventure that Kiki and Cooper aren't impressed. They're not jumping with enthusiasm and excitement like I'd witnessed before when Charles said we'd be switching boats. In fact, judging by the way Kiki clings her backpack to her chest, her appearance reflects how I'm feeling. Scared, insecure, wondering what our next step is. And as per usual I'm the only one who knows how to make things better for my children. Through a hot chocolate and marshmallows during a thunderstorm, through lemonade after a heavy bout of gastro, through a Band-Aid and Mummy kiss when they scrape their knees. He's the absent, distant father who doesn't kiss, or even notice them. Doesn't build forts, doesn't kick a football, doesn't mutter anything more than, 'Morning, Cooper,' and, 'How was school, Kiki?' while scrolling through his phone.

Charles can't tend to them. He doesn't have the magic touch. And this is what I believe most mothers pride themselves on. Our children are connected to us with an invisible umbilical cord that never severs, no matter how far away they are. It's an energy that's felt. A quiet knowing. Men and fathers like Charles are jealous of this connection, and are forever trying to tie it to themselves by purchasing presents, playing games, cracking jokes. He's never even tried to form a bond, a true bond that I can imagine Jack having with this baby.

My children turn their worried faces to me, not him. They cling to me. They ask me. They want me in the dead of night. I'm staring at the back of his hair, where it's thinning at the crown, and smile with disgust. And when he turns to ask for our baggage, I think my face shocks him. Because I see him jolt a tad, just a tad. Just enough to know that he knows I hate him. And I'm swelling with satisfaction, a beautiful revenge that swirls and dances around my body like liquid black, an all-encompassing hatred towards him. I imagine it seeping into his body, and I swear it does. That's why he looks away, blinking a few times, brow wrinkling like crepe paper. I hate you, Charles. I hate you with all my being. And they will too. You will be forgotten too easily when this is over.

◆ ◆ ◆

It's sickening. We all feel it. The imbalance in our ears making us dizzy. Now what? What does he plan to do with a vomiting Cooper, who's often suffered motion sickness?

A new man joins us. They shake hands, Scott says goodbye and I watch as *Lady Luck* sails back the way we came, its pristine whiteness glaring in the sun. And I can't believe the sadness that sweeps over me. Each mode of transport – the car, *Lady Luck* and now this small boat – is a stepping-stone away from our real world, away from my business, my appointment at the doctor today, my wellness wake-up class, my Friday-night drinks, my daily walks, my fluffy dressing gown.

'It's okay, buddy,' I say to Cooper, who's hanging over the side of the boat, throwing up his breakfast. I wipe his mouth with a tissue and ready myself with a new one. His small body shudders over how disgusting he feels and Kiki sits on the step to the boat entrance, watching with her backpack on her lap. Little dots of tears squeeze out of Coop's eyes and a string of vomit blows out of his mouth, into the salty wind. I wipe his face.

'It's okay.'

Two words. How often do I repeat them? Do they make me feel better? Do they work? Do they remind Charles to treat us okay? I'm saying it all the time and yet it doesn't stop another bout of vomit projecting out of Cooper's mouth.

I've started hating the way I think, the way I talk. I think in negative waves of hopelessness that only diminish any confidence about surviving this. I think of killing Charles. Often. I talk in trembles. I'm really worried about my state of mind, the way I'm imagining it's me killing Ariella. And she's eyeing me and wondering why. And I'm shrugging and pulling the trigger. It's all my fault.

'It's okay,' I say to the air. Cooper shudders and I wipe his vomit, letting the tissue drop from my hands into the foam. The boat lingers to the left and then lingers to the right. It dumps down like a horse, ready to buck.

My hair is always in my face and my eyes leak from wind. The boat lurches, leans, stays that way.

'It's going to be okay.'

PART TWO

ACT TWO

Now

The water is tranquil, allowing the boat to slice through without effort. Cooper's small body is still drained and empty, on the downstairs bed, almost sleeping. A sickly sourness wafts from his breath. I'll have to brush his teeth when he wakes, yet I want him to just stay here awhile. The stillness is what I've been craving, but it doesn't last.

Kiki sits beside us reading a novel while I'm trying to nap. The turning of the pages rouses me and the second my eyelids open, I'm remembering: Ariella's skull. Blood. Her vegetable patch now neglected by its caregiver. Tracy. The letter.

I roll over, and the baby rolls with me. The bedsheets smell of dank mould, as though they've been carelessly left wet from salty swims and never hung out to dry. The eighties colour-splattered pattern makes my vision blur. I'm sick. It hasn't happened yet today, even with Cooper vomiting nonstop. And I've just eaten a bag of corn-chips before Cooper fell asleep, so I don't need carbs or salt or anything weighing my gut down.

No, this feels different. Not so much nausea, more a cramp, radiating around my pelvis. I sit up and Kiki lowers her novel.

'You okay, Mummy?' I love how she still calls me that.

I force a smile and hold my tightening belly. It bunches up like it's been wrapped up in cloth, twisted and pulled. 'Fine,' I whisper. 'Keep reading. I just need the toilet.'

The baby is getting bigger. And I don't want to imagine what the adrenaline is doing. Doctors all over have studied the effects of stress on unborn babies, especially survivors of trauma, whose stress and pain ripples through their lineage like a rotten spreading illness. I have to remain level-headed, even if these past days have been a living nightmare of ill-equipped events. I think I've handled everything quite well. Even before, as Cooper hung over the boat, I kept up the durable persona for Kiki. Her mother is strong. She can rely on me. This is everything that I teach my clients – find your inner strength, find it during hardship. If the baby senses panic, it'll want to come out. It's nature's way of protecting me, protecting mothers in bad situations. Most of the time their babies are premature, but as long as the mother is surviving, that's what nature mostly intends.

The bathroom is feral. A brown stain smudges the toilet bowl rim and pubic hair is curled in places by the sink. It makes me want to spew. However, I'm here to get away from Kiki's worried gaze while I get to grips with what's happening to me. The pain isn't severe like an intense contraction. But it *does* feel like the start of one.

'No,' I whisper to my belly. 'You can't come now.'

Closing the toilet lid, I sit down, holding my stomach and speaking to the baby in hushed, relaxed affirmations. 'If you come out now, we won't be ready for you. You deserve the best chance at life and it's not here and it's not now. Wait for your father. He'll love you so much. I promise when we get back home, I'll leave Charles and finally be with your dad. I don't care about anything now except giving us all a normal, sane life.'

And as I'm sitting atop the toilet bowl, with surging water outside the window rushing past in blue, I reflect back to before now. The ungrateful attitude I lived with each day, waking under high-thread-count sheets, in a house warmed in the winters and cooled in the summers, with views over a river and a garden so lush it took three gardeners to maintain. My breakfast was made for me daily, a bowl of colourful berries, seeds, coconut yogurt. My coffee brought to my bed most mornings by Georgia. I had it all. I hated it all. And now look.

Now

The sea has somewhat flattened into a bearable moving surface, which results in Cooper's cheesy grin. There's no more seasickness, for now, and my cramping has thankfully backed off. I've thrown his tissues in the wake and he's ready to enjoy the breeze, the freshness of the sea.

Coop's out on the stern, while Kiki stands with her backpack by the stairs to the flybridge. My crappy belongings, which Charles packed last week, have become a vital connection to our previous lives back home. Even my lacy undies, which he picked, are only one of four which I've washed and dried. Each object is sentimental to me now. Carting my belongings with me like a shell on a turtle's back has me realising how much I take for granted. My closets back home, brimming with the latest seasonal fashions and attire I can't even remember purchasing, have never been so far removed from the reality we now face. I don't know how long we'll be here, and Charles hasn't given me a definite answer. The food I've brought from *Lady Luck* is packaged at my feet and will soon dwindle. Biscuits will be eaten, bread and fruit consumed. Who provides the supplies for this island and from where?

There's another island to the left of us, looking attractive and inviting the way most Queensland islands do. Tropical, stunning, a sunny paradise. The clear water is the kind you can't stop marvelling at. I want to drink it, bottle the colour and bathe in it.

That island to the left is not the one we're going to, though. It's longer, higher, greener. From here, I can't distinguish whether it's a resort island or a vacant piece of nature, left untouched. There's no obvious infrastructure, no boats, no jetty. I turn my attention to the island we're headed for. There's a white home on the hilltop and what looks like a jetty and another smaller building on the beach.

Why here? Why has he chosen this place? And more importantly, how does he know about it?

The only positive aspect I can use to relax myself is the fact we'll be able to disembark onto dry land. Because the threatening part, the part that tells me we're now trapped, is too terrifying to address. Everything from the constant drone of the engines, the rocking, slapping of water against the hull when you're trying to sleep, to the unsteadiness on board a moving vessel is tiring, uncomfortable and far removed from what we're used to.

Maybe I'm looking forward to solid ground, and a bed that doesn't sway, and trees. Not that I believe this island will be a holiday in paradise. I'm guessing it's a staging post for us to recalibrate and to sort out the strife Charles has put us in. Equally, I'm worried it's the end point. The place we stay and set up a new life.

When he climbs down the ladder from the flybridge to ready the ropes, I ask him what this place is called and how long we'll be here. I'm assuming *Lady Luck* has returned to Sydney. And when it does, I'm hoping the police will be waiting. They'll arrest and interrogate Scott to determine where he brought us because the boys on the boat would've told the police the name. A boat that size is hard to hide.

'I don't know,' Charles says.

191

I lean against a pole, while Kiki and Cooper rummage in her backpack for a lost lollipop, arguing over who it belongs to. 'You don't know the name?'

He blows hair from his eye. 'It has no name.'

'Then how long are we here for?'

'I don't know,' he snaps, yanking large ropes from the side of the boat. 'There's no point in asking.'

I shake my head, folding my arms, getting sick and tired of the bullshit. 'Why not?'

'Because there is no time frame yet.'

'*Yet?*'

'Until I know more.'

I'm screaming inside, screaming. I want to wrap the rope around his neck and strangle him. He's not on drugs, he's not high, not intoxicated with booze, and that's why he looks bedraggled, seedy, rumpled, grey, ageing, ugly, pallid, sweaty and irritated by my questions. Well, too bloody bad. 'I'm not giving birth on this island,' I tell him.

He ignores me, asking Kiki and Cooper to argue about the lollipop inside. Why? So he can lash out in privacy? Tell me to shut up. I'm heaving with fury, now gripping the pole until my palms hurt.

'I've started having cramps and I think I'm miscarrying,' I say. I like provoking someone I hate. And I hate him. Yet does it work? I can't tell. But I'm guessing his silence has a bit to do with its efficacy.

'Who'll deliver it?' I say.

He turns with the ropes and says, 'Would you just be quiet, for fuck's sake, and let me figure this out?'

'The baby's not waiting,' I tell him.

'Well, you better keep your legs closed then.'

192

I don't know what he means by that, however, a memory of Jack on top of me flashes through my mind. I'm guessing his comment has nothing to do with labour. Is it to do with the affair? Cooper calls out that he's starting to feel sick again and the swell has him stumbling towards me. I clutch my son and wait for his body to convulse and all the while I'm staring, staring, staring at Charles with the hope that he feels my rage.

Now

From a distance, the tiled tops of a mansion emerge from behind the hill. It's exactly as Charles described it on the way here. Large, rambling, modern. It'll be fit for Hollywood movie stars to reside in absolute privacy. I can already imagine the kitchen. Pearly-white counters, wicker furniture, large coral pieces and shells, adorned perfectly amongst beachy coffee-table books. A faint wail touches my ears and I face my husband.

'Birds,' he says.

A man stands waiting at the end of the long pier, large ropes in hand.

'Who's that?' I say.

'Wallace.'

When the boat pulls up to the jetty and Charles goes about throwing ropes and shouting orders, I stare at the latest man. There have already been two others, men I've never met before. I'm in the company of strangers and my husband is one of them.

Wallace has thick black hair and an auburn beard. The contrasting colours make me smirk, yet I'm not in the mood for humour. As the boat bumps against the pier, Wallace loops the rope around the cleats and then catches the luggage as Charles throws it over. Wallace wears his sleeves rolled up to his elbows. His fingernails are dirty at the ends from gardening or maintenance or whatever other jobs he's employed to do here. And who the hell employs him? My husband? Wallace doesn't make eye contact with me, just holds his hand out while assisting me onto the pier. Afterwards, I wipe my hand on my shorts.

'They'll be staying in Barque,' Charles says, stepping onto the pier and helping Kiki and Coop off the boat. He passes Wallace my case. 'Make certain their luggage gets there.'

Wallace trudges off down the pier with some of our cases.

'Barque?' I say.

Charles gestures with a nod. 'Behind the boathouse.'

'We're not staying with you?'

'You'll have more privacy, Emma.' Charles gazes out over the ocean, his fringe swept back off his forehead. 'Better get in. Rain's coming.'

The pier is long, weather beaten with splatters of bird droppings and sharp splinters. Underneath, the water is a cool blue, slapping up against wooden pilings. It's enticing and clear and I want to dive in fully clothed. I clutch Kiki's small hand. Closer to the shore, palms sprout in clumps amongst white sand and limestone rocks. I'm not noticing that. The boathouse is to the left of us, and behind it a building made of pale stone. A cluster of palm trees surrounds the area, their leaves a shade of emerald. A fringe of straw hangs over the roof, and I almost imagine reggae music playing. The door is blue, chipped and worn from salt and tropical storms. An island home. I hold my breath.

'That's Barque?' I say.

'You'll be happy here, kids,' Charles says, stepping off the pier onto the pebbled path. He's already made up his mind that we're not staying up in the big house with him.

'What about us, Dad?' Kiki says. 'Are we staying with you?'

Wallace disappears around the boathouse.

'It's up to you.' Charles makes a smile, ignoring me. 'You can come back and forth.'

Coop leans his head against my hip. 'I'm staying with Mumma.'

Kiki nods. 'Same here.'

Charles shrugs, lugging a bag over his shoulder. 'Suit yourself.'

Somewhere on the island, a wailing bird cries.

◆　◆　◆

'Why's it called Barque?' Kiki asks me.

'French for *small boat*,' I tell her.

The iron plaque is slightly askew above the blue door. The stone walls are damp and discoloured with an unfamiliar creeper. The path is littered with palm fronds, a stray coconut and blushing flowers that have fallen from the creeper, but all of this adds to its charm, its deceptive beauty, like everything else that's happening right now.

The wooden boathouse is in front of Barque, a gaping hole with a triangular tin roof. We walk down to it and balance our way along the side. Underneath, the water is azure and gently sloshing against the walls. Across the ocean, the resort stares back.

'You could be sleeping with the fish tonight,' says a deep voice from behind. Wallace stands at the shore with his arms crossed. 'Sometimes at high tide the water comes right up to the front door.'

He has a penetrating stare, one that makes me glance away. Normally I'd respond to someone's comment. But I have a feeling he knows why we're here, more than I do. And this makes me instantly dislike him. So, I don't respond. I face back to the shoreline. Charles is nowhere to be seen now. He's left us here, the way he's abandoned our children and any fatherly duties.

Rain starts flattening the sea. The tin roof catches the sound of it.

'We better go inside,' Kiki says, holding herself. It's not even cold and the rain is hot tears. I wrap an arm around her shoulder and Coop's, aware that Wallace is watching us. Because that's what I believed he's paid to do. Mind us. Ensure we won't leave this island. This is my husband's way of kidnapping us, without really making it obvious. And I stare down at the bump starting to extend below my breasts, heavier with moving life and a future responsibility. Five and a half months. There's no way I can swim away from this place.

Now

Strangely, the fridge is stocked with essentials. Butter, white bread – which I'll never eat – jam, eggs, milk – not almond – fresh apples, a bowl of carrots, spinach, cherry tomatoes, celery, avocado.

I slam the fridge door, making the things inside wobble and chink. Who stocked the fridge for me? Was it Wallace? I'm tempted to throw it all into the sea and starve as a form of protest. But obviously I can't. The kids need to eat, as does the baby in me. Plus I've started thinking differently now. Smartly. Since the last place we stopped at, I've already started forming some connections, some strategies that could work to get me and the children to safety. All I need is time. A little more time.

The rest of Barque smells tired and dusty. Kiki and Coop are on the floor with their backpacks, arguing over who gets to read their new book first. I want to yell at them. *This is not a holiday*. But I can't. I have to pretend to be the peaceful one, even if I know what's happening.

'I'm just going upstairs,' I tell them.

'Can we go exploring?'

'No.' My voice cuts into the air. 'Not yet. Not without me. You're not going anywhere yet.'

Coop has that look on his face. Like when he first asked to walk to school alone, and I told him absolutely not.

I smile faintly. 'Why don't you come up too, and we can see the bedrooms.'

They both nod and leave their backpacks to join me up the creaking staircase. There's only one bedroom with one large bed. The duvet is crinkled with a dent in the middle. Someone has slept here before me.

'Where are our beds?' Kiki pouts with her hands on her hips.

'Well, how about we all sleep together?'

Coop rejoices in this. It's been months since I've allowed him to share a bed with me.

There are views over the boathouse and across to the other island. I attempt to work out the distance between here and there. Five kilometres, possibly more? I've never been good with distances. I touch my belly. I've never really been good at long-distance swimming either. Fuck.

'Come on,' I say to the kids. 'Let's make our bed.'

I hand Kiki the pillows and bundle the duvet up, taking care not to inhale the dust and old scent. I ask Coop to go and shake it outside and then grab the bottom sheet, scrunching it up. And then I stop. And Kiki notices it too, pulls a face, makes an *ewww* noise.

On the mattress are spots of blood. At the end of the bed, the middle and top. My throat clenches tight and I remind myself to breathe. Breath is the only thing needed to placate the body.

'Is that blood, Mum?' Kiki says.

'I doubt it. Probably just mould. Here, let's flip it over.'

We flip it, a cloud of dust forms, Kiki sneezes, I hold my nose. Coop returns with a shaken duvet and I pull the sheet over the corner of the mattress, while Kiki places the pillows back. All of this makes me puffed. This bed, these sheets, the blood spots remind me of Tracy, Mateo, the strip club and Ariella's gun-shot head. My mind is screaming, screaming, screaming.

Now

Dusk. The sun has descended behind the island, making the temperature drop, making the ocean like ink. We've unpacked the backpack and placed the novels on the empty bookshelf and folded trousers and shirts and arranged them on the shelf underneath. We close the door to Barque, and I'm well aware that Wallace will probably go in and scope and scour our belongings while we're off exploring the island. Still, I have nothing in there and nothing to hide – not now that Charles has taken everything from me.

'Let's go to the beach,' Coop says, running ahead along the path.

'Just wait, Cooper,' I say. 'I'd like to see where your dad is.'

'Same,' Kiki says. 'Let's see the big mansion.'

I pull my jacket closer around my neck. Charles followed the boardwalk up, so the house must be in that direction. Everything about this seems foreign and has done since we left Sydney. I can't quite arrange the pieces of memory together and I partly remind myself of John, my client, who often disassociates from reality. Trauma has that effect on people. Sometimes your attention sticks on something meaningless like the weeds growing from a clump of pebbles, like the crunching of shoes over rock, like the pattern of a shell. It's a way of coping. If you look up from the shell, the weed, the pebbles, you'll face an overwhelming threat which will debilitate. I can't allow myself to weaken with my kids present. They're the only things keeping me sane and they need me as much as I need them. I can't stop wondering how this will affect them later on in life. I have to make it light, make it fun.

Cooper runs along the sand, hopping over limestone rocks with arms out while Kiki crouches to collect a stone. She weighs it in her hand, turns to me and smiles. A stone is a good weapon, and I hate that I'm even considering that. But when the time comes, I'll have to be thinking of ways to protect us from him.

Now

The island across the expansive blue has just turned on its lights. Holidaying people in a resort, or privately owned? Soft yellow dots, running evenly along a line indicate it's a working island with people on there. So close it teases me. So close I can almost smell the cooking prawns and coconut sun cream.

Judging by the colour of the water and the many islands we passed on the way here, we're somewhere in the Whitsundays or perhaps even further up near Cairns.

There are dangerous, lethal jellyfish in that water. It's a trick of nature to look so beautiful and yet not allow swimming. I'm guessing it depends on the seasons. I just wish I could remember which season they frequented these waters. I need to find that out, but without my phone, I'll have to ask Charles.

When Kiki and Cooper follow me up the boardwalk, I take in the sandy area either side of the decking, palms bent above us. Browning palm fronds litter the sand. The decking is splintered and hasn't seen an oiled varnish brush in years. There are no lamps or fairy lights leading the way up the boardwalk like you'd expect from a resort island.

And it's when we reach the top, and the palms open up to a large area of grass and a rectangular infinity pool, that I can see this place is privately owned. There's no pool boy strolling past sunloungers, balancing trays of cocktails. The house is modern, large and stretched, with open windows overlooking the amazing sea view. It's stylishly designed, meant for a honeymooning couple or A-lister who can bring their entourage to pamper them.

'Awesome.' Coop leaps, kicking off his thongs. 'Can we go swimming, Mumma?'

He's attracted by the pool toys and waterfall trickling down a makeshift rockery running from a tropical garden above. Still, I pull back his arm and stop him.

'Just wait,' I say.

'Can't I just dunk my feet in?' He looks up at me, blinking. I nod.

There are voices coming from a building behind the pool. One of them is Charles, and the other two I don't recognise. Is Jack here? God, the thought of him being here, holding me and assuring me, makes my eyes sting. I can't hear his voice. I get snippets of information that I'll write down later to form more of a picture that I've been trying to sketch for days. He'll find out eventually, and then what? Then we'll be ready. We need another boat.

Is he talking about Mateo? Or Jack? When the men see us, Charles stops walking. The other two, Wallace and a man I've never seen before, look up.

'Hi, Dad.' Kiki waves. 'We want to go swimming.'

'I told them to wait,' I say. My voice has lost the power and volume it used to have.

'It's fine,' Charles says. Is this new man the owner of the island? I hold Cooper against my belly while Kiki stays beside me. 'They can go swimming.'

Kiki and Coop don't have to wait to be told. Coop's struggling to rip his t-shirt off while Kiki steps out of her sundress and neatly places her thongs beside me. I want to wrap a towel around her skinny little body.

There's a creepiness in the way Wallace stares at us, her, me. And now another man, with red hair slicked back off his long forehead. He wears glasses that I haven't seen since the eighties and a Hawaiian shirt. I can't see his eyes. I like to see eyes to make an assumption about a stranger. Except he doesn't take them off. In fact, he doesn't even speak. Instead, he walks in the direction of another building at the far end of the pool while Wallace follows him. These men seem worse than Mateo's minders.

Coop jumps into the pool with his knees tucked into his chest. Water droplets spray onto my legs. Kiki climbs carefully in while Cooper surfaces and swims to the floating donut. This could be a postcard picture. Happy family in paradise.

I half imagine Jack standing beside me, placing his arm over my shoulders. And then I exhale slowly. I'm standing like a guard, waiting to protect myself, or the kids from the husband behind me. I can't ask him why we're here or how long for or what plans he has for us. I'm stuck to the warm concrete, feet heating through my thongs. My teeth are on my bottom lip and I'm waiting for him to speak, to tell me anything, just to instruct, make a noise, fucking *talk* to me. And then his shoes shuffle off and he joins the two men.

We're not in good company and I cannot trust these men. The redhead's arms were covered in tattoos and that's all I need to build an accurate picture. Because it's not so much the tattoos, it's what they're all about. Guns, knives, blood drops. Naked women with huge, overly exaggerated breasts, legs spread. Words like 'murder' written in Latin.

I tell Kiki and Coop to get out. I wrap their pale, pure bodies in my shawl and tell them we'll swim off the shore if it's safe. I don't want to come back up here. I want Jack. I just want to go home.

204

Now

The humidity is thick and suffocating. Kiki's leg weighs my shin down while Cooper's hand fans my face. Their skin sticks uncomfortably to mine and this heat is penetrating, I won't be able to sleep. Not in this bed, not stuck between them, not with this headache thumping my temples. I can't think about the fact that I don't have painkillers, or a Band-Aid, or a toothbrush, or a hairbrush. In less than sixteen weeks' time this baby will come, and it'll wait for no one. Still, I can't think about that because I'll be off this island by then. Jack will find us. Or Mum. The police.

On *Lady Luck*, we had everything. Not now. Now we only have each other. There's rain hanging heavily in the air, and I wish it'd dump down and wash everything away.

I'm thirsty. Prying their limbs off me, I leave my babies and heave myself up off the mattress. Hoping to welcome any cool breeze off the ocean, I've left the window open. In the distance, behind the resort island, lightning splinters across the clouds, yet it's too far away to generate thunder. How long before the storm comes?

My gaze scans the area below for any hint of movement – Wallace? The ginger bloke? Who's out there minding us? It's as though mine and Ariella's lives have switched. I'm now being tracked, scrutinised. My watch reads ten thirty, which means I've only been lying in bed for an hour. Kiki and Cooper spent the evening beachcombing for shells and bits of reef, fraying rope and stones with peculiar patterns. I made them a sandwich each and cut up some vegetables with the cheap butter knife, almost slicing my finger as I chopped a carrot.

There's a television that only plays VHS movies, still at least it's something. But it means I can't get the news on here, can't find out what the media are alleging. Everything else about Barque is sandy, worn and it has obviously been unoccupied for months, if not years. The kitchen holds simple utensils, only two plates, two glasses and a coffee mug. There are three forks, two bread knives and one spoon. One couch, the colour of rust and mildew, sits in front of the television, and there's no dining table. That's how Kiki knows we're no longer visiting a sick friend. Something is most definitely up. But still, I lie: *This is the halfway point, we're going to a better island soon.* I don't want her staying up in the house with Charles and the other two. I want to keep my daughter close.

Downstairs, I turn on the tap and fill a glass with water. Rust and salt taints the flavour, however, I need to keep hydrated. On the cruiser, everything was provided. Food, clean water, coffee sachets with different types of sugar. Netflix, board games, cushy beds with Egyptian-cotton sheets. Now the everyday comforts have been ripped from us, still I need to try and keep it normal, routine and comfortable for the kids and myself, before I can figure out how to get off this island and away from my husband.

That's why dinner will be at dinnertime and bed will be at bedtime. And they will dress in new underwear in the morning and I will wash them with the one bar of soap that I have. They will read their books and make up endings and write the sentences on a piece of paper that I'll demand from Charles. To keep up their learning, to keep them distracted while I sort this out. They can build sandcastles and palm houses and rockpools made of shell and coconut

206

skins. They can swim in the pool and laze in the Queensland sun, but I have to figure this all out, I just have to.

My nausea starts up again, churning my guts as the baby flips inside me. And there's the pain, clenching tight. I clutch the kitchen bench and my stomach with the other hand, curling over. I can't believe this. I just don't believe how quickly and dramatically my life has altered. But I won't let the tears come, I just can't. Once they start, I won't be able to stop. Jack always says to stay calm. Being calm is having power. Being calm means making rational decisions, and everything will work out. So, I straighten and sniff back the tears.

This fear won't own me. *I* own me. I'm the queen of my own thoughts.

Now

The boat's gone. Has Charles gone, too?

Kiki and Coop skip over the rockpools, bending to collect a shell or two while I scan the ocean. The resort opposite is glaring white and wondrous, wearing a halo of sun. Would he leave us here alone? Was this the plan? Part of me rejoices in this while the other part panics. If we're alone here, then who will replenish the food? And the baby. How will I deliver this baby?

'Wait here,' I say to the kids and run past them, treading hard on a sharp rock. 'Ouch.' I wince, checking my soles. A nasty gash spills blood onto the sand and like all sharp slices of skin, I don't at first feel the stinging. But then the salt bleeds into it, along with the sand and I know, this cut needs stitches. It's deep with flapping skin and I want to cry, but suck it in.

'You okay, Mum?' Kiki calls.

'All good.'

Rinsing it quickly in the sea, I wince as salt needles the wound. Peering under my palm to the blue horizon, I search. No boat. I didn't even hear it leave. I'd fallen into a coma at about one am on the sandy couch downstairs. I woke, eyes crusted in dried tears, to Kiki's and Cooper's footsteps padding down the stairs. I made breakfast in a quiet daze, pouring milk into bowls of Weetabix. There was no honey, only a sprinkle of sugar to keep their complaints at bay.

They'd watched cartoons and I'd stared at the back of their round heads and shed a few silent tears into my coffee cup.

'I'm going to see where Dad is and check the pool's warm enough to swim.' I lift my foot out from the water and turn to Kiki. 'Will you stay here, please?'

She nods and then crouches to scoop sand into her lap.

Sand sifts into the cut as I run towards the boardwalk, though I don't care. I'm numb from pain, it has no effect on me anymore. The boardwalk is already warm from humid heat and I run up the wood, chest slightly tight. I shouldn't run with the baby and with the cramps starting, but there's a desperation to see if he's left us and I want to get back to the kids.

My feet find the grassy area and I wander to the pool, dipping my bleeding foot in. Red mixes in hypnotic swirls. Then, after I've washed the cut, I continue to the veranda. The doors and windows to the house are shut, yet not locked. The sliding door opens and I'm hit with burnt toast and coffee. Someone's home.

'Charles?' I call out. A radio plays somewhere in another room, country music with a drawling singer. The tiles are pristine white and cool. I'm accidentally stamping blood marks on them, but I don't care. Where is he? The kitchen is tidy, organised, designed in expensive stones, chrome and copper. The views out the glass windows and doors are incredibly eye-catching. There's almost a one-hundred-and-eighty-degree view across the island, a high vantage point displaying gardens and palmed slopes. This island isn't very big. You could probably walk the perimeter in less than an hour. Another small island sits behind this one, empty and flat like a muddy, barren marsh. From here, I spot waves crashing almost over the centre. It's more like a spit than an island.

'What the fuck are you doing here?'

I swing around. The man with the ginger hair walks out of a room beyond the kitchen. His glasses are off now, and his eyes are red, bloodshot and I'd know that anywhere. He's high, twitching awkwardly, mouth pulling and pinching, nose sniffing. Charles has left us with him. I wish I'd never come here.

'I'm sorry, I was looking for—'

'Charles said you'd be attractive. All legs.' He points to the floor behind me. 'But you're fucking up my floor.'

I back away. 'I'll clean it up.' He takes three large steps towards me, plants his hand on my belly and I freeze. The country music drags out like a dying cat, and this is not what I expected. I don't know what to do, still I have to think quick. He's high, dangerous and the words on his arm appear 3D and real now.

'Love myself a preggo one.'

I lick my upper lip, tasting salt and step back. This time he lets me create distance, dropping his hand and watching with a sly smile that says everything. Tilted head, Hawaiian shirt unbuttoned displaying red curls. I think about a knife. I think about a forceful object in the kitchen I'd use if I had to. But then I think about Kiki and Coop, alone down there on the beach.

My hands quiver as I crouch to wipe the blood smudges off the tiles with my skirt. He watches, sniffing. There are four stains. My belly is heavy. Where is Charles? For once, I need him here. I don't think he'd let this happen, even after everything, I don't think he'd approve of another man touching me, perving, trying to get close.

Rising, I avoid facing the man who's right in front of me. Instead, I turn and limp out the sliding door with the feeling that at any moment he'll lunge and pull me back.

Now

Kiki and Cooper aren't by Barque when I hobble off the boardwalk. I scan the area, the rockpools, the palm trees off the sand, and listen. I can't hear them. I can't bear to think they're with Wallace or another strange man after the ginger gave himself permission to touch me. I still feel his handprint on my top and want to shower. I'm surprised he let me walk out. I'm guessing it's because he knows Charles will be back. My foot's stinging now, and I'll need to bandage it up and wear shoes to prevent infection. But the kids. I need to know they're safe. I call out to them as I start walking briskly along the sand, careful to not stamp my sole.

'Kiki, Cooper,' I yell.

When Kiki shouts back from the boatshed, 'In here,' I drop my shoulders and slow my steps. Thank goodness. Every moment, every day, seems like a new version of suspense I can't relax from. The stress and adrenaline coursing through the baby will be felt. That much I know. It's the same with pregnant women who have lived through wars and horrific situations. It carries through to the baby. I hate knowing this.

Sweat pools between my heavy breasts and I stick a finger in there to wipe it away. Even after everything that's happened, I'd rather Charles be here. With the other men on this island high on drugs and power and masculine supremacy, I need a familiar face.

Even if he doesn't care about me anymore, I think he cares for the kids.

'Where's Dad?' Kiki asks. They're pointing their feet into the water's surface and I want to bundle them in a baby blanket and float away.

'Come here,' I say with my arms out. I'm braced for the impact, for the sand in my face and thumping hugs. They both run to my open arms and snuggle in.

'I think Dad's gone fishing,' I say.

'Why are we here, Mum?' Kiki asks, looking up at me. Faint freckles dust her nose. If only she knew. Her little video has probably gone viral. Police watching it and checking the man in the balaclava, his stance, the way he walks, any feature that'll lead them to their suspect. I'm trying to think back. Was it Charles under the mask? But why?

'We're on our way to visit—'

'I don't believe you.' Her voice is quiet and soft and Cooper watches us both for a reaction. I let out a silent breath and hope they don't feel it.

'There's nothing to disbelieve.' I jiggle them playfully. 'Dad will be back soon and we can have some lunch and maybe play in the pool?'

She doesn't smile, though Cooper is easily pleased and jumps off me. Kiki fiddles with my hair and her eyes meet mine.

'Something's happened. You won't tell us, but I know it.'

Kiki's unaware of what she posted to the world. Even in the footage I could see how oblivious she was to the murder occurring in the background, while she bent to collect her crown. And then she uploaded it immediately. Posted a video that changed our lives. Usually, what she's saying would cause me stress, but I'm distracted. A young woman is stepping out of Barque with a pile of dirty clothes. Our clothes that I'd bundled by the door, ready to clean. I set Kiki down and stand.

'Excuse me,' I call out, walking to her and forgetting about my cut. Recoiling with the pain, I lift my sole and hobble over. She glances up and doesn't seem at all fazed by our presence.

'They're our clothes. I was going to wash them—'

She flaps her hand and speaks in a stern, gruff voice as though she's telling me off. She's not speaking in English. She points to the washing basket of clothes and gestures over her shoulder. I'm guessing she's going to take them and wash them? She's scruffy in a faded floral dress which hangs off bony shoulders and looks like clothes you'd find in an op shop. Her upper lip is swollen and thinly crusted in blood. Bare feet, stringy hair. Who is this woman? Why is she hurt? She reminds me of the two young women in Mateo's strip club bathrooms. Young, petite, attractive with sad-looking eyes.

'Emma.' I press my chest and then offer my hands to her. 'You?'

She purses her lips and shakes her head. 'No,' she says and walks off.

'Wait,' I call and follow. 'Do you speak English?'

She flaps a hand behind her. 'No.'

'What's your name?'

She ignores me, but I want to pull her back, I want her attention. I'm sick of backs facing me and people not being straight and I'm sick of lack of honesty and not having Jack and not having a comfortable bed to lie on. And her frame is so like Ariella and I want female company. Not men, not kids, I want this woman.

'You do know what I'm talking about.' I speak tightly, with a fury so strong, I'm stomping after her, down the path behind Barque, and I'm no longer caring if my sole hurts or how hot it is. 'I'm Emma. What's your name? What's that island over there called? Do you have a phone—'

She whirls around and snaps a sharp, final, 'No.' It echoes through the palms and cuts me. The young woman keeps going, holding our washing on her hip. And I already know, after she can't see me anymore, I'll get the kids, and we'll go looking for her. This woman might be the only hope we have.

Now

Limping back to the boatshed, I call out to Kiki and Cooper, asking them to come with me. They can't be alone out here, not now that Charles has gone. That's if he has. An ulcer on my inner cheek has turned nasty and red. I can't help chewing, dragging my tongue across it. Has he really gone and left us here? I stop for a moment, hands on hips, eyes on the choppy waves. There's no boat in sight, only the island. If I close my eyes and strain my ears, will I hear music, voices, carrying over the water? I test it out, hoping that if I do, it won't seem so far away. But there's nothing. Only the gentle slap of waves against the sand. Kiki humming a tune. Cooper dragging a stick into the gritty sand. I open my eyes, defeated, angry, biting my tongue.

'Where are we going?' Cooper marks a cross with the stick in wet sand.

'I want you to be super quiet, okay. We're going to follow that lady.'

'Why?' Kiki says with her hands on her hips. She's starting to get that fed-up look about her. Like she knows I'm hiding secrets and she wants in on the lie.

'Kiki, do you have to question everything I say and do? Just do it, okay?'

I catch her rolling her eyes before she follows with crossed arms. She deliberately walks slowly, sliding her feet behind her, while Cooper ditches the stick and joins me, little warm hand clasped in mine. We head back behind Barque and he bends to pick up a coconut and then throws it with a thud against the trunk of a palm.

'I said to be quiet.' He shrugs and keeps moving.

This is the first time we've been down this path, and it could be anywhere, any tropical romantic island in the Barrier Reef. I can imagine holding Jack's hands under here, coming back from a five-course dinner and wandering back to our beach-side studio apartment.

I shake my head. There's no point in dreaming. This nightmare is real and I need to face it head on instead of fantasising.

We climb a small slope, then the path breaks down into sand and small prickly shrubs. The woman's footprints are small and immature. What is she doing on here? Why the cheap clothing and bad hair? More importantly, the bleeding lip. That's what worries me most. I'm scared I'm about to step into a scenario I'm not prepared to witness. My body pulls itself back and when the path stops and ferns and tropical plants shield the area, I tell Kiki and Coop to stay here and not move a muscle.

'Just sit here,' I say, pointing to a small boulder.

Kiki sits down with a pouting lip and Coop plonks himself on her lap. For once, she actually lets him, so I kiss her head. 'Back in a sec.'

She has every reason to be annoyed with me, but one day, when we go home and things go back to normal, she'll know I only lied about the boat trip, this island, to protect her.

Pushing through the ferns, I continue tiptoeing over smaller shrubs until I detect from the bent branches where the woman has ventured. When the trees give way, I'm able to peer through to the other side. A small tin building and a few large gas bottles – outdoor machinery such as wheelbarrows, lawnmowers and a trailer are kept over here, away from the main house. And the woman is meandering down a slope with my washing basket jabbed in her side. She calls out to someone. I move the branches away from my face, just enough to be concealed from my neck down. Another woman appears, lugging a baby on her hip. The baby is poorly dressed in a weighty nappy, sucking on a hairclip. The woman wears baggy male shorts and an orange bikini top. She has big breasts and a winged tattoo sprawled across her back like a fairy. It's tacky, showy and reminds me of Ginger's arms. And just when I think that's all, another older woman exits the tinned building holding folded white sheets. She's dressed like an old-fashioned maid in a stiff grey dress and white apron. She yells at the other two women.

I'm guessing they're hired to be here as cleaners and housekeepers. But what else? Mateo's club springs to the forefront of my mind again. Do they speak English? My eyes move to the baby. How long have they been here? These questions roll in my head, directing me back to the bedsheets in Barque, the blood stains I'd tried to forget about, the woman's bloody lip, Mateo's strippers.

There's an altercation of some sort that I can't understand. But the older maid slaps the woman with my laundry basket hard across the face, so she drops the basket. Clothes spill out and I hold my mouth and want to sob. I'm possibly piecing it all together. And what I'm seeing scares me more than when we first stepped off the boat.

Now

I'm verging on vomiting again, and it's not just the morning sickness progressing since first trimester – it's this island, the women, the bloodied bedsheets, the men, this situation. Mostly, it's how blind I've been for ten years. How long has Charles been connected to people like this? It wouldn't make it any better if he told me only a year, or three. The fact is, he's involved in something sinister. I grip a palm tree and hang my head, as the onset of sickness dizzies me.

'Go back to the house,' I say to the kids, closing my eyes. 'I'll meet you there.' They run off like the good kids that they are. It's too much. I gulp three times, exhaling steadily through my nostrils while the Weetabix I'd eaten earlier starts travelling up my throat. I crouch while I convulse, allowing my body to take over. The noise interrupts the lapping waves, the hum of a boat. A boat?

I blink the tears away and cover sand over the mess with my good foot. Wiping my mouth, I scan the area. There are no boats out on the water, but Charles could be back in the boathouse. My stomach instantly settles and I start limping back down the path. Please be back. I've never been more excited to see someone I now despise.

The shade of palms ends when I step back onto the sand. Dazzling sun hurts my eyes, so I gaze under my hand. There's a smaller white boat in the boatshed and Charles is definitely in there, talking to one of the men inside. I'd recognise that laugh anywhere.

Kiki and Cooper are balancing along the edge of the shed and Charles carries a large suitcase, rolling it along the wooden boards. We have another visitor. When Charles notices me, he stops.

'I thought you'd left us,' I say and can't control the way my chin wobbles like a child. He doesn't like the look of it, I know, because he stares down and keeps pulling the case towards me. The emotion I'm showing hits him hard and part of me revels in it. Look what you're doing to me, look what you've done. How will you ever fix this mess you've created?

Biting my top lip, I wait for him to respond, only he doesn't and a strong choking smell of sweat drifts off him as he continues past me. I stare back at the boatshed. Who else is with him? Another crim?

A man's leg stretches out of the boat and I'd recognise those shoes and shins anywhere. The hairs I've licked and kissed. The legs I've massaged. Oh God, he's here. I stifle a sob. Jack. Jack's here. Where has he been all this time? I want to ask him but then remember I can't. With Charles around, he is only my husband's silent business partner. I have to act normal, when really I'm in disbelief.

A part of me feels saved, yet I know the truth. We can't talk, touch or do anything with Charles watching. And all I want is to collapse against Jack for a while and allow his strength to hold me upright. Where has he been? I need him to quench my fear with safety. I'm stuck on burning sand, sweating and wanting.

He steps onto the side of the boatshed, ruffles Cooper's hair and looks over to me. And I can't read his face and I can't stop the tears because he's here for us. I hold a fist to my mouth and silently sob, smiling, hoping Charles won't look back and catch me. He goes to smile back and Charles calls, 'Come on,' and a sharp twist of confusion kills me.

219

His eyes stick on me and yet I can't interpret the gaze. Us or Charles? Water reflects over his skin like swirling snakes, and I want him to come closer so I can smell him. *Us or Charles?* I want to touch him; I want to slap him. *Who are you here for?* Or is he in danger too? What if he's a part of all this?

No, Jack's not here for us. He's here for Charles. My kidnapper, the person we were escaping to live our lives together. *You hate Charles, remember?* I want to say. *You know what Charles has done and yet you're here for him.*

Is there such a thing as being loyal to a husband *and* a wife? A mother *and* a father? A brother *and* a sister? If one disappoints the other, whose side do you take? Whose side has Jack taken? Ours or Charles'? I don't know whether I can trust him anymore and this breaks me. Images of him lifting me into bed like a baby, drawing circles over my belly with his fingertips, filling my belly button with water in the bath, seem to shatter like the illusion of magic.

Kiki and Cooper follow him out of the boatshed, seemingly excited by his arrival. Coop's asking if they can go for a boat ride later or maybe fishing. Jack says, 'Sure,' and keeps heading towards me, carrying his case. Kiki does a cartwheel and the joyous innocence makes my heart thaw. They have no idea what surrounds them, how on edge everyone is.

I flick my head, glancing over my shoulder at Charles. On the edge of the sand and decking, he's waiting for Jack with the suitcase by his side. Tense face, balled fists, like he's ready for a fight. With me, Jack or Mateo?

Jack walks past me, close enough to hear him mutter words I can't quite catch.

Wait or *save* or *babe*?

I want to tug him back around and ask, but Charles starts talking to Jack and all I can do is stare at the back of him. Down his spine, sweat dampens the t-shirt he's wearing. I caught a hint of his spicy deodorant and I'm back in our hotel room after we've showered together.

How can he not want to touch, reach out or hold me? I want to imagine he does. He wants it just as much as I do. He's simply pretending for Charles. But he's really here to rescue us. Still, he follows my husband up the decking with his suitcase bumping behind and doesn't glance back at me. Usually, a glance back would indicate a special message, a secret signal, an emotion I could read. But nothing.

'Jack, look at this,' Cooper calls out, running behind Jack with a giant shell. 'Do you think a crab lives in here?'

Stopping, Jack crouches, twisting the shell around. 'I don't know, buddy, let me take a look.' His back faces Charles and he uses this position to finally peer at me from beneath furrowed brows. But Charles is there, and I can't make it obvious, so I kick the sand. 'I think some sort of creature lived in there before, but they've swapped out homes.'

'Dad, Mum's foot's bleeding,' Kiki says with another cartwheel. She leaves foot and handprints on the wet sand. Water pools into them and they vanish as though she was never there. 'We need Band-Aids.'

'I'll grab some soon.' Charles gestures with his head. 'Come on, Jack.'

Jack rises, brushing his hands down his shorts. He's the type to clean my foot up for me and bandage it thoroughly.

'I really need some antiseptic cream,' I tell Charles.

He nods as though I'm a nuisance and keeps moving up the decking. And Jack gifts me one long look and a nod. Something I've been wanting, an indicator that says he may be here to help us.

Now

We eat lunch on the bent trunk of a palm. Ants make a trail past our bottoms, carrying tiny eggs on their backs. Up the top, four unripe coconuts are bunched together like party balloons. I've never really liked Queensland or the burden of its humidity – but the foliage, the ocean, the islands and white squeaky sand is almost alien compared with Sydney. It's beautiful. I don't know whether I can appreciate this beauty now that Jack's here, helping me to take a moment, or because I'm sitting and facing it. But if I was going to be on the run by choice, I can't think of many places I'd rather be. Cooper accidentally drops his sandwich in the sand and I sigh. I'll have to make him a new one. He's sorry, almost crying and I want to join him. I'm tired, restless and my foot's throbbing.

'It's okay, Coop.' I pat his knee. 'We'll go for a swim after this.'

'Can you make it for me now?'

I chew and swallow a chunk of bread, so it gets trapped. 'Let me just finish mine first.'

Cooper waits for me to finish my sandwich by filling a rockpool with shells. They go in with a splash. He's play-acting Minecraft while Kiki chews her sandwich beside me. Her legs are in the sun, so I fling my towel over them. It's so bloody hot. This humidity is oppressive. I want to dunk myself in the sea and live there. I need to ask someone about the jellyfish.

'I'm glad Jack's here,' Kiki murmurs with a mouthful of bread. 'I was starting to get scared.'

Her brown fringe moves in the sea breeze. 'Of what?'

'I didn't know where we were. And those men and women are a bit weird. And you losing your phone and mine smashing and not being able to talk to friends and stuff. But now Jack's here, I get it.'

Get it? Get what? She thinks she has it all figured out, and maybe that's what I need to do. Just be like a ten-year-old and believe I have the answers.

I smile. 'What do you get?'

She brushes the fringe from her eyes. 'That we really *are* only here for a stopover. We'll be going to your friend's house soon.'

I kiss her head. 'I don't much like it here, either.'

She seems happy I'm agreeing with her. 'It's a gross beach house.'

'I know.'

'And nothing to play with.'

'I get that,' I say. 'But it's nice to have to make your own fun, right?'

She nods and points over the beach. 'Here's Jack now.'

I stop eating and place the sandwich on my lap. Jack's holding a bandage and some cream and the woman with the tattoo is behind him with a bucket of steaming water. He ruffles Coop's hair and bends to the rockpool. I hear him comment on the coral while the woman carries the bucket past him.

'They're here to clean my foot,' I tell Kiki and place my sandwich on her plate.

I stand, hobble over to Barque and hope that Jack and I can do this in private. We need to speak. But the woman shouts no, no, no, and orders me to sit back on the palm trunk. It's like she's a spy sent to watch over me and Jack. It then occurs to me, what if Charles knows about Jack and me? What if Mateo told him? Is that why he acts like I'm a stranger now?

I sit back beside Kiki and the woman flicks her hand to lift my foot. Kiki laughs beneath her breath. The water is warm, trickling down over my sandy foot. It's faintly perfumed and warmly fresh. Jack straightens and heads over to us, staring at me.

'How'd you hurt yourself?' he says.

'Stepping on a sharp rock.'

He tuts, bending to inspect my foot, but doesn't touch me. Faint freckles cover his nose and his face appears greyer, tired, like he's stressed. And Jack doesn't get stressed.

'Jack, where are we going next?' Kiki asks, finishing her sandwich. 'Where's the next island?'

He smiles and tickles her foot. 'It's a surprise, Kiks.'

'Home?' I say.

The woman looks up at him. And he doesn't say anything. But why? Why can't he bloody talk to me? A seagull cries overhead, searching for sandwich crumbs. So, he's here for Charles. I'm blinking away tears and I cannot look at him.

'I'll dry it and bandage it for you.' He has a towel and I snatch it off him.

'Don't bother.' I pat my foot dry, examining the cut. I bite my teeth together and Kiki watches me.

'Well, then let me put the cream on—'

'Kiki, can you please make Coop another sandwich?'

'But, Mum—'

'Now, Kiki.'

She sighs and knocks her plate, so it falls to the sand. Jack reaches to pick it up and I grab the cream and bandage from his other hand.

'Thank you.' I speak to the woman. But she just stands with the bucket, watching us, eagle eyes black and glaring. I think she

224

was the one with the baby. I pass the towel to her and peer up at him. The sun is like a halo around his head.

'What is *happening*?' I ask.

He smiles. 'Nothing. Just hang tight while Charles sorts this out, okay?'

'Where have you been, Jack, I needed you—'

He taps the woman's arm and turns away. 'Let's go.'

'What?' I hiss, going to stand, but then I remember my clean foot and stay seated. He ignores me and stomps off and I could scream. The woman's fairy wings give the illusion of flapping as she swings the bucket in one hand. Jack marches in front of her and I know there's nothing more I can do. I don't want Cooper to see me cry, so I face the waves and remember a time when I was little, when my babysitter took me to the beach.

No matter how fun she tried to make it, with Neapolitan ice cream, beach balls and boogie boards, nothing seemed as fun as the mother and father riding the waves with their children beside me. She wasn't my mother; she was a teenage girl working during university breaks. My parents let me down time and time again and so do most people.

Jack was my saviour and now he's neglecting me, and in a way, I always feared he would.

Now

Dusk sets the ocean in a palette of apricot and peach. The setting sun casts a golden filter over the island, faking paradise. We haven't gone exploring today. Since I've bandaged my foot and cleaned it, we haven't seen anyone down near Barque and I'm trying to keep the kids occupied here. Up at the big house, Charles, Jack, Wallace and the ginger stay put, snorting drugs, drinking or fucking the women – whatever they plan to do while we're here. And what about Jack, will he have to pretend to take part in it? Sick images of him being dragged into a bedroom, his body being explored, kisses, moans, licks, revolve in my imagination. I can't handle it.

I'm going to wait until it gets dark before I sneak through the palms and watch them, check to see what Jack's up to. I could have the kids go up and swim in the pool and snoop but I don't trust these men around my daughter and I don't want my kids witnessing anything disturbing.

It's been tricky keeping them busy, especially when my mind's distracted by the women behind the hill, Jack's arrival and dismissal of me. We've built sandcastles and mini-forts that occupy five metres of beach. We've built a tent out of palm leaves and collected every coconut, piling them up so they balance. Tomorrow we can do bowling, or weave palm fronds, or bury Kiki's legs in sand.

Just the simple arrangement of keeping the kids busy reminds me of movies where the family are stranded on a deserted island. I'm grateful for the stained toilet, the grotty shower with mouldy grout and dismal hot water. I'm grateful for the food in the fridge, which I hope will get replaced when it runs out. That's if we stay here for longer than a few days. Being left in the dark, without answers or explanations is not only soul-destroying, but also frustrating in the sense that I constantly want to cry. As children, we have boundaries, rules, routine. This follows through to adulthood. Breakfast, the commute to work, lunch, coffee break, a jog after work, a yoga class, dinner, bath, Netflix and reading. We know what comes next, we know what to expect. To have that ripped from me makes my mood and personality disordered and anxious, as though the coconut we last found fills my chest, clogging it.

So, I leave Barque after making us another sandwich each with a floppy carrot and a cucumber and arrange a spot in front of our palm tent. The only solution to a disordered mind is silence, stillness and clarity. I need to keep reminding myself of that. As long as I'm practising what I preach to others, I can keep going and figure out how I'll get us out of this nightmare.

'Let's have a fire,' I say to excite them, to excite myself.

'How?' Kiki asks, carrying her plate to the sand. It's still warm from the afternoon sun.

'We'll gather some dry sticks and, Coop, you get some rocks. Leave it to me.'

They set about gathering twigs, dried grass, palm fronds and dead leaves while I hunt around the kitchen for some matches. There are none. But there's a gas stove. I test it out, pressing down the knob and ignition until a flame coughs out. I smile down at it. I'll have to use an object to transfer the flame to the fire – rolled toilet paper or a small stick, but I'll make us a fire, it'll make us happy.

Kiki assists Cooper, clunking rocks into a small circle and they both dump the sticks and twigs in the centre. I layer them all neatly into a tepee style arrangement and tell the kids to wait while I get the fire.

Using twisted toilet paper, I light the ends and quickly dart outside to drop it onto the dry contents. And it works. The grass sizzles and curls into orange flames and the palm fronds catch on, curling and whipping into life. Kiki and Cooper smile widely and I beam, hands on hips. We crowd around with our plates and sandwiches, watching the little fire we made. And I knew it'd make things better, because nature has a way of doing that. The fire goes with the surroundings, and all I can do is pretend, the way the sunset does, the way the water does too, so flat now it moulds with the sky. I pretend we're in paradise and for a moment, the knot in my chest untangles.

But come nightfall, once the kids are asleep, I'm venturing up to the main house.

Now

Bits of gritty sand scratch my legs whenever I roll on the mattress. Kiki and Cooper have brought the sand in with their feet, but it can't be helped on an island. Sand gets into your hair, fingernails and ears.

The curtains waver in the wind and outside the clear black sky whispers to me. It's late again, and I can't sleep. When will I ever have a sound night's sleep again? Home feels like a million years away. I'm picturing people back there searching for us. Tracy must be beside herself, but what is she doing about this? Did she contact the police? Do Mum and Dad lie awake, worried sick about me? Imagine what they're thinking, imagining, believing. Everything the media accused appears reasonable. Our family *is* on the run. Our neighbour *was* shot in the head. My husband *was* the head of their security. I *was* her friend. Our housekeeper *was* hushed. And Charles was the one in the footage, holding up the gun, I'm sure of it now. How long until the police find and arrest us with Kiki and Cooper watching?

I can't just lie here and accept it. I need answers. I need Jack close to me, holding me, telling me everything's okay. Music. A rhythmic thump that matches the beat of my heart. It's them. They're probably high, drunk.

Without waking Kiki and Cooper, I roll from the bed and into my shoes. My foot feels bruised and tender, but it's the least of my problems. Treading carefully down the stairs, I stop at the bottom and stand still, listening. If Wallace's outside, I won't be able to leave Barque. Distant music thuds. Surely he's with the rest of them, partying, loosening up, off their heads on drugs and power and stress.

Opening the door slowly, I peer out to the silver beach, greyer and more mystical at night. No one's here watching over us. Closing the door behind me, I creep around the side of the house to check for Wallace or the old maid. No one. We're alone. It feels horrible to leave the kids asleep inside, but I have to be quick and see for myself what's going on here. Who are these men and what do they get up to? I limp quickly up the boardwalk, biting down hard on my lip with each painful step, aware of my breathing, aware of being quiet. The closer I get to the top, the louder the music becomes. Thump, thump, thump. They'd never hear me, even if I screamed. At the top of the boardwalk, I stop, standing behind a palm, and stare into the brightly lit residence. It's so white, sterile and opposite to our natural surroundings. The men can't see me out here in the dark, in the shadows behind the trees, but I see them. Crouching, pinching my lips, trying to look away, but can't. I shake my head.

The older maid is smoking a cigarette and ordering the two younger women to perform for the men. They are naked, dancing around, dancing on Charles' lap, breasts in his face as he smokes, nodding his head to the rhythm of the music. Beer in one hand, cigarette in the other, Charles delights in the attention while Wallace pulls the tattooed woman against him. They're being pulled, yanked, spanked and twisted like dolls between bratty children and I don't even realise I'm crying until I taste salt between my lips.

Jack's at the back of the room, standing, drinking a beer with a face so solemn and dark, I almost don't recognise him. He's either

230

hating this or off his face on drugs, I can't tell. But he's involved. He's here for Charles and I can't stand the sight of him. And it's then I wonder who these women are and what they're doing here. What if they're prisoners from another country? What if they've been brought here and can never leave?

Now

I'm back in bed, red-faced and sick, wide awake and worrying. There are footsteps, creaking on the stairs. I sit up, stirring Cooper and hold my breath. Thoughts quickly piece together: if the ginger one steps through that door, I'll scream and use the rock I've stored under the bed. A sharp white hunk that hurts even holding it. I'll slam it against his forehead, and it'll pierce his skin. It won't kill him, but it'll give me enough time to wake the kids and run. Run where? To Jack? Charles?

I'm about to reach under the bed when Jack steps into the room. I gasp and he holds up a finger. 'It's just me.'

'You scared me so much,' I say and then crumble like a toddler, sobbing in convulsive motions. Kiki and Cooper's bodies jiggle from it and he crouches beside the bed, reaches to hold my face and shakes his head.

'Come here,' he says and we kiss without caring. Because he's here like I wanted him to be, even if it's not for me. He's here. Tears get in the way of our kissing.

Pulling away, I gently roll myself out of the bed and Jack takes my hand, helping me up. I hug him so tight it hurts my breasts. And I cry into his shirt until he tells me to follow him downstairs. 'We'll wake the kids,' he whispers.

We hold hands all the way down and when we get to the bottom, I can see he's pulled the curtains downstairs closed. 'I have to be quick,' he whispers, kissing my cheek, nose and mouth. 'Christ, I was worried about you.'

'What's happening?' I cry. 'Are you a part of all this? Please tell me you're not.'

'I'm not. Of course I'm bloody not.' He wipes my tears with a thumb and holds me against him again. 'The guys here have taken everything off me. My phone, wallet, everything. That was the deal. I come here for Charles and they keep everything. The cruiser's gone, we're stuck here, and I don't know who these men are, but I'm going to find out. I just need to get Charles alone.'

I thought Jack would come here with answers, a rescue plan, a risk assessment. But he's clueless, almost as much in the dark as I am. I stare up at him and frown, unknowing what to think.

'The police are after you all,' he says. 'Charles is a major suspect because he's left so suddenly. No one saw him at work that morning and there's rumours circulating that Charles was in love with Ariella.'

'I don't believe that he was,' I say. 'But I still think he might have killed her. I saw the footage and it looked like Charles. I just don't know why yet.' I eye him carefully. 'Why are you here?'

'I got your messages and Charles phoned me telling me to come.'

'Did he?' I ask, pulling back to read his face. 'Did he kill her?'

He shrugs and whispers, 'I don't know. There's so much I didn't know.'

'Ariella wanted to meet me just hours before she was murdered,' I tell him, speaking so fast my words collapse over each other. 'I got a note saying she wanted to talk to me. She said she knew everything and that my friend Tracy told her something. We went to Mateo's strip club last week.'

'I told you not to get involved—'

'I didn't tell you because I knew you'd be mad. But Mateo was there, and he did something to Tracy. I don't know what happened to her, but she told Ariella something and I don't even know how they got in contact with each other. But they somehow did and then Ariella was shot.' I shake my head. 'It's all related, it has to be.'

He's gazing at me as though trying to figure out what it could mean. 'I agree.'

'But if Charles killed her, then why?' I ask. 'And why would Mateo set Charles up?'

'He's a crim, Emma,' he says. 'Mateo's a bad piece of work. Perhaps it had something to do with not protecting his wife and maybe it was more than that. I had no idea that Charles was so involved with him. Charles and he have been doing other shit on the side.'

'Like what?'

'Drugs, money laundering. It's bad.'

'And you didn't know?' My voice is quick and shaky.

'I didn't know.' He shakes his head. 'And I have no idea what he plans to do now. I've been trying to get it out of him without him suspecting my investment in you and the kids.'

'What is this place?' I gasp a lungful of air, finding it hard to talk and get everything out. 'There are women here, and the men—'

'I don't know these men.' He looks at me grimly. 'Charles has been doing shit behind my back it seems for years, Emma. I only came here for you.' He scratches the stubble on his chin. 'I'm trying to figure out how to get you away from here.'

'Why didn't you tell the police?'

'I was worried if I did that he'd take you somewhere I wouldn't be able to find you. As soon as he phoned me, I came.' Jack shakes his head, running his fingers through his hair. 'I need to get you away from him, but I have to pretend I'm on his side, you've got to understand that. It looks like I'm helping him, but I'm not.'

I nod, relieved, crying an emotional wreck. I lean my forehead against him.

'These men aren't good people,' I say. 'The red-haired man—'

'What?' He pushes me back to examine me. 'Did he touch you?'

I nod. 'My stomach. Said he loves pregnant women. And those women—'

'I know.' He nods. 'I know.'

'This baby can't be born here,' I say. His hands hold either side of my belly and he kisses me softly.

'We just need to pretend a little longer, okay?' he says. 'We'll get you home.'

I nod, wiping the snot from under my nostrils. 'I wish you could stay.'

He kisses my hand. 'Me too. But if they find out about you and I . . .' He trails off and I know. It's so risky him even being here.

'Go,' I say.

Jack kisses my head hard and leaves out the back door. And I stand in the living area shivering even though it's warm. Because he's here for us, here for me, but even that knowledge can't help us get off this island.

Now

Morning light streams onto my face like a heater, ready to prove its ultraviolet danger. A bird I don't recognise sounds like an alarm, rousing Kiki. I just want to lie here awhile. There's really no need to get up anyway. Aside from my full bladder and need for water. Closing my eyes, I breathe gently, hoping my stillness will send Kiki back to sleep. Jack's here. That thought alone supports me mentally, enough to rest. The baby sleeps inside me.

The door downstairs opens and my first thought is Jack. If I move, the kids will wake up, but I want to see him. Gently, I roll off the mattress and make my way downstairs. I'm halfway down the stairs when I stop. The woman with the baby is in the house, returning the basket of washing from yesterday. There's no redness on her cheek from the hard slap she'd received.

Last night she was naked, being forced to perform to my disgusting husband. Now, she's a mother folding the clothes while her baby crawls over the tiles. My heart aches. I clear my throat and she looks up and then goes about her business as though she doesn't care. The baby stops and sits, big eyes on me. He or she makes a 'dada' sound and I can't help but smile. Its mother gives a nose snort, semi-smiling and I continue down the steps to the baby, where I crouch and hold out my hands.

'Hello, little one.'

The baby reaches out and the mum scolds it. There's a nasty nappy rash stretching from its inner thigh down. Raw and red and in need of ointment.

'This,' I say to the mother, pointing to the rash. It occurs to me the baby smells of urine, needing his cloth nappy changed. She stares and then keeps folding.

'I have cream for this,' I say, standing and moving to my hand-bag. I always carry paw-paw cream and I used it on my kids to soothe nappy rash and skin problems. I find it deep in the depths of my bag and pull it out, showing the mother. 'For that.' I point.

She considers me, neither nodding nor dismissing, just watches.

I flip open the lid and go back to the baby, lifting him; he looks like a boy. She lets me lift her baby, and he just stares at me, milky, raspy lungs, tiny fingers touching my nose. I'd like to kiss his button nose, because he's adorable, but I don't. I set him on the kitchen bench, enjoying the chubby folds of fat on his thighs and squeeze the balm onto my finger.

'This will help you, bubby.' I softly speak and rub it over the rash. He pulls away and then lets me continue. 'It's okay.'

A sheen of ointment coats his skin and I set him back down.

'Here,' I say, handing it to the mother. 'Take it.'

She looks at it and then purses her lips before snatching it off me. 'Thank,' she says.

I lean in. 'You speak English.'

'Can, but no good,' she says, folding Cooper's t-shirt.

I could cuddle her. I hold my mouth and then decide the best way I can get her to talk to me is over a coffee. And we have coffee. And milk. Do they get that sort of food in that shed? I want to know how long they've been here, too. And why. And who these men are. And where's this island? Filling the kettle with water, I set two coffee mugs on the chipped plywood bench and fill heaped spoonsful of coffee into them. I pour milk into both and stare at the kettle, willing it to boil before she leaves. The baby is over by the dining chair, pulling himself up and babbling.

When the kettle clicks, I pour steaming water into the mug and mix it around. I offer it to her. 'Here,' I say, hoping the coffee beans will tempt her. She sniffs and shakes her head, folding the last of my clothes. 'Please.' My voice sounds pathetic, and I feel that way too.

She finally looks at me and my stomach. She takes the coffee and sips it with her eyes over the rim. She licks her lips and I sip mine, looking at her. I start with gentle probing, like asking the baby's name.

She says, 'Akmal.' And takes another sip. She has sad eyes.

'Cute.' I smile and we watch him crawling to the next chair, grunting with the effort.

'Thank you.' I point to the washing. She shrugs a shoulder and takes another sip.

'I have two children,' I tell her. 'Sleeping.'

She gives a nod and a faint smile.

'They used to get rashes like Akmal.'

I don't want to push it. I don't want to worry her or scare her away from me. I'm so tempted to ask about herself and the other women, so tempted to ask where we are, but I don't. I painfully leave it there, hoping by doing so, she will return and talk more.

'Kiki, my daughter, could play with Akmal,' I tell her. 'If you come back later.'

Again, she raises one shoulder and finishes the last of her coffee, placing it on the bench. It's a final sound, but I think she'll be back. She collects baby Akmal from the dining table and I notice her back, purple bruising like dotted paint. I bite my lip. I hope she changes his nappy. I hope she comes back later.

She could be our way out of here. And I could be hers.

Now

The island across from us has a ferry-shaped boat which arrives and departs around ten am each day. A passenger ferry wouldn't travel further than thirty minutes, forty at most, from land. It's dropping off passengers, holidaymakers, honeymooners, and if I were them, staring over here, I'd ask the ferry operator, 'What's that island over there?' Holidaymakers would stare at us over the channel on their daybeds, with the sun tanning their thighs and the cocktails making them merry. They'd sip their drinks and squint through the sun, trying to make out the private island across from them. Must be expensive to own a private island, they'd think. Someone from big money owns islands.

Kiki and Cooper eat their late breakfast beside the fire from last night, as though imagining it still burns. Her hair's teased at the back and Cooper's little skinny legs are sunburnt. But we don't have sun cream. Because that's an item Charles didn't buy along with the lacy knickers. I'm at the kitchen window, sipping my third coffee, noting the level of the coffee jar diminishing, trying not to put too much pressure on my injured foot as the ferry arrives at the island opposite. It would be five to eight kilometres away, I'm guessing. I drop my attention to my stomach. This baby isn't as big as Cooper was. Kiki was average sized, Cooper was a whopper, but this one – it's smaller, as though too afraid to develop and come out. And I'd like it to stay put. Kiki was on time and Cooper was ten weeks premature. I'm over five months pregnant and capable of running, swimming, cycling. But the pains I felt on the boat are what worry me.

The toast they're eating is developing furry blue patches. I gave them the last two slices, from the bottom of the loaf, the least mouldy. But we need more. And milk, and fresh vegetables. The carrots are pathetically limp and wrinkling. The cucumbers squishy. I set my coffee mug down and head out to the sand.

'I'm going up to the main house,' I tell them.

Cooper perks up. 'Can we come?'

Kiki drinks the milk from her cereal bowl, but there's no use in correcting her. At home, that'd never be allowed. But we're not at home. And I don't know when we'll return. Asking for more carrots, more bread, more milk, means I can gather an indication of how long Charles plans to keep us here.

'No, just stay here, buddy.' I bend to kiss his hair, which is stiff and sandy. I'll need to wash it with the conditioner. 'Go and collect coconuts. We can play tenpin bowling.'

'Yes.' He jumps up, dropping his bowl so the sand sticks into the wetness.

'When's the baby coming to play?' Kiki has a milk moustache.

'Soon.' I hope. 'I'll be back in a minute.'

Kiki watches me as I limp off and I close my eyes for a moment. She's good at pretending, like I am. I don't know how long Kiki's picked up on the danger, the unclear future, the sudden upset of life, but she play-acts for me, for Cooper, and for that I'm grateful.

If she asks if her dad is dangerous, I don't know how I'll answer.

Now

The woman with the winged tattoo balances a tray of steaming coffee. She places two mugs down on the outside table in front of Ginger and Charles. The woman with bare feet displays her thick thighs in bright-pink bike shorts. Her black tank has missing sequins. She's not a regular waitress, but she behaves like one, silently serving, bowed head, careful not to trip over the obstacles of Charles' feet. Charles' legs are splayed, bare-footed. He crosses his arms over his chest as though he's relaxed, content to be here. Like he's on a holiday. Just the sight of his posture causes my body heat to soar.

He hasn't come down once to visit the kids – not that they've asked. They'd expect this – the distant, cold, unloving attachment he gives off. He's always been this way. Bastard. Perhaps it's because Jack's here, but a cockiness in me, an anger, surges down my legs, generating confidence. When it comes, I can't stop it. I stomp forwards, ignoring the pain in my foot, allowing the hurt to fuel my rage.

'We're out of bread, milk, the vegetables are off.' I hotly speak. 'The kids are going to be hungry.'

Ginger leans forwards, hands clasped between knees, as though he's watching a performance and getting to the good bit. A purple mark under his eye mottles over pale skin. He's been punched. By

Charles? Doubt it. It'd be Jack, because it wasn't there before. I almost have the desire to point and laugh at it.

The milk and sugar bowl rattle on the tray and the woman glances over her shoulder at me. Do I spot a hint of fear?

'Just calm down.' Charles patronises, flapping his hand as though waving a fan. Then he smirks over to Ginger, a piggish grunt that has Ginger grinning.

'Feisty.'

That redhead repulses me so much because I know this is his island and these are his women, and that baby is probably his, with one of the women. I want to give him another black eye. I picture the rock under my bed cracking against his temple. My feet tingle on the asphalt.

'No, not feisty,' I say. 'Just human.'

He goes to stand, but Charles stops him with a touch to the hand. He's appeasing this attack dog like a master would. It makes me realise how dangerous this tattooed man really is. What was he planning to do to me? Slap me? Tie me up? The dynamic between the men is unsettling because it appears Charles is in charge here.

The woman with the tattoo and I are equals. We've been reduced to nothing. Perhaps she notices this as she slowly pours a stream of white milk into my husband's coffee, flicking a quick glance my way. And where is the other one, the older maid who's aggressive and siding with the men?

'We'll bring you down some milk,' my husband says.

'And vegetables?' I ask.

Charles chews his cheek. 'We'll get some soon.'

Soon? How long is *soon*? A day, a week, a month? The boat he and Jack came on is gone again. Who's coming to drop off supplies?

'How long are we staying here, Charles?' I ask.

He flaps me away and Ginger shakes his head, saying, 'You need to reel her in.'

The sliding door rolls open and Jack steps out. I swallow. His soft face makes my fingers tempted to clutch him. Perhaps Jack senses my distress as I stand there, lost for words, fists clenched in sweaty balls. He seems fresher than these two. Hair brushed and wet, peeling an orange and giving me a look as if to say, *Keep it cool. Keep pretending.* But it's hard to. Citrus spray wafts from his orange, tangy and sour.

'I only ask because I love it here and so do the kids.' I smile. I won't let Charles know he's affecting me. The ginger sits back, setting sunglasses over his injured eye and Charles sips his coffee, staring at me.

'It's a perfect place.' I grin. 'We don't want to leave. Who cares about Sydney and our home. Barque is all we need.'

'Cut the sarcasm, Emma.' Charles speaks into his cup. 'You should be grateful you've got a bed down there. Two-timer that you are.'

'Two-timer?'

'You're a cheating bitch and you're no wife. So, go back down to Barque and wait patiently.'

Jack shifts awkwardly on his feet, stops peeling the orange, but I don't know that Charles is referring to him. Regardless, Jack resumes his composure. He peels the orange, and the citrus scent reaches me. He'd want to kill Charles, he'd want to pull me away from these men, yet he stays solid, placing the peel on the table. He doesn't look at me.

'You're imagining everything, Charles. Yes, we were miserable, but I've never cheated on you—'

'Go,' Charles barks at me.

Ginger watches, twiddling his thumbs on his stomach and a bird screeches from a palm. That's why he tried to kill me, left me stranded in the ocean, because he knows. He knows I've been having an affair. And now that he does, he's capable of anything. Charles doesn't care if I die, but does he care about the kids?

There's only one way to find out. I turn and walk away from the men, eyeing the toys in the pool: the inflatable bed, the floaty rubber rings.

Jack better have a plan. And if he doesn't, then it's up to me.

Now

Out the front of Barque, the baby and mother relax on the sand with Kiki and Cooper. Kiki's passing Akmal shells and a rock, which he takes and puts in his mouth. My daughter takes it back off him with an, 'Ah, ah, ah.' There's a pile of coconuts gathered by Cooper's feet, ready for his tenpin bowling game and I smile, relieved that she's decided to come back to us.

From a distance, it could be Ariella sitting there with her own baby, playing with my children. I wonder if, under different circumstances, we would've been close enough to travel with our kids. She had something to tell me. Something life changing. I'm grinding my teeth. It's a habit that's been developing since we left Sydney. My jaw's sore and tight, so I practise resting it.

When the woman spots me heading towards them, she looks away, as though ashamed she's here. Or is it fear of being caught with us? Whatever it is, her expression proves she's uncomfortable, so I don't push, I don't prompt a discussion. I simply say hello, and then continue into Barque where I take the remaining cookies from the yacht and place them onto a plate. Outside the window, she's speaking to Kiki, and I can't quite hear the words but Kiki nods and smiles. If Kiki's understanding, then Akmal's mum is speaking English articulate enough for Kiki to respond.

Heading back out, I offer her a butter cookie, which she looks at for a second before accepting. Akmal notices it and she breaks off a small chunk and places it in his eager, gummy mouth.

'Here, Kiks, Coop,' I say, holding the plate out. They both scramble up to snatch one and we all sit together, chewing on cookies. There's a list of questions, so primed to leap out of my mouth. And because Jack can't come and be with us here, this woman is my only hope. I can learn through her and pass on the message to Jack. I hope he comes tonight, or finds a snippet of time and space to see me. He's so close, yet so distant, it hurts.

'Mum, look.' Cooper points to the pile of coconuts.

'Good on you, bud.' I smile as the baby uses his mother's legs as a lever to pull himself up and bounce. He's happy with his cookie and thinks he's clever standing up. I touch my stomach, with the urge to meet this little one. But not yet. Not until we're safe.

'Jellyfish?' I point to the rippling water. It always seems so flat, so inviting, so crystal bright.

She nods at the ocean. '*Obor-obor.*' So, she's aware of the venomous, deadly creatures.

'Here now?' I ask.

She eats the last bit of cookie and nods.

'Always here?' Kiki listens, scooping sand over her feet.

The woman nods and then looks at me, as though reading the question. She then signs heavily and continues talking. '*Obor-obor* get my sister.'

I wish Kiki hadn't been listening. But she perks up, mouth open, and I ask her to go in and get the last of the cookies. She's reluctant, wanting to listen, but goes.

The woman brushes a fly from her forehead. 'She swim, she bit and no save.'

'How long ago?' I ask, swallowing.

'Long time.'

246

'Did she see a doctor?'

The woman shakes her head and lifts her baby up when he plops down on the sand. I make two mental notes: the jellyfish are there, and the woman has been here a long time. And another, more sinister record – a woman died, and the men didn't save her, didn't take her to hospital.

'I'm sorry,' I say.

She doesn't respond, just bounces the baby up and down until he's babbling.

'The other women, are they your sisters?'

She shakes her head and then we both snap our heads over our shoulders when a woman yells out, 'Oi.'

It's the older maid with Wallace, by the bottom deck, hands on her hips, calling out to whom I presume is Akmal's mother. Is the older woman their guard, ensuring they do the right thing? Akmal's mother stands, brushing the sand from her lap and lifts Akmal to her hip. Quickly, she leaves us, darting behind Barque and back up the path to where they live. And Wallace and the older woman stare at me for a while, as though telepathically warning me to stay away from her. And I ask Cooper to stick dying palm fronds into the sand and make them be the pins, and Kiki comes out with more cookies, and Wallace and the woman just stand there watching, watching, watching.

Now

Tonight, I'm going to see where Akmal's mother lives. I want to know what's there, how she sleeps, what she eats, what brought her here. I don't think she'll admit to me how they came here, yet. I need to build a relationship with this woman, and this is something I'm good at, good for and specialise in. I didn't get to the top of my game, owning one of Sydney's top wellness clinics, by being vindictive or standoffish. No, my company has been built on a foundation of relationships and trust. And I believe those two qualities are needed now, to save us.

It always feels good to have a plan. I'm not one to sit blindly, ignorantly, unable to care for myself. Jack taught me this: don't rely on a man, don't rely on anyone, only rely on yourself.

I did what I could on the cruiser: the escape to the smaller craft, texting Jack, notifying the young fishermen to alert the police about the danger we're in. But now, being on this island and meeting these strange women, who I believe shouldn't and don't belong here, means if we work together, we can manage a way off this place. It only takes courage and a plan.

Kiki and Cooper have showered and are lying in front of an eighties movie I don't recognise, drawing and reading in their pyjamas. Earlier, Wallace carried down two boxes of fresh fruit, snacks for the kids and milk. I know Charles has packed everything the kids love, and I despise in this box. It's my punishment, a shopping gift of hate. Sweet biscuits, crackers, peanut butter, lollies, hazelnut spread, fizzy drink. And the kids' favourite fruit: apples and mandarins.

They were more than thankful when Wallace left the boxes at the front door and sauntered off, running his hands through his thick hair. I shuddered as I watched him go, not daring to open the door until he disappeared up the boardwalk.

Now, they have a bowl of snacks each, delighting in their treats while a roaring dinosaur movie resounds from the television. On the dining table, I've stuffed a backpack full of goodies: lollies, leftover tea and a row of chocolate biscuits. The deodorant from the cruiser, the hand wash and shampoo are also loaded inside, along with three mandarins. I'm hoping this small gesture, this gift of treats, will open these women up to me. Because whether they know it or not, we both share hell.

Even at night, the temperature refuses to budge. The stubborn humidity creates a gleam over my skin, a stickiness under my pits. Being pregnant doesn't help either. Hot, always so hot. I walk in my shoes, careful not to tread my sore foot onto something I can't see in the dark. Because I can't use a torch, candle or light. I don't want to be seen, more importantly, I don't want the women to be seen with me.

The backpack sticks to my skin, chafing as I wander up the hill to the ferns. There's crickets and other strange bugs and insects making noises beside me in the bushes. The palms shift like fans, the fronds scratching against one another above.

When I reach the ferns, I push them apart and step through, catching a spiderweb in my face. I blow it away, careful not to make a noise and brush it from my face and hair. If a spiderweb scares me, then escaping isn't an option. I need to gather courage, an emotion I've never had to use in normal circumstances. Bravery over opening a business, bravery over giving birth, bravery over speaking at a wedding – none of this equates to the courage I need now.

Once I'm through the ferns, I wait at the top of the hill and assess my surroundings. The grass slope is dark, which is good. No one will spot me walking down it. However, the shed where Akmal's mother lives is lit up with white fluorescent lights which flicker and twitch. And there are voices, accents and a language I can't understand. Baby Akmal wailing. An aroma of cooking: ginger and fish sauce. A radio playing pop music. I clutch the straps of my backpack and wonder how they'll react when they see me. I don't want them to cry out or scream. Through the doorway to the shed, the woman with the winged tattoo is clomping around in her bikini top and black skirt, smoking. She's doing all the talking. Baby Akmal crawls past in a nappy.

I can't see any of the men: no Ginger, no Wallace, no Charles, nor the older maid.

So, I step down the slope, ready to introduce myself.

Now

I'm right outside their shed, and cigarette smoke and chilli wafts from the building. Food sizzles inside and the scraping of a pan means they're in the middle of cooking dinner. From here, I can get a better picture of how they live, and these women live rough. Akmal's mother spots me through the doorway and steps backwards, glancing to the other for authorisation. The tattooed woman hasn't noticed me yet. She stirs something meaty in the frying pan, hand on her hip while a cigarette tray, crowded with butts, smokes from a shitty white plastic picnic table.

Akmal's mother shakes her head at me, as though warning me off this place, but I ignore her and knock on the tin door. The woman cooking looks up, leaves the plastic spatula resting in the pan and starts yelling, shooing me away with her hand. She's missing a tooth at the front and she's livid.

I step away and open my backpack, pulling out my gifts. 'Here, wait. I have this for you.'

Akmal's mother speaks to her friend in an appeasing tone that has the tattooed one arguing back. They're snapping at each other, gesturing to me and towards the main house and Akmal watches from the floor in his nappy.

'Go,' his mother tells me. 'Go.'

'It's okay,' I tell her, stepping forwards with my backpack open. 'I just came to bring you these.' I show them all and hold it up. 'Take it. It's for you.'

The tattooed woman pushes past Akmal's mother and snatches the packet of biscuits. She doesn't smile, doesn't speak, just carries them back to the table.

Akmal's mother faces her friend and mutters. And the tattooed woman just glares at me and makes her way back to the frying pan. She's not happy I'm here, and I understand now the danger I'm putting them in. Nevertheless, I need them to trust me, even if it happens slowly. So, I crouch to the grass, and start pulling the goodies from the bag, laying them on the doorstep. They watch me and the baby gurgles, crawling over to inspect what I have. I then zip up my bag and pull it onto my back, standing.

I smile at Akmal and then leave them to it. The grass is muddy and soaks my shoes. They're living in a swampy area here, a place I can imagine infested with sea snakes. Their shed is tiny, with only the plastic table and chairs revealing any traces of home life. The concrete they cook on and sleep on and walk on is cold and crumbling. And through the door, I spotted a mattress, just like I'd imagined, covered with a flimsy piece of fabric disguised as a sheet.

'Hey,' Akmal's mum calls out in a whisper. I stop and turn around, shoes slurping. Her short silhouette stands between the doorway to their home. Akmal pulls himself up with her legs. 'Come.' She holds a finger up to her lips.

Heading back towards her, I hear the faint rustle of grass, the croak of a frog and the breeze, hot and suffocating, dominates this island they call home.

Now

The shed is worse than I imagined. They cook on a campfire stove connected to a small gas bottle with a frying pan so charred the meat sticks. They have a blocky eighties ghetto-blaster radio, no television and no computers or devices. The baby plays with a hairbrush, lifting it into his dirty mouth. The plastic chairs have frayed cushions, and only on two. There's a disgusting old seventies brown couch reminding me of what you'd find under a bridge at night. I wouldn't sit there if they paid me.

Behind the small area is another shed with three mattresses squished together to form a giant bed they all must share. There's no windows, no ventilation and no cooling.

My tongue thickens in my mouth. How did they get onto this island and into this mess?

Akmal's mum offers me a seat at the dining table and I sit on the one without the cushion. I can't be long here. I need to get back to Kiki and Cooper. I tell them this. I will come back, I'll come back with more food. This makes the tattooed woman's hard face soften slightly. She has a face that's weathered terrible circumstances and a harsh life. Her hands are dry, knobbly and scarred in places as she flips the meat on the pan.

She can't speak English. While I talk to Akmal's mother, she constantly stares with pulled brows, asking her what we're saying.

Akmal's mother interprets and, based on that, I can observe from her nods and mannerisms whether the woman's happy or dissatisfied with what I'm saying.

The woman leaves the pan and goes through the supplies I brought along, opening the conditioner and sniffing it. She places some on her hand and rubs it in. I don't comment. And I face Akmal's mother, who sits fanning herself with an old newspaper.

'How long have you been here?' I ask her.

She takes a while to respond, as though she's thinking, *I guess we're both doing this: opening up to one another.*

When she speaks, she displays gums and a missing canine. 'Year.'

'You came here last year?'

She nods. 'From Malaysia.'

The frying pan hisses out garlic and burnt meat and Akmal talks to himself. She interprets to the tattooed woman, who's stopped fossicking to listen. I clasp my hands together on the table and take a deep inhalation.

'Are you married?' I ask. Not that the answer will make this any better, but I need to know whether this baby is Ginger's. And if it is, have they been brought here, knowing what conditions they'll be living in? If so, then I'll feel better. And if they didn't, then why is my husband friends with someone that does this?

Akmal's mother shakes her head and looks to the tattooed woman.

'She's his wife?' I ask.

She nods.

'Akmal is his son?'

Her eyelids fall and her lips purse and she doesn't need to answer. They're in a twisted, sick mess on this island.

'And the other older woman?'

Her expression changes to fury and she shakes her head, clenching her fists. 'She trick.' She's madder at the older woman than she

254

is at the men. Trick? Trick how? Led them here to the island? Told them a story to have the women follow? I've heard about this kind of racket – being promised a new beginning, a fresh life and better opportunities to then have a passport removed. So, Ginger has all of them: Akmal's mum, who he obviously got pregnant; the tattooed lady, who he probably married back in her country; and the older woman who manipulated them to come here. It's hard to know exactly, but I'm trying to piece it together.

'Were there other women? Your sister and—'

Akmal's mum nods, blinking down at the table and this all makes clear sense. I believe this island is a staging post for trafficking. Other women have come and gone, possibly shipped off to small farms, people who've paid to have them. I'm sure that's how this works. And Mateo's strip club? Those girls in the bathroom looking young enough to be in high school. Could they have been trafficked from Indonesia and brought here first? I'm wondering if that's what Tracy saw, what Ariella discovered. *I know everything.* This could have been the evidence needed to imprison Mateo and also a significant reason to have Ariella silenced and shot. *By Charles.* She was going to tell me what he was involved in. How my husband was involved in this operation. I'm tensing my jaw so hard I'm getting a headache that wraps itself around my skull.

I can't look at the women here. Because if I do, the real nature of what I'm doing here with my children is too terrifying to admit. I can't look at them because in them I see myself, trapped, alone and frightened. And how stupid have I been to not know this about Charles? And I'm sitting here in a tin shed with smoke filling my nostrils, while the crickets chirrup outdoors and the radio shrieks Katy Perry. And my manicured fingernails need filing and the diamond ring on my finger needs throwing away and the hair falling across my sweaty brow has seen a hair stylist who works on top celebrities. And I can't look at them because we're lifestyles apart and yet we've been forced into the same hell. And I think I know why they're here and I think I know why I am, too. And a single stupid tear squeezes over my eyelid and drips onto my lap and she spots it. We're women, and we can work together. I need their strength, just like they need mine, the strength we don't see right now because it's been stolen from us. It's been stolen from them. And it was stolen from Ariella too. But it's there, buried and we just need to blow over it to reveal it.

So, I say to her, with my gaze stuck on that useless diamond ring, 'I'm Emma. What's your name?'

'Maryam.'

'Maryam, I need your help.'

And for the first time since our car pulled away from my home, I believe I've found my saviours.

Now

I've lit myself another fire. Kiki and Cooper aren't awake to enjoy it, and that was the point. I wanted this fire for myself. If I'm going to do this, I'll need strength and that means a strong sense of mind. Jack will be proud. Ariella would've been proud.

I gaze up in the direction of the main house, as though my concentration will summon Jack to join me here. I'd love nothing more than to be sitting with my back against his chest, his hands on my belly, the fire toasting our feet with the clear sky displaying its diamonds. I imagine the kids asleep in our hotel room and we're here alone on this island and after talking quietly, we'd have sex on a rug by the fire.

He is so close, yet I haven't seen him since this morning, peeling the orange and giving me a look of caution. What's Charles telling him? And is he aware that it's Jack who I've been with during our marriage? Jack who I want to leave him for? If he knows, I'm worried what he'll do to Jack with his posse of crims around him. I know Jack's up there, doing all he can to get down here to me, I'm just concerned that something's gone wrong. Charles has found out about us.

I throw another piece of wood onto the fire and the sparks fly up, popping into nothing. It takes a while for the wood to glow, but it eventually catches on, raising the strength of the flames.

Akmal's mother, Maryam, told me they'd help. I have to go back tomorrow night and see what we need to get away from the island. It was only after I'd left, my backpack empty, my feet slogging through the grass and up the hill, that a sullen sensation stopped me walking. What if they tell the men? What if Maryam and the woman set me up? What if the old maid finds out?

I remember the way the tattooed woman watched on like a prison guard as Jack helped clean my foot. If she's married to Ginger, I don't know that I should or can trust that she won't spill the truth. But what other option do I have? I'll only know tomorrow, if Maryam keeps her word and helps to find equipment, tools needed to leave this place. Perhaps I should've only relied on Maryam, but judging by the state of their living conditions, I'm betting the women aren't happy about their lives here. We all need to leave together.

The island resort opposite is all lit up with yellow-dotted lights that blink. Citronella candles? Fairy lights? I like that I can see them. I like that the island is there, far, yet not too far. That's how I have to keep on looking at it. An attainable goal.

'This looks cosy.'

I notice the voice before the scrunching footsteps on sand. And when I glance up, I smile, getting to my feet. I want to throw my arms around him and kiss him. But I hesitate. We aren't the only people here.

'Come here.' Jack motions with his finger over to a shielded area of trees, shrubs and bushes that'll cover us securely from view. I leave the fire and follow him. A cobweb clings to my forehead and I quickly brush it off. He pulls me into him and I'm home.

I close my eyes, comforted in an instant the way a baby is upon returning to its mother. A kiss to my head. A tight squeeze. A heavy sigh. He feels it too. I don't even notice the tears until he wipes them away.

'I've been wondering where you are,' I whisper. 'I just miss and want you so much.'

'Shh.' He soothes me. 'I'm here. I'm not going anywhere.'

'Tell me what's happening. Does Charles know about us?'

Jack shakes his head. 'No. I think he's bluffing. He hasn't mentioned anything to me, and he's still treating me the same. Yet there *is* something.'

I don't want to know, and at the same time I do. *Something.* Something bad. Something Jack's come to tell me, warn me about. It's the way he says it that makes me shrink.

'Sit down,' he says, finding a space under a bush where he lowers himself and collects me onto his lap.

'You're scaring me.'

He kisses me again from behind. 'That's exactly what I don't want to be doing.'

I fiddle with his fingers, the ridges of bone and coarse hair. 'Tell me.'

'Firstly, I want you to trust that I'm going to get us out of this mess.'

I nod, unable to look at him. If I look at him, I'll know how bad this is. It's the same at the doctor's. They always have to mollify the fear before dishing out the bad news. Jack's news is bad. It's in the way he's set me down, in the way he keeps kissing the back of my head like he's nervous. And he's never nervous.

'Charles was helping Mateo with a little business on the side, business I think he's been dabbling in for a while, even before Mateo came along.'

'I already know, the women here told me. And I think that's why Charles killed Ariella. She found out about this from Tracy.'

'Possibly. I don't know who killed Ariella. But these men, Brad and Wallace, have been trafficking girls over here for years. And Charles is okay with that. When he found out Mateo is in the same dirty business, Charles started doing the security for him, safeguarding it all. I had no idea about any of this, Emma.'

I want to throw up. I hold my mouth as my tongue stiffens inside. The women on this island, was Charles a part of this? I tell Jack about them and he says he doesn't know about Charles' involvement in their illegal entry into Australia. It seems likely. And if I didn't already hate Charles enough, my body is brimming with it now. Jack too looks sick as he tells me what he's just learnt from Charles.

'Not only has Charles been protecting Mateo, he's also been smuggling Mateo's drugs and storing them here on the island. Mateo has no idea about the drugs. These three men here are a team, working together.'

I tell Jack about the living conditions of the women, the mattresses, the dirty floor, the fingerprints on Maryam's back, their relationships to one another, the baby belonging to Brad, the sister who died after being stung by a jellyfish. And as I do, I'm forgetting where I am and how much danger I'm in. Because right now, it just feels good to have his arms around my belly. The baby rolls and he smooths a thumb over the protruding elbow or foot or knee. It's like we're back home and all is real and right. 'We all have to get away, Jack.'

Jack agrees and holds me tighter.

'Why did Charles bring us here?' I ask the darkness. We maintain low voices, barely moving, both with the shared understanding that if someone comes, we leave one another. We simply cannot be seen. 'Because he shot Ariella?'

'He's hiding from Mateo, so that's a strong possibility.' The fact that Jack considers Charles to be a murderer is frightening. What the hell are we up against here on this island with these men?

'I don't trust the other men. I bet they'll tell Mateo we're here.' I turn to him. 'And then what?'

He looks beyond me. His cheek tenses in and out. 'That's what I'm worried about.' I hate that he's not reassuring me. His admissions are dark and factual and he's not sprinkling sugar on this dire situation. I'm used to him lifting me up, boosting my morale, talking positively. But there's nothing positive and jovial about this.

'How long is he planning on keeping us here?'

'I'm not sure. He said he's trying to figure things out while he's away from Mateo and the police.'

'Can't we take a boat out of here?'

'I would. But Brad and Wallace keep everything under lock and key. Like I said, they took everything off me. I have no way of communicating with anyone.'

I'm almost crying and I have to pull it together. 'If he finds out about us, Jack—'

I hear him tut, impatience growing and the cuddle slackening. His arm hairs are tickling me, making me itchy. It's hard to be romantic when there is so much tension surrounding us. 'It's going to be okay.'

I stare out beyond the trees to the island opposite. I'm cold as a breeze skims across the ocean, ruffling the leaves above us. I hug myself. I can't help this annoyance that's stopping me from loving him more, and I'm trying not to show it. I thought he'd come with answers, a solution to this shit. I'm relying on him to make this better, and he's not. Like me, Jack's lost for answers. He hugs me again, bringing me and my hope and faith back to him. Although it's hard to be positive and uplifted. I'm rigid, biting down hard on my tongue.

'Just sit tight. I'll know more soon.'

'We all need to get off here,' I repeat.

'And we will.'

And I have to believe him, I have to trust, because what other choice do I have?

Now

Jack's visit is not enough to keep me going as I wake with the kids, make them a sandwich, pour milk into cups and stare at the movie playing on the VHS. There was no plan of escape, no clutching of boat keys and a quiet urgency of *we have to leave right now*.

I spread butter over white bread and stop. The new information about Charles and his seedy, underworld connections has kept me awake all night. It's akin to discovering your husband is a serial killer or rapist. Someone you've shared a bed with, felt the leg hairs prickle against your skin. Someone whose shower fogs the mirror you apply your make-up in front of in the mornings. I've accidentally used his toothbrush, and I don't know why that mental image sticks in my mind more than having sex with him, but it does and it repulses me. He killed our neighbour and I don't know what's worse, that or what he's embroiled in here. I'm finding it hard to inhale. These are the type of men who surround me now, men who are capable of killing their own wives, men who steal women from their own countries and retain them for sex and slavery. Charles is one of those men.

Imagine what my parents will say. Imagine the parents at school. Everything will have to change. Once we're back in Sydney and he's locked up, we'll start fresh and just this little sparkle of hope allows me to stand taller. To slather my piece of bread with

honey and bite a big chunk of it. To taste its sweetness and appreciate the stillness of the ocean outside the window.

The movie continues with cheerful music and the kids sit
bonded to the screen, so I step outside of Barque and onto white
sand to eat my sandwich. We still have our beach house. And Jack
has always loved the idea of retiring in the country. He's mentioned
the Blue Mountains more than once. It doesn't matter, the possibili-
ties are endless. Charles won't be around anymore. And our affair
won't be the focal point of discussion. It'll be Charles' dirty deeds,
his criminal, disgusting acts, that they'll discuss. I'll be pitied by
the press. People will send baskets of coffee and chocolate and face
cream. They'll ask if they can care for Kiki and Cooper, to give me
space alone with the baby. And when Jack and my relationship
finally does come out, they'll nod their heads and smile and say, of
course, they're the perfect match and Emma deserves to be loved
and be happy.

The bread sticks to my palate and I pull it down with my finger.
It'll all work out eventually because it always does. I step into the
water and then back out, remembering the dangers of this pretty
ocean.

Instead, I go to sit on the bended palm tree, to rest my ankles,
which are collecting a bit of fluid lately, and that's when I see it.

At first, it'd felt like water, moistening my skin, although it's
red. And it's dribbling down my thigh, calf, ankle, foot, toe. The
sand gathers the colour, forming red gems with my blood. I lift my
dress and notice my knickers, coated in a deep, rich, earthy amber.
Blood. I swallow, eyeing the beach, as though the ocean, the rocks,
the bright sand, the curved palms will resolve my dilemma. And
if we were at home, I'd call the hospital now, and ask to speak to
my doctor. It's too early. It's too premature. I'm miscarrying. And
I'd call Georgia in from cleaning one of the rooms and ask her to
grab me a towel and a fresh pair of knickers. And I'd be worried

about the bleeding but I'd be ten minutes away from the emergency department. The doctors would care for me and stop me from delivering.

Not here. Here I'm miles from anywhere. I'm bleeding when I shouldn't be and there is no pain yet, so I'm not sure that I'm in labour. I pace along the beach, each step dripping blood into the sand. And now I'm frightened.

And there's only one option. The women.

Now

Maryam is outside, flapping a sandy rug. The thump of it sounds like a helicopter from a distance and I wish that were the case. Baby Akmal is by the doorway, chewing on a piece of coconut. His knees are red and dirty, scratched from crawling and I imagine my own baby here, doing the same. That's not going to happen. I'm getting off this island, with or without Jack.

I've had to leave Kiki and Cooper back in Barque. I told them to lock the doors behind me and when Kiki asked why, I told her, 'When I come back, I'll tell you everything.' Because I have to now. Everything is unravelling and I can't hold this in any longer. There's a level and I've reached it and this baby's arrival is speeding what I'd wanted to keep hidden into reality. I can't keep lying to Kiki. And if we're getting off this island, she needs to be prepared.

Maryam looks up and when she sees me, she checks the surroundings to ensure the men and the older maid aren't around noticing my presence. I do the same, yet part of me is done caring. I feel like fighting back.

Most of the blood's been washed off my skin by the shower water. I didn't want my children noticing it. It doesn't matter how dire this situation is, I intend to remain collected for them.

'This baby is coming. Soon,' I say to Maryam. She looks at my bloodied hands, the few spots on my dress. 'Bleeding isn't good.'

She shakes her head; a look of sadness covers her eyes, and she places a hand to my belly. God, the touch feels so good, so needed. Skin on skin. Affection. The love of a woman. I can't stop myself when I pull her into my arms. She smells strongly of sweat and shampoo, the one I'd gifted them. But I block it all out, because with her small figure in my arms, it's like I'm hugging Ariella and saying goodbye. Because, really, I feel like this is all my fault. Getting involved in Ariella's entangled life, spying on her controlling husband. The notes. The communication. Whatever Tracy endured that night. Ariella's death is on my hands. Maryam holds me tight so I can cry on her shoulder. Tears tangle her hair and yet she allows it. It's a release that's needed. Because afterwards, when I pull away from her, I'm refilled, boosted and ready.

'Do you want to leave this place?' I ask her.

She chews the healing part of her lip and I wipe my eyes, waiting. I want her to say yes because I don't know how it'd feel to leave them all here. She inhales deeply and then stares down at Akmal, who's pulling himself up on her legs.

'We can leave all together and safely,' I say, unsure how I can fulfil that promise. I've started imagining ways of escape while lying in bed awake at night. Cooper and Kiki are asleep, the hot breeze touches my skin and belly like a kiss and I lie, thinking. There are two possible ways of getting to the island opposite us. Each of them a huge risk and dangerous, but our only options.

'Do you like being here?' I ask her.

'No,' she says.

'You weren't supposed to live this way,' I tell her. 'They've trapped you here.'

She nods and touches Akmal's head. I sense by her shaking hand how scary this sounds. And I'm under no illusion this won't be dangerous. Except I can't sit here and wait for Jack or for the authorities to realise where we are. This baby is coming, and we all need to get to safety. I need their help to do this.

'You can go back home, or somewhere safe. We can help each other.' I'm worried they'll want to stay and when they find out about my plan, they'll tell the men.

'Is your friend happy here?' I ask her, wondering by her response whether I can trust them.

She shakes her head over and over. 'No. Not happy.'

'Then we can all leave,' I say.

She nods and looks me in the eye. 'Together.'

Together is the only way. I'd be too scared to do this alone. Having Maryam and her friend with me gives me more strength than she can imagine. And I truly believe if it weren't for baby Akmal, Maryam would have done this too, chosen to escape this hell. Together, we can work as a team to support the baby across the water. I believe it's doable. People swim across channels all the time, and yes, they are good swimmers and no, they aren't pregnant, but I'm fit and I'm capable. And this baby's health and safety has now become the driving force motivating me to do this.

Maryam leads me around the back of the shed to the gas bottles, a trailer, bricks, limestone blocks, a shovel. There's not much here. I was expecting loose tin, parts that I could somehow work with, however there's nothing here but an old mattress, paint cans and shelving that's chipped and bubbling from rain and humidity.

Even if there were material here, we don't have time or privacy to build something safe enough. Especially now that I'm bleeding. We'd need ropes, or flat, light material to hold us, and I just don't see how I could effectively build a raft that'll withstand the journey over.

There's a more likely option though; a quick, somewhat effective and probably only realistic option. Except the idea of actually doing it scares me no end.

I shake my head at Maryam and tell her to try and come up with an idea, while I think too. I'll be back later tonight, when it's dark and I can speak to the other woman. And she points to my belly and says, 'Soon.' The bleeding has stopped. For now. And I nod, realising tonight may be too late.

Now

I ask Kiki to take a walk with me and gather coconuts for another round of tenpin bowling, and although she's reluctant and rolling her eyes, she notes the way I raise my eyebrows and this little sense of intrigue has her leaving a crappy movie and her brother on the faded couch.

'Just a small walk,' I tell Coop. 'We'll be back in a short while.'

He nods, barely listening and we head outside to the path where the pink flowers fall like confetti and Kiki picks one up, breathing in its naked scent and I watch her. I finger a piece of hair from her eyes and can't believe I'm about to do this, except I know if I don't, we're done. She stares back, brown eyes wide and innocent.

'What did you need to tell me?' she asks.

'You're just so young.' It's the only thing I can say because it's true. She's too young to know such things and too young for this to not affect her later on in life. She'll be in therapy in five years' time, possibly with anxiety and blaming me. Her therapist will turn her against me and she'll be spiteful and tense up whenever I say anything that's deemed a 'trigger'. Because we all go through that stage, me included. It's almost unusual *not* to blame parents for issues in your life. Your addiction to biting your nails that came from trying to impress your father with his own nail-biting addiction. My nails are shorter than yours. Your addiction to bingeing because you were told to watch your weight. Your addiction to toxic relationships because your parents' was so messed up. Blame is easy. Ownership of emotions is something else altogether. That comes later, when you realise blaming does nothing to move you on in life. It keeps you stunted in that childlike body, afraid to step up and grow up. I see it all the time. I see it in me.

'We're not going to another island, are we?' she starts. Good, we can begin slowly. That's probably the better way. Best to take baby steps before admitting her father has kidnapped us and killed our neighbour.

'No, we're not.'

'There wasn't a sick friend, was there?'

I collect a flower myself and realise it bears no scent. 'No, there wasn't.'

'So why are we here, then? When are we going home?'

I pull her over to a rock, which I sit on and take her onto my lap. I practised this speech last night, when I knew we were going to have to escape the island, with or without Jack. Her bottom is bony and my belly gets in the way of a real hug, yet she lets me hold her there and kiss her hair. Kiki doesn't smell like herself anymore. I'm used to her perfume from the girly retail shops and the expensive soap she always made me buy to turn the bath pink. Now, she smells like an island. Wet shells and limestone.

'Kiki, you filmed something last week that's got us into a lot of trouble.'

She turns to face me on my lap. 'What?'

'You filmed yourself in the treehouse and something bad happened to Ariella in the background. It's absolutely not your fault. In fact, I'm sure the police are using the footage to try and work out what happened.'

'Like a break-in?'

270

I fiddle with the flower petals, bending them back so they crease and damage. I can't admit she was killed. I'll have to just pretend they moved house until she hears it from her friends. I nod. 'Ariella was injured. And you filmed it.'

She frowns. 'But what's that got to do with us?'

'Well, your dad does the security for Ariella's husband, Mateo. And because this happened, he let Mateo down.'

'So, Mateo is angry?'

'Very. In fact, we had to leave our home immediately, because Mateo is not a good person. He's dangerous.'

'Well why was Dad working for him?'

I press my lips together in a tight line. It's the most difficult thing I've ever had to do. 'Since your dad's been friends with Mateo, I've found out he's been doing some pretty bad things too. Dangerous things that really worry me.'

I can see she's about to lose it. However, she regains her composure and stares at me. 'Like what?'

'You don't need to know the details. The fact is these men on this island are bad men. And your dad doesn't believe they are, but I know they are. They're keeping those women here as . . .'

'Yes?'

'These women are trapped here.' My eyes start to sting. 'The fact is, Kiks, we're trapped here too. Your dad is really worried about Mateo coming and I don't think we're going to get home unless you and I and Cooper do something.'

'But, Mummy,' she says, starting to cry. Her nostrils flare in and out and she's terrified, clinging on to me for dear life.

'Shh, it's okay. We're going to be just fine, Kiki. Look at me.' I hold her face. 'Jack is doing all he can to get us back home, but we also have to try.'

'How?' Her voice is loud and I shush her gently. 'I'm scared.'

'And you have every right to be, but not with me looking after you. I'm not scared, Kiki. We're going to get away from here. I know you'll have a lot of questions and I'll answer everything when we get off this island.' I wipe the tears falling down her cheeks, trying to contain myself. 'It has to be something we do in secret.'

'Is Dad a bad man?' she asks, face red and wet.

My tongue sticks to the roof of my mouth. If only she knew. If only. 'He's making really bad choices and he's not considering us. And you and I have to be really brave for Cooper, Kiki.'

'How are we going to get off here?' She's sobbing and sniffing and if one of the men comes down and sees us, we're screwed. So, I tell her to calm down and she needs to be big and brave and listen to my instructions. This seems to work, slightly. She nods, sniffing and wiping her snotty nose on the back of her hand.

'When Cooper is asleep, we have to wake him up and go. We can't tell him now, because he'll just panic. We only tell him when we're leaving. That way he'll just have to do it.'

'How are we going to do it, Mummy?' she asks.

'See that island over there?' I point across the ocean to the island, now cast in a shadow. I wish it was bright and sunny, that way it'd make it look closer, attractive, a paradise for us to want to get to, without trouble. Kiki blinks out a few tears as she stares over to it. 'We're going to swim there.'

She turns to me, face horrified, body trembling. 'What? How?'

'We'll need to practise, get good at it.' I smile a false smile, yet she doesn't know that. I've become quite good at morphing my face into expressions they'll believe. 'But it's completely doable. We'll see if Jack can help us and if he can't,' I say kissing her head and wiping under her eyelashes, 'then we leave in two days.'

Now

Before the sun sets fully and the crickets start chirping, before the full moon rises out of the ocean like a spotlight over the opposite island, before any of that, I take Cooper and Kiki with me to the women's shed. We're going to play with Akmal, I tell Cooper, as we trudge down the hill.

My bleeding's stopped, and I haven't seen Jack. Nonetheless, I need to somehow get information to him: this baby is either in danger of dying or ready to introduce itself to us. Cooper mentions the state of the place, asks why they live in such a yuck shed. And by the time we get to the front door, I've taught him to keep his honest opinions to himself. They're privileged young kids and I'm a privileged mother and I'm hoping if we can take anything positive out of this nasty place, it'll be to never take our privileged lifestyle for granted.

I've already made a promise to the universe. I'm not ready to voice it until we're in that water, swimming away from this prison.

Maryam invites us in, cautiously as usual, checking behind me on her tiptoes. The other woman is missing. Well, that's what I think at first as we step into the small area, but I'm wrong. Maryam points into her bedroom, to the mattresses inside, where the tattooed woman is sprawled out on top of the tropical pattern covers.

'Siti hurt,' Maryam says.

I ask Kiki and Cooper to take Akmal to the far end of the shed, away from the view of the main house. I ask them to find me a pretty flower or a hidden treasure on the sandy flats. After they leave, Kiki peeks back inside and I shoo her off.

'What happened to Siti?' I ask Maryam, going to her friend and crouching beside her. There's no blood that I can see. I stroke Siti's bare foot. 'What did they do to her?'

'They slap. She get things and they see.'

Amazing the way anxiety appears like an old cancer. I'm constricted from all angles, a tightness I can't seem to loosen.

'Do they know?' I ask, swallowing repeatedly. A lump sticks and that's when I know it's not a lump. It's my throat constricting. 'Maryam, do they know? The men, do they know we're trying to escape?' The room is getting blurry, like a television with no reception.

She shrugs and shakes her head.

'I was supposed to do this, not you. Not Siti, I was supposed to be the one. I didn't want you or Siti getting in trouble, and now they know.'

I'm about to faint, I think. This has never happened before, yet the loss of blood, the cramping, the fear – it's getting under my skin, into my thoughts and taking any sense of control.

Slouching against the wall, I close my eyes and lean into my hands. One chance. There would only be one chance to do this, and now it's gone.

I scream, bursting up and kicking one of the plastic chairs in the eating area so it bounces off the tin with a wild clang. 'I'm so angry,' I cry. Anger disrupts the fogginess and rage enters, pulsing through my hands and legs and feet. I'm crying and Maryam runs back out to me, saying *shush shush*, and I don't listen, because why should I? They know, they already know and now we're never getting off this shithole. I cry into my hands, not knowing where to

274

step in this tiny shed. I want to run, bolt. Instead, she pulls me into her skinny arms and holds me there like a mother, shushing my cries. It's only then I realise what I'm mumbling, over and over like a child, lost and sinking. 'Help me, please, help me.'

'We help,' she says.

'How?' I ask.

'Siti say they hit her and done.'

I pull away from her sweaty neck and blink. 'They don't know we're trying to leave?'

Maryam shakes her head. 'No.'

Sniffing, I wipe my eyes on my arm and don't know whether I can trust or believe them or whether Maryam even understands what I'm asking. Maryam sits me down at the table and picks up the chair I kicked, pushing it back in its place. We need to plan this escape before the men find us together. If the men didn't know I was here, they'll surely know now. My screams would be heard. The kids will wonder. I'm unravelling here. I don't know myself anymore.

After I've checked on Siti again and she's up sipping water on the mattress, I ask Maryam to come with me to the palm trees on the hill. From there we can plan in peace and work together to invent a solution to the complicated grief we're all in.

Now: 4:02am

I'm almost asleep when there's tickling on my forehead. I slap my
hand over it, waking in a frenzy. Was it a spider or insect? I open
my eyes. No, it's Jack. Standing above the bed like a creepy intruder,
about to pounce on me. He holds a finger up to his mouth and I
nod, waiting for Kiki and Cooper to settle back into a deep sleep.
When they do, I roll out of bed with Jack helping me up.

The usual ocean breeze wafts through the curtains and it's weird
that I'm noticing the routine of this place, having been here only
a few days. The squawking of the same bird outside the window
each morning. The humidity setting in by seven am, smothering
the air with domineering heat. The tide rolling in and out, twice
a day displaying miniature shells that poke out like sharp cones.

We sneak downstairs together, never letting go of each other's
hands. The last time we made love was in the hotel room, with
me packing my bags after and leaving in a huff. With him calling
me back down the hallway, making a fool of himself. We fought
because I had to leave him and couldn't bear the thought of it.

When we reach the kitchen area, I notice the blinds are down.
No one can see in, regardless, we still whisper.

'The baby. Did Maryam tell you?'

Jack drags out a chair from the dining room and takes a seat,
pulling me onto his lap. His action imitates my own when Kiki

was upset this morning. He nods and touches my stomach. 'How are you?'

'It's not good, Jack. Bleeding is serious. I'm not supposed to bleed. It means something's happening inside.'

His eyes are downcast, and he sniffs. His fingers hover over the skin as though he's worried he'll damage me further. It's in that touch that I'm aware he's frightened. This baby and the idea of it being hurt is moving him deeply.

'We need to get you off this island and to the mainland.'

'This is all my fault.'

'Don't be silly, Em.'

'It is.' I stand up, starting to cry into the wall. Jack gets up from the chair and comes to me, covering my back with his body, holding me.

'Because of you, the police will have uncovered a massive trafficking ring.'

'I couldn't save her.'

'No, but you'll save hundreds of other women.'

I nod, and I should be happy about it, I know, except I'm not. Knowing Ariella had to sacrifice her own life for others isn't fair or equal. I don't even realise how much I'm shaking until Jack spins me around and holds me tight, saying, 'Calm, just calm. This isn't good for bub.' I listen and try to moderate my skipping pulse by sucking in large breaths and slowing everything down. I sink my head into his chest and then lean into it. I give myself permission to cry on him. There's only one focus on my mind, driving me towards escaping this island. If any doubts creep in, I'll lose my nerve. And it's easy to do with the plan I've established.

Realistically, there's no boat here; Jack can't overpower three men, one who I've noticed carries a gun on him like a newborn baby attached at the hip and ready to disarm. He needs to keep pretending for a little longer.

This'll be the last time we're together until I reach safety.

While Kiki and Coop remain asleep upstairs, with a distant rumbling echoing over the steamy ocean, I relay to Jack each element of how the women and I are going to escort the kids to safety. He doesn't comfortably agree, in fact, he scrutinises my plan for flaws, danger and my ill-preparation.

He also knows I have no other choice. It has to be done, risky or not. Even if it worries him, even if he says it's nearly impossible.

'Nearly, but not impossible, right?' I say.

He sucks a cheek in as he considers it. 'Nearly.'

'Great.' I brush my hands down my dress and stand from the lounge. 'Then it's doable.'

'But the baby,' he keeps saying. 'The bleeding.'

'I either deliver the baby here or there.'

We agree to disagree and, eventually, Jack *has* to let me do it. The only job he needs to consider is distracting the men so we can leave unnoticed, and we plan to leave tomorrow night at eight. By that time, Jack will have the other men dosed up on booze by playing a drinking game. Prior to that, Kiki and Cooper will swim in the pool. We'll practise, all without Cooper knowing. We'll judge how well they can float on the two pool beds, large, bright-pink, heavy-duty floatation devices that we'll be using to cart the both of them and baby Akmal over to the island. Behind them, the women and I will swim, using our legs to kick and push us five or more kilometres over to the opposite island in darkness. And this is the part that worries me most. Not the lack of strength we'll have, the baby bleeding, the risk of losing it – but the jellyfish, the current; the dangers that lurk beneath in the deep, rising with the scent of blood in the water.

Now: 7am

As if I want to be here, bathers on, insides bruised and worn like the baby's head is crowning. As if I want to be striding into the pool, the colour starkly aqua. The men are inside slurping coffee and burnt toast, and bacon fat wafts from the sliding doors. As if I want to be dipping in here with Ginger's eyes on my body, my swollen breasts and stomach, my bare skin.

Yet this is all part of the plan.

Kiki dives in first like an Olympic swimmer and starts doing laps. I don't know whether she's showing me how good she can swim, how capable she is, yet all I'm thinking is, go easy, Kiks. Don't tire yourself out today. They'll have a rest later. I'll force them to.

I've had to tell Kiki that tonight is the night. What started as tears ended with confidence as I pitched the trek as an adventure. People do this all the time, I'd said. Night-time scuba divers swim across rivers, under wrecks, into caves. It's no different to you being at the beach or in the pool all day. And you won't even be the one who's swimming. The women will be with us and we'll work as a team.

'But it's deep,' she'd said and, in that moment, I had to change the subject. Because I can't picture the deep. I can't picture how it's going to feel. I have to psych myself out of it like those people who prep for channel swims. Do they ever consider what's below? Surely. Well, I can't. I won't be able to do it otherwise.

Cooper delights in having me there. He swims around me, clinging on to my shoulders and accidentally pulling my hair. He squeals and I remind him to be a little quieter. I'm certain they'll all have hangovers. I don't want his sounds to pierce their patience.

Their eyes are on me, and I'm trying not to peek inside. Because how could Charles do this?

I dip my head underwater, imagining it's later on and I'm safe and it's dark, but I'm safe. Closing my eyes, I roll my shoulders, collecting the water with my palms and blow and inhale air with every head-turn. My arms windmill over my head while my legs kick and churn the water. And then, I leave the surface, leave my kids and their splashes and Cooper's squeals and I keep kicking, down, down, deep, further down until my lungs become tight with air, until I know the chlorine water surrounds me from all angles, above and below. Now, I stop kicking, just hang there underwater in the pure silence that only underwater can offer. I have to be one with it, not fight it, just accept it. It's the only way it's going to work.

When I surface, one of the pink floating beds is just centimetres from my nose. Our raft. I clutch the side, as the rubber stretches and groans. It's pumped enough, I hope. It's thick, not like a flimsy, cheap version, it's a good-quality type. I don't even care why it's here or who decided to purchase the toys in this pool. I only care that it's going to work for us.

Kiki swims up beside me and gives me a look.

'Don't wear yourself out,' I whisper. Little droplets of water spill down her cheeks like tears and I kiss them, tasting salt. 'Hop on. Then ask Coop to join you.'

I help her to get her legs over where she lies flat like she's about to paddle out to surf. She fits beautifully, all limbs free from water. I smile.

'Hey, Coop,' she calls out to Cooper, who's bobbing up and down on a pool noodle. 'Come on here with me.'

'Good idea,' I say. 'We can have a race.'

'Nah, I don't want to,' Cooper says, skimming water with his hands, making rocket sounds.

'Please,' I say.

He bobs like he's riding a horse and shakes his head. I swim over to him and say quietly, 'I bet you can't fit on there with Kiki. I bet you'll knock her off.'

He grins and slips off the pool noodle. 'I can.'

I grab the noodle and place it under my shoulders and kick towards them. This would also work well, keep me upright. With this under my arms, it wouldn't be so tiring. Maryam and Siti are going to bring the pool bed to the boatshed later on, when the sun goes down. They'll pretend to be cleaning up the pool area with the leaf scoop and pretend to pack the toys away into the pool shed, a small tin space occupied by the pump and chlorine bottles. One of them will bring the pool bed down and hide it under the jetty. And this noodle is an implement that'll benefit me during the crossing.

Cooper clambers on, almost knocking Kiki off and I tell him to wait before pushing his sister off.

'Let's see if I can race you from this end to the other. You have to paddle the bed together, okay?'

Cooper loves the idea and beams at my competing with them. He hasn't seen the bubbly, friendly mother that he's normally used to. The one who's all hugs and kisses, and Lego building and cake-making beside Georgia. This small interaction lifts his face into normalcy. It's like seeing my son again for the first time in weeks.

They both wait for me to join them, and I start the race with a ready, set, go. While I'm bobbing beside them, I'm noticing the rubber pool bed and how it's holding up, how it's holding them. It's doing its job, mainly because it's meant to comfortably support an adult male. They can both lie there without getting wet while I push them from behind, using my legs to propel them along.

And then I look up from them and Jack's at the doorway, clutching a coffee and clamping his lips down on a smile. It works. I told him it would. I'd cry if I wasn't smiling.

Now: 8:11am

On the bed in Barque are three outfits, a knife, an old beach towel and twelve hair ties. I stand at the base of the bed studying them, considering whether this is going to work. Maryam's words haunt me. *They kill my sister.*

The jellyfish are always there, no matter what season. This is why we all need to be well-covered and protected from their fatal stings. I have the kids' pyjamas Charles packed from home. We left when it was cold, unlike here and so they haven't even worn them. I'm grateful for their length.

Taking the flimsy towel, I use a knife to saw through twenty-four pieces of cloth, enough for all of us. Outside, Kiki and Cooper's voices echo from the beach. Rocks are being clumped on top of one another as Cooper constructs a fort or village or sea pool.

It's hard to get the pieces of towel perfect, but they'll have to do. Some are jagged and small, and I'll use those pieces for Cooper and Akmal's hands. The cloth will be bundled around their hands, like makeshift gloves. I'll tie them securely with hair ties. They'll be wearing their school socks tucked over their pyjama pants to stop the jellyfish from slipping in, with hair ties bonded around for extra strength. I can't risk the socks rolling down or falling off. We have a long way to swim without protection. And most Queensland resorts hire out stinger suits. This is the best I can do. I'm praying the floating bed will keep the kids entirely dry and out of the water, nevertheless, I need to prepare for worst-case scenarios. Jack taught me to be prepared for anything.

For instance, the bed may deflate. Which is why I need the pool noodle. Currents, stings, and the worst – sharks and salt-water crocodiles – are also a factor. It's unlikely, Jack said, still, they need to be respected. That's why I'll take a small knife with me, tucked in my pants. I close my eyes tightly, holding the towel in my fists. I can't think this way, it only terrifies me; just stop, Emma. Bending over with my hands on my knees, I open my eyes onto the island across the ocean. It's not too far. The resort is clear now, like white light. Our haven. We only need to get there, and we'll be supported. The vision of them phoning the police, sending a helicopter, putting us up in a secure room with good food and warm baths fills my body with heat. And then later, Charles being sent to prison, along with Mateo. Jack and I living together with our baby. I smile down at the bump. The cramps and bunching sensations aren't there, and last time I checked, there was no sign of blood either. He or she needs to hold out a little longer and it's my duty to keep serene.

Laying the cloth together, I fold them all and stash them under the bed, ready for tonight, when we'll all need them.

Now: 10:08am

Kiki and Cooper are outside eating a sandwich with wet hair and goosebumps when Charles comes sauntering down the boardwalk. Cooper almost drops the sandwich as he leaps from the palm trunk and bolts towards his father. I didn't expect to see Charles before we make our move from this place. To have him barefooted, collecting Cooper in his arms, makes me drop the butter knife.

For a split second, I can imagine that this was all a mistake. Jack has got it wrong. Charles would never do anything to hurt me, let alone any other women. And Cooper throws his arms around Charles' neck, loving him, even though his dad's never around, even though he barely listens when they talk to him; the boy loves his father. And this hurts.

I spin away from the window, gripping the counter with greasy butter fingers and gawk at the fridge. How will I explain this all to Cooper on the way over, while I drag the pool bed from under the jetty and push him onto it? We're just going for a late-night swim? We've just decided to race across the ocean?

'Fuck. Fuck, fuck, fuck.' The cramps below start up again, twisting my guts and I hold my stomach. 'Not now. Please stop.' The pain parallels anxiety. The baby senses danger as my adrenaline surges through to its heart. It wants to flee. But not yet, it can't come yet.

Charles' voice creeps closer to the kitchen window and I spin around again, pick up the knife and continue spreading butter over the bread. He steps inside. Nicotine seeps from his clothing. He hovers by the front door, watching me.

'We're going back home tomorrow,' he says.

I look up, clanging the knife down on the board. 'What?'

He scratches an eyebrow and nods. Grey stubble makes him look homeless. 'A boat's coming first thing to take you back.'

I don't believe this. 'Just me?'

'You're the one with the baby.' He gives a tiny smile, finally acknowledging it. And I'm useless, gullible and wanting to be. Just this little smile from him gives me hope.

'What about the kids?'

His bottom lip scrunches up to the top and he nods. 'They can go too.'

'What about you?'

'I'll come back with Jack. Mateo and I have spoken. I think he did it and I know how to prove it to the police.'

I can't fathom what he's saying. Because it's an unexpected contradiction, a misleading trick, negating what Jack's told me. He's lying. I'm sure of it. I'm standing, blinking and he semi-smiles, crossing his arms.

'I thought you'd be happy,' he says.

Outside Cooper's singing a song. Singing connotes happiness. I'm sure it's because his father is here, paying him attention.

'I am,' I say. 'I'm just shocked.'

'Well, instead of being shocked, maybe you should start packing.' He goes to leave. 'I'll tell the kids.'

'No wait—' I hold up a hand. I can't have him telling Kiki and getting her hopes up. I can't have him lying to her. Our plan will go awry. I've finally got her mental state the way I require it to be. Strong, positive, trusting in me.

He's lying. He has to be. Still, I have to act ordinary, like I would if what he was saying were true. Which it's not. Is it? My head hurts, a deep throb that kicked off this morning, and is still building.

'I'll tell them,' I say. 'They're really not happy about all this. Kiki is moody and Coop is tired and I'd rather sit them down and tell them.'

He frowns. 'But this should perk them up.'

'It will. But I'd like to tell them myself.'

He shrugs. 'Suit yourself.' He knocks on the glass window. 'Get packing.'

Out the window, Charles lobs a shell to Cooper, who collects it and grins, twisting it in his fingers. Kiki warily sits back from the trunk, sandwich up to her mouth. Charles tries to talk to her and she looks away and kicks the sand. He laughs a quick laugh, a laugh of insecurity and keeps walking away, to the boardwalk. And I'm left standing, stunned, not knowing what or who to believe. If it's not true, then why does he want to tell the kids? Kiki puts her sandwich aside on the trunk and clasps her little hands on her lap. She's lost her appetite and I don't blame her. But what about Jack? Would he lie about this?

There's a minor detail hinting at deception. Charles never mentioned the affair he thinks I'm having. Just now, he was too enthusiastic, too forgiving.

For someone so bitter by the pool a few days ago, accusing his wife of being a two-timing bitch, he's certainly transformed into a happy soul now. Then again, maybe he's sorted everything. Still, that's how I discern the lie from fact. I just need Jack to confirm it.

Now: 1:17pm

Cooper doesn't understand why he must nap. He's dragging his toes across the tiles and whining like a brat. It's little things like this that irritate me to the point of making me hot and sweaty. I can't have him stuff up our plan. And usually I wouldn't care, I'd brush this behaviour off, yet right now I'm not in the mood. I can't be the settled, encouraging mother that I need to be.

'You need a nap; I don't care what you say, Cooper.' I'm dumping their breadcrusts in the small compost bin and wonder why I'm even bothering. I'm cleaning the kitchen, acting as though I'm still at home. Although perhaps it's these ordinary acts that keep me from crumbling.

Kiki places an arm around his shoulders like a little therapist and says, 'I need one too, Cooper. How about we nap together?'

She's being such a good girl, better than me. I'm proud of her maturity and then guilty that she possesses it. She's too young for this. Too young to play the character of mother, to chaperone Cooper into napping. I give her a tired smile.

'But I don't wanna sleep,' Cooper says. 'I'm digging a channel through my town and about to build a bridge.'

'It's fine, Kiki.' I nod. 'Just let him go.'

'But, Mum—'

'I know,' I say. 'But he'll be all right.'

She drops her hands from his shoulders and Cooper runs back outside. In an instant, the singing resumes.

'I'm going to have a nap,' Kiki says. 'That way I can help you.'

I take a step towards her, kiss her glistening forehead and sniff her. She smells like herself again. Smells like home.

◆ ◆ ◆

Eventually Kiki falls asleep because she needed to. Last night, she'd been tossing in bed, unable to get comfortable. It'd taken her hours to finally get to sleep. Stress tends to do that. While she's sleeping, I ask Cooper to come with me to see baby Akmal. Maryam is the only person who can discreetly ask Jack to come and speak to me. I need to know that Charles is telling the truth, that Jack's got it all wrong and we're leaving tomorrow to go home. He'll be upset with me for asking, even doubting his story. However, if Charles *has* changed his mind, then perhaps Jack knows now.

Wouldn't it be easier just to play along until we reach Sydney, pretend that everything is okay and then contact the police once we're back in the warmth of our home?

I hope it's true.

Maryam isn't in her shed; neither are the others. Cooper picks up a stick and thrashes it against the grass bushes while I inspect their space. Garlic and meat lard lingers in the air, as well as the floral hint of incense. Two empty coffee mugs, stained and rimmed with lipstick sit on the round plastic table. The women must be up at the main house, doing their chores for the disgusting men who force them.

I'm about to ask Cooper to join me back up the slope when I spot Maryam running down the hill with Akmal on her hip. She waves at me and I sneak back into the shed, in case one of the men spots me.

'Coop, come here.' I motion for him to follow.

He brings the stick with him and sits on one of the chairs.

Maryam enters, flushed faced and grimacing. She's puffed and sets Akmal down at her feet before holding the doorframe. There's something she wants to say, a reason for her running.

'Are you all right?' I ask.

She shakes her head and points towards the main house. 'They fight. Make Akmal scared. Much scream.'

I swallow and my voice almost disappears. I already know what she's going to say. I can picture it now. 'Who is fighting?'

She takes a breath and looks at me front on. But she doesn't say who.

'Jack?' I ask, holding my hand up high. 'Tall man?'

She nods and Cooper's listening and so I ask him to take Akmal outside for a moment. Jack's in trouble. I don't know how badly, and I doubt Maryam will be able to explain it in depth. My hands are sweating. Charles must have found out about us, that's all I can assume. Why else would they be arguing? I can't believe I doubted him. I wipe my hands on my dress.

'Who's screaming at him? Wallace? Charles?'

'Yours.' She nods at me. She means Charles. 'He say.' She can't find the right words and agonises over it as she searches my face. 'You love Jack,' she finally states.

I hang my head. Shit. Charles is a lying son of a bitch. He's known all along that Jack and I are together, I'm sure of it. That's why he invited Jack here. Not for support, not for partnership. For revenge. Why else would they take his keys, wallet, phone, everything from him? He's been a prisoner without even being aware. Or maybe he was, and maybe he didn't care. Maybe he came knowing that would happen, yet came for us regardless. Two beads of water drip from my eyes. I need to get to him and at least try and help.

Charles discovering our affair has now lifted this perilous situation to another height.

'Where are they?' I ask her as she rubs my arm.

She shrugs. 'Akmal.'

Cooper runs in, barely holding Akmal, who's slipping from his little arms and trying to wriggle free. The baby is grunting in annoyance and Cooper sets him down.

'Mum, there's a woman coming down the hill and she looks grumpy.'

Maryam and I stare at each other and I quickly step outside as the old maid storms down the hill. She's coming towards us and I take Cooper's hand and run. The woman sees me and doesn't care because she's only got her mind stuck on one person. Maryam.

'Stay here,' I tell Cooper and run back towards the shed. The woman enters and I hear screaming. I run faster, my insides splintering as I do. She has Maryam by the hair, and she's saying she's not allowed to speak to the Australian bitch, and I push her in the back, hard. She releases Maryam, turning to me.

'Take your fucking hands off her,' I scream.

I cop a slap to the side of my face and I'm thankful it's nothing more. Still, it stings, jolting me. My ear rings as I clasp my cheek. Just as long as Cooper doesn't see, I think. It's okay. It's okay. It's only pain.

'I came asking for milk,' I yell. 'It's not her fault.'

She reaches out and surprisingly grips my other cheek between her fingers, pulling the skin tight making me close my eyes, wincing. 'Keep away,' she says and then lets go, face fuming and red, weathered like an old strap of leather. What abuse did she cop as a child to make her so cruel? She thrusts out her finger, pointing at me to leave and I obey. I hear Maryam sobbing and the old maid yelling.

I can't wait until they're all in prison. They'll be there for life. This notion uplifts me, makes me that much more determined. These men locked up, Charles taken away. This woman punished.

These are the thoughts I'll choose, like trying on a favourite coat. I'll think about this while we're swimming, while I'm fearing what's beneath me. That'll get me to the other side of the ocean. Guaranteed.

Now: 1:37pm

Kiki's still asleep when Coop and I enter Barque and I want her to stay that way. I want Cooper to sit in front of the television, watch a movie and be hypnotised by the movement, the sound. There's an urgent need to go and find Jack and make certain he's okay. And already my body is revving from the old maid, so I'm prepared for the wrath of Charles. I'm ready for anything.

I always knew this would happen eventually. The moment Jack's tongue curled against mine, I knew my future. Charles would one day discover our affair, our relationship, our connection. I'm ready for the abuse.

I switch on the television for Cooper, load an old video tape, then close the front door and stop, hanging there a while.

When that gruff voice appears, it takes me right back to the cabin, him crushing my phone and screaming. Charles is coming. My fingers clench the doorknob. I don't need to guess what mood he's in, the tone of that voice now tells me everything. When to run, when to defend the kids, when to block my ears. I lock the door and turn the TV up. Then I move to the kitchen window and peer at an angle, shielding myself. Is he coming for me? No. Jack's in front of him, charging along the sand towards us, bits kicking up like dust.

'You're not going anywhere near her,' Charles roars behind Jack's back.

But Jack continues towards Barque and for a moment I stand, immobile. A child again. Only I'm not. I've been waiting for this moment. One year since we started our affair. I understood the conditions: one day, somehow, my husband would clue on. Now, fronting Jack, I know Charles is ready to prove his possessiveness, a quality that's never introduced itself in all the time we've been married. Out at parties, there was never any jealousy, no quiet corner chats about staying clear of certain men or accusations of flirting. Charles has never cared. But he cares now.

As he beelines for Jack, my mind screams to step back. He's going to kill him. I can read his face, wild and twisted and ugly. One finger on Jack and he'll never stop. He's killed people. He killed my friend. He traffics women. He's a drug addict. A criminal. He's capable of anything.

'Leave her alone, Charles,' Jack says and Charles kicks him in the back of the leg, but misjudges. Jack spins around. 'Are you out of your fucking mind?' He shoves Charles' shoulder and laughs with contempt. 'Look at you. A psycho druggie. She deserves better.'

Charles lunges, gripping Jack by the collar and I'm thanking the universe that Kiki is sleeping, that Coop's distracted by the TV. But it won't be long until he hears them fighting. And now Wallace and Ginger join them, stomping down the boardwalk and I'm by the window, wondering how I can help Jack. Because it's getting worse. I glance around the kitchen for a knife, for anything I can use to protect Jack. There's nothing. What would I do with a knife anyway? It's two against three.

Charles pins Jack up against the brick wall beside the kitchen window, he must feel stronger, taller than Jack. But he's not. That's why he has hired muscle for back-up. To intimidate.

'She hates you,' Jack says.

Charles punches Jack in the face and smiles. 'That felt really good. Like taking a shit.' Charles is aroused by the violence. It makes me want to hurt him. But Jack is strong, he'll recover from whatever Charles dishes out.

'I'll fix you good.' Saliva sprays out of Charles' mouth, landing on Jack's bloodied nose. 'And that cheating bitch.'

Jack spits out blood. He goes to hit Charles, but my husband is quicker, grabbing a fistful of Jack's hair and knocking his head against the brick wall, like cracking a coconut. The sound of skull hitting brick makes me sick and I bring a hand to my mouth. It was very hard, blood to the brain hard. Charles' knee jerks up between Jack's legs and Jack bends forwards, but there's no more grunts. The pain is too intense, either that or he's unconscious.

I try to run out and stop Charles, but my feet are planted to the floor, unable to shift. My eyes zoom in on the little details, images I'll unfortunately remember. Fingers tightening around Jack's neck. Sweat patches on Charles' shirt. Bared yellow teeth. Fingers pressing hard, pinching skin and reddening Jack's cheeks. Another smash of head against bricks will do it. Gone. Forever. Jack is suffering greatly, most probably haemorrhaging, and I can't breathe anymore.

I can see it's taking incredible willpower to release Jack's sobbing body. The way Charles remains there with his hands around Jack's neck, teeth gritted means he's enjoying this moment. When he does release him, Jack falls into a heap against the wall. Head hanging, eyes closed. But it doesn't end there, and that's when I pull away from the window. The others step forwards, their feet kicking against a hollow body, the grunts and wheezing gasps coming through the kitchen window. I hear Charles tell Jack that cheating is the ultimate betrayal.

And I can't hear anymore. Because the character is singing on the television, masking the kicking, masking the laughing. I collapse onto the floor, hands over my face and silently weep.

Now: 3:13pm

Kiki wakes from her sleep, groggy yet emotional. Her crying can be heard downstairs while I'm using ice on my cheek and sitting against the wall, snot dribbling down onto my lip. I don't feel like getting up for her. I, like her, am a child needing comforting. They've taken Jack and I don't know where. They carried him away from Barque and I can't leave this stupid house. There are droplets of blood on the sand and the sea suddenly doesn't seem as hazardous as staying here.

The crying upstairs continues and Cooper's in front of the television eating a snack and I'm hoping this rest will be all he needs to get through the night. Because we leave tonight, whether they want to or not. We leave tonight.

My cheek and face are sore, red, although nothing compared with my stomach, which now aches with on-off spasms. They don't seem like contractions yet. And I had Braxton Hicks with Coop, so it could be those. I'm hoping that's all it is: just the baby and my body preparing for the new arrival. If I rest awhile, and stop moving, it tends to soften again into a natural ball of weight. I'm guessing the stress, the run back from Maryam's, the horrible sight of my love being beaten is what did it.

'Mum,' Kiki calls out now, so I stand and wipe my nose on my arm.

I take the steps, two at a time, to Kiki, who's sitting up under the covers, puffy-eyed and crying. Her hair is teased into a puff at the back, and I brush it down and kiss her forehead.

'Bad dream?' I ask. Stupid, really. This whole experience is a waking nightmare.

'I'm scared, Mum. What if a shark comes, or we drown?'

'There's no sharks around here,' I lie. 'They're only in cooler waters. Queensland is too hot for them. As for drowning, how can we when we have the bed and noodle?'

She sniffs, leaning her head onto mine. 'I'm just scared. I hate swimming deep at the beach. This is my worst nightmare.'

'I know it is, but we'll get through it and you'll feel so brave.'

'Do we really have to do it? Can't we just speak to Dad? He seemed happy before, like he loves us.'

'That's not what this is about.'

'He'll listen to me. He won't want us to do this, Mum.'

'You can't back down now, Kiki, okay? He does love you—'

'Then I don't understand.'

I now realise I'm going to have to go deeper with her. Reveal something that'll make her believe me, trust me. I point to my cheek, which she hasn't yet noticed. She's too busy playing with the ends of her hair, now stiff and crusted from chlorine and sun and salt.

'See this?'

'What happened?'

'These men and people here are dangerous. They did this to me. And Jack's been badly beaten too. We need to get off this island, Kiki. It's too dangerous to stay now.'

Her eyes study the impact marks on my cheek and her little chin wobbles again. I stop her by holding her face between my hands. 'You must stay brave for all of us. See that island?' I point through the window. Across the glittering sea is our destination, still sun-soaked and beckoning. 'It's not that far.'

She nods and I cuddle her, shielding her head from another view outside, something unexpected. The men, Wallace and Ginger, are carrying Jack by his arms and legs. I release Kiki and move to the window, using the sheers to block me from them. The two men cart him to the end of the jetty, just beside the boathouse, where they dump him, violently dropping him like a sack of potatoes. His head thumps down hard on the boards and he's not moving. *Please*. I take a sharp gasp. *Please be okay*. And I have to wait until they leave to see how badly injured he is.

Now: 3:30pm

The sand burns my toes as I sink into it, quickly peering over my shoulder. I don't want them to spot me running. The wind between the palms is picking up, lifting the fronds like fingers as they start to shake. However, there's no one there, or on the boardwalk and I've waited long enough before venturing out here.

Kiki and Cooper are watching the dinosaur movie together with a packet of chocolate biscuits spread out between them. She's woken up now, appears fresher and I leave them there while I bolt out to Jack, trying to slow my pace as the baby jerks inside me.

When I reach the jetty, I step faster, eyes examining his body for movement, anything that'll mean Jack's alive and okay.

'Jack,' I call without yelling. His body is still, with his arms outstretched, as he was left when they'd dumped him here. When I get to him, I crouch down to his shoulders and touch his battered face. I feel for a pulse on his neck and find it strong and obvious. Very much alive.

'Jack,' I whisper, resting my head on his hard chest and hear him moan, a rattly sound that vibrates through his pecs. He's badly beaten with dark-red patches all over his temple, cheek and lips. One eye is swollen shut. Open cuts are bleeding where the men have split his skin with their fists. Come tomorrow, they'll turn a nasty purple. I've made a wet patch on his t-shirt where my eyes have leaked.

'Talk to me,' I whisper. He may be alive but who knows what internal damage has been done. He could have head injuries, internal bleeding. I kiss his sticky hairline, suddenly unfazed if the men see me here. It's painful seeing him this way. A strong man, reduced to this.

'Just make a noise if you're okay,' I say. I take his hand and he gives me two squeezes. It's enough. That's all I need for now. It sets me off crying. I kiss his fist and rest it against my swollen cheek. 'We're all going to get off here. Tonight. I'll use the pool bed and you can float on it and we'll swim behind.'

He makes a sound like *nahhh*, a breathless no.

'Yes.' I pat his hand and lower it. 'The kids will feel better knowing you're with us. Even if you can't do anything. I'm getting us away from this place.'

I'm preparing a list in my head of everything I need to remember. I'll make extra cloth pieces to tie around his hands and feet, to protect him. The sun isn't as strong now, regardless, he'll still need protection from the sun's heat, water to drink. The salty ocean will do the cuts good.

But there's two thoughts sneaking in, rattling my confidence. What if he falls in? He's too heavy to roll back on and he won't be able to move. He'll drown. And the other thought, springing into my mind like one of Wallace's slaps – the kids will now have to swim with me.

I start to cry again on his chest. Because I want to take him with me, take him to safety. I want us all together and off this island. I stare down at his badly injured body, red and purple and finger-marked skin. I can't take him. Cooper wouldn't make it. And the fear in Kiki is much too strong. And I think he knows. That's why when I hear him again, a clearer, 'No,' I stare down at my belly, poking against his side and have to agree with him. This is his baby. And those are my children. They come first, they always will.

I kiss his head, sweaty and greased as guilt surges through me.

'We'll come back for you,' I say.

And it's a pathetic statement even if true. Because we both know what will happen come tomorrow. Jack will be gone, the jetty empty and all that will remain is the memory of him feeding me scrambled eggs on the first morning we'd slept together. It means I'll have to swim faster, get back here quicker. It means I'll have to be more determined.

Now: 6:32pm

The rest of the afternoon pans slowly and I'm caught between three activities: gazing out my window to check if Jack's okay; running out to offer sips of water; and staring at Cooper and Kiki as they listlessly watch television. Kiki's as nervous as I am, constantly turning to face me. I smile, she smiles at me, and then she looks back at the television. She's started biting her nails, her legs wiggle and she's refusing dinner.

'But you have to eat something,' I say. 'To give you strength.'

Eventually she accepts the plate of vegetables and fruit and nibbles slowly while Cooper scoffs his down. To keep her spirits up, I play a game of I-spy with them and read some pages of their novel aloud. I've cut their vegetables into shapes and arrange them on the plate to look like a clown face. Cooper loves it. Kiki weakly smiles.

I'm ignoring the pain in my stomach. I'm ignoring the blood. It's started up again, needle-prick drops that dirty my underwear. I wipe it away with toilet paper, drink lots of water, eat lots of food and lie down on my bed, propped up with pillows, face turned to the jetty where he lies. The sun's setting. Storm clouds help with the orange and pink picture. Water turns to blood. Sand goes yellow. Palm trees lift their swaying fronds.

Eventually, two pink pool beds enter the window view, bouncing as Maryam runs to hide them and the pool noodle under the jetty, piling handfuls of sand over the top. I can barely move to thank her, but I do. Standing by the window, I make a *pssst* sound and she looks up; I wave the bits of cloth I've cut. I watch as she faces Jack, a large shadowy figure at the end of the jetty.

Because of her, we're doing this together. We'll make it off the island okay. She doesn't know how thankful I am to have met her.

Now: 7:16pm

Kiki's spotted me outside, coming back from Jack with a wet face and runny nose. She's holding the doorframe and the light behind her spills out onto the sand. Her silhouette waits for me.

'How's Jack?' she asks.

And just the question, just the idea that someone is asking and caring has me stopping on the sand and crouching. I can't always be the brave mum for her. It's okay to show emotion. Maybe not rage, maybe not aggression, but sadness, grief, fear – yes, those are good things to admit to your kids. I have to remember this. I'm not always strong. I am always human. And seeing Jack slipping in and out of consciousness has battered my strength. I can't get up from this sand. So I sit. And she comes to me. And her little hand is hot on my shoulder. And it pats me. Follows with a, 'Shhhh. It's okay, Mummy.'

'He's not good, Kiks.' I sniff and tilt my head back to face the stars. Maybe if I acknowledge how vast that sky is and how small my life is, it'll help lessen the stress. Is this all just ego? We don't really matter, not in time. Still, my man who I love is metres away lying stiff and sore on a jetty in darkness, possibly on the way to death.

'Why did they do this to him, Mum?' she says, crouching. 'Why did Dad let them?'

'It's adult stuff and it's complicated, but Jack did not deserve this.' I stare at her. I hope she can read my eyes, without me having to confess anything. 'I really care about Jack.'

She nods. 'So do I.'

I take her hand. 'We've become really close over the years.'

She blinks down at her hands. Perhaps she knows. Perhaps she doesn't want to just yet.

'We should take him with us,' she says.

I shake my head. 'We can't.'

'But he needs a doctor. And what if they do something to him?'

I lift a shoulder and drop her hand. She crosses her legs in front of me, so our knees touch. Kiki scoops sand into one hand and pours it into the other. 'I could swim.'

'Stop it.'

'I could,' she says.

I go to stand and she tugs my skirt. 'I will.'

'Stop it, Kiki.'

'We can't leave him, Mum.'

We look at each other and I sit back down and touch her little cheek with my knuckles. 'You're very brave. But it's too far and there's not enough room. Maryam and her baby can lie on one bed, but you and Coop need to be on the other. I'm not having you in the water with me.'

My voice is wobbly, yet hers is strong when she says, 'I can do it. I'm a good swimmer.' I laugh tiredly and she stares, a look of solid concentration stopping me. 'Mum, we can't leave him. Let me swim with you.'

'No, Kiki.' I stand, kicking away her hand. 'It's not happening.'

She calls out to me as I walk away. 'You want to protect us all the time, and you don't trust that I can do this.'

'I know you can do this,' I snap, spinning back to her.

'Then let me swim.'

306

I turn away. 'No.'

'See? You're brave and you don't want me to be.'

I'm brave. She thinks I'm brave. She wants to be brave. She wants to be like me. I slowly turn around to her and place my hands on my hips. She's sitting there staring up at me and behind her, Jack is a collapsed heap on the jetty. She wants to swim? But how will she make it? This changes everything. Kiki demanding to be brave means we could take Jack with us. But she's too small and what if something happens?

'You are brave,' I tell her. 'Very brave.'

She smiles, only for a moment, before rising and dusting the sand off her lap. 'Cooper can lie on Jack. But I'll swim beside you, Mum.'

I don't need to ask if she's sure about this, I don't need to tell her what to do. I've raised a daughter who's determined, strong and capable. And this is her showing me that. She pushes past me and enters Barque and I'm left standing, watching her go.

Now: 7:30pm

I'd like to leave some mementos here. Gross acts such as my blood-stained knickers, a shit on the tiles, the house trashed and the fridge emptied all over the floor, smeared into the lounge and over the walls. I'd love to do it, and I've never thought like this before, so deluded and evil, so calculated and motivated by defacing this island and all that it means. The hatred I have for this place and these men, my ex-husband, who doesn't even deserve the name, is boiling so hotly inside me.

When Maryam comes to the door, breathless and sweaty, motioning for me to hurry up and go, I close my eyes and leave the fabric pieces on the table. What now? How can there be anything more critical than what we're doing, than what Jack's just endured? I tell Kiki to stay put and lock the door while Cooper sits eating a chocolate sandwich in front of the television. And then I follow Maryam quickly across the sand to the boardwalk, and she's urging me to shush and I'm checking Jack's silhouette is still there at the end of the jetty. He is. A big lump at the end. So, if it's not Jack, then what is it? Her friend, Siti? I'm seriously concerned that anything I'm about to face will prevent us from going through with our plan. We're so close to leaving, it hurts. My stomach also aches as I follow Maryam up the boardwalk, half powerwalking, half skipping. Holding it tightly, we finally reach the top, where loud, booming voices, aggressive and volatile, have me pausing. I recognise the voice – cocky, arrogant, authoritarian. Yanking Maryam behind a cluster of ferns, I peer out, squinting, unable to believe what I'm witnessing.

Mateo is here. Gun down and pointed to a kneeling Charles' skull. On the white tiles, a puddle of red pools beneath Charles' face. He's here. He found us. He arrived so silently no one knew. My toes curl under my feet. He's about to shoot Charles. And then he'll find me. The kids. I knew I couldn't trust these men, but Brad and Wallace are themselves parked against the wall, hands behind their heads with Mateo's men holding a gun to each of their backs. The old maid is kneeling, face at the floor, hands behind her back, silently sobbing so her shoulders shake. How the hell did he find us? My lips are dry when I lick them.

'You take my drugs from me.' Mateo spits as he yells. 'You hide them here. You think you can cheat me?'

'It wasn't—'

'Shut the fuck up.' Mateo kicks Charles in the ribs and readjusts the gun, pressing it against his head. 'You steal from me after only three months of working for me. You were supposed to bring the packages to me. Instead, you and these fuckers hide them here. And you run when my wife is shot. You betray me. And you know what happens to people who betray me? Vanish. Boom.'

He's referring to his ex-chief of security and Ariella. But what about the women? Is this island his staging post?

'I didn't kill her,' Charles splutters. 'I didn't want you to think I let you down.'

Mateo laughs and his men all snigger. The gun on Charles' head wobbles. 'I know you didn't kill her, you dumb prick.' He leans down to Charles' head. '*I* killed her.'

I've lost my breath. I thought it was Charles, all along I thought it was him. Really, he was just running from Mateo.

'She was going to go sneaking on me to your wife. Tell her all my secrets. Where *is* your wife?' Mateo glances outside and for second, it's as though he looks directly at me, us, behind the ferns, holding our breaths. He's coming for me. The kids.

'We . . . we dropped her and the kids off in Brisbane.' Charles speaks to the tiles. He's protecting us and I don't believe it. My face scrunches with anguish. 'They were too much hassle.'

'I concur there. A nosy, prying, snooping bitch. But I don't believe you.' He presses the gun down harder against Charles' dipping head. 'Do you know why I know you're lying? Because we've been tracking you since you left. You never went to Brisbane.'

'Coffs Harbour. We stopped there—'

'We'll find her.' Mateo nods to his other two men.

And that's all I need to hear. He's after me and Charles. He killed his own wife and Charles had nothing to do with Ariella's death. Clutching Maryam's hand, we quietly run down the boardwalk, my heart drumming so loudly in my ears I feel faint. Shaking my head, blinking my eyes, warm water trickles out of them. I whisper to go and grab Siti and Akmal, the cloths and their bag. He's coming for me and he's coming for my kids and he'll kill us all like he did Ariella. We have to get off this island right now. Right now.

Now: 7:48pm

The pyjamas are on the dining table and I call Cooper over. He goes to bring his plate up from the floor and I tell him to leave it. I help Cooper into the pyjamas, little fluffy ones with planets and rockets all over them, and my fingers are shaking. And then he points to the cloth pieces I've stacked on the table.

'What are those, Mummy?'

I button his little top over another long-sleeved shirt and press my lips thinly together. This is going to be hard.

'Coop, we're not going to bed tonight,' I tell him, holding his leg up and pulling his socks over his pyjamas.

Kiki starts dressing in her own pyjamas, ballerina ones, pink, fluffy, girly, soon to be drenched in sea water and trauma. I tell her to hurry. I haven't been looking forward to this at all. I don't think I can talk to Cooper when he says, 'Where are we going?' Instead, I bow my head and start to bawl my eyes out. His little hand rests on my head, warm and rubbing. And I cry into my hands for a moment while Kiki takes over once more. The guilt rips my heart apart.

'Cooper, something a little bad has happened here today on the island,' she says.

'The angry man?' he says. 'I heard him yelling at Mum.'

'There're lots of angry men on this island, Coop,' she adds.

His little hand stops stroking me. 'What about Jack and Dad?'

'Jack's not one of them,' I say, wiping my eyes. 'But Kiks is right. These men are scary and I'm a little worried. We don't have a boat, so you know that island across from us?'

He nods, chubby cheeks smothered in chocolate spread.

'Well, we're going to have to get to that island.'

Cooper giggles, almost losing balance as I slip the second sock over. 'How, swim?'

I don't laugh, I just nod and I can't look at him as I say it. There's nothing worse than seeing a child fear for their life. 'That's right. That's how we're going to do it.'

'Stop joking, Mummy.'

'I'm not joking, Coop.'

'It's going to be fun,' Kiki says.

'No,' he shouts, kicking my hand away. 'Stop lying.'

I finally meet his eyes and his face falls as he searches to find the truth in what I'm saying.

'Cooper, I promise I'm not lying to you, and I know this sounds really scary and you're very frightened, but you have to listen to me.' I grab his face hard. 'If we don't go now, we will never see our home again, do you understand me?' I've jumped from doing this in gentle steps like I did with Kiki. Time is precious, Mateo is going to come looking for us, Jack is out there injured, this baby is coming and this is all I can be right now: the bearer of bad news.

Cooper screams, pulling away and this is everything that I expected from him. Kiki goes to grab him, and he tries to run, opening the front door and I stop him, slamming the door and pulling him into me. He thrashes about, kicking and screaming and crying.

'I don't want to swim,' he cries. 'I don't want to.'

'You don't have to, you'll be safe,' I yell, startling him into shock. He stares, face wet, when I beg, 'Please, Cooper. Please. I'm trying to keep you safe, and this is the only way. You will be on a floating pool bed, but you have to do as I say.' I kiss his face as snot dribbles down his nose. He's shuddering with fear like we all are. 'Jack's going to be there too. He's hurt, so we have to help him. You want to help him, don't you? We have to make sure he gets to the island safely, but he'll be there with us.'

'But I want Daddy,' he cries.

I tell him we'll see Dad later, when we get there. I tell him to be my brave boy. I tell him it'll be like an adventure. And as much as he protests and sobs, he eventually permits a small nod. And he lets me quickly tie the cloths around his hands and feet. I'm dropping them. Picking them up. I'm struggling to work quickly knowing Mateo is up at the main house with a gun. Kiki helps me and then lets me tie them to her too. And we give each other one last, longing hug. And I'm so proud of them and I tell them this. Everything will go back to normal soon, I promise. We'll all be okay.

I close the front door to Barque. Maryam, Siti and Akmal are already on the jetty. This is it, we're finally on our way. I look to the ocean and feel it stare back with Mateo's presence pressing down on my spine.

Now: 8pm

I'm very clear about what I expect and one of those expectations is silence. They're not to cry, scream, argue or do anything noisy until I know we're far enough. You can cry on the way over, but not when we're leaving, that's what I told them. We have one chance to do this and do it right. I'm relying on these small humans to take on an adult task that I'm not even confident about. Akmal is wondering what we're doing, twisting his head around while he rests in Maryam's arms, little hands and feet bundled in protective cloth. And I'm so conscious of the boardwalk, the men coming down and spotting us.

The only belongings I have in my backpack are the kids' teddies. They'll be washed and dried in no time. I've snuck a knife in there too, without them noticing, and some water that'll have to last for all of us. I've also put three apples in there for energy. I plan to use everything, except the knife.

When we get to the jetty, I instruct Kiki and Cooper to wait by Jack until I find the rubber bed underneath. Siti helps me. Maryam's buried it well. I'm careful to not make any noise as I smooth piles of the sand off its surface and tug it from under the jetty. Siti grabs the other, along with the pool noodle.

Small waves lap around us and I'm thankful for the weather. There's no moon, no stars and the water's smooth, as though holding its breath. If it were windy or swelly, it'd make the crossing almost impossible.

Sweeping one last look over my shoulder, I see nothing, hear nothing. Only the rustle of palm fronds and a distant bird. But that could mean they're sneaking down to find us. I pad out onto the jetty in my long clothes and wrapped hands and feet. I'm warm, shaking with sweat that moistens my underarms. I'm not sure how cold it'll be out there. With the pool bed under one arm and my backpack on, I'm panting, brimming with anxiety, adrenaline and shock. Although I can't let those emotions take over. I have to force myself to stay focused and confident. The message and reason are clear: I'm doing this for each person on this jetty.

'I help get him on,' Maryam whispers, handing Akmal to Siti and nodding towards Jack, who holds up an arm.

I bend to him and when he quietly speaks to me, I want to kiss his hand, but don't with Kiki and Cooper watching. I'll tell them about us soon, now's not the time. Jack's no longer groggy and out of it. Still, what he's saying is stupid. 'You should leave me here.'

I squeeze his hand. 'Don't speak. Mateo is here. He's got men with him and they're holding guns.' This stops him talking because he knows – he'll also be killed if Mateo finds him.

Luckily, the tide is quite high, meaning we can easily slide Jack down on the pool bed. Except I'm worried about it ripping on the boards. We'll have to be super gentle. Kiki's beside me, carrying the pool noodle and shivering. The kids couldn't speak, cry or argue if they wanted to. They're in shock, total, utter shock. We need to get in and get going.

'Roll him onto this,' I tell Maryam.

She helps and Jack stops her. 'No. wait. Lift me. I think they've cracked some ribs but lift me up, I'll help.'

I hold his head down and whisper in a hiss, 'Stop being a hero, Jack, and stop moving. Come on, Maryam.'

315

Maryam nods and helps to roll Jack on his side while I stuff the pool bed under him. He groans in agony and Cooper blocks his ears. He's on, yet not fully, so I get Maryam to help me pull him on by scrunching his shirt and tugging. Jack slides on and I bend down again to quickly kiss him before the children see.

Maryam climbs quietly into the black water. She's going to help balance Jack into the water from the side while Kiki and I lower him and the bed in. She pulls the front part while she's holding on to the jetty and I'm wincing, afraid to hear the pop of the plastic. It scrapes over okay with Kiki and I lifting the end where Jack's feet are. As it lowers, it almost jiggles and I steady it with all my might, straining my stomach muscles as I do. But he's in. And he's steady.

Next, we lower the other pool bed into the water and Maryam holds out her arms to take Akmal, who squeals with delight. She plonks his tiny body on the bed and waits for Siti and me to follow. We both climb in together. Siti is silent, clearly in shock, yet I'm grateful for their company.

It's cool, but not cold and I'm well protected in these clothes, even if the water does instantly seep through the fabric, weighing me down. I'm holding on to the side of the pool bed when Jack's fingers clutch mine and squeeze.

'Proud of you,' he very quietly says. I kiss his fingers and then look up to my kids, who're standing above me holding hands. It breaks me to see them like this, yet I smile and with arms out-stretched and I ask them to trust me and come into the water.

Now: 8:15pm

The crying starts up as soon as Cooper sinks under the water as I knew it would. After all, the sea is black ink surrounding us and our only guide is the island opposite with its dotted lights winking.

'It's cold,' he says, shivering more from shock than temperature. His teeth chatter. 'And my clothes are all wet.' He's speaking too loudly and saying things that are obvious, however, not when your body's going into shock.

'Shh, it's okay, Coop.' I pull him between Kiki and me. He's splashing too much and he's not monitoring the level of his cries and I'm worried they'll hear if he doesn't pull it together.

Regardless, I use my feet to push away from the jetty. The quicker we start swimming away from here, the less likely they'll hear Cooper crying and splashing like he's forgotten how to swim. Blood pumps rapidly through my heart. I'm shaking, teeth rattling too, as I start to push the bed with Jack on it.

'You're going to climb on Jack, but you need to be really careful,' I whisper to him. 'If you flip the bed, there's no way we can get Jack back on there and he could drown.'

I don't look back. The island and Mateo are the chaser in hide and seek, ready to yank us back and catch us. Cooper's doing nothing but hanging on and crying while Kiki also shivers, face etched in horror, little legs kicking behind her like a baby duck.

We're in the water and it's cold and I want to cry, and it's dark, so dark I can barely see the smaller waves approaching. I swallow a mouthful of salty water and almost vomit. Maryam is shushing Akmal, trying to prevent him from crawling off the bed, Siti is blubbering beside me with a childlike cry, trying to kick and push the bed and everything just seems disastrous. They'll hear us. They'll spot us. We're going to be shot dead.

'You have to be careful of Jack's ribs,' I tell Cooper. 'I think they may be broken.' Cooper's already trying to pull himself on and I tell him to wait. 'You're going to lie between his legs and rest your head on his lower stomach. And then when you're on there, you can just close your eyes and relax.' I force a smile and kiss his wet cheeks. 'Got it?'

'Okay.' He shivers, going to pull himself on. I assist by lifting his bottom while he clutches the sides of the bed. It's rocking and Jack's holding the sides and then Cooper comes off. He slips under the water, surfacing and calls out, 'Mummy.'

I hope the men are distracted by violence and aggression and revenge. Please just don't hear the commotion happening here. I want to yell at Cooper to shut up, but then remember to keep him pacified. I push with my arms and start kicking underwater as he clutches on to me.

'You need to hold on to the bed, Cooper, do you understand me?'

It's only then that I realise Kiki is silently crying as she pushes the bed and thrusts her little legs. She's trying to stay quiet and she's terrified and God, so am I.

'Let's try again. This time we have to be really careful. Kiki, can you help hold the bed steady while I lift Cooper on?'

She nods and holds the sides while I, again, gently push underneath Cooper's bottom. This time he makes it and I hear Jack grunt as he spins around to lie on Jack's abdomen. But I can't help it. I can't help everything and everyone all at once. I want to cry.

318

'I'm sorry, Jack,' I say.

'Hey,' he whispers from the other end of the bed. 'Come up here near my head and swim beside me.' He talks like he's in a lot of pain, a tight, constricted voice. I'm certain just breathing would hurt his ribs.

There's only water and more water beneath me and the lights of the island appear hugely far away. It's the most dreadful, out-of-control feeling I've ever encountered. Out here, we have no control. We only have the option of swimming. Maryam lies back on the bed, attempting to placate Akmal by patting his back, singing a soft lullaby. Siti cries and kicks beside me. We look at each other, mirrored in fearful emotion.

'Come on,' I whisper to Kiki, holding her as she edges around the bed towards Jack's head. 'You can't pull too tight. We have to even the bed out.'

'But, Mummy,' Cooper wails. 'My legs are dangling.'

Doesn't he realise our whole bodies are submerged? I want to tell him off. Tell him to be quiet. Anger is there and hot, yet only because I'm so scared.

'Emma, you go at the front and pull,' Jack softly says. 'Kiki, you stay by me. Lie down, Coop.'

I'm leading the bed at the front, struggling to grip the sides with my fingertips as I kick underwater and pull at the same time. It's easier to push from the rear, but I understand what Jack's trying to accomplish. He's trying to settle them both down, me down. Trying to distract them from where we are and what we're doing.

Siti's swimming is strong and they're keeping up with us, two beds floating side by side. But her crying won't stop and it's making my chin wobble. Eventually, hopefully, the fear will dissipate like the waves on a shoreline, and we'll simply swim without thinking. Eventually we may accept that underneath us is nothing but more black water. Still, I have an urge to tuck my legs under the bed and

319

stay that way. Having them loose and dangling to the deep is what has me trembling.

'When we get to the island, it'll have a pool and comfy beds and warm spas and ice cream,' Jack says. 'And it won't be long until we get to have everything.'

Kiki's sniffing, while Cooper is unable to listen. He's crying, while every now and then a salty wave splashes Kiki's face, making her gasp. She's not swimming, she's just clinging. And it could be like this the whole way there. And if it is, I have to accept it. Regardless, I don't want to turn back, because if I do, I'll see how close we are to the boathouse, how we've barely even left. How Mateo could still come and punish us.

Now: 8:45pm

According to Jack's watch, we've been swimming for thirty minutes. I've asked him to stop telling us the time. Out here, we can only judge time by the distance from us to the island. I'm scared to turn back around – similarly, I'm addicted to doing it. It's like being chased during a game of hide and seek. I always want to know how far away I am from danger.

When Jack mentions the time, I turn back and I'm surprised by the distance we've covered. Jack said the wind and current's probably helping us. Yet there's another problem, a thought that hangs below me, tingling my feet. The further away we are from the island, the further into the deep we venture. I'm bordering on panicking when I jerk my head behind and measure the distance from Barque. It'd be five hundred metres away, possibly more and the ocean's colder, darker, more menacing. And when we hear a loud gunshot echoing over the water, I freeze.

'What was that?' Kiki asks.

'I don't know,' I lie. I'm picturing Charles' head blown to pieces the way Ariella's was.

I think I'm having a panic attack, and I've never experienced one before, still I'm aware of the symptoms. Hallucinations, tingling, tightness of throat. Panic attacks mimic heart attacks and that's what has most people in hospital. Dizziness clouds my vision and I'm hyperventilating and sobbing. This only peaks Cooper's cries, which haven't stopped since we've left. He can talk a bit more now and all I'm hearing is, 'I want to go back. I want to turn back.' But noise travels and we're not far enough away to be inaudible. So, I shush him and reach for Jack's hand. I squeeze it and he lifts it to his mouth. His hot gasps warm my fingers, which are wet and trembling. Now is not the time to be panicking. Mindfulness is the only strategy left to combat a panic attack. Just concentrate on the heat, on the skin, the prickles of hair beneath his lip. Gradually, the tingling fades, the dizziness clears, I can smell again. Rubber, salt, Kiki's shampoo from last night.

'You're doing so well,' I hear him say. His voice is drawling, like he's drunk. I'm sure he's dipping in and out of sleep. I let go of his hand and keep pulling. Kiki has stopped for a minute, laying her head on the mattress and sobbing. She'll be regretting this, I'm sure. I kiss her head three times, loving her so much with the echo of the gunshot lingering.

'We're all doing so well,' I say, shaking my head under the water for a second. It wakes me out of the panic. Words of positive affirmations are what we need, what I need, right now. 'Look at how brave we are. When we get to the island, can you imagine what they'll say?'

Kiki lifts her little head, eyes barely distinguishable in the darkness. Just two black holes stuck on a pale face. And Siti tries to understand what I'm saying, but can't. So I just smile and pat her hand and that has her kicking harder. Maryam is with baby Akmal, who seems to have drifted off to sleep on a floating dream. She can only lie down with him lying on top. The minute she sits up, the bed could tumble. I keep reminding her of that.

'We got away, we rescued Jack.' I rub Kiki's cold cheek and kiss her wet hair. 'Imagine what you can tell your friends at school about this?'

I'm worried about her open collar, water getting in there, stingers and jellyfish getting in there. But I push it out of my mind. It's too late now. We're here and we're doing this. I keep pulling, scooping the water, striking the water with my legs and realise how hard it is. I ask Kiki to stay up that end with Jack while I push from behind. But she wants to follow me, so I let her.

'Let's let Jack have a nap,' I say, dragging her back with me. 'He needs it. And what I need is turbo-kicking. Are you ready?'

Kiki starts kicking, rhythmic slaps that spray over us.

'Good, Kiks.' I kiss her head. 'The quicker and harder we kick, the quicker we get there.'

This motivation pushes her and she's thrashing her legs and pushing the bed and we're finally moving further onward. And I ignore the cramps in my belly, the spasming back. I'm certain there'll be blood, the scent of it leaking through the ocean. Every now and then, I catch myself, panting, because I know this feeling now, and it's no longer practice. This sensation is familiar and vivid. It's the start of labour.

Now: 9:42pm

I think we're about halfway when Kiki asks to lie on the bed with Jack. She's exhausted and can't keep going; she's scared of how dark it is now. We've been swimming for an hour and the water's choppier with the wind out here picking up. There's no coves or bays or mountains to protect us from the gusts.

We're now midpoint between the islands and there's a roller-coaster of similar emotions that tend to plummet and dip, before rising. Fear of where we are, dread over what swims beneath, confusion over the gunshot, panic over what they think they see, hear, feel. Is that a shark fin? There are no sharks. I think I felt something. That was my leg. Something splashed over there. There're waves out here, they make noises.

Emotions then level out, with adrenaline petering into exhaustion. My affirmations are the only substance keeping us motivated to keep swimming and kicking. And even then, they don't work.

Now, Kiki is tired, the third emotion that creeps in, and I can't blame her for this. Her little legs are not used to swimming for this long. Sometimes I tell her to just rest and hang on to the back.

I'm getting tired too. Jack wakes and tells me to lean my upper body on the back and kick that way. I'm worried about leaning too much on Cooper and knocking him into the water. If he falls in, there's no way I can roll him back on. And my own panic tends to move in swells. I too think about sharks and wonder whether my bleeding is attracting them, whether the vibrations of our kicks and splashes will entice them.

I push it out of my head and continue hitting the water with my legs, alternating between frog kicks and straight leg thrusts. I'm deciding to concentrate on what will happen once we arrive there. A hot cup of tea, a bowl of salty chips, a cushy bed with white crisp sheets and a fluffy gown. Slippers, a hair wash in a steamy hot shower, moisturiser over my wrinkled hands. Lip balm. A hair-brush. A doctor. I need a doctor. My stomach starts again, pulling up and radiating around my back. I can't help but groan this time.

'What's wrong, Mumma?' Kiki asks.

'It's just the baby,' I say. 'Let's keep going. Not long now.'

She flops her head down on the bed and the rubber squeaks. I tell her to rest there. Cooper is quiet and I wonder if he's fallen asleep. Jack's resting now with his hands clasped on his chest. He needs a doctor too. I'm concerned about internal bleeding.

The night's unagitated and quiet, unlike us. Only splashes disturb the peace. Such a weird sensation being out here. I'm cold, yet hot and almost feverish. My skin stings from the salt and I'm sick of swallowing mouthfuls of it. The tips of my fingers are prunes, starting to peel.

Siti is quiet now, no longer crying. Kicking on autopilot, eyes vacant and staring. It's the best way to be. Don't think about what's below. Just kick. And Maryam sleeps and wakes with jerks that have her clutching a sleeping Akmal. Thank God he's sleeping. When he wakes, and grizzles to sit up, I'm not sure how we'll hold him in place.

'I can't keep going,' Kiki says, her cheek rubbing against the rubber.

'Come on, Kiks.'

'I can't. I feel sick.'

'I feel sick too.' Cooper finally talks. He's been quiet for the past little while.

'You may be seasick.' I pull the backpack off my back and rest it on Coop's legs. I tug the drink bottle out again. It's already half empty. I search around for the apple and take it out. I hand one to Siti and grab one for us. She smiles and bites a huge chunk of it. Fresh sweetness breezes past my nose. Its skin is salty, but it'll give them some strength.

'Here, have a bite.' I hold it against Kiki's lips, and she takes a big bite, licking her lips. She makes an *mmm* sound. I then offer it to Cooper, who takes a chunk of it. I have some myself and hold the apple in my mouth as another contraction starts up again. They're inconsistent. Fifteen minutes, then twelve then twenty. This is my fourth now. This one is closer. I ride through it and when it eases, I chew the mouthful and swallow. It's sweet and a welcome change from the saltwater.

They finish off the apple and the freshness boosts their morale. I throw the core away and zip up the bag, pulling it back onto my shoulders. And then we keep going, and I tell them both a story about scuba divers who explore caves at night, about how they do this kind of thing all the time. I don't know if it improves their confidence, but it certainly enhances mine.

Now: 10:44pm

It's a cliché moment in films, the kind you'd expect. We're close to the island now, so close I'm starting to make out the details. Fairy lights hanging over a bar. Distant music. Laughter and clinking glasses from late-night drinkers. I can distinguish the infrastructure, the resort, the bedrooms, the lamps across the island. It's so close, the seafood cooking for guests at the restaurant enhances my hunger. What a shock when they see us, scrambling up the beach in blood-soaked clothes with a pink floating mattress. But the wind is also gearing up, pushing the island noises towards us, chopping the waves. We're still in the deep depths, half a kilometre from the shore, with a persistent current wanting to pull us back out to sea. This is what Jack notices. We're floating sideways. We'll have to defeat the current and push in the other direction. And if we scream for help, our voices will be carried off with the wind.

We're so close Kiki is kicking faster, knowing that the harder she goes, the quicker we'll get there.

And that's when we see it. Because sharks are often found closer to the shoreline. And we're close, however, not close enough to touch down on sand. And Jack looks up because he's spotted something, and I notice.

'What?' I say, glancing behind me.

'Nothing. Just keep going.'

Kiki faces me and Cooper's asleep on Jack. I keep having to hold him on and wake him each time he goes to roll around.

'Did you see something?' I ask Jack.

'Just relax.'

Siti flicks her head around, seeming to understand what we're alluding to. Her breath becomes tighter, wheezy.

'Mum,' Kiki moans.

I pat her hand. 'Jack, I'd rather you tell us if you've seen something.'

But he doesn't have to tell me because I see it myself. A fin that moves through the water about ten metres away and dips down so silently, you'd never know if you weren't anticipating it. Yanking the backpack from my shoulders, I unzip the bag while Kiki starts screaming. I tell her to shush and Jack yells to *calm down*. Siti screams, letting go of the bed and Maryam wakes. I grab the knife in my shaking hand and don't care about the backpack now. It almost falls off, but Jack reaches and grabs it. And I'm turning and scanning the area, waiting for it to come. My heart is in my throat, almost making me sIck. Kiki is screaming and Cooper starts crying and the waves all look like fins to me. Black and slithery and pointed. I'm ready. Even if it comes up from underneath us, I'll stab it with the knife. Kiki's trying to clamber on the bed with Coop and Jack, yet that'll only mean they'll roll in and Jack will drown. So, I tell her to stay steady and focused. I tell Cooper to lie back down.

'We're so close. Hear the music. We're almost there. Keep going. Keep going.'

Their cries turn into sobs and Kiki's little head rotates around to search for the fin.

We're swimming towards the island and Jack's saying how rare it is to be hurt by sharks when a puffing noise startles me from behind.

It's not a shark. It's a dolphin. Its blow hole puffs again and Kiki turns to look. I dip my face into the water and laugh into it. When I lift it back out, I say, 'It's a dolphin.'

I cry out with joy. Siti laughs, huffing and puffing and holding her a hand to her throat. The kids both burst into horrified laughter and Jack does too. I honestly thought it was a shark. We were done for, almost at the finish line. Except the dolphin's appearance somehow makes me feel safer and I hang my legs for a moment and kiss the kids. 'That's good luck. Dolphins mean good luck.'

Kiki and Cooper smile and talk between themselves about maybe being able to ride it. We're laughing, smiling, forgetting what we've just endured, where we currently are.

'We're going to be okay,' Jack says, reaching his hand out to me. I swim around and take it, bringing it to my lips. He's dry and warm. And Kiki lets me swim to him, without hurrying behind. And that's how I know.

'We *are* okay.'

And in that moment, with the island drawing nearer and the dolphin keeping us company, with the wind carrying delicious scents of fried seafood and vanilla candles, I smile, thinking of Ariella.

We've made it. I did it. I did it for her.

Now: 11pm

To have our feet settle on sandy ground is not only surreal, it's emotional. While I force Jack and the mattress up the sloping beach, Kiki and Cooper crawl out of the water, collapsing onto the sand. Waves break over their feet. Maryam helps Siti pull their bed out of the water and the two women cuddle and weep. Once I know that Jack's secure, I do the same, on my hands and knees, scrunching sand into my fists as I shakily make my way up to dry sand.

And then, I fall on my side and cry. Exhausted moans flee my mouth and Cooper and Kiki copy me, crying into their hands. It takes a while for me to open my eyes and ask them to come to me. My energy is so low, I can barely breathe, let alone talk. It's a struggle for Kiki's weak body to even move, but they both do, flopping beside me, hair in the sand.

I kiss their heads, over and over, countless times, gazing up at the stars, the fairy lights behind me. To have the earth hold me and my back, to have the earth be solid under our bodies is the greatest feeling. Tears mix with salty ocean.

When I finally sit up and crawl to Jack, I notice he too has tears trailing down his cheeks. I hug him tight, crying on his face as he tells me how proud he is.

'Aren't you something,' he tells me. 'So strong.'

The baby kicks me hard and I'm heavy and aching. And then a voice speaks up behind us, a woman who stops with her husband.

'Oh my gosh, are you all right?' she says.

And I can't even talk. I'm just sitting up and crying, gawping at them with disbelief. Kiki and Cooper are lying exhausted on the sand, curled in balls. Maryam and Siti hold each other with Akmal sitting beside them.

The couple are well-dressed in heels and a dinner jacket. They've just had a romantic meal and her hair is blow-dried and her nails sparkle with silver polish.

'Help us,' I finally say. 'Please.'

Her husband runs off and she nods and removes her heels before stepping onto the sand. She's blond and pretty. Her perfume smells expensive. She holds out her hands to me and I take them.

The warm breeze carries a pungent frangipani perfume, matching the woman's. Tropical music tinkles through the palms. Nearby laughter settles my nerves. And it's exactly as I imagined. An island of safety.

Now: 8:05am

Days, hours, seasons blur into a useless abstract of time. All I'm aware of is this present moment. Heat from a beady fabric under my spine, the whiff of hand sanitiser, incessant beeping, cracked lips coated in a slippery substance, coffee in Styrofoam cups, sharpness in my wrist, a ball in my gut.

And there's murmuring from two unfamiliar voices, one uttering that she's waking up. Who is she? Ariella? Kiki? Maryam?

A peppermint breath hovers over my nose and I'm met with a soft peck of lips. The mattress creaks and then stiffens. My breasts tingle.

'Emma,' the first voice says.

'Mumma,' comes the second.

'Sweetheart.' A brush over eyebrows.

The light, when I open my eyes, has them closing again. And in that eyelid moment, I've seen who's around me. Kiki, Cooper, Jack and two other figures standing by the end of the bed. I'm so exhausted I could sleep forever. I'm in hospital, tucked tightly under hard sheets that reek of disinfectant washing powder. I finger around to my bump and notice the hardness. It's there. Still there.

I open my eyes, vision clearing and darting to the faces. Kiki, Cooper, Jack, the other two. 'The baby?'

Jack's there, bruised, wrecked, yet by my side. He takes the needled hand and smiles. His skin is grey and he grimaces, in pain.

'Bub's safe,' he says. 'Hear that strong heartbeat? Just like her mother.' A whooshing sound becomes clear. And there's a band around my lower belly, obviously monitoring the womb. Bub's alive. I can't help crying with utter, emotional relief. She's alive. My baby. We're all alive. How did we manage such an ordeal, such a long crossing, to be sitting here now, safely surrounded by doctors, medicine and help? We did it. Jack wipes my eyes and I notice he's also crying. I go to sit up and it hurts, but I don't care. Kiki and Cooper step around to join me. They don't look like themselves, dressed in strange clothing, pale faces and hollow eyes. I touch Cooper's face and pull Kiki into me. They don't smell the same, either. Their hair has been washed in simple soap and they are gaunt, yet smiling. We're all in hospital clothing.

'We saw our new baby on the machine.' Cooper shyly sticks his fingers in his mouth. I want to see the ultrasound footage, but my other two babies need me more than ever.

When I talk, my voice feels like it's been scratched by sand. 'And how are my other babies going?'

Kiki nods. 'We're good. We had a big sleep and when we woke up, the doctor gave us treats.'

'And we got ice cream for breakfast.' Coop jumps and I hold his hand.

'No way. Ice cream. Aren't you lucky?'

To think only a short while ago we were in the ocean, swimming for our lives. I kiss them both again. How easy it would have been to lose one of them, including our new baby.

Jack clearly can't move. He takes a seat beside me. 'It was touch and go for a bit,' he says. 'You lost a lot of blood.'

All I remember is the helicopter flight back to the mainland, the bleeding, Kiki and Cooper sleeping on the police officer's lap.

333

The darkness. The rough blanket over my shoulders. And then they took Kiki and Cooper away to one ward and Jack to another. I remember passing out as they wheeled them off in wheelchairs and I remember not wanting to be separated.

'What about you?'

'They wanted to check me over for internal bleeding. By the time I got back to you, you were heavily sedated.'

I can vaguely recall snippets of memories, still, it doesn't matter now. We're safe. We're together. But what about Maryam and Siti?

I blink towards the police officers. One wears plain clothes, the other is in uniform. I recognise her from the helicopter. 'I need to know that the women are okay.'

The detective nods and clings on to the back of the bed base. 'They're fine. They're just down the hall. You've been through an ordeal together.'

I close my eyes tight and let it sink in. They're fine. They're safe.

'We need to ask you a few questions.' The detective is about my age and fit-looking. She wears a V-neck, long-sleeve top over a business shirt. She has a warm face when she thinly smiles. 'I know this is bad timing, but before you forget anything, while it's still fresh, it's good to ask.'

I'm certainly not fresh. Thirsty, hungry, needing a wee – I think, I think there's a catheter attached to me. But I want to be with Jack and my kids. Can't they give us a few moments?

'They've already questioned me.' Jack smiles, squeezing my shoulder. Just that act makes him wince. He looks badly beaten, as I knew he would. He can't even open his puffy left eye.

'Could we have a moment?' I plead with the police. 'Please.'

The kids look to them, as does Jack, and eventually the kind detective nods.

'Okay. We'll go and get a coffee. Take a few minutes.'

The woman smiles and the other police officer follows her out and it feels good to be safe and well with my family. Cooper sits up on the bed and Kiki plays with my hair.

'What did they ask you?' I say. I want to be here without the police because this moment is the one thing I've looked forward to since we left Sydney. To be safe and together. Jack switches the television on for Kiki and Cooper.

'Everything. I told them everything,' he says, nodding. 'They knew quite a bit anyway. Apparently, the young boys who were fishing and spotted you in the water went straight to the police and told them what happened. The skipper on *Lady Luck* was taken in for questioning the minute he landed back to Sydney.'

'Oh my gosh, those young boys,' I say. 'I wasn't sure they'd do anything. And did the police go back to the island?'

He rubs above his eyebrow and faces his feet. Then he exhales and I know what he's going to say. It reaches into this secure room, darkening the moment. I taste something sour in my throat.

'They got away,' he admits.

'They got away?' I'm trying to be quiet, so Kiki and Cooper won't hear. 'Mateo and Charles? But what about the gunshot?'

'The island was empty. Who knows what Mateo did to Charles, but he's gone. No one's there. Maryam and Siti told the police everything.'

It's probably supposed to bolster me, and it does, for a second. Maryam and Siti are safe, so are we, and my promise to protect us all is preserved and achieved. I close my eyes and give thanks. Yet what Jack also mentioned tarnishes this happy news. Mateo and the men got away and this can only mean one thing: if they return, they'll be imprisoned. But what about Charles? Did Mateo kill him, Brad, Wallace and the old maid and then get rid of their bodies?

The thought snags me, looping around this bittersweet moment.

Seven Months After

There will be a dinner tonight. Candles will be lit, and the outdoor balcony table will be set with fine cutlery and linen napkins. A bowl of fine white roses will combine with the scent of vanilla candles and seafood. Wine glasses will be filled, cheese-platters picked and soft music will serenade the company.

We are really good at hiding our past. The kids are good at accepting their new family.

I sip my wine and adjust one of the knives straighter. In ten short minutes, three people will enter this home and gush over its brilliance. The beach views to die for. Everything so wonderful and Instagram worthy. I take another sip, massage my temples and gaze at the flat ocean. Nature has made it bright this evening with sunsets and pink-streaked skies. White seagulls whisk the sea with their feathers. The hum of boats and the rhythm of waves are our soundtrack.

We wanted a fresh home that mirrored the transformation in our lives and now we have it. And after the police investigations, Jack resumed directing the security company. With the other owner now a wanted man, Jack could take over the business as sole owner while I continue to run my wellness clinic.

Ariella's house remains vacant, the herb and vegetable garden decaying, the grass browning, leaves being blown into the pool.

And our old house is cold, as though the shade of Charles lingers throughout. The river views are ugly, only reminding me of our morning walks together, our terrace coffee-talks. I'm glad we're in a new place, a new home.

Jack comes out to light up the barbeque, clutching a bottle of beer. He's still limping from his injuries, but his face has recovered well.

Kiki and Cooper are in the lap pool, lobbing a ball over a net that stretches across the water. And baby Ella is in her bassinette, watching as I set the table, chubby legs thrashing at the sight of me. I bend to kiss her milky skin, the folds beneath her chin and breathe her in. At three months old, she's healthily developing the chubbiness around her knees and thighs.

'Do you think they'll like sausages?' Jack asks, opening a packet up with the tongs.

'I'm sure they're not fussy,' I say.

When the doorbell rings a little while later and I know who's arriving, I still stiffen at the sound. It could be a delivery, the new neighbour bringing a bouquet of flowers, a visiting friend. Yet, when that door opens, I continue to picture him there. Jack says it's normal to envision these things. I'm suffering some sort of trauma. The fact is, Charles still hasn't been caught and neither have any of them. They've either gone to ground here in Australia or fled overseas. But even with police and investigators trying to find them, they're alive and free and that bothers me.

Georgia answers the door and escorts our guests out to the balcony. And it's like being back there again, only without the sand, heat and constant sweat. The women are clean, smiling and well-dressed.

Maryam's in white pants and a floral top. Her hair is chopped in a trendy bob and she wears lipstick and strong perfume. She holds her arms out to me, with Akmal squirming to run off. Siti hangs back, allowing us to greet one another, but I reach for both of them.

'Oh my God, it's so good to see you.' I hold them both tightly. Maryam squeezes me back and we stare at one another. There're memories between us all, yet we don't have to voice them here and now. We embrace, and each thank one another, and I offer them soda and cheese while Akmal waddles over to Ella. He's grown into a chubby toddler now.

The rest of the night passes easily, with no talk of the island, no talk of the men. We discuss their future, whether they'll fly back home. We discuss fashion and hair styles and laugh at similar jokes that only Maryam can interpret. We smile, clinking champagne glasses together. It's because of them that we're here and safe. And when the doorbell rings again, I know who's behind it.

Tracy stands with a bottle of champagne. 'I think this is a celebration, right?'

I nod and I don't stop holding her. We've caught up each week and met Barbs at the wine bar and still, each time I see her, I feel tempted to sob. Because I took her there. And she saw it all. The girls down the hall, the men twisting them around and paying for them, the dirt and scum and filth of the place. He took her down there and took her hard and although at first, she wanted it, what she didn't expect was to be drugged, kept for twenty hours, locked up with the other women there as punishment for spying. He made her stay quiet. Threatened her life.

And when Ariella appeared at Tracy's yoga studio on the morning of her death, to 'practise yoga' for the minder's sake, she found her. The minder waited outside while Ariella practised her poses. But what she really went there for was Tracy. Ariella wanted to know if Tracy was all right after I'd taken her to the strip club, after Tracy went missing the whole next day. She wanted to know what Tracy had seen and heard, what she'd experienced there. And Tracy told Ariella everything. The girls. The strip club. The buying and selling. The apparent drawer full of passports, according to one of

Mateo's girls. And this is what Ariella planned to tell me at the fence at ten am on the morning of her death.

There may be a lasting sadness in Tracy's eyes, a smile that doesn't quite touch the soul, and I sometimes wonder if she blames me for pulling her into the muck and mud and mess. But she holds me now like I'm a life-raft and whispers in my ear, 'They've found Mateo.'

I pull back, studying her face. 'You're kidding?'

'They phoned me just now, and I bet they're phoning you. They've arrested him and his men.'

'I cannot believe this.' I beam. 'I cannot believe he's been found.'

I squeeze Tracy's shoulder and she inhales, holding in a breath, nodding, grinning, eyes wet. I kiss her head, because I can't imagine what she's feeling, what she's remembering, what he did to her. All I know is what he did to Ariella, how he treated her and it's enough to fill me with relief. He's been caught. Locked up. He'll never get out. We did it.

'But what about Charles?' I ask.

She shakes her head and shrugs. 'No mention of him.'

I believe the gunshot was the final sound linking me to Charles. Mateo would have killed him, I'm certain now. And mixed emotions dip and soar as I stand before Tracy – irrational guilt, surprise, shameful relief and a deep sadness for the kids. Even though Cooper and Kiki still question where he is, what he's doing, toss with sleepless nights and times of terror, I watch them now and weakly smile. Playing, jumping in the pool, squealing, enjoying freedom. They'll get through this, just the way Jack and I planned. With continued therapy and loving care. Still, it's a shock, and I don't know what to do with it, where to put these irregular emotions.

'I just cannot believe this.' I take the bottle from Tracy. I want to tell Jack that Mateo has been found. Is this a celebration? Tracy

339

seems to think so. We eat, drink and ignore the news for now, promising to enjoy the company and freedom we share.

There may be the language barrier, with Maryam required to interpret our conversation, but it doesn't matter because they're here on my balcony, eating salad and laughing. And as I watch them enjoying one another, chatting while I clear their plates, I suddenly smile to myself. Maryam reaches for a plate, I pat her hand and tell her, 'You're a good friend, Maryam.'

And her touch warms me when she squeezes my hand back. And no matter where we end up, what we've been through together means we're tied now. Maryam, Siti, Tracy and me. The kind of bonded friendship I've always wanted.

Jack tops up mine and Tracy's champagne glasses, the kids splash in the pool with Akmal, Maryam jiggles Ella on her lap and I sit at the end of the table, noticing the fine details of this life we've created. The apartment, the ocean view, the happiness. I'll tell the kids about their father, and one day they'll understand. But for now, we're welcome to enjoy what we've built without sadness.

Because this is who we are now, and this is what we do. Safely settling in as though we've always been this way.

ACKNOWLEDGEMENTS

I don't know about you, but I always flip to the back of a book to read the acknowledgments. In a way, they are the author's mini life story. I am so thrilled I get to sit here, writing my own as a published author. Little eight-year-old Holly, you did it! There are many people to thank and it's tricky knowing where to begin. Wherever you come on the list, just know there is no scale of importance. You've all helped me so much.

I am so grateful to my awesome, lovely, supportive and dedicated agent, Jade Kavanagh. Your enthusiasm, excitement and dedication in pushing and championing this book (and the three others I quickly wrote) has filled me with so much joy. Getting that first email from you is a moment I'll cherish. You instantly 'got' me, and you have made my dreams come true. Seriously.

Thank you to the whole team at Darley Anderson. Camilla Bolton for kindly passing me on to Jade (and supporting us both along the way) and to Mary Darby and the foreign rights team for taking THE SHALLOWS to Frankfurt Book Fair. Thank you for accepting a little Aussie writer into your incredible, professional, superstar agency!

Thank you to my publisher at Audible UK, Harry Scoble, who loved THE SHALLOWS enough to request the manuscript! And to my wonderful, positive and passionate publisher at Thomas &

Mercer, Victoria Haslam, for also making my dreams come true! You have no idea how long I've wanted my very own publisher! Your vision for THE SHALLOWS was spot on and I couldn't have had a better first experience through every stage of edits. Laura Gerrard, you're amazing and I'm so lucky I had you doing my structural edits! Thanks also to Frances Moloney for your eagle-eyed edits, Sarah Rouse and Sarah Conkerton.

Thank you to the new authors I've met and become friends with (in person and online), especially my DA sisters: Liv Matthews for your positive encouragement and Paula Johnston (you belter) for making me laugh. And to ALL the new writers I've met this year: Nerida, for your professional advice, 'The Furphies', and all the writers of The Write Club who have trusted me to teach you (and spoilt me rotten!). We are so lucky to be a part of such a supportive community.

Louise Allan. What can I say, if it wasn't for you, this manuscript would never have got published. I needed your eye and professional advice to spur me on, and you never pushed me away. The best mentor an author could have.

Polly Phillips. Thanks so much for the belly-aching laughs, the podcast *Off The Page*, the special friendship we've formed over rosé wine, hot chocolates and cheeseboards. I can trust you, bounce off you and I'm so happy we found each other.

Natasha Lester. Thanks for your generous advice, ongoing support and wealth of knowledge. I love our Wednesday writing days. Thanks for letting Polly and I gatecrash your OG writing group.

Special thanks to my university supervisor, Brett D'Arcy, for being one of the first to tell me, 'You'll get published one day.' I believed you, I always reference you. You taught me the techniques and skills to become a better writer. And it worked. Our uni days were the best, right, Jono and Caitlin?

Thanks, Dad and Darryl for letting me use your house as a writer's retreat! And thanks so much, Darryl, for reading and providing feedback over the past few years.

Thank you, Michael, for designing my awesome website, which I use every day! I appreciate it so much.

To my besties who were there the night I got my offer. Lou-Lou, Shandy, Kel, Aims, Jules, Kinga (sorry I stole your fiftieth, Kel). I'll write you all into the next books, promise (and I won't kill you). And Mellypops, Shellen, Nic, Carls, Kim, Kat, Kad, Sharon, Nat for knowing and asking and reading my work over the years.

Mum. You were there when I was eight years old, listening to my handwritten stories about toast with dripping honey, always 'oohing' and 'ahhing' at just the right places. You gave me the ego I needed to carry on with my dream of doing this. You always knew I'd get here eventually. Thanks for always believing and encouraging and supporting. Aren't I lucky? Wish Nan knew.

And Ez, for always asking and being interested in the process.

Tiff. Thanks so much for motivating (forcing) me to keep writing so you could have something 'decent to read'. Even while you lived in London, and I had to send over hard copy manuscripts! You've never grown tired of it, you've never said no – reading whatever I sent you. You were and ARE the ultimate beta-reader.

Kurt. You are the one person who has completely, one-hundred-per-cent supported me, not just in life, but over every sentence, every word. Number one editor. Number one plotter. I love our walks together where we invent stories. I could write a novel of acknowledgments thanking you and it still wouldn't be enough. We really were meant to meet that first day at uni. You are not only my partner, you are the best writer, my best friend, best supporter and motivator I could ever ask for. You make me safe and happy and I will thank you my whole life. Now it's your turn to write.

And lastly, the sweetest daughters a mum could want, Milly and Emme. Thank you for teaching me to be the best mother. For letting me write. For being just as enthusiastic about this book as any adult. For teaching me to nurture my own inner child so that I can nurture you. Mil and Em, everything and anything is possible if you want it badly enough. This is proof.

To the readers who bought and are reading this book. I hope I've satisfied you enough that you'll continue to follow my stories for many years to come.

Holly x

ABOUT THE AUTHOR

Holly Craig lives on the Western Australian coast. She spent her childhood on boats and on Rottnest Island, inspiring her second novel *The Rip*, which is out in 2024 with Thomas & Mercer. The beach and river were her playground and have shaped the settings in her novels. Holly is an English teacher and now teaches adults how to write their novels, preparing their manuscripts for publication. She also co-hosts a podcast, *Off The Page*, which focuses on the highs and lows of author life.

You can follow Holly on her website: www.hollycraig.com, Instagram: Holly Craig (@hollycraigauthor), and Twitter: Holly Craig (@hollycwriter).

Follow the Author on Amazon

If you enjoyed this book, follow Holly Craig on Amazon to be notified when the author releases a new book!
To do this, please follow these instructions:

Desktop:

1) Search for the author's name on Amazon or in the Amazon App.
2) Click on the author's name to arrive on their Amazon page.
3) Click the 'Follow' button.

Mobile and Tablet:

1) Search for the author's name on Amazon or in the Amazon App.
2) Click on one of the author's books.
3) Click on the author's name to arrive on their Amazon page.
4) Click the 'Follow' button.

Kindle eReader and Kindle App:

If you enjoyed this book on a Kindle eReader or in the Kindle App, you will find the author 'Follow' button after the last page.